MW01250676

background, and, in the process, the temporal world of Mrs Gibson's drawing-room, no matter how briefly, becomes palpable and real.

The quintessential adage of nineteenth-century domesticity was that there was 'a time for everything and everything at its right time', and it is tempting to take this as a starting point for an investigation of domestic temporality. It is true that the Victorians were fond of this phrase, which is repeated again and again in advice manuals, Sunday school books and, among many other famous novels, in Charles Dickens's *Bleak House* (1852–3). It suggests, to modern eyes, a very clean and ordered universe, if somewhat naively mechanic; but then the Victorians liked to think of their homes as machines (or so received wisdom likes to remind us). However, what this memorable phrase also implies is a rhetorical emptying out of domestic time. Only the timetable is left, nothing of the negotiations within it – and thus no thought is given to interruptions, delays, or improvisations. Nineteenth-century writers could not rest on their laurels after quoting this platitude. Just as domestic work required rethinking as well as repetition, so too was the representation of that same work a perpetual series of negotiations. These negotiations did not just take place in narrative form, such as in the two epigraphs to this chapter. In both fictional and non-fictional writings, authors and publishers were experimenting with forms, layouts, and rhythms of publication that could conceptualize domestic practices as processes enmeshed in time. How, for example, could you best present a recipe for pickles that took months to make? How could you arrange the hours of the day on the page of a domestic manual? What about serialized works, which were in themselves (at least metaphorically) interrupted – since they were divided up into monthly or weekly instalments? Did the structure of interruption in fact form part of their representational power?

Although nineteenth-century domesticity is a familiar area of research, scholarly inquiries have almost exclusively focused not on time but on space: on the functional subdivisions within the home, the politics of who goes where, and the gendered and classed lines which intersect in rooms, corridors, and doorframes.[3] When critics have discussed temporality in connection with domesticity, they have tended to focus on choreographed practices such as morning calls (which skews the picture towards rigid timetabling), or on the idea of the cyclicality of women's time (an argument which veers towards essentialism). Alternatively, scholars have argued extensively for the sheer non-narratability of certain temporalities, whether those timings are associated with women, the everyday or the 'timeless' Victorian domesticity that was so heavily

Introduction: Timetabling and its Failures

> Mrs Gibson had once or twice reproved them for the merry noise they had been making, which hindered her in the business of counting the stitches in her pattern. [...] 'Mr Roger Hamley' was announced. 'So tiresome!' said Mrs Gibson, almost in his hearing.
>
> Elizabeth Gaskell, *Wives and Daughters* (1865)[1]

> [Light and ornamental needlework] may be put aside and resumed without much inconvenience.
>
> Mrs William [Frances] Parkes, *Domestic Duties* (1825)[2]

In a nineteenth-century novel, a morning caller interrupts a middle-class woman while she is doing needlework. In a nineteenth-century domestic manual, female readers are assured that needlework is excellent employment for those who are liable to be interrupted. The situation is so well known to readers of works from the period as to require no explanation. And yet, from another point of view, the assumptions behind this predicament are singular. Why must women be interrupted? What structure of time makes that interruption possible? What does it mean to put your work aside, and to choose occupations that allow, even ensure, interruption? And would we even learn of Mrs Gibson's embroidery if it were not for the fact that the plot, in the shape of her daughter's suitor, interrupts her diligent work? Both passages cause the narrative – whether the book is a novel or an advice manual – to linger, however briefly, on the temporal aspects of domesticity: the durations, timings, and negotiations of temporality within the middle-class home. The narrator divulges something that ostensibly belongs in the

Acknowledgements

I am eternally grateful for the warm support and invaluable suggestions of Clare Pettitt at King's College London. Everyone should have someone like Clare on their side. Also at King's, I owe special thanks to Ian Henderson, Cora Kaplan, Josephine McDonagh and Mark W. Turner for their comments on my work as it was progressing. I'd like to thank Lene Østermark-Johansen at the University of Copenhagen, Matthew Beaumont, Louise Lee, Francis O'Gorman, Caroline Levine and Tania Ørum for help along the way.

At archives and libraries, I owe a debt of gratitude to Helen Peden at the British Library, to Sonia Gomes at the London Women's Library, to Claire McHugh, Shirley Nicholson and the Leighton House Museum, to the curators at Manchester Metropolitan University Special Collections, and to the Bodleian Library. I would also like to thank King's College Graduate School, Knud Højgaards Fond, Krista og Viggo Petersens Fond, Augustinus Fonden and Carlsbergfondet for funding me through a number of projects.

Many thanks to my editors Ben Doyle and Joseph Bristow, to Tomas René and everyone else at Palgrave Macmillan, including anonymous readers, for invaluable help and kindness. An earlier version of material from Chapter 4 appeared in *Serialization in Popular Culture*, edited by Rob Allen and Thijs van den Berg (New York and Abingdon: Routledge, 2014). I want to thank Rob and Thijs for their suggestions and dedicated work, and Routledge for the permission to republish.

Special thanks to Sarah Crofton, Jordan Kistler, Jennifer Lo, Mary L. Shannon, Anne Spangsberg, Will Tattersdill and Esben Wilstrup for tea, jokes, conference support and useful suggestions, and for reminding me to have fun with what I do.

Finally, I would like to thank Camilla Damkjær and Anne Duch. I wish my father, Søren Damkjær, were here to see this book be published – I know he would have enjoyed it. More than anything, the book owes its existence to my mother, Susanne Engstrøm, who never once doubted it was possible, and who has read more drafts of my work than anyone. It is dedicated to her, with all my love.

List of Illustrations

Contents

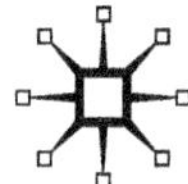

TIME, DOMESTICITY AND PRINT CULTURE IN NINETEENTH-CENTURY BRITAIN

First published 2016 by
PALGRAVE MACMILLAN

Palgrave Macmillan in the UK is an imprint of Macmillan Publishers Limited, registered in England, company number 785998, of Houndmills, Basingstoke, Hampshire RG21 6XS.

Palgrave Macmillan in the US is a division of Nature America, Inc., One New York Plaza, Suite 4500 New York, NY 10004-1562.

Palgrave Macmillan is the global academic imprint of the above companies and has companies and representatives throughout the world.

Hardback ISBN: 978–1–137–54287–8
E-PUB ISBN: 978–1–137–54289–2
E-PDF ISBN: 978–1–137–54288–5
DOI: 10.1057/9781137542892

Distribution in the UK, Europe and the rest of the world is by Palgrave Macmillan®, a division of Macmillan Publishers Limited, registered in England, company number 785998, of Houndmills, Basingstoke, Hampshire RG21 6XS.

Library of Congress Cataloging-in-Publication Data

Names: Damkjær, Maria, 1983– author.
Title: Time, domesticity and print culture in nineteenth-century Britain / Maria Damkjær.
Description: Houndmills, Basingstoke: Palgrave Macmillan, 2016. | Includes bibliographical references and index.
Identifiers: LCCN 2015038162 | ISBN 9781137542878 (hardback)
Subjects: LCSH: English literature—19th century—History and criticism. | Periodicals—Publishing—Great Britain—History—19th century. | Home in literature. | Time in literature. | Domestic relations in literature.
Classification: LCC PR468.H63 D36 2016 | DDC 820.9/355—dc23
LC record available at http://lccn.loc.gov/2015038162

A catalog record for this book is available from the Library of Congress

A catalogue record for the book is available from the British Library

Typeset by MPS Limited, Chennai, India.

Time, Domesticity and Print Culture in Nineteenth-Century Britain

Maria Damkjær
Post-Doctoral Fellow, University of Copenhagen, Denmark

Colin Jones, Josephine McDonagh and Jon Mee (*editors*)
CHARLES DICKENS, A TALE OF TWO CITIES AND THE FRENCH REVOLUTION

Jock Macleod
LITERATURE, JOURNALISM, AND THE VOCABULARIES OF LIBERALISM
Politics and Letters 1886–1916

Kirsten MacLeod
FICTIONS OF BRITISH DECADENCE
High Art, Popular Writing and the *Fin de Siècle*

Charlotte Mathieson
MOBILITY IN THE VICTORIAN NOVEL
Placing the Nation

Natasha Moore
VICTORIAN POETRY AND MODERN LIFE
The Unpoetical Age

Kristine Moruzi and Michelle J. Smith (*editors*)
COLONIAL GIRLHOOD IN LITERATURE, CULTURE AND HISTORY, 1840–1950

Sean O'Toole
HABIT IN THE ENGLISH NOVEL, 1850–1900
Lived Environments, Practices of the Self

Tina O'Toole
THE IRISH NEW WOMAN

Richard Pearson
VICTORIAN WRITERS AND THE STAGE
The Plays of Dickens, Browning, Collins and Tennyson

Laura Rotunno
POSTAL PLOTS IN BRITISH FICTION, 1840–1898
Readdressing Correspondence in Victorian Culture

Laurence Talairach-Vielmas
FAIRY TALES, NATURAL HISTORY AND VICTORIAN CULTURE

Marianne Van Remoortel
WOMEN, WORK AND THE VICTORIAN PERIODICAL
Living by the Press

Palgrave Studies in Nineteenth-Century Writing and Culture
Series Standing Order ISBN 978-0-333-97700-2 (hardback)
(outside North America only)

You can receive future titles in this series as they are published by placing a standing order. Please contact your bookseller or, in case of difficulty, write to us at the address below with your name and address, the title of the series and the ISBN quoted above.

Customer Services Department, Macmillan Distribution Ltd, Houndmills, Basingstoke, Hampshire RG21 6XS, England

---

Palgrave Studies in Nineteenth-Century Writing and Culture

Palgrave Studies in Nineteenth-Century Writing and Culture is a new monograph series that aims to represent the most innovative research on literary works that were produced in the English-speaking world from the time of the Napoleonic Wars to the *fin de siècle*. Attentive to the historical continuities between 'Romantic' and 'Victorian', the series will feature studies that help scholarship to reassess the meaning of these terms during a century marked by diverse cultural, literary, and political movements. The main aim of the series is to look at the increasing influence of types of historicism on our understanding of literary forms and genres. It reflects the shift from critical theory to cultural history that has affected not only the period 1800–1900 but also every field within the discipline of English literature. All titles in the series seek to offer fresh critical perspectives and challenging readings of both canonical and non-canonical writings of this era.

Titles include:

James Campbell
OSCAR WILDE, WILFRED OWEN, AND MALE DESIRE
Begotten Not Made

Margot Finn, Michael Lobban and Jenny Bourne Taylor (*editors*)
LEGITIMACY AND ILLEGITIMACY IN NINETEENTH-CENTURY LAW, LITERATURE AND HISTORY

Adrienne E. Gavin and Andrew F. Humphries
TRANSPORT IN BRITISH FICTION
Technologies of Movement, 1840–1940

Joshua Gooch
THE VICTORIAN NOVEL, SERVICE WORK AND THE NINETEENTH-CENTURY ECONOMY

James Grande
WILLIAM COBBETT, THE PRESS AND RURAL ENGLAND
Radicalism and the Fourth Estate, 1792–1835

Jason David Hall and Alex Murray (*editors*)
DECADENT POETICS
Literature and Form at the British Fin de Siècle

Mary Henes and Brian Murray (*editors*)
TRAVEL WRITING, VISUAL CULTURE AND FORM, 1760–1900

Yvonne Ivory
THE HOMOSEXUAL REVIVAL OF RENAISSANCE STYLE, 1850–1930

Stephan Karschay
DEGENERATION, NORMATIVITY AND THE GOTHIC AT THE FIN-DE-SIÈCLE

mythologized in nineteenth-century culture.[4] Domestic time, if thought about at all, tends to be described primarily in negative terms: not public, not historical, not productive, not measurable, not narratable, not there. *Time, Domesticity and Print Culture in Nineteenth-Century Britain* argues that as the middle decades of the nineteenth century progressed, writers, far from asserting non-narratability, increasingly attempted to represent the middle-class home as process, not stasis – as an entity dynamically bound to time as well as an entity in space. Writers might continue to claim that 'everything' had a 'right time', but what that rightness consisted of was no longer self-evident.

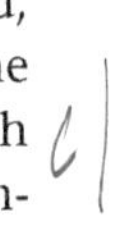

Time, Domesticity and Print Culture traces the process by which domesticity took a temporal turn around the 1850s. Different kinds of narratives traced out practices of domesticity; for some writers of this period, the intersection of time and place in the home was a central part of the realist drive to describe and define. In this regard, I follow Elizabeth Deeds Ermarth, who sees a qualitative shift to the representation of temporality as a defining characteristic of literary realism in the novel from 1850 onwards.[5] The works discussed in this book all participate in that shift in representation. The formation of realist fiction, however, is only part of the picture. The novels analysed here participate in a broader concern of print culture (whether periodical, advice manual or cookery book) to give a temporal dimension to domesticity. Three tendencies worked together to push the representation of domestic time further. The first, as Ermarth suggests, was the popularity of literary realism, through which the mechanisms of daily lives became in and of themselves worthy of elaboration. The second was the sharp rise in the sheer volume of print media that was produced and consumed in Britain. The third was the consolidation of the middle classes into a system of practice increasingly centred on the home. These three tendencies conspired to produce more detail and more depth in the conceptualizations of domestic temporality found in novels, periodicals, manuals, and private albums.

Time, Domesticity and Print Culture focuses on the mid-century period, a time when a full description of domestic practices seemed possible. However, even the works discussed here were shot through with uncertainty under their confident posturing. Soon, the fullness of realist description turned to anxieties about consumerism and impostors in Mary Elizabeth Braddon's sensational *Lady Audley's Secret* (1862), and to satire in the Grossmith brothers' *Diary of a Nobody* (1892). And yet the present study uncovers an urge to push description and representation further in order to account for the complexities of domestic time.

Although the basic tenets of mid nineteenth-century domestic practice were an inheritance from previous generations – early rising had ever been a moral imperative, and washing day was still disruptively time-consuming – they were now urged in new media to new readers. As modernity and new class structures took people away from their parents' experience, people sought printed manuals to teach them how to be middle-class.[6] Advice books reiterated long-held convictions, but such manuals had continually to find new ways to urge middle-class systems of value (partly to distinguish each manual from its competitors). The increasing number of publications is in itself a sign that people could no longer rely on personal experience to build the temporal structures of the home. The order of chores, the interruptibility of certain work, the ongoing struggle to keep disorder in check were addressed and re-addressed. The tendency emerges concurrently with realist fiction, which bulked up its description of the processes involved in running a household.

As Rosa Mucignat has argued, nineteenth-century British novels saw a qualitative change in description, a change fuelled by the pressures of realism, which 'elevat[ed] [...] everyday life to narratable status'.[7] Nicholas Shrimpton has argued of material culture in literature that a simple list in the eighteenth century became an accumulation of narrative possibility in the nineteenth.[8] A similar deepening of significance, I argue, happened with time and timings. The realist impetus to show how things function heightened narrative involvement with temporal dynamics, with practices of timing, and with time-bound processes. A domestic setting was no longer a stage on which drama was played out, as it is in Henry Fielding's *History of Tom Jones, a Foundling* (1749), but was instead a part of the workings of plot. Whereas in *Tom Jones* domestic spaces are what Ermarth in another context has called 'rhetorical *topoi*, literally sites of arguments', in Gaskell's serial novel *Wives and Daughters* the dynamics of space and time have become vital to any conversation.[9] Gaskell places scenes with particular care: the news of the death of a major character in Chapter 51 is brought by a housemaid to the daughters of the house, Molly and Cynthia, who are standing in their father's consulting-room (he is out) because it is the only place that they can have a confidential conversation while their mother occupies the drawing-room. In this careful mapping of timed spaces, the temporal dynamics of the home 'takes on flesh', in the words of Mikhail Bakhtin.[10] Realist writers, in other words, give temporality a descriptive and qualitative thickness. This phenomenon arose in response to modernity, to advances in print technology, to the spreading print marketplace (which touched on all areas of modern life), and not least to the continual urge towards realism.

In nineteenth-century print culture, to describe something was ostensibly to master it. But description is never plain and simple; it always encodes reality in a particular way. New media, formats, and layouts were used to present a coherent system of knowledge in a self-conscious teleology, where domesticity and its temporality could become more and more detailed and complete. Modernity, during this period, could be seen as a move from a less organized body of knowledge to a more intricately organized body of knowledge, mapped out in print. Of course, such a teleology is a fallacy, and, as I show here, the ambitious project of describing the everyday in a heavily detailed manner led to its own failure, since the more closely one looks at something, the more unknowable it becomes. At this time, however, fulfilling this ambition still seemed possible. A proliferation of printed media went into more and more elaborate detail to describe the wheels and cogs that made domesticity tick.

Domestic time

In an 1860 book entitled *Homely Hints from the Fireside*, Henrietta Wilson equates domestic management to the workings of a clock:

> Be regular in your time for giving orders, be as early in doing so as possible, state your wishes precisely, and as far as possible, let one winding-up of the domestic clock do for the day. Neither watches nor households go on well when they are perpetually interfered with, interrupted, and altered as to time.[11]

Wilson posits the middle-class household manager as a supervisor of domestic cogs, with a bird's-eye perspective on the grubby details (implied, not described) of scrubbing, boiling, and sweeping. The metaphor of 'winding up' the clock of domestic time allows Wilson to suggest that domestic time can be mechanized – that it can be scheduled and made logical and unproblematic, given enough time discipline. Yet, as other writings from this period reveal, the clockwork household could not encompass all of domestic time, since the practices of the everyday were not always reducible to schedules, or amenable to strict timing. Although certain temporal coordinates are relatively fixed – eating times, rising and bedtimes, the breadwinner leaving for work and coming home, last time for posting letters – they are still not enough to fully tether all of domestic time. Advice literature that praises regularity and precision does so in the fear that domestic time is in fact dangerously discretionary. Sarah Stickney Ellis, in *The Daughters of England* (1842), is particularly worried about

> [those people] who, coming into a room for a particular purpose, and finding a book there by chance, open it, and sit down to read for half an hour, or an hour, believing all the while that they are going to do the thing they first intended; [or people who start out on a walk, but fall in with friends on the way]. Now, in these two cases, there may be as little harm in reading the book as in calling upon the acquaintance, and nothing wrong in either: but the habit of doing habitually what we had not intended to do, and leaving undone what we intended, has so injurious an effect in weakening our resolutions, and impairing our capacity for making exact calculations upon time and means, that one might pronounce, without much hesitation, upon a person accustomed to this mode of action, the sentence of utter inability to fill any situation of usefulness or importance amongst mankind.[12]

Even though Ellis is eager to reduce the problem to one of personal habit, this passage reveals the double difficulty of middle-class domestic time: its lack of temporal structure, and its peculiar flavour of vagueness when narrated. Ellis uses this vagueness as an aid in description – 'half an hour, or an hour' – to underline how sloppy timekeeping injures one's moral fibre. Drifting time remains a challenge to representation itself. Ellis's prose, with its meandering syntax, exemplifies the desire to describe the fluidity of time in order to do away with it. Simultaneously, it highlights the somewhat conflicting need in print culture to provide the schematization that proves woefully absent from domestic time.

I use domestic time as a shorthand term: for my purposes; the phrase designates points in a work where the representation of domesticity becomes temporal. In Wilson's clockwork metaphor, and in Ellis's drifting half-hours, the temporal dynamics of domesticity emerge before our eyes. Their remarks alert us to the fact that domestic tasks frequently add significant temporal structures to narrative. Sociologist Elizabeth Shove writes that 'temporal arrangements arise from the effective reproduction of everyday life, or, to put it more strongly, *practices make time*'.[13] When a character in a Victorian novel performs a domestic task (such as setting out a meal), she is making domesticity temporal through that performance. Moreover, such tasks involve conceptualizing time.

When Mrs Gibson experiences an interruption, domestic time binds together wider fields of association – space, time, gender, the genre of domestic fiction and the unspoken assumptions about what is, and is not, an important event – into a politicized whole.

Mid-century writers did not set out to describe domestic time. Instead, they aimed to reach the heart of something (household management, the English middle-class home, psychological experience) that appeared more pressing than ever before in English culture. In the process, they produced an incidental representation of domestic time. Emily Brontë's *Wuthering Heights* (1847), for example, constructs incidental domestic time through a series of inexplicable glimpses. The characters are always coming upon unexplained activities (or unexplained inactivity). The two narrators, Lockwood and Nelly, move through the baffling temporal functions of Wuthering Heights as if they will never penetrate its workings. For example, it is inexplicably difficult for Lockwood and Isabella to be allocated bedchambers upon arrival in their separate parts of the story.[14] The threatening unreadability of domestic time stems partly from this novel's Gothic heritage. Works of fiction in the Gothic mode tend to conceptualize domestic time as something dramatically incoherent – since writers have not yet turned towards the realist impetus for unified systems of time. In Gaskell's first novel, *Mary Barton* (1848), the author's use of melodramatic traits similarly colours domestic time. The narrative unfolds a series of stark tableaux: first, there is the cosy kitchen when Mrs Barton is alive, and then we witness the pinched scarcity after her death. The transition from one situation to the other – of pawning Mrs Barton's domestic treasures after her death – is implied, not described.

The shift I have identified between *Mary Barton* and *Wives and Daughters* informs my selection of materials. My study begins with two distinguished works of fiction. *Bleak House* focuses on a self-contained bourgeois domestic centre as an alternative to the never-ending bureaucracy of the Courts of Chancery. It is also a novel where Dickens peers so closely at domestic practice that such practice begins to look seriously odd. Meanwhile, Gaskell's *North and South* (1854–55) is a novel about the jarring meeting of two middle classes (the pseudo-genteel and the industrial) with entirely different modes of operation, and the internalization of that clash in the protagonist Margaret Hale's psychology. In both *Bleak House* and *North and South*, domestic time is coming together at the point at which old certainties are simultaneously coming apart. These two novels, however, draw attention to a further urgent debate about domestic time, which relates to the way they were printed, distributed and consumed. *Bleak House* was serialized in monthly instalments surrounded by advertising; *North and South* was printed weekly in *Household Words*. As Stuart Sherman has argued, 'a given narrative will inevitably, by the particulars of its form, absorb and register some of the temporalities at work in the world that surrounds its making'.[15] Just as much as textual representation 'makes' time, so too does the embodied text in its material format make time. I explore the connections between domestic time and print culture by shifting my focus from novels over periodicals to household manuals and, finally, private albums. Although the works are treated in chronological order within a concentrated period (1840–70), an equally significant trajectory is from narrative to non-narrative genres, as I explain in the next section.

Morning hours in print

In 1863, Barbara Hutton published a small book, *Monday Morning: How to Get Through It*. Pocket-sized and with an embossed blue cover, it promises to guide middle-class women – flatteringly and anachronistically called 'gentlewomen' in the subtitle – through the choppy waters of household management. It does so chiefly by dividing the day into portions, constructing a comforting sequence of times and places. For instance, Hutton advises that from 'ten to half-past ten may be spent in your drawing-room'.[16] *Monday Morning* attempts to reconcile the spatial and temporal dimensions of domesticity through its structure: each chapter is an hour-long interval, and each hour has its own specialized purpose. Hutton places the various spaces in the home in a chronological sequence from daybreak to afternoon tea, taking the reader from breakfast room to drawing-room, then from drawing-room to kitchen, and then from kitchen to larder. Hutton gives each hour its correct use, and the book moves through the working parts of the house with confidence.

It was a truism that morning hours in the middle-class home should be devoted to household management. The tradition was handed down to Hutton's early-1860s readers from previous generations. Maria Rundell, in her bestselling and much-pirated *New System of Domestic Cookery*, first published in 1805, tells us that 'if orders be given soon in the morning, there will be more time to execute them; and servants, by doing their work with ease, will be more equal to it, and fewer will be necessary.'[17] Frances (sometimes 'Fanny') Parkes in *Domestic Duties*, a hugely influential conduct book first published in 1825, informs her readers: 'The morning is the best part of the day, for the discharge of every employment connected with the business of a family.'[18] In 1835, Anne Cobbett remarks in *The English Housekeeper*: 'As soon after breakfast as she conveniently can, the mistress of a house should repair to the kitchen.'[19] Making a round of the kitchen, larder, storeroom and other 'offices' after breakfast was a practice firmly entrenched in early nineteenth-century advice literature. By 1863, however, Barbara Hutton clearly believes that more detailed instructions are required. In giving them, she reveals that this daily visit to the nether regions was not as problem-free as Rundell, Parkes and Cobbett had made it sound. Hutton's remarks often seem to be a covert response to besetting uncertainties about what this morning visit actually entailed:

> It is now half-past ten; so, leaving your writing or your flowers, you go down into the kitchen. Many young wives find this one of the most irksome of their duties; but it is one that cannot be shirked by any mistress of a household, except in establishments where a housekeeper is kept. I do not, however, advise *ladies* to be always in the kitchen; and the morning's visit, once paid, need not be repeated, unless something unusual occurs.[20]

Hutton has expanded what was once a simple one-sentence suggestion into an anxious exhortation. By 'irksome', Hutton means 'awkward' or even 'daunting'. Entering the space where the domestic staff worked most hours of their lives, a young and inexperienced housekeeper might well expect silent hostility, implied ridicule or other intractable behaviour from her unfamiliar, antagonistic servants. Sixty years later, in Denis McKail's novel *Greenery Street* (1925), these middle-class tribulations were satirized when a newlywed woman's awkwardness with her servants leads her married life to near ruin.[21] In 1863, though, Hutton still only hints at the possibility of humiliation while she demarcates the borders between the classes both spatially and temporally.

When writers in the nineteenth century manipulated the divisions of the day, they often chose to manipulate the divisions of their books to help them. However, as is evident from Figure 0.1., at a micro-level of organization, Hutton's volume lacks structure. The announcement that 'it is now half-past ten' occurs at an odd place, following immediately after an anecdote instead of opening a new paragraph, as would seem more logical. Throughout *Monday Morning*, Hutton's recipes, which are otherwise clearly marked with headings, tend to run straight into the more narrative parts of her text; in comparison, *Beeton's Book of Household Management*, published four years earlier, has a much more

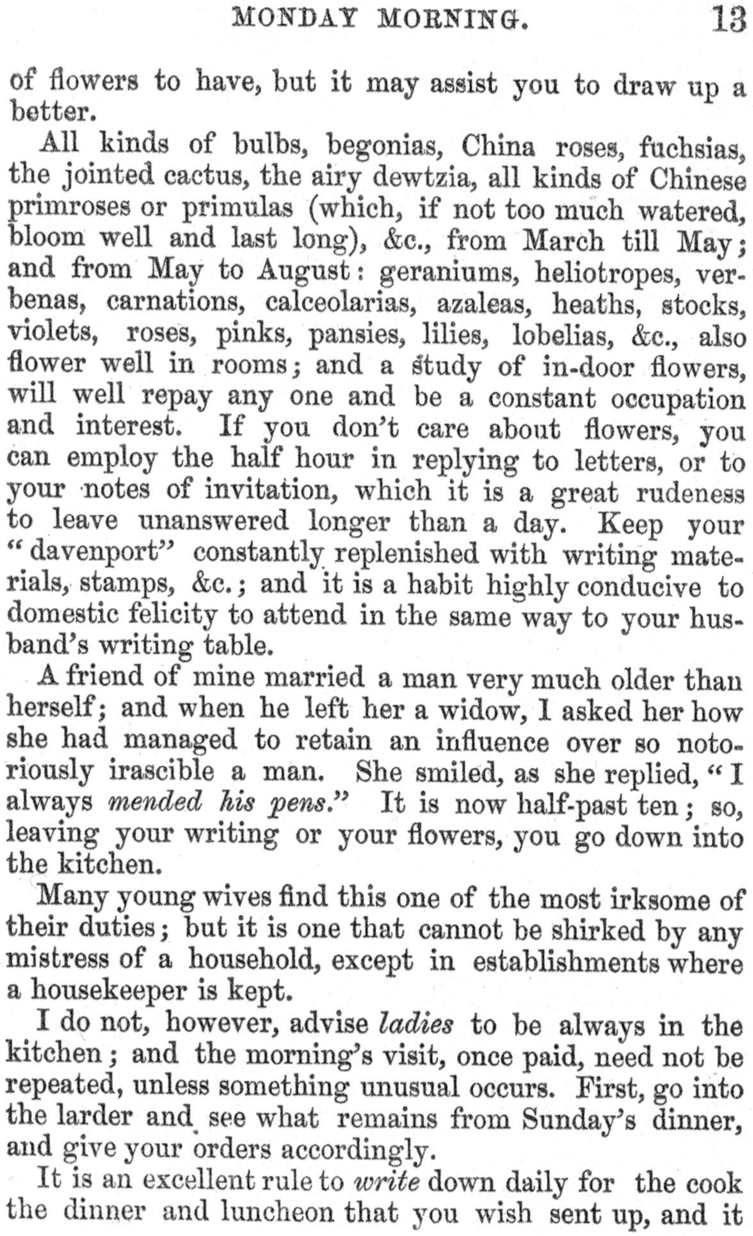

MONDAY MORNING. 13

of flowers to have, but it may assist you to draw up a better.

All kinds of bulbs, begonias, China roses, fuchsias, the jointed cactus, the airy dewtzia, all kinds of Chinese primroses or primulas (which, if not too much watered, bloom well and last long), &c., from March till May; and from May to August: geraniums, heliotropes, verbenas, carnations, calceolarias, azaleas, heaths, stocks, violets, roses, pinks, pansies, lilies, lobelias, &c., also flower well in rooms; and a study of in-door flowers, will well repay any one and be a constant occupation and interest. If you don't care about flowers, you can employ the half hour in replying to letters, or to your notes of invitation, which it is a great rudeness to leave unanswered longer than a day. Keep your "davenport" constantly replenished with writing materials, stamps, &c.; and it is a habit highly conducive to domestic felicity to attend in the same way to your husband's writing table.

A friend of mine married a man very much older than herself; and when he left her a widow, I asked her how she had managed to retain an influence over so notoriously irascible a man. She smiled, as she replied, "I always *mended his pens.*" It is now half-past ten; so, leaving your writing or your flowers, you go down into the kitchen.

Many young wives find this one of the most irksome of their duties; but it is one that cannot be shirked by any mistress of a household, except in establishments where a housekeeper is kept.

I do not, however, advise *ladies* to be always in the kitchen; and the morning's visit, once paid, need not be repeated, unless something unusual occurs. First, go into the larder and see what remains from Sunday's dinner, and give your orders accordingly.

It is an excellent rule to *write* down daily for the cook the dinner and luncheon that you wish sent up, and it

Figure 0.1 Detail from Barbara Hutton's *Monday Morning*, p. 13

logical relationship between typesetting and content. In spite of its inconsistencies, *Monday Morning* encapsulates several tendencies developing in print culture at this time. First, it responds to a need to parcel out domestic time. Second, the book combines different forms – time schedule, narrative, and recipe – into a hybrid genre. Third, Hutton shows a tendency to elaborate what had previously been taken for granted, and makes up her own, somewhat idiosyncratic, structure in the process. In some ways, *Monday Morning* responds to the teleological move towards more organized writings on household management; in other ways, though, it is a haphazard mixture of forms and genres. Hutton's structure must have appealed to some readers, at least; a quarter of a century later Elizabeth Garrett plagiarized *Monday Morning* in her book *Monday Mornings in India* (1887), which rewrites Hutton's volume in order to conform to the realities of colonial life. Borrowings and echoes were an intrinsic part of the genre, but the plagiarism also speaks to an important truth about domestic practice, and this is my fourth and final point. Like print culture, domesticity points both into the past and the future. Wilson's clock metaphor attempts to simplify what Hutton has taken upon herself to elaborate: the need for domesticity to run on in a cycle of repetition, and the need for print culture to reiterate that need again and again. Whenever narratives of domesticity become temporal in the mid-nineteenth century – whenever description runs into domestic time – they tend to try to balance the discrepancy between the safely repetitive and the worryingly fluid.

Modernity, time-discipline, and the novel

Nineteenth-century experiences of modernity triggered conflicting needs to make domesticity feel stable and to represent it as realistically dynamic. Constructing stable conceptualizations of domestic time was to a certain extent a desire borne out of an experience of change accompanied by inherent contradictions, as Marshall Berman has observed.[22] On the one hand, modernity was associated with transience – embodied in flimsy handbills and newspapers, and symbolized by the much-proclaimed impermanence of the Crystal Palace – and, on the other hand, it was linked with drastic alterations in the material fabric of the everyday, such as the many new railways, the building of factories where before there were fields, and suburbs sprouting in every direction. Modernity always has two sides: increased mobility is never far from the desire for stability, and growth is welcomed just as the erosion of old certainties is abhorred. As a consequence, nothing and no one can ever be wholly modern within modernity. As John McGowan argues, 'the very notion of the modern inevitably places us in a moment of transition. The modern is always out in front of us.'[23]

The impact of modernity on time experience has been described in much scholarship as a shock, a jolt, or a process of alienation: the spread of time-based technologies such as clocks and watches heralded a profoundly 'new' time experience, incompatible with older timekeeping practices.[24] Lately, however, this view has been challenged. Paul Glennie and Nigel Thrift have argued rather that once clocks and watches became more widespread, two developments took place. Not only did time experience become 'denser'; people also increasingly navigated this dense time environment with ease throughout their everyday lives.[25] Glennie and Thrift find no evidence that those who had just bought a new timepiece found the change particularly troubling. Moreover, clocks were just one aspect of time experience through which people faced up to new urgencies. Print culture, too, was an integral part of the texture of modernity and simultaneously formed a space for reactions to modernity. As scholars such as Mark Turner, Laurel Brake and Margaret Beetham have argued, print culture manipulated temporality, enforcing different rhythms and periodicities – from transient ephemera to the fixed and seemingly 'timeless' volume.[26] Nick Hopwood, Simon Schaffer and Jim Secord have argued that new print technologies, especially seriality, were becoming the central systems of knowledge – literacy in the nineteenth century was 'primarily a way of participating in a serial culture'.[27] In the material texture of print media, time was constructed – just as it was within the writing itself.

Print media were not the only means by which nineteenth-century people negotiated time. They had clocks, trains, postal services, office hours, meals, and growing children to remind them of time passing. But print was a sophisticated way of constructing a cultural consensus of temporal experience, and, as the print industry expanded, it was an increasingly effective one. In an era when so many sciences and institutions were gathered into totalizing systems of knowledge, to describe was to understand, and to understand was to master. We find such teleological optimism across print culture at this time. At mid-century, a new class had sprung up: a culturally strong middle class, which had not existed fifty years earlier. For many observers, a new class affiliation brought with it a pressure to conform to a new set of rules that people could not learn from their parents' generation, from whom they were socially and often geographically separated. A wealth of publications sprang up to cater to this new demand, and a large part of the print boom in the mid-nineteenth century went into the process of class consolidation. There was an increasing pressure to describe the smallest of practices that made the middle classes what they were. Routines and habits held the key to middle-class status, and a proliferation of print media promised to make the mechanisms of the bourgeois home comprehensible.

From the birth of the industrial age, the effective use of time had been a central concern, perhaps most prominently in Adam Smith's *Wealth of Nations* (1776), which continued to influence political economy throughout the nineteenth century. Smith's book famously opens with a discussion of the division of labour to make work time more productive. As E. P. Thompson has shown, the split between a labourer's work hours and leisure hours became contested ground in the factories of the first industrial revolution.[28] The discourse often incorporated a religious tradition of timekeeping. Here it could borrow from a strong Puritan tradition for self-disciplining diaries from the seventeenth century onwards. Nineteenth-century time management, especially for the new middle classes, was to a large extent a question of self-discipline or self-help, to borrow the title of Samuel Smiles' 1859 book. In a domestic context, self-help became a question of class discipline as well. Modern scholars often quote the preface to *Beeton's Book of Household Management*, where Isabella Beeton likens the middle-class housekeeper to 'the Commander of an Army' – a militaristic metaphor that suggests that domestic time is largely about troop deployment. Thad Logan suggests as much in *The Victorian Parlour*:

> the importance of "timing" for the performance of Victorian middle-class life can hardly be overestimated. [...] A finely tuned routine was considered of paramount importance in household management and child care. Social relations, too, were governed by the careful management of time: consider, for example, the stipulation that formal calls last twenty minutes. Clocks, then, played an important role in the home and were frequently situated at what is arguably the most prominent site in the parlour, the center of the mantelpiece.[29]

While these observations are perfectly valid, the inference seems to be that the timetable is the most appropriate model for domestic temporality. In this respect, Logan's observations find support in Michel Foucault, who, in an aside in *Discipline and Punish*, suggests:

> ([O]ne day we should show how intra-familial relations, essentially in the parents-children cell, have become "disciplined", absorbing since the classical age external schemata, first educational and

military, then medical, psychiatric, psychological, which have made the family the privileged locus of emergence for the disciplinary question of the normal and the abnormal.)[30]

To the contrary, *Time, Domesticity and Print Culture* argues that no easy transference can be made from ideal institutional structures to real everyday practices. Furthermore, representation in nineteenth-century print culture, supposedly so eager to show schematization and machine-like efficiency, reveals major uncertainties about how time in the home actually worked. Beeton's 'Commander of an Army' is in truth a manager in the midst of threatening chaos, not the capable emblem of order that she might appear to be. Charles Dickens satirizes the idea of perfect domestic scheduling in his description of Mr Podsnap in *Our Mutual Friend* (1864–5):

> The world got up at eight, shaved close at a quarter-past, breakfasted at nine, went to the City at ten, came home at half-past five, and dined at seven. Mr. Podsnap's notions of the Arts in their integrity might have been stated thus. Literature; large print, respectively descriptive of getting up at eight, shaving close at a quarter-past, breakfasting at nine, going to the City at ten, coming home at half-past five, and dining at seven. Painting and Sculpture; models and portraits representing Professors of getting up at eight, shaving close at a quarter-past, breakfasting at nine, going to the City at ten, coming home at half-past five, and dining at seven. Music; a respectable performance (without variations) on stringed and wind instruments, sedately expressive of getting up at eight, shaving close at a quarter-past, breakfasting at nine, going to the City at ten, coming home at half-past five, and dining at seven. Nothing else to be permitted to those same vagrants the Arts, on pain of excommunication. Nothing else To Be – anywhere![31]

While Sarah Stickney Ellis might have celebrated such rigidity, for Dickens it was an experiential void: the daily schedule symbolically emptied out domestic time. Schedules, in everyday life, are states of exception: they contain no chance visitors, no travel, and no emergencies about dinner. Such abstractions purposely exclude the accidents of lived time.

Temporal margins: untold time, gender, and servants

The problem, of course, was that domesticity – or its close associate (that other critical construct), the everyday – was difficult to represent.

Social historian Hans-Joakim Voth, in his study *Time and Work in England: 1750–1830*, ignores housework because it is for him 'discretionary', and thus resists measurement.[32] As Elaine Scarry has argued of work (a concept which touches on domestic time), there are some categories that resist representation:

> The major source of [the difficulty of representing work] is that work is action rather than a discrete action: it has no identifiable beginning or end; if it were an exceptional action, or even 'an action', it could – like the acts in epic, heroic, or military literature – be easily accommodated in narrative. It is the essential nature of work to be perpetual, repetitive, habitual.[33]

Activities that are not 'events' or 'actions' prove to be non-narratable – an insight that illuminates domestic time as well. Like work, domestic time is composed of 'perpetual, repetitive [and] habitual' actions. As Scarry goes on to show in an excellent reading of Thomas Hardy's fiction, nineteenth-century realist writers aimed to discover some way of representing the unrepresentable. They confronted a pressing question. How do you write non-events into the fabric of a novel? In a related vein, Bakhtin describes the production of novelistic 'eventless time' in a style that suggests that he was writing a nineteenth-century realist novel:

> The petty-bourgeois provincial town with its stagnant life is a very widespread setting for nineteenth-century novels [...] Here there are no events, only 'doings' that constantly repeat themselves. Time here has no advancing historical movement; it moves rather in narrow circles; the circle of the day, of the week, of the month, of a person's entire life. A day is just a day, a year is just a year – a life is just a life. Day in, day out the same round of activities are repeated, the same topics of conversation, the same words and so forth. [...] This is commonplace, philistine cyclical everyday time. [...] The markers of this time are simple, crude, material, fused with the everyday details of specific locales, with the quaint little houses and rooms of the town, with the sleepy streets, the dust and flies, the club, the billiards and so on and on. Time here is without event and therefore almost seems to stand still. [...] It is a viscous and sticky time that drags itself slowly through space. [...] Novelists use it as an ancillary time. [...] It often serves as a contrasting background for temporal sequences that are more charged with energy and event.[34]

Bakhtin makes us aware that novels produce 'ancillary time' in order to activate plot time. As Bakhtin shows, 'markers' of time give the novel's temporality a texture (in this case, 'viscous and sticky'). In the opening of the same essay, he argues that 'in the literary artistic chronotope, spatial and temporal indicators are fused into one carefully thought-out, concrete whole. Time, as it were, thickens, takes on flesh, becomes artistically visible'.[35] By describing such strategies of visualization, we can uncover the politics that lie beneath representation.

Eventlessness is no less culturally constructed than event. In Bakhtin's example, which synthesizes the works of several European realist novelists, eventlessness is equated with provinciality and stagnation. Domestic time is similarly marginalized when it is associated with interruptibility, circularity, and endless repetition. Understanding domestic time as an absence of event can be productive without falling into the fallacy that the dichotomy of eventfulness/eventlessness is necessarily true. One way of representing domestic time in a novel is to note it when it falls away – 'ancillary time' is only necessary to narrate when something happens to disrupt it. In Elizabeth Gaskell's novel *Wives and Daughters*, the narrator describes domestic details in order to prepare the way for an interruption:

> One day, to Molly's infinite surprise, Mr Preston was announced as a caller. Mrs Gibson and she were sitting together in the drawing-room; Cynthia was out – gone into the town a-shopping – when the door was opened, the name given, and in walked the young man. His entrance seemed to cause more confusion than Molly could well account for. [...] Mrs Gibson was at her everlasting worsted-work frame when Mr Preston entered the room; but somehow in rising to receive him, she threw down her basket of crewels, and, declining Molly's offer to help her, she would pick up all the reels herself, before she asked her visitor to sit down.[36]

Here we see a juxtaposition of event and non-event. The narrator represents the non-events, the enduring actions, in the past progressive tense – 'were sitting' and 'gone . . . a-shopping' – thus relegating them to the background. In contrast, the narrator depicts the positive action through the preterite: 'walked' and 'entered'. This ground-and-relief becomes evident in the words that associate Mrs Gibson with her 'everlasting' worsted-work and Mr Preston with contrastingly short and decisive actions: 'the door was opened, the name given, and in walked the young man'. The confusion into which Mrs Gibson is thrown only underlines the sense of disruption. In Bakhtin's terms, the interruption makes domestic time 'artistically visible'.

Such narrative contrast often reflects gendered nuances in plot construction. Conventionally, novels tend to align men with plot, and women with non-plot. Nina Auerbach argues that in *Pride and Prejudice* (1813) Jane Austen defines female experience as one of waiting for men; for an heir to Longbourn to be born, for a marriage proposal, or (more obliquely) for a war to be won.[37] Although mid-century novels, especially those written by women, give female characters more agency, narrators often describe such agency as a struggle against the social grain. In Charlotte Brontë's *Shirley* (1849), for example, the title character is a wealthy, independent female employer, and yet her independence is subsumed in a marriage plot. Meanwhile, the heroine Caroline Helstone spends large portions of the novel literally wasting away at home waiting for Robert Moore to propose.[38] By comparison, Anthony Trollope's *Doctor Thorne* (1858), aside from its inheritance plot, is structured around Frank Gresham's deliberations over whether to marry the socially inferior Mary Thorne. Mary waits patiently for Frank to persuade his family to consent. Certainly, Gaskell's female characters have more agency to move plots forward, but even in *North and South* that agency is either thrust upon Margaret Hale by hard circumstances or won through tiring fights with her more conventionally minded relatives. This is not to argue that women characters had no power over plot; it is simply to point out that the gender of a character affects the genre of representation available to them, just as it affects the way characters of different genders experience domesticity. On this matter, I depart from Ermarth's *English Novel in History*. Since Ermarth links men's time with 'the professional's time, common time, universal time, the time of public affairs, and wars, and heroics' – the neutral, non-gendered temporal medium that became the norm in nineteenth-century self-understanding – she leaves women forever shut out not just from economic and legal life, but from the shared medium of time itself. Women's time 'conforms to local and private conditions; it is not neutral; it is flexible, defined by others, their needs, their schedules, their ambitions'. Ermarth sees women's time as entirely non-narratable, since it cannot be accommodated within a public temporal logic.[39]

As Julia Kristeva warned in her seminal paper 'Women's Time', such gendered distinctions of time have the effect of essentializing women's position as 'other', thereby risking a symbolic retreat into mysticism. She explains:

> By demanding recognition of an irreducible identity, without equal in the opposite sex and, as such, exploded, plural, fluid, in a certain way nonidentical, this feminism situates itself outside the linear time of identities which communicate through projection and revidication. Such a feminism rejoins, on the one hand, the archaic (mythical) memory and, on the other, the cyclical or monumental temporality of marginal movements.[40]

Kristeva's article is a critique of this binary division of time into linear (male) and cyclical (female).[41] While *Time, Domesticity and Print Culture* acknowledges that women's practices in the home are often associated with cyclicality – occasionally even with non-production and stasis – my discussion also demonstrates that in the ever-shifting field of representational print culture, such mysticism could not uphold itself. The pressure to specify and particularize everyday practices meant that the comforting ideal of the unchanging domestic realm and its ever-youthful Angel in the House either unravelled or stagnated. Print culture could not, by its very nature, tie anything permanently down, since the drive to control domestic time through description merely fuelled the persistent strangeness of domestic time.

Domestic time gains its evocative power by stretching the capabilities of realism. Domestic time pushes towards the margins of what can be told. As William Morris insisted, 'you can't have art without resistance in the material'.[42] In this respect, the manipulation of narrative is like the movement of the nib of a pen over paper – it only truly works when it meets friction. As Rachel Bowlby has argued, the problems inherent in representation are written into the very fabric of realist writings:

> realism can never be simply codeless in its claimed replication of reality [...] It is always presenting a particular theory of what will count as a picture of reality, and it is always attached, if only by counter-positioning, to rival forms of artistic representation that it is out to replace.[43]

The idea that writings present a 'particular theory of what will count as a picture of reality' is true not just of the realist novel, but also of all the other genres which have an explicit stake in representing reality – non-fiction like Hutton's *Monday Morning* included. As I argue, different genres have to confront different limits of representation. In Caroline Levine's terms, different forms have different 'affordances'; forms allow certain uses and latent actions.[44] What I have found particularly fruitful is to explore how works edge towards the limits of their affordances. For the realist novel, there is a limit to how much of the fullness of everyday experience can be narrated; specifics must be curtailed to allow the plot to flow. Another limit to the mediation of domestic time relates to the lives of the people labouring beneath stairs. These are the domestic servants whose vital labour emerges in diverse ways in the sources I analyse.

Nineteenth-century print culture was almost exclusively produced by the middle classes, and in the eyes of most commentators, working-class domestic practices, though often deplored for lack of good habits, had little or no impact on middle-class experiences. There was, however, a substantial subsection of the working classes which did directly influence middle-class experience, but which barely surfaces in narratives: the hundreds of thousands of domestic servants who kept middle-class homes going. The myth of the smoothly running home was maintained off-stage, as it were, by endless hours of back-breaking work; the ideal of a stable household was upheld by work which was repetitive, hard and often singularly thankless. If there is one thing the nineteenth-century domestic novel struggles to represent, it is this vital work behind the scenes.[45] As Bruce Robbins argues, 'servants come to represent the realm of unrepresentability itself: The presence of servants signifies the absence of the people. Signposts left at random in the no-man's-land between what can and cannot be represented, they indicate only that the other side of the border is inhabited.'[46] In *Bleak House* and *North and South*, and in the pages of domestic periodicals, we encounter these shadowy servants in the corners of each narrative. While novels tend to be reticent on the matter, advice literature can be much more forthright. Manuals frequently, and with relish, give heart-rending specifics of a servant's day. In contrast to the clockwork logics of such representation, middle-class time is made to seem free-flowing; and very few writers ask themselves what a servant's experience is actually like. The limit to representability for manuals lies not in daily fullness, as it does in the domestic novel, but in the experience itself (which the realist novel would be perfectly equipped to represent – if only it represented servants at all). Almost uniquely, Anne Cobbett makes the attempt in *The English Housekeeper* (1835):

> Ladies who shudder as they meet the cold air, in descending to their breakfast rooms, forget, too many of them, the sufferings of

> the female servant, who has, perhaps, the night before, gone to bed exhausted by fatigue, but whose duty compels her to rise again, some hours before she is sufficiently rested, to begin her work afresh, and to do all over again all that has been done the day before. A lady who thinks that her servant is sufficiently *paid* for all she endures, has never known what it is to get up in the dark of a cold winter's morning, and to spend half an hour on her knees, labouring to produce a polish on the bars of a grate, which bars were burnt black yesterday, and will be burnt black again to-day.[47]

Cobbett recognizes the backbreaking and heart-breaking repetition of cleaning and dirtying, soiling and scrubbing. It is the untold-ness that gives the passage its emotional power, since Cobbett is writing at the limits of representability.[48]

Time, Domesticity and Print Culture: From Narrative to Non-Narrative Forms

The chapters that follow each combine textual analysis with an understanding of the mediation of that text in material print. In Chapter 1, 'Repetition: Making Domestic Time in *Bleak House* and the "Bleak House Advertiser"', I discuss Dickens's construction of domestic time as a repeatable practice in conjunction with Dakin & Co.'s audacious full-page advertisement that echoed the *Bleak House* cover. The advertisement underlines the coordination of readers' time into an imaginary simultaneity, in which tea, coffee, and Dickens instalments produce a national (domestic) time. Dickens's novel itself, through its reliance on repetition and its tendency to linger lovingly on domestic tasks, makes time in the home drawn-out and enduring – and very odd. Of all the chapters, this one touches the most on the marginality of servants. Chapter 2 similarly treats a thematic pattern: interruption. By charting the trope of the 'spare moment' in domestic periodicals between 1845 and 1865, the chapter examines the discourse that domestic time for women was necessarily interruptible, and that this central fact set a challenge to representation. With recourse to extracts from George Eliot's *Felix Holt, The Radical* (1866), I discuss how domestic time became porous. My analysis then turns to periodicals and advice manuals to show that porousness was a representational challenge that in turn pushed at the boundaries of realism. Women and their sewing became shorthand used to fill the holes left behind in interruptible domestic time.

In Chapter 3, 'Division into Parts: Elizabeth Gaskell's *North and South* and the Serial Instalment', I turn to Gaskell's third novel. Serialized weekly in *Household Words*, the novel caused friction between Gaskell and Dickens, in a manner that illuminates Gaskell's unique attitude to serial division. The divisions underline the particular quality of *North and South*'s conceptualization of domestic time: in this novel, domestic time is often equated with eventlessness, but a particularly charged version of eventlessness. Finally, the chapter turns to the coincidental synchronicity of novel and war, as it reflects on the similarities and differences between Margaret Hale and Florence Nightingale, who rose to fame in the Crimean War as a nurse and hospital administrator. By comparison, chapter 4, 'Decomposition: Mrs Beeton and the Non-Linear Text', takes us from serial novel to serial cookery book. *Beeton's Book of Household Management*, so central to late-Victorian self-understanding, was published serially before finally being collected into volume form in 1861. A cookery book, since it is both non-linear and non-narrative, does not fall naturally into monthly segments. My discussion examines the complications arising from the instalment scheme during its 24-month run. This reading expands into a wider exploration of how the material text constructs domestic time, both in words and in paper and cardboard.

Finally, the Coda, 'Scrapbooking and the Reconfiguration of Domestic Time', builds on the findings in the cookery book chapter and expands the argument that non-narrative genres challenge our understanding of the work of print culture. Albums and scrapbooks, while evidently a kind of record of domestic time, yet capture print culture in a wholly different way to the genres we have been used to discuss in academic criticism. I use a selection of albums from the Harry Page Collection in the Manchester Metropolitan University Special Collections to examine the album's construction of domestic time. The Coda calls for a more inclusive style of literary history, arguing that criticism of novels and other narrative genres can benefit when it juxtaposes these sources to non-narrative, non-fictional, even non-printed genres.

1
Repetition: Making Domestic Time in *Bleak House* and the 'Bleak House Advertiser'

> In the distribution of [the boiled pork and greens], as in every other household duty, Mrs Bagnet develops an exact system; sitting with every dish before her; allotting to every portion of pork its own portion of pot-liquor, greens, potatoes, and even mustard; and serving it out complete.
>
> Charles Dickens, *Bleak House* (November 1852)[1]

> Boiled beef and greens constitute the day's variety on the former repast of boiled pork and greens; and Mrs Bagnet serves out the meal in the same way, and seasons it with the best of temper.
>
> Dickens, *Bleak House* (January 1853)[2]

If domestic time has a basic structure, that structure is repetition; its backbone is formed out of routines. Dinner, for instance, must be prepared every day; yet novels, for obvious reasons, do not tend to give details of every single meal. Charles Dickens, however, is unusual in his elaboration of banal everydayness, and *Bleak House* (1852–3) is a novel with a peculiar stake in narrating what is normally invisible. The narrative uses repetition as a structural element and as a trope in itself. Mrs Bagnet's two family dinners – pork and greens followed by beef and greens – occur two monthly numbers apart (November 1852 and January 1853). The repetition serves three purposes. First, such repetition is part of Dickens's endeavour to bring all characters before the reader's eyes at regular intervals during the 19-month-long run. Secondly, such repetition supplies Dickens's well-known method of characterization, one that tends to associate characters with idiosyncratic actions and particular speech patterns. And thirdly, on a formal level such repeated actions are the mainstay that produces virtuous domesticity – the primary hope for the nation as a whole.

In *Bleak House*, domestic time is located in repeated actions: the codified ringing of bells for meals, the rhythms of cooking, account-keeping and supervision, and the small tasks which characters are engaged in when the narrative lingers on them. The novel is shot through with references to Esther Summerson's jingling bunch of keys, making her domestic management a base beat of recurrent significance. As a counter-rhythm, the ominous step on the Chesney Wold terrace is a recurring sign of the decline of aristocratic power in the face of new, active bourgeois self-fashioning. Time is measured out in *Bleak House*. The project of the novel is the making of the middle-class home, and the narrative follows characters who are deliberately and painstakingly filling up time. Whereas Agnes Wakefield in *David Copperfield* (1849–50) conducted her home silently and unobtrusively – linked, in the narrator's mind, to an eternalized ideal of domestic womanhood, silently pointing towards heaven – domestic time in *Bleak House* is obtrusive in its repetitive insistence. Mrs Bagnet is militantly exact in her management. Similarly, Esther's keys, which act as her self-disciplining subconscious, also link her to the rhythms of daily life. Partly, this insistence on routine tasks is a function of the novel's aim: to narratively construct the middle-class home as a bourgeois power centre. But it is also partly owing to a historical tendency to establish the details of everyday life, and to restate them more emphatically, which came to a head in the 1850s. The net movement was towards length and detail. Household manuals projected confidence in their ability to be all-encompassing. *Beeton's Book of Household Management* was only one of a long line of manuals intended to describe every aspect of everyday life and solve every query. In a spirit of class consolidation, fiction as well as non-fiction took part in this drive to be specific, exhaustive, and authoritative. In *Bleak House*, Dickens uses the topos of repetition to suggest an easily reproduced household, one running on a logical plan. In the process, repetition is pushed as far as realism will allow it. Characters duplicate their own actions, clearly expecting similar results. Henri Lefebvre has cautioned that repetitive rhythm inevitably incorporates change over time: 'there is no identical absolute repetition, indefinitely [...] [T]here is always something new and unforeseen that introduces itself into the repetitive: difference.'[3] Dickens's characters in *Bleak House*, especially Esther Summerson and John Jarndyce, work actively to deny dynamic change, as we shall see.

Repetitive activity, such as humdrum housework, is problematic in narrative because it can lead to monotony; when domesticity is described as repetitive it takes on an association with pointlessness, making it seem as if household tasks are never finished and domestic time never goes anywhere. Dickens has often been identified as a writer who traps his female characters in profoundly undynamic loops, denying them growth and change. In an attempt to give this idea a positive spin (and based on a misreading of Julia Kristeva's 'Women's Time' which ignores Kristeva's warning against gender essentialism), Elizabeth A. Campbell has argued that:

> rather than envisioning time as history, moving in a linear fashion (the temporality traditionally associated with men), Dickens's narratives [of women] give priority to time's cyclicality, to the representation of time as a space that emphasizes at once repetition and eternal return.[4]

As this chapter will show, I profoundly disagree with this statement. The first part of my analysis may in fact seem to confirm that *Bleak House* aligns 'repetition' with 'cyclicality' and 'eternal return', as Campbell suggests. But as the repetitions accumulate, and as Dickens elaborates domestic tasks more and more (to the point of absurdity), these loops begin to look strange. Repetition and cyclicality are not, in fact, synonymous: no repetition can ever be perfect, and so repeated actions or events always carry a seed of change with them. A household manual may require users to repeat their actions every time a recipe is revisited, but the dish will never work out the same way twice. Writers of household manuals must abandon any idea of complete reproductivity and aim for a universal discourse of active, sometimes inventive, performance.

In *Bleak House*, Dickens purposefully works against this consequence; the narrative is straining against change, even as the narrator repeats individual acts in elaborate detail. In other words, the novel shows cyclicality to be a construction, borne of a wilful dedication to repetition that denies repetition's inherent dynamics. As I shall show, *Bleak House* is a novel which acknowledges the constructed quality of repetitive time, and which hints, at various points, at the erasures that make this possible. One erasure is the possibility of a future or a past; another erasure is the work of the novel's shadowy servants. Finally, the chapter links the novel's production of time with a particular advertisement in the 'Bleak House Advertiser', the advertising supplement which was sown into the covers of the initial serial publication in 1852–3. *Bleak House* was published in 19 instalments, each containing 32 pages of the novel (apart from the 19th, which was a double number). Each instalment was bound in blue-green paper covers with a cover illustration by Hablot Knight Browne, under the familiar pseudonym 'Phiz' (Figure 1.1). The 'Bleak House Advertiser' both precedes and follows the novel. The advertisement I want to focus on below, for the tea and coffee company Dakin & Co., both invests in and elaborates on Dickens's desire to construct a reproducible domestic time for the nation.

Bleak House has a stake in representing domestic time as a national allegory. Not only can domestic time be repeated in time (being inherently repetitive), but it can also be repeated across space, in other domestic spheres, by other families, simultaneously. Dickens had a well-documented dream of the many simultaneous domestic readings he could achieve with his serial format each time a new number was released. In the 'Preliminary Word' to his periodical *Household Words*, he writes:

> We aspire to live in the Household affections, and to be numbered among the Household thoughts, of our readers [...] We have considered what an ambition it is to be admitted into many homes with affection and confidence; to be regarded as a friend by children and old people; to be thought of in affliction and in happiness; to people the sick room with airy shapes 'that give delight and hurt not', and to be associated with the harmless laughter and the gentle tears of many hearths.[5]

The periodical text, being reproducible, will produce near-identical affective responses from its many readers. The aspiration is that synchronous readings will tend towards uniformity. Similarly, the monthly parts of *Bleak House*, with their recognizable blue-green wrappers and the distinctive cover design by 'Phiz', created a nationally synchronized reading time which could be domestically situated. The paratext of the *Bleak House* serial – the blue-green covers and the numerous advertisements in the 'Bleak House Advertiser' which accompany the letterpress – thus informs the novel's aim to construct a national (domestic) time. Matthew Rubery has even spoken of a '*Bleak House*-time', one produced by the novel and its paratext together. All 19 months were unified by their implication in the print run of *Bleak House*.[6] In this chapter, I follow the lead of Laurel Brake who has similarly argued that 'publishing histories of individual texts themselves may [...] be said to participate in

Figure 1.1 Cover of the *Bleak House serial,* no. VI (August 1852)

the paradigm of the timespan of the series which marked the period'.[7] By 'marking the period' of *Bleak House*, both visually and through explicit references to Dickens's novel, the 'Bleak House Advertiser' helped build the paradigm of that timespan, as Brake suggests.

Contemporary buyers of Dickens's serial novel would be familiar with the engraved cover illustrations, which often contain oblique references to the novel's themes. But in the sixth number, published in August 1852, the first sight that meets the reader upon turning the green front cover is a visual echo of that same front cover. It is an advertisement for Dakin & Co., tea and coffee sellers, deliberately designed to resemble the *Bleak House* cover (Figure 1.2). Dakin & Co., the firm behind this visual imitation, was a habitual and somewhat audacious advertiser in the 'Bleak House Advertiser'. This particular illustration in the sixth number is so similar in design to Browne's cover that a first-time reader is likely to pause for a moment, confused at the unexpected new beginning; in fact, there is little doubt that Browne is the artist responsible for both Dickens's cover and Dakin & Co.'s advertisement. That the tea warehouse is using the Dickens serial as a vehicle obviously suggests how recognizable the Dickens brand had become. The Dakin & Co advertisement shares Dickens's investment in the dream of innumerable domestic spheres, all of them leafing through the latest Dickens serial at once. Domestic time is central not just to the novel-text itself. As we shall see below, the Dakin & Co advertisement ties domestic time to the commercial distribution of print – novel, flyer, and advertisement – and suggests that ideal domesticity is reproducible (given the right brand of tea). Similarly, in *Bleak House*, repetitive actions are a model of behaviour. By using repetition formally, the novel posits that with the right practices, readers can reproduce Esther Summerson's ideal domestic sphere, in synchrony, across the nation. Repetition, in other words, is set up as a producer of stasis and sameness. As I explain below, the narrative goes to inordinate lengths to maintain a viable stasis.

This chapter examines, first of all, traces of repetitive action in *Bleak House*. Repetition, by the very nature of the novel genre, is always represented *pars pro toto*; a novel that contained every instance of repetitive actions would be literally endless. Gérard Genette, in *Narrative Discourse*, distinguishes between narratives with recurrent events, and narratives where a single instance of an event is made to stand for many recurrences – he calls the latter 'iterative narrative'.[8] The distinction is a useful one: almost all of the instances of domestic recurrence in *Bleak House* are iterative (not every meal in the Bagnet family is narrated).

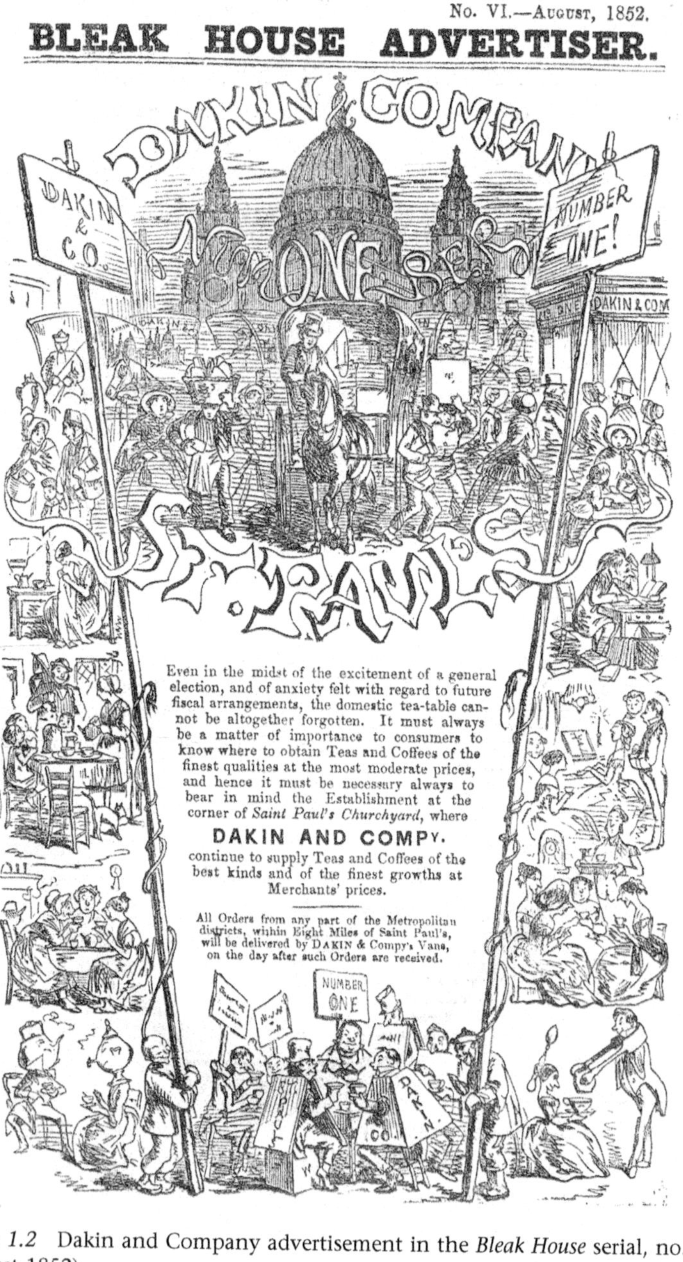
No. VI.—August, 1852.
BLEAK HOUSE ADVERTISER.
DAKIN & COMPANY
DAKIN & CO.
NUMBER ONE!
NUMBER ONE ST. PAUL'S
DAKIN & CO
ST. PAUL'S
Even in the midst of the excitement of a general election, and of anxiety felt with regard to future fiscal arrangements, the domestic tea-table cannot be altogether forgotten. It must always be a matter of importance to consumers to know where to obtain Teas and Coffees of the finest qualities at the most moderate prices, and hence it must be necessary always to bear in mind the Establishment at the corner of *Saint Paul's Churchyard*, where
DAKIN AND COMPY.
continue to supply Teas and Coffees of the best kinds and of the finest growths at Merchants' prices.
All Orders from any part of the Metropolitan districts, within Eight Miles of Saint Paul's, will be delivered by DAKIN & Compy's Vans, on the day after such Orders are received.
NUMBER ONE
ST PAUL
DAKIN
CO

Figure 1.2 Dakin and Company advertisement in the *Bleak House* serial, no. VI (August 1852)

Susan Stewart, in *On Longing*, discusses such narrative sleights of hand that represent repetition:

> The temporality of everyday life is marked by an irony which is its own creation, for this temporality is held to be ongoing and nonreversible, and, at the same time, characterized by repetition and predictability. The pages falling off the calendar, the notches marked on a tree that no longer stands – these are the signs of the everyday, the effort to articulate through counting. Yet it is precisely this counting that reduces difference to similarities, that is designed to be 'lost track of.' Such 'counting', such signifying, is drowned out by the silence of the ordinary.[9]

When a narrative represents repetitiveness, individual instances are erased. One example of a dreary evening must stand for months of monotony in, say, Elizabeth Gaskell's *North and South* (1854–5). As Caroline Levine and Mario Ortiz-Robles have recently argued, nineteenth-century novelists became increasingly interesting in repetition both as a formal quality of narrative, and as a trope in itself:

> repetitions might seem to act as a drag on narrative, unnecessarily elongating the text – making too much of the middle. And yet, narrative cannot do without repetition. Narrative theory has insisted on this point at least since Gotthold Ephraim Lessing, who argued that there can be no narrative without a subject who appears again and again, marking the passage of time for us through successive appearances. And the nineteenth-century English novel allows us to reconceptualise this property of narrative not only as a formal fact but also as a fact of social life. Repetition allows Victorian writers to reflect, and reflect on, the problem of mundane contemporary existence: such as the ordinary sameness that characterizes daily life, or the recurrent habits and manners that allow us to identify distinct social groups, or the dreary mechanical routines of factory labour.[10]

Repetition, Levine and Ortiz-Robles point out, seemed particularly pertinent to modern experience: it coloured work life, social interactions, the daily commute, and it characterized the everyday experiences that nineteenth-century novelists came to elaborate and investigate. Here Levine and Ortiz-Robles outline the two main meanings of the word 'repetition': first, the denotation of a narrative strategy, and second, as a trope in itself. Repetition can mean both repetitions of events and repetitive events. Following this argument, repetition becomes a trope of mid-century modernity itself – one associated with quotidian urban life and with the middle class's self-identified perseverance. *Bleak House* aligns with this careful tracing of repeated actions which single-mindedly produce the same thing over and over again, regardless of place or circumstance, as I will show below. What later in the century would become tedium – in *Our Mutual Friend* the soulless drive of Podsnappery – is here the key to stability in the face of accelerating change.

Round and round: *Bleak House* and cyclicality

There is politics and poetics in repetition. In *Bleak House*, repeated actions are productive: if they produce nothing else, such actions produce sameness, the important maintenance that props up middle-class domesticity. Without seemingly working towards anything, characters in the novel seem to be working to prop up time itself. Early in the novel, the narrative can make do with an idealized archetype for uncomplicated domesticity: the school to which Esther Summerson is sent after her aunt's death. Greenleaf becomes Esther's first real home, and the place where she identifies herself with the role of comforter and manager. It is a little haven of exactness, reduced to narrative cliché: 'Nothing could be more precise, exact, and orderly, than Greenleaf. There was a time for everything all round the dial of the clock, and everything was done at its appointed moment' (34).

We recognize the model from Wilson's clockwork house in the Introduction: a sparse and simplified conceptualization. At this extreme low end of representation, order is absolute. The 'dial of the clock' works as a simple visualization to link domestic time with circularity, recurrence, and stability. One thing follows another like beads on a string: nothing overlaps or spills or grinds to a halt. The school suggests an unproblematic, translatable, and essentially unproductive conceptualization of domestic time. When reduced to a clock-dial symbol, repetition can produce only stasis – tropes of repetition allow for narrative erasure of actual activity. However, it is only in such a foreshortened form that domestic time can uphold such stasis. Once repetition is articulated, and no longer just iterative or symbolic, stasis must be maintained by hard and imaginative work.

Bleak House presents two rival systems of governance. The one is the long-winded, perverted and self-serving machine of injustice, the Court of Chancery. Here the extended Jarndyce family, and numerous other claimants (including Lady Dedlock), have been tied in an inheritance dispute for generations. The other system of governance is the beneficent alternative, the middle-class home which forms an allegory for an ideal national household. These two systems – a centralized Chancery and a decentralized domestic sphere – are diametrically opposed, but share some qualities. The likeness is most striking in the first chapter of the novel, where the Chancery 'cause' of Jarndyce and Jarndyce, running as it has for untold generations, has usurped, by semantic substitution, the place in the sentence where 'family' ought to be:

> Innumerable children have been born into the cause; innumerable young people have married into it; innumerable old people have died out of it. [...] The little plaintiff or defendant, who was promised a new rocking-horse when Jarndyce and Jarndyce should be settled, has grown up, possessed himself of a real horse, and trotted away into the other world. Fair wards of court have faded into mothers and grandmothers. (14)

Like the family, and like time itself, Chancery is a swallower of generations and a leveller of men. It is through its similarities to the family unit that Chancery becomes so insidious, allowing it to pervert family dynamics. It insinuates itself into sibling squabbles and blows them out of proportion, as in the case of 'the man from Shropshire', whose entire estate was swallowed up by costs while Chancery deliberated on what should have been a minor point of law. It stands in the place of parents to Ada Clare and Richard Carstone, as it did, to terrible effect, to little mad Miss Flyte, a faded spinster who has spent her life awaiting judgement, and now confidently expects it 'on the Day of Judgment' and not before (43). John Jarndyce tries to save the three young people, Ada, Richard and Esther, from Miss Flyte's fate at the opening of the novel by becoming their guardian and taking them to Bleak House. The house itself has erased its tragic past (the suicide of its owner) and kept only the name Bleak House as a reminder.

It is precisely the shared characteristics between Chancery and the paternal family unit that is so dangerous. Jarndyce warns Esther, Ada, and Richard of Chancery, but in words that suggest this parallel. He could as easily have been talking about Victorian domestic ideology when he explains: 'And thus, through years and years, and lives and lives, everything goes on, constantly beginning over and over again, and nothing ever ends' (109). While this statement spells horror for the inmates of Chancery, it is also the hope of domesticity – never-ending, constantly renewing itself through the generations. Like Chancery, the ideal Victorian home is able to substitute one person for another. 'Jarndyce and Jarndyce' will run on regardless; the households of *Bleak House* are similarly constructed to run on perpetually. When John Jarndyce in the beginning of the novel assumes the guardianship of Ada, Richard and Esther, it is to thwart Chancery's perversion of the parent-role and to rebuild the family that Chancery has usurped. Unfortunately, Richard has already been the victim of false parental influence from Chancery. He has been educated to no profession, because of the vague hope that the case will be settled in his favour. This predicament is remarkably similar to the position of first-born sons under the system of primogeniture, who would rarely be expected to choose a profession, and yet could wait years to inherit their estate.

The novel is narrated alternately by an omniscient present-tense narrator, and by Esther Summerson in the first person. It is especially in Esther's portions of the novel that domestic time is produced. As soon as Esther arrives at Bleak House, she becomes enmeshed in its temporality. Her central trope is the bunch of housekeeping keys given to her upon arrival. She repeatedly alludes to her keys, and they signal a repeated cycle of daily or weekly household management. The labels on the keys designate a route around the house:

> Every part of the house was in such order, and every one was so attentive to me, that I had no trouble with my two bunches of keys: though what with trying to remember the contents of each little store-room drawer, and cupboard; and what with making notes on a slate about jams, and pickles, and preserves, and bottles, and glass, and china, and a great many other things; and what with being generally a methodical, old-maidish sort of foolish little person; I was so busy that I could not believe it was breakfast-time when I heard the bell ring. (105–6)

While we never see this progression through the house again, Esther evokes it every time she jingles her keys as a reminder to herself of her duties: 'So I said to myself, "Esther, Esther, Esther! Duty, my dear!" and gave my little basket of housekeeping keys such a shake, that they sounded like little bells, and rang me hopefully to bed' (95). The association with bells, marking time for Esther, is pronounced. While these keys symbolize social control over the domestic staff because of the access they grant to domestic valuables, they also extend spatio-temporal control over Esther, sending her on a daily or weekly circuit around the house, opening and closing each room and cabinet methodically, over and over again. Each key, then, represents one station in a sequence of domestic progression, a succession of spaces, and the whole bunch represents the whole circuit or temporal cycle. This is labour that does not go anywhere, which exists only to be repeated. The bunch represents Esther's determined belief in the cyclicality of her household management, and hence her wilful erasure of change and difference.

Esther retains the power to repeat the cycle endlessly; indeed, her keys remind her to do so. As a narrator, she brings these housekeeping keys to the fore again and again – particularly when in need of self-chastisement. She uses the keys to remind herself not to be ungrateful or unhappy:

> Finding my housekeeping keys laid ready for me in my room, [I] rang myself in as if I had been a new year, with a merry little peal. 'Once more, duty, duty, Esther,' said I; 'and if you are not overjoyed to do it, more than cheerfully and contentedly, through anything and everything, you ought to be. That's all I have to say to *you*, my dear!' (562, emphasis in original)

Whenever Esther finds the need to ring her keys as encouragement, she does it to conceal from herself her desperate unhappiness.[11] In fact, ringing her housekeeping keys becomes a very literal sounding of Esther's super-ego. She is an unreliable narrator not least because such self-control masks the denial of her own desires, especially in her romantic plot developments. As James Buzard says, Esther is 'aggressively self-effacing'.[12] But the sound of jingling keys always grounds her psychological distress in domestic temporality – a temporality characterized by determined circularity.

One of the cautionary tales Esther meets in the novel is that of the Jellyby family, who live in perpetual domestic confusion. Philanthropic Mrs Jellyby cares only for the correct management of the African colonies, and nothing for household management. But like Bleak House, the Jellyby household is essentially unchanging. The daughter of the house, Caddy, can make nothing run right even though she aspires to be like Esther. Each time Esther visits, the house presents essentially the same chaos: letters scattered everywhere, household utensils in the most peculiar places, children coming to grief by falling down staircases. When Caddy Jellyby moves away to marry, nothing in her parents' home changes. Children still hurt themselves, the letters still stream in, and utensils and dinner times remain comically misplaced. Adding or subtracting a person from a household makes next to no difference to the way it runs. The Jellyby household is always disintegrating, but never disintegrates completely: even the resultant bankruptcy essentially changes nothing. The household runs on a short-circuit. In Bleak House itself, the seed for domestic disruption – for division of the domestic nucleus – is sown from the very beginning. On the very first evening in Bleak House, Esther senses the future rift prompted by Richard's faulty education:

> The room in which they were [...] was only lighted by the fire. Ada sat at the piano; Richard stood beside her, bending down. Upon the wall, their shadows blended together, surrounded by strange forms, not without a ghostly motion caught from the unsteady fire, though reflected from motionless objects. Ada touched the notes so softly, and sang so low, that the wind, sighing away to the distant hills, was as audible as the music. The mystery of the future, and the little clue afforded to it by the voice of the present, seemed expressed in the whole picture. (85)

The shadows 'blended together', the 'strange forms' and 'ghostly motion' are all species of fortune-telling. The 'unsteady' firelight does not, as one might have supposed, make the prophecy unsteady but foreshadows, accurately, the unsteadiness of Richard. The phrase 'little clue' has a double meaning: it can either mean 'next to no clue', or a clue small in size (but definitely present). Even without pre-knowledge of the plot, readers are alerted to trouble ahead, but beyond such narrative prefiguring, the passage also has vast implications for domestic time. It suggests that the things that can build or destroy a home are always already in the home. Even external forces, like poisonous Chancery cases, have been brought into the home by one of its inhabitants. In spite of Jarndyce's attempts to replace the tainted Chancery guardianship with a family relationship, a chip of it travels into the heart of Bleak House. External forces of destruction have been allowed into its short-circuit. Esther's keys become a symbol of the wilful maintenance of a past-less domestic time; the bunch of keys is a symbol of her determination to erase the past. Instead of asking Jarndyce for information about her own secret parentage – the burning question in her first few chapters – she jingles her keys and immerses herself in the daily running of Bleak House: 'It was not for me to muse over bygones, but to act with a cheerful spirit and a grateful heart. So I said to myself, "Esther, Esther, Esther! Duty, my dear!" and gave my little basket of housekeeping keys such a shake, that they sounded like little bells' (95). It is clear to neither Esther nor the reader why Esther becomes Mr Jarndyce's ward, and yet the bunch of keys signals Esther's suppression of curiosity and the attempted erasure of the past.

There is a counter-rhythm to Esther's determinedly ringing keys in the present-tense portions of the novel. The counter-rhythm is the ominous dripping on the Ghost's Walk at the aristocratic Chesney Wold, the seat of Lord and Lady Dedlock. The omniscient present-tense narrator describes the sound of drops of water falling, 'drip, drip, drip, upon the broad flagged pavement' (18). Where Esther's keys symbolize cyclicality – repetition of essentially the same actions over and over again – the dripping represents linear time. The family is old and aristocratic enough to have ghosts and to collect ancestors, unlike Jarndyce's little family at Bleak House, which does not even acknowledge the identity of Ada's or Richard's parents. But possessing a linear past can be dangerous. The drips, which sound like the steps of a ghost, are a warning of the fall of the Dedlock family, according to the housekeeper, Mrs Rouncewell. The steady drip counts out time, and it connects the present Dedlock family with a stain on its family history. Esther's keys erase the past; the step on the Ghost's Walk keeps the past alive. After having related the legend of the Cromwellian Lady Dedlock and her base treachery of King and family, Mrs Rouncewell explains:

> 'That is the story. Whatever the sound is, it is a worrying sound', says Mrs Rouncewell, getting up from her chair, 'and what is to be noticed in it, is, that it *must be heard*. My lady, who is afraid of nothing, admits that when it is there, it must be heard. You cannot shut it out.' (104, author's emphasis)

The old curse becomes literal and temporal, a persistent and never-ending aural blot on the house, and one from which the present Lady Dedlock very pointedly cannot escape. These two rhythms, the jingling quotidian keys and the slow inexorable counting out of linear time, become entangled when Esther inadvertently walks onto the terrace at Chesney Wold and becomes, herself, the step of doom to the Dedlocks through the secret of her parentage; she is Lady Dedlock's illegitimate child, a revelation that causes Lady Dedlock's downfall. The dripping step thus links with a sensation novel's insistence on revelation and on payment for past sins – on a linear plot development driven by mistakes made years before the present time of the novel. Jarndyce's Bleak House does everything to negate and neutralize the past, but the past must be heard.

Esther's erasures

Esther's housekeeping keys symbolize the ease with which bourgeois domestic time – the centre of stability in the novel – can be repeated. This ease is belied, however, by the fact that the keys do not necessarily connote a specific place, in spite of their labels, which link each key to a press or cupboard at Bleak House. Much key-jingling takes place not in Bleak House itself, but in lodgings off Oxford Street in London: 'I was very busy indeed, all day, and wrote directions home to the servants, and wrote notes for my guardian, and dusted his books and papers, and jingled my housekeeping keys a good deal, one way and another' (256).

The trope of the keys is jingled slightly askew in this passage. Where are the cupboards and presses to which the keys belong? If the jingling is in fact figurative, rather than literal, this is the first we hear of it. When key-jingling drifts into metaphor, it migrates not only into all aspects of domestic management, but also into geographically remote domestic and semi-domestic spaces. Esther herself is remarkably mobile in this novel, and walks with complete ease into a variety of households. For instance, she makes an unannounced morning visit to Harold Skimpole's house, which prompts no comment. She interviews Mr Turveydrop Senior on behalf of Caddy Jellyby and her suitor Prince, with no prior acquaintance (and finds him wanting). This easy intrusion into other people's homes is a function of Esther's unquestioned middle-class mobility. Bourgeois women were expected to pay calls, and make visits of charity; their social inferiors were expected to receive these visits gratefully. But Esther is extraordinarily welcome in all domestic spaces. When the overbearing neighbour Mrs Pardiggle takes her on a charity visit to some bricklayers, Esther's tact ensures her a welcome from the bricklayers' wives which is not accorded to the sanctimonious and rude Mrs Pardiggle. There is no obvious reason for the bricklayer families to trust Esther, and yet her narrative makes it clear that they do. In all of these scenes of domestic visiting, Esther exhibits more than just proper middle-class behaviour; her status as narrator lends her a near-omniscient ability to travel between spaces. She never acknowledges that she could, in fact, come as an interruption into other people's domestic time, just as she rarely acknowledges the time it takes to travel between places. Boarding trains to jingle her keys in London lodgings poses no problem to her. Similarly, Mrs Bagnet, the splendidly stoic soldier's wife, is equipped at all times equally for a trip to the local market and a trek across a continent.

Such excessive mobility points at an erasure of difference between spaces. Class differences remain intact, but for Esther there is nothing challenging or difficult about crossing thresholds. She moves between different domestic spaces as if they were spatiotemporally and socially aligned – as if they all existed in easy simultaneity. In contrast, the novel's present-tense narrator – who is omniscient – takes great pains to paint different spaces in the novel as profoundly different realms, which are causally but not temporally connected. The time at Chesney Wold is treacle-like; the time at Tom-All-Alone's, the city slum, is one of inexorable entropy. We learn that both Chesney Wold, the home of Lady Dedlock, and Tom-All-Alone's are entangled in the Jarndyce Chancery case, but in the omniscient narrator's parts of the novel, there is no easy simultaneity between them. They may be economically connected by Chancery, but they pay a very different price for the same social rot. The omniscient narrator paints spatiotemporal difference. Esther, in her narrative, erases it.

Esther's narrative erases spatiotemporal difference in order to insist on simultaneity and reproducibility. This is the first of three significant silences in the novel that have to be maintained in order for the stable domestic centre to function. The second silence is introduced in the second instalment of the novel. Esther, Ada and Richard are on their way to Bleak House, but a nameless messenger stops the carriage to deliver three identically worded notes from their guardian:

> 'I look forward, my dear, to our meeting easily, and without constraint on either side. I therefore have to propose that we meet as old friends, and take the past for granted. It will be a relief to you possibly, and to me certainly, and so my love to you. JOHN JARNDYCE.' (74)

Esther and the others take this to mean that Jarndyce dislikes being thanked for his benevolence – as indeed Esther continues to stress throughout the novel. But the notes have another function: they allow Bleak House to spring into existence, fully formed, from nothing. The 'past taken for granted' alludes not just to Jarndyce's kindness in taking them in, but also includes the household – complete with Esther, Ada and Richard – in its becoming. Bleak House is never seen forming, only already formed. It is thus both complete and disintegrating at the same time. In order to achieve this, Esther, Ada and Richard must be warned never to question the making of the family unit: they must perform its inevitability. Esther, Ada, Richard and Jarndyce are acting out their domesticity by deliberately ignoring its strangeness and constructedness.

Throughout the novel, Bleak House stands on the border between being a literal family home and a metaphoric, idealized space. All of the work that maintains the house balances on this line between actual work and metaphorical labour. The activity in the house when the young people first arrive bears this out. We hear of a fully functioning household, but all of the work is performed by servants who remain nameless and curiously shadowy. This is the third erasure: the elision of servants in the novel. As Alison Light has pointed out, the middle-class home's air of unchanging comfort was made possible by invisible or repressed labour.[13] The anonymous messenger on the road who delivers the three notes is one of the many indeterminate individuals who populate the house and make it seem real. When Esther is first given her housekeeping keys, she stresses that the maid who delivers them is a stranger to her:

> I was dressed in a few minutes, and engaged in putting my worldly goods away, when a maid (not the one in attendance upon Ada, but another whom I had not seen), brought a basket into my room, with two bunches of keys in it, all labelled. 'For you, miss, if you please,' said she. (81)

The scene relies on the strangeness of being in a new place where everybody seemingly knows more about you than you do about them (and possibly more than you know about yourself). However, Esther's narrative persists in keeping the house oddly unfamiliar, peopled by a shapeless and nameless group. Towards the end of the book, when Esther arrives at Bleak House after a long night's hunt for Lady Dedlock with Inspector Bucket, she makes the following observation:

> The whole household were amazed to see me, without any notice, at that time in the morning, and so accompanied; and their surprise was not diminished by my inquiries. No one, however, had been there. It could not be doubted that this was the truth. (811)

Who are these people that staff Bleak House? Why is it necessary to emphasize (somewhat grudgingly) that their words can be trusted? Relegated to the background, this silent group (how many? mostly women? how long have they worked for Jarndyce?) makes the house seem inhabited. Their anonymity is a guarantee of the ongoing existence of the house, but they also remain a strange 'other' – never named, not quite trusted.

Bleak House itself is permeated aurally by their presence, but the house and servants are always inextricably linked by their essential strangeness. The sounds of activity in the very first description are a case in point:

> Out of [Mr Jarndyce's room], you came into another passage, where there were back-stairs, and where you could hear the horses being rubbed down, outside the stable, and being told to Hold up, and Get over, as they slipped about very much on the uneven stones. Or you might, if you came out of another door (every room had at least two doors), go straight down to the hall again by half-a-dozen steps and a low archway, wondering how you got back there, or had ever got out of it. (79)

It is not so much that the house defies logic as that the operating logics are being produced behind the scenes, only dimly grasped from the upstairs rooms. Significantly, the spatio-aural elements are carefully synchronized towards gender. In the above passage, Jarndyce's room is accompanied by sounds with masculine associations, such as grooms and horses, whereas Esther's final impression is more bent towards feminine pursuits:

> Such, with its illuminated windows, softened here and there by shadows of curtains, shining out upon the star-light night; with its light, and warmth, and comfort; with its hospitable jingle, at a distance, of preparations for dinner; with the face of its generous master brightening everything we saw; and just wind enough without to sound a low accompaniment to everything we heard; were our first impressions of Bleak House. (80)

The feminine quality of 'comfort' and 'curtains' is associated aurally with the sounds of 'preparations for dinner', a female concern. The shouts in the courtyard, the jingle from the kitchen, and the moans from the wind: all these sounds add not just interlinked spatiality to the house, revealing surprising adjacencies with every new room or passage; they also add temporality. Without these sounds from the near-distance, Bleak House would have been a static house; with them, the description is temporally placed (near dinner time), and divided into gendered temporalities as well as gendered spaces.

The shadowy but (probably) trustworthy servants thus form a kind of temporal tethering. Similarly, auditory sensations of housework sometimes tell time in the narrative. On Esther's first morning, she is called from her bustling and key-jingling by a significant sound: 'I was so busy that I could not believe it was breakfast-time when I heard the bell ring' (105–6). In the background, domestic periodicities are operating persistently. It is somehow unlikely that John Jarndyce has laid down the workings of the house before Esther arrives, since his organization of space and time within the home seems altogether more idiosyncratic. He attributes all negative feelings to the East Wind, and the main space in the house that he has defined is the Growlery. The Growlery's function seems chiefly to be containment of Jarndyce's unpleasant moods; it is, according to him, 'the best used room in the house' (107). As the master of Bleak House, he has the undisputed right to make the house an extension of his mental landscape. However, Esther's description of the Growlery underlines its marginality to the general workings of the residence: it is 'in part a little library of books and papers, and in part quite a little museum of his boots and shoes, and hat-boxes'. Part study, but mostly boot room, the Growlery is Jarndyce's personal space where he can indulge his fits of depression without interfering with the machinery that runs the household. Jarndyce has in fact performed the male middle-class prerogative of designing a space for himself, one secluded from the business of domesticity; in other words, his moods are maintained within the house, but away from its vital functions.

A smoothly running household was only possible because someone, always just out of sight, swept the carpet every morning and turned down the beds every night. Bleak House is in a sense mediated by servants, the medium forgotten over the untroubled message. When Esther sends her maid Charley for the letter that she knows will contain Jarndyce's proposal of marriage, Charley's trajectory through the house paces out the long passages in an equally long sentence:

> When the appointed night came, I said to Charley as soon as I was alone, 'Go and knock at Mr Jarndyce's door, Charley, and say you have come from me – "for the letter."' Charley went up the stairs, and down the stairs, and along the passages – the zigzag way about the old-fashioned house seemed very long in my listening ears that night – and so came back, along the passages, and down the stairs, and up the stairs, and brought the letter. (637)

While this narrative device adds suspense, it also adds the sense of how a household goes about its business, one measured spatiotemporally through servant-mediated domestic time. Domestic sounds and practices construct the time in which the house exists. But they do it incidentally; we come upon these practices almost by accident, each time we take three steps down a chapter or turn a corner in the narrative. The implied assumption is that household temporality continues even when it is not narrated, and especially when it is not in the hands of the middle-class household manager.

The temporal structure of Bleak House is thus achieved not just by Esther's jingling of her household keys, but also by actual sounds of work. These sounds highlight Esther's ambiguous status within the house. She is not the person ringing the breakfast bell, but she does hover in an odd 'no-man's land' between servant and lady. She is in charge of some temporal markers – most notably, keys and weekly accounts, the remits of either a housekeeper or of the lady of the house – but not of others: bells, dinner itself, or all the shadowy upkeep of the house. Her status is a mixture of three elements: housekeeper (servant), companion to Ada (semi-servant), and eligible young woman (not-servant). Ada has a maid 'in attendance' from the first evening, underlining the fact that Jarndyce interprets her as a lady, but only later does Esther receive the 'gift' of little Charley, an orphan whom Esther and Jarndyce decide to help. Esther proceeds to train Charley more as a housekeeper than a lady's maid. All of these nuances make it difficult to gloss Esther's class position. As D. A. Miller has pointed out, it is the very insecurity of the subject within Bleak House that maintains the stability of the family. Esther's insecurity, Miller observes, 'supplies the constant vigilance wanted to keep the contractual family from lapsing into the subjection of tutelage'.[14] This comment suggests that in order to represent a viable, workable domestic unit, as *Bleak House* patently attempts, one cannot but show what Miller calls the constant 'neurotic' work that must be performed in order to stabilize it.[15] Ultimately, the novel's emphasis on anxious repetitive work signals a larger truth: that domestic time is actively made – that the way to represent it is to show how it is performed. Habits and routine thus become elaborated in the narrative because it is these elements that make time happen.

Making time

Dickens's representation of habits and routines often makes them seem like expressions of immovable dogma: domestic managers in *Bleak House* are methodical to the point of single-mindedness. By repeating certain practices in a deliberate manner, they establish the habits that individuals should live by. We can see this assumption clearly when

Mrs Bagnet is first introduced into the narrative. Trooper George sees her and reflects: 'She's as usual, washing greens. I never saw her, except upon a baggage-wagon, when she wasn't washing greens!' (405). Even the diet of the Bagnets is invariably the self-same 'greens', served with some species of boiled meat. Repetitive practices become repetitive diet. It is clear that the narrative approves of her single-mindedness. The 'greens' operate so powerfully on her psyche, that, according to her husband, she cannot be consulted on serious matters until, in his words, 'the greens is off her mind' (409). Mrs Bagnet goes through an elaborate preparation and serving of dinner, all of which requires her utter concentration and thus excludes the possibility of conversation. After dinner has been eaten, the narrator even more elaborately describes the preparations for sitting down quietly:

> The dinner done, Mrs Bagnet, assisted by the younger branches (who polish their own cups and platters, knives and forks), makes all the dinner garniture shine as brightly as before, and puts it all away; first sweeping the hearth, to the end that Mr Bagnet and the visitor may not be retarded in the smoking of their pipes. These household cares involve much pattening and counter-pattening in the back yard, and considerable use of a pail, which is finally so happy as to assist in the ablutions of Mrs Bagnet herself. That old girl reappearing by and by, quite fresh, and sitting down to her needlework, then and only then – the greens being only then to be considered as entirely off her mind – Mr Bagnet requests the trooper to state his case. (408–9)

Not only does Mrs Bagnet take her time, but the narrative voice also delights in taking its own time in describing her domestic practice. Whereas habit and routine such as this ought to release Mrs Bagnet from having to think about it, such rituals and repetitions have the opposite effect. Dickens represents domestic practices as wholly absorbing, extravagantly elaborated sequences of concentrated work, and in the process of describing them in such detail he makes them strange.

The most peculiar housekeeper is Trooper George's batman, Phil Squod, who was dragged up in the gutter and is deformed from a literally indescribable series of accidents. Squod is incapable of crossing a room in the normal manner, and instead shoulders himself around the periphery of the shooting gallery:

> He has a curious way of limping round the gallery with his shoulder against the wall, and tacking off at objects he wants to lay hold of,

> instead of going straight to them, which has left a smear all round the four walls, conventionally called 'Phil's mark.' [...] Phil cannot even go straight to bed, but finds it necessary to shoulder round two sides of the gallery, and then tack off at his mattress. (324–5)

Phil's movements mimic the jerky zigzag motion of sailing, but on dry land and indoors. When Phil makes breakfast for himself and Trooper George, his compulsion to circumnavigate the shooting gallery makes cooking a significantly enduring process:

> It is not necessarily a lengthened preparation, being limited to the setting forth of very simple breakfast requisites for two, and the broiling of a rasher of bacon at the fire in the rusty grate; but as Phil has to sidle round a considerable part of the gallery for every object he wants, and never brings two objects at once, it takes time under the circumstances. At length the breakfast is ready. (386)

Both Phil Squod and Mrs Bagnet make domestic tasks enduring and fulfilling, since their routine activities deliberately slow down and protract temporality. In her own narrative, Esther uses the same strategies to describe and elaborate domestic practices for her own purposes. For instance, she particularizes her duties with the household accounts in order to distract herself from disturbing thoughts after the young clerk Guppy has startled her with a marriage proposal:

> I sat there for another hour or more, finishing my books and payments, and getting through plenty of business. Then, I arranged my desk, and put everything away, and was so composed and cheerful that I thought I had quite dismissed this unexpected incident. (141)

The reader, of course, is not fooled. Esther also attempts such tactics towards other characters. When she suspects that her love for Allan Woodcourt is too obvious to Ada, she transparently uses her 'bustling' as a means of feigning indifference to the handsome doctor, as well as communicating her contentment with her peculiar betrothal to Jarndyce:

> What could I do to reassure my darling (I considered then) and show her that I had no such feelings? Well! I could only be as brisk and busy as possible; and that, I had tried to be all along. [...] I resolved to be doubly diligent and gay. So I went about the house, humming

> all the tunes I knew; and I sat working and working in a desperate manner, and I talked and talked, morning noon and night. (716)

This is a temporality entirely of Esther's own making, one that can, apparently and improbably, be doubled for extra suspicion-allaying effect. Soon afterwards, this making of time occurs again, during a conversation about Woodcourt's career prospects:

> As there was a little pause here, which I thought, for my dear girl's satisfaction, had better be filled up, *I hummed an air as I worked* which was a favourite with my guardian. 'And do you think Mr Woodcourt will make another voyage?' I asked him, *when I had hummed it quietly all through*. (717, my emphasis)

This is patently an example of Esther taking her time for her own purposes, stretching or suspending time with a 'hummed [...] air' while working. Domestic work is thus a show, a performance, and for one's own benefit it must look as single-minded and absorbing as possible.

All this labour that ostensibly achieves so little, and the protracted temporality that results from such detailed representation, stands in stark contrast to the inexorable progression of the sensational plot surrounding Lady Dedlock. Her past life is a mystery, and the revelation that she had a child out of wedlock with the mysterious Nemo who dies in penury at the opening of the novel – and that that child is Esther Summerson – drives the suspense that runs through the novel. Domestic practice and domestic time in Esther's narrative are the dull and repetitive ground against which the melodramatic plot is played out in stark relief in the omniscient portions of the book. Towards the novel's end, the two storylines converge when Esther goes in search of the missing Lady Dedlock, her mother. The mundane details of everyday life appear colourless when juxtaposed with the forbidden passion, self-destruction, spontaneous combustion, threats, murder, swapped identities, concealment and flight that characterize the sensation novel that *Bleak House* also is. But the determinedly anti-sensational domestic sphere also itself conceals Esther's history and negates it. The fact that domestic time is boring is a positive boon in the face of dramatic denouements: repetitive labour at least produces that retreat from, and reworking of, the tainted past. Because of the novel's ground and relief effect, singular events become alien to domesticity and repetition becomes anathema to sensation. By making dull, ordinary time intersperse the sensational plot, the mundane can offer its alternative. As a result, domestic time, at the end of the novel, naturally becomes unnarratable – happy families are all the same – and the novel can finish. In fact, pragmatically improvising domestic time is what allows it to stay safely unproductive. Governed by easy translatability and simultaneity, middle-class domestic time can be produced and reproduced as alternative centres safely sheltered from the hubbub of dramatic novel time.

Constructing a national domestic time: the 'Bleak House Advertiser' and Dakin & Co.

Constructing a workable domestic temporality that functions within a national setting is not only the concern of *Bleak House*, the novel. It is also an important aspect of the commercial serial venture called *Bleak House*. As Emily Steinlight has argued, advertising, by borrowing from and referencing novels, helps the novel genre create itself as a form with cultural capital.[16] The 19 instalments in their blue-green wrappers, filled to the brim with advertisements, were part of a canny business plan that made the Dickens serial a recognizable brand: the many tie-in advertisements which explicitly mention *Bleak House* bear testament to the success of this scheme. Moreover, Dickens frequently emphasized the ability of serial publication not only to give a wider spectrum of readers access to his work, but also to synchronize reading. Dickens's favourite vision of his readers was of scores of simultaneous readings in front of diverse domestic hearths, from all stations in life. Dickens, his publishers, and his advertisers were invested in this idea of the Dickens serial's potential to call simultaneous domestic spheres into being – to crystallize the dream of domestic comfort by the simple expedient of uniting all readers in time. The advertisements in the 'Bleak House Advertiser' that surround each instalment assist in this construction of a nationalized domestic sphere, one firmly situated within the marketplace.

The Dakin & Co. advertisement (Figure 1.2) is designed, most likely by Dickens's own illustrator Phiz, to look exactly like a serial instalment of a Dickens novel. But this allusion to the medium in which it appears is not the only topical element on the page. The advertisement also refers explicitly to the 1852 General Election, informing the reader that:

> Even in the midst of the excitement of a general election [...], the domestic tea-table cannot be altogether forgotten. It must always be a matter of importance to consumers to know where to obtain Teas and Coffees of the finest qualities at the most moderate prices.[17]

This central copy is framed by two outsize placards, which read 'Dakin & Co.' and 'Number One!' The latter is a reference to their shop's address at No. 1, St. Paul's Churchyard, but it is clear that the advertising slogans are meant to evoke the slogans of election campaigning. At the very bottom of the page, jovial men with 'Dakin!' placards and sandwich boards are enjoying a tea-fuelled respite from the bustle of the streets. In order to suggest the colonial origin of tea, a stereotypical Chinaman holds each outsize placard, complete with hair whips snaking up the staffs. The central street scene, which shows the Dakin & Company shop and a hurrying crowd, is dominated by hansom cabs emblazoned with 'Dakin' and an image of St. Paul's on their sides. Dakin & Company has, it seems, managed to infiltrate not only the elections and their advertising methods, but also advertising across the city. This scene reminds readers of various contemporary husting practices that skewed the democratic process by monopolizing the vote. Dakin and Company could resort to a number of Dickens's previous novels for satirical sketches of election cheating, including, perhaps most famously, the Eatanswill Election in *Pickwick Papers* (August 1836).

As the crowning piece of infiltration, the ampersand in the large-lettered 'Dakin & Company' dominating the image has managed to snake itself around the lantern on the dome of St. Paul's. In its enthusiasm for advertising, this enterprising company implicates election campaigning, street advertising, and an iconic London landmark in its puffery. Finally, the panels on each side are taken up by illustrations of domestic tea-drinking, both high and low: eager gossiping in a cosy kitchen, haughty elegance in drawing rooms, a cheerful working-class family and a solitary seamstress. All the clocks depicted in these domestic scenes point to approximately four or five o'clock – tea-time. But the really important, and indeed unifying, product on display is, of course, not actually visible in the picture. Tea, that thoroughly domestic article, insinuates itself into the everyday lives of all stations. It unites the many little side panels into a uniformity of purpose – more than that, a shared and simultaneous temporality. All these simultaneous acts of tea-drinking construct homogeneous time, mediated through commodities. This shows the fantasy of the reach of the marketplace: the dream that consumer products, whether tea or a Dickens novel, may homogenize domestic practices across an entire nation, aligning different classes and spaces into one, coherent, temporality. The visual spectacle of tea-drinking is thus an exercise in making time.

The advertisement, in other words, is heavily allusive. It references many things simultaneously: the General Election; the tea duty; the exotic provenance of tea and its domestic consumption; the busy trade, advertising, and street life in the capital; the iconic London landmark which is also practically the logo for Dakin & Co.; and the well-known covers of a Dickens serial. The deliberate echo of Dickens's front page labours a point that Dakin & Co. was always keen to suggest: Dickens had done the company a great service by writing another novel. Three months previously, in May 1852, also on the first page of the 'Bleak House Advertiser', Dakin & Co. ran an advertisement that rather audaciously thanked Dickens for *Bleak House*:

> For the facilities that this excellent medium of publicity has allowed us for making known the above particulars, we sincerely thank you, and we trust and hope that by our care and attention, and by the excellence of the Goods we supply, those readers of 'BLEAK HOUSE' who may turn their favourable patronage to 'Number One,' will never regret having glanced over the first page of its white paper, on this 1st of May.[18]

The phrasing is deliberately ambiguous.[19] Which 'white paper' – the 'Advertiser' or the novel itself? Which 'Number One' – the first number of *Bleak House* or the address of Dakin & Co.? Already in this earlier advertisement, Dakin & Co. is relying on heavily entangled referents, thereby staking a claim to the 'white paper', just as Dickens has become known by his green covers (which Dakin call 'green leaves', another allusion to tea). As a result of these tangled referents, the advertisement encodes the first page of the 'Advertiser' as another sort of beginning, one that will, if perused correctly, prove a favourable beginning of a seller-consumer relationship. The company's reference to 'Number One' plays on both their address and on the 'No.' of *Bleak House* with which the reader presumably decided to give their 'patronage' to Dickens, the purveyor of fiction. The advertisement builds up a deliberate confusion between the objects for sale. Setting the pleasure and benefit of reading an advertisement on a par with that of reading a novel, it becomes unclear what, in Dakin & Co.'s eyes, the primary goal of the *Bleak House* serial really is. Buying practices and reading practices are already, in the May number, inextricably linked; in the August number, they are completely intertwined.

Dakin & Co. was clearly taking advantage of the recognizability of the well-known Dickens serials, as Gerard Curtis has observed:

> The Dickens serials [...] made almost continuous use of green covers with pictoral illustration – strongly controlled by Dickens for

> illustrative hints to the structure of the story – which were designed to be read [...] as a visual primer to the narrative. These covers served to make the serials an eye-catching and well-known feature on Victorian bookstalls, a necessary feature given the competitive periodicals market.[20]

This already established continuity and coherence proves too good an opportunity for Dakin & Co. to miss.[21] By August 1852 and its General Election advertisement, Dakin & Co. is in effect starting its own one-issue (and cover-only) Dickens serial. By relying on the fact that Dickens has become associated with the green covers and the illustrations by George Cruikshank or 'Phiz', the company is claiming a similar association for itself. For contemporary buyers, a Dickens novel started with the cover illustration – laid out with hints of the story and inviting close scrutiny – and not simply with the first page of letterpress. Similarly, the Dakin & Co advertisement can be read as a novel *in spe*. In fact, readers could be forgiven for feeling a certain disappointment that Dickens did not write a novel to suit such a glorious cover. While the Dakin & Co. advertisement does not offer many indications of an actual plot, it is still considerably more readable than the *Bleak House* cover proper. Furthermore, it is strongly reminiscent of one of Dickens's actual novels, *Dombey and Son* (October 1846–April 1848), the serial cover for which (also by Phiz) carried the full title: 'Dealings with the firm of Dombey and Son, Wholesale, Retail, and for Exportation. By Charles Dickens'. Dickens's joking mixing of referents for this earlier novel seems almost to invite the opposite move. *Dakin & Company*, the novel, has only a front cover and no plot. But that front cover suggests a setting and a background of action that every novel needs, even if all the characters are unnamed and they have no actual plot lines. This advertisement lifts into prominence the ground of the storyline's relief; the novel without the plot, signalled by a front cover with no letterpress; the reality effect of everydayness; the teeming, quotidian and richly ordinary. The ease with which the advertisement calls up the possibilities of a novel – and calls up the novel's capacity for capturing the essence of everyday life in the background – alerts us to the fact that at least part of the novel's powers are shared with advertisements: the power to evoke practical life in its formation. In a novel, this practical life would fall into the background. The advertisement suggests to me that the evocation of everydayness is only possible by *not* writing the novel; this advertisement is a perfect everyday novel exactly because it is a 'not-novel'. By visual representation of the reach of tea and novels, everyday life and print culture are inextricable intertwined.

The Dakin & Co. advertisement represents a simultaneous moment of tea-drinking in a series of domestic spaces, set apart from a busy street teeming with the markers of modern life (transport, print, consumerism and colonialism). In thus setting the domestic sphere apart from the public spaces, and suggesting domesticity's reproducibility, the advertisement offers an analogy to the ideological work of *Bleak House*. In the advertisement for Dakin & Co., repetition is spatial: the same printed material, the same product, the same social situation can be circulated and transposed across multiple thresholds. While this spatial repetition mirrors the ease of Esther Summerson's travels between domestic spaces, it is also a markedly different vision of society than the one Dickens constructs in his novel. There is no levelling in *Bleak House*: only an alternative centre of power, the middle-class home, which functions as a retreat rather than a general and unifying principle of society. As Andrew Williams has pointed out in his reading of the same advertisement, the Dakin & Co. illustration emphasizes sameness and equality: 'Class and sociopolitical tensions are erased by the universal assertion of the domestic ritual of taking tea. Social inequality is glossed over to posit a universal middle-class consumer.'[22] According to Williams, the same erasure of difference does not happen in *Bleak House*. Nor is translatability entirely denied, however. As I have argued, Esther's narrative performs hard work to make different spheres exist in simultaneity – in fact, only Esther's narrative has the power to synchronize, and only because it simultaneously obscures things (pasts, servants, causal relationships).

Repetitive domestic time is central to Dickens's novel because it offers both an apotheosis of, and a respite from, modernity. It becomes a haven not only from a destructive aristocratic past, but also from a destabilized modernity where bricklayers have to tramp miles for very little work, where Jo the crossing-sweeper can be cast out from institutionalized charity, and where Mrs Jellyby represents a global exoticism that ignores domestic needs. Jarndyce's and Esther's two Bleak Houses at the end of the novel provide a model of replication that can subsume and neutralize the troubled souls that have been unmoored by spinning modernity, and by the stagnating tendencies of aristocratic Society and bureaucratic Chancery. *Bleak House* constructs domesticity as a product of forward-thinking individuals who focus intensely on what is close, what can be ameliorated, and what can be salvaged from the old order and into the new one. Domestic time in *Bleak House* must be purposefully built, not least in order that it may be a pattern in the British order of the world, as hinted by Dakin & Co.'s two Chinamen. The serial novel, implicated in the global spread of a British domestic ideal, suggests that stability must be built by paying close attention to everyday things, and by spreading a reproducible domestic time through the print arteries of the Empire.

The topical advertisement and serial time

While Dakin & Co. jokingly destabilizes the point of a Dickens serial – hinting that the most rewarding information to be obtained may very well be 'Number 1, St. Paul's Churchyard' – the firm's advertisement and the rest of the 'Advertiser' form a temporal, ephemeral, and topical tethering of *Bleak House*. Advertisements link a serialized novel very closely to its role as a commercial product, soliciting buyers in what is supposedly not a common consumer object. The advertisements also situate *Bleak House* in a temporal flux of printed matter. The *Bleak House* serial contributes to the construction of national domestic time in the very format by which it achieves its commercial success.

The ephemeral elements of the publication – dated covers and advertisements – tie *Bleak House* to its 19-month publication span, not only by making instalments a monthly event for readers and by making the instalments themselves more transient and ephemeral, but also by hinting towards topical events, seasonal changes, and print culture time. The seasons are noticeable in the 'Bleak House Advertiser', especially in the advertisement for clothes, parasols, and umbrellas that anticipate seasonal needs. Topical events also find their way into the 'Advertiser' whenever it suits companies' interests. Various advertisers use the 1852 General Election as a hook, notably 'Parr's Life Pills' and the clothing warehouse E. Moses & Son. Sometimes, topicality is justified by an important current event with direct influence on products: from July 1853 (No. 17), tea sellers announce that the tea duty is now reduced by 4*d.* per pound. Several merchants explain to customers that the reductions in price will probably be short-lived, as wholesale prices are increasing, and urge them to make their purchases now. Similarly, in September 1852 ale brewers are eager to extricate themselves from accusations of adulteration:

> As a general rule, Salt & Co. have been content to let their Ales speak for themselves; but the agitation which has been going on for the last few weeks in the shape of what may be called the Strychnine

> Controversy, has placed them in a position which seems now to call for a few remarks.[23]

While Salt & Co., by its own admission, is unused to advertising, fellow brewers Allsopp's are not. In the very same number they run four pages of testimonials, and they continue to advertise heavily in the following numbers, adding more testimonials and explanations of the intricate controversy. Topical references in the 'Advertiser' temporally tether the novel itself to its historical moment, infiltrating the serial letterpress with periodicity and topicality. In the babble of generic incoherence between many different advertisements and competing visual effects, the 'Advertiser' filters topical themes through the needs of individual advertisers. The temporal moment of publication is thus put in the service of the logic of selling consumer products. Advertisements take part in the discursive construction of a moment in national history (including the General Election) for their own purposes.

One of the most interesting temporalities we find in the 'Advertiser' is print culture time. First of all, of course, *Bleak House* itself is referenced, as many critics have noted.[24] The clothing sellers E. Moses & Son eagerly references current events in their regular advertisement on the back inside cover, but also Dickens's novel itself. The company's headline often punningly refers to the title and themes of *Bleak House*, mostly without showing evidence of having read the novel. The wording of their first advertisement, 'Anti-Bleak House', seems to suppose that Bleak House is truly 'bleak': 'Woe to the inhabitant of the Bleak House if he is not armed with the weapons of an OVERCOAT and a SUIT of FASHIONABLE and substantial Clothing.'[25] In the last number, E. Moses & Son ran the headline 'The Closing of the Story', thus wrapping up the *Bleak House* serial publication as effectively as Dickens's own 'THE END'. Like Dakin & Co., E. Moses & Son sees a Dickens serial as a golden opportunity, and takes the chance to echo and mimic the cultural capital of novel-writing. What these advertising strategies suggest is the eagerness for each company's products to resemble print culture, and for print culture to be a product.

Topical references tether the serial in an incoherent and partial 'now'; intertextual links between advertisements and the medium in which they appear serve to bind the two discourses – Dickens's and the advertisers' – into a semblance of collusion. Visually, the advertisements help construct coherence across the run of the serial *Bleak House*: the back cover, for example, is taken up by Heal & Son, the furniture warehouse, which runs stylistically identical images of bedsteads throughout.

The aesthetic contribution to the format of the 'Dickens serial' by this visual consistency is considerable. The 'Bleak House Advertiser' is full of doggedly repetitive advertisements, changing little or not at all from instalment to instalment. The aim of an advertisement is to cause change – to alter the practices of readers. Taken en masse, however, the advertisements suggest that alteration is pervasive: a constant state of flux. This emphasis on changing practice becomes, in itself, a ritual or a repetitive habit. The advertisements summon up a range of products, asking readers to believe that they are all perfect in their way, improved beyond imagining ('Best Ever', 'Beware of Imitations'). This language of superlatives presents a contrast to 'life-as-we-know-it': where ready-made shirts fit badly, tea is disappointing and hair oil is greasy. Advertising time is always open, but it also promises closure: it suggests an endless succession of new beginnings. In a sense, since the 'Advertiser' is constantly asking readers to reassess their consumer and domestic practices, it dramatizes the extent to which such practices can be questioned and (ostensibly) perfected.

The assertion of authenticity was of primary importance not just to advertisers of consumer products, but also to Dickens as a working author who made money from his book sales. Dickens was famously incensed by the plagiarisms and piracies under which his works suffered, arguing again and again for stronger copyright laws both nationally and internationally. Viewed in this light, the strong visual branding of the Dickens serial was not just to ensure as many readers as possible, but also to allow readers to choose the genuine article. In advertisements of the time such anxieties are also ever-present. Consumers are constantly warned of the snares that are laid out for respectable tradesmen and their customers. Thomas Harris & Son, makers of opera glasses, urges prospective customers to memorize their address:

> CAUTION.–Number 52, is directly facing the New Entrance Gate to the Museum. Recollect this, and you will avoid mistaking the house; there being a person in the same street who displays the words '15 years with Harris & Son.' designed to cause mistakes.[26]

While practice is made to seem simple, the fear of fraud and marketplace misdirection suggests a back-story to this culture of consumption shared by novels and advertisements – a dark side where frameworks for practice can be and are manipulated. The reading moment thus becomes, by extension, suffused with the possibility for practical (and pragmatic) decisions of trust or mistrust, imitative desire or resistance, and self-referential questions about domestic practice. As a child, Dickens himself witnessed the importance of branding and consumer manipulation surrounding Warren's Blacking and its rivals. The fact that *Dakin & Company*, the almost-Dickens-novel, sits so audaciously within the *Bleak House* covers is even more startling in light of the author's concern for authenticity. However, while playing with deception, Dakin & Company is in fact announcing the authenticity of the Dickens serial by honouring it with a direct address. This is not a case of an advertiser responding to a fixed or stable form, but one of participating in the construction of recognizability and trustworthiness.

The practices readers are invited to change are often (but not exclusively) domestic in nature. Gerard Curtis establishes that towards mid-century Dickens's serials carry more and more advertisements for household goods, and suggests that this reflects 'the broadening out of the middle-class domestic market for luxury goods'.[27] But it could also be seen as an expression of the increasing coexistence of serial print culture and everyday life. In one representative number of *Bleak House*, No. 17 (July 1853), the advertised domestic goods run to an impressive list: papier mâché and iron tea trays; lamps and candles; 'ice safes'; 'royal Turkish towels'; a sponging bath; tea; 'Soyer's Relish'; 'Every article for the dinner table in Diamond Pressed Glass' (an imitation of the more expensive cut glass); and, finally, 'Mott's New Silver Electro-Plate, Possessing in a pre-eminent degree the qualities of Sterling Silver, from which it cannot be distinguished; at a fifth of the cost'. It is notable that not all of these items are luxury goods as Curtis suggests: some are cheap imitations of consumer desirables. Authenticity is not always an object in itself; imitation can be just as good. These advertisements, then, indicate that the domestic ideal can be achieved in a multitude of places, and that imitation wares and imitation practices would help consumers achieve a result virtually indistinguishable from the 'real thing'.

Advertising uses a multitude of voices, and thus it can never be coherent; as Kevis Goodman says of daily news, advertising is always noisy.[28] The serial novel, surrounded by chatter, startling fonts, bad puns, and eye-catching illustrations, made monthly interruptions into the reader's spatiotemporal setting, and thus noisily solicited attention. All of these elements combined to make the form of the serial temporal, and to bring this noisy temporality into the reader's domestic time. Advertising, too, carries its own interpellation of the form it is participating in, and among other concerns, it discursively domesticates practice. Reading a Dickens serial is an everyday practice that in itself has implications for readers' domestic time. The advertising supplements to *Bleak House* are thus part of a discursive move to make Britain domestic, which they share with *Bleak House* itself. Not only did magazines and serial works continually emphasize the domestic situation of their consumption; the advertisements that partly funded these publishing ventures also interpellated the domestic setting into which they entered by suggesting consumer products whose purpose was to idealize domesticity. In *Bleak House*, Dickens represents a workable domestic ideal that can be imitated by the lower class of household manager – Caddy Jellyby and Charley – until this class has internalized it and can transplant it to new places. Implicitly, *Bleak House* suggests that a broad distribution of its text can cause a broad distribution of domestic influence. Similarly, the Dakin & Co. advertisement works to represent, by visual juxtaposition, a series of temporally aligned domestic spaces, united around a single idea. In this case, the idea is not 'Esther', but tea. The Dakin & Co. advertisement aligns the way tea is sold and consumed with the way novels and MPs are sold. The veins of the body politic flow with words and monthly numbers as well as with tea, coffee and members of Parliament. Synchronous tea-time produces nationally aligned domestic time.

In *Bleak House*, Dickens uses repetition to suggest sameness, but also, crucially, to show that sameness must be the result of constant labour. *Bleak House* goes further than any other of Dickens's novels to show that domestic time is made through repetitive actions, and in his later works Dickens conceptualizes domesticity very differently. With *A Tale of Two Cities* (1859), he abandons the detail-oriented domestic time for a more conventional mystification of housework, embodied in Lucie Manette and her 'golden thread'. This is not just a reflection on the change in genre – *A Tale of Two Cities* is a historical novel and emphatically not a novel of domestic realism – but also reveals a realization that realism could not be pushed any further before domestic repetitiveness would become conceptually problematic and overload the narrative.

As Chase and Levenson have argued, in Dickens's last completed novel, *Our Mutual Friend* (1864–5), conventional domestic ideology, some of it remarkably reminiscent of Dickens's earlier oeuvre, is mocked by the anti-hero Eugene Wrayburn. Eugene facetiously praises the ineffable 'domestic influence' of a fully equipped kitchen where no one will ever cook. Chase and Levenson comment that these ironies are 'nothing like a repudiation of an earlier Dickensian axiom, but they too indicate the changing circumstances of affirmation. [...] [Dickens] must now flee from his own rhetoric that had once found easy comfort in sentimental conventions.'[29] Even more intriguingly, the heroine Bella Wilfer steps out of the stereotype of effortlessly domestic heroines by improvising housework, playing at housekeeping, and failing at cooking:

> Persisting, Bella gave her attention to one thing and forgot the other, and gave her attention to the other and forgot the third, and remembering the third was distracted by the fourth, and made amends whenever she went wrong by giving the unfortunate fowls an extra spin, which made their chance of ever getting cooked exceedingly doubtful. But it was pleasant cookery too.[30]

Unlike poor Dora in *David Copperfield* (1849–50), Bella is allowed to learn from her mistakes and redeem herself. *Our Mutual Friend* repeatedly emphasizes the performative aspect of domestic work. By this late stage in his career, Dickens has moved to a mode of representation where the illusion of easy repeatability cannot be maintained. In *Bleak House*, the performative aspect is still hidden, hinted at in the humming of a song or the circumnavigation of a shooting gallery for breakfast bacon.

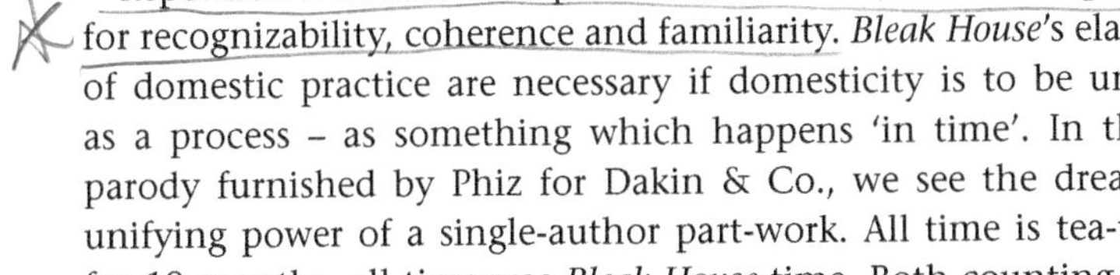

Repetition is difficult to represent in narrative, but as a trope, it allows for recognizability, coherence and familiarity. *Bleak House*'s elaborations of domestic practice are necessary if domesticity is to be understood as a process – as something which happens 'in time'. In the loving parody furnished by Phiz for Dakin & Co., we see the dream of the unifying power of a single-author part-work. All time is tea-time, and for 19 months, all time was *Bleak-House*-time. Both counting out time, and pulling time together into a coherent whole, the serial forms a visually striking set of recurring print events. Seriality becomes a fantastical sameness. When taken together, *Bleak House* and the 'Bleak House Advertiser' suggest, therefore, that domestic time and print culture time belong to the same circuit.

2

Interruption: The Periodical Press and the Drive for Realism

> Nor is it only the *regular* demands made upon the store and housekeeper, for which a mistress should be prepared; in a thousand unexpected forms, the *good* wife and mother is liable to be *interrupted*, and she will submit to these interruptions with the better grace when she considers them as *an important part of the business of the day*; of more consequence to the happiness of her household than any sedentary employment, she must lay aside for their sake. General order and forethought will, indeed, do much to *limit* these applications, but no housewife can expect to be exempted from them. And let her not overlook the *dignity* and *privilege* of being thus wanted and called upon continually.
>
> 'M.B.H.', *Home Truths for Home Peace* (1851)[1]

The interruptibility of domestic time was a trial for the nineteenth-century household manager. As the anonymous writer of *Home Truths for Home Peace: Or, Muddle Defeated* admits in 1851, timetabling and forward planning will only limit interruptions, not eliminate them. The temporal mainstays of middle-class domestic time – daily meals, for instance, or the weekly laundry – cannot tether all of domestic time into strict schedules. Because of an underlying realization that this is perhaps not the most satisfactory way of running things, interruptibility also posed something of a problem to representation. As we can see, *Home Truths for Home Peace* invests considerable narrative energy on what is, when it comes down to it, a call for submission to the constant invasion of the unforeseen. In the passage above, we can trace the implied hierarchy between enduring employment and annoying interruptions; a hierarchy which 'M. B. H.' tries to turn on its head by calling interruptions *'an important part of the business of the day'*, and by urging the *'dignity* and *privilege'* of being in such constant demand. Aside from noting that 'M. B. H.' has a fondness for italics, one can conclude that interruptibility is difficult to present as a coherent and logical system. The paradoxical reference to *'dignity* and *privilege'* reminds us that, unsurprisingly, interruptibility is gendered – that the woman at home must learn to read constant interruption as a function of her exalted position at the hub of the middle-class British household when, in fact, interruption is generally less than dignified.

Contemporary commentators pointed out the gender-political bias of interruption. John Stuart Mill touches on the topic in *The Subjection of Women*, first published in 1869:

> The superintendence of a household, even when not in other respects laborious, is extremely onerous to the thoughts; it requires incessant vigilance, an eye which no detail escapes, and presents questions for consideration and solution, foreseen and unforeseen, at every hour of the day, from which the person responsible for them can hardly ever shake herself free.[2]

Over and above this exercise of vigilance, however, a woman 'is expected to have her time and faculties always at the disposal of everybody'. Such a trial, Mill argues, would not be suffered by a man, even in his leisure time. For women, it is otherwise: 'Are a woman's occupations, especially her chosen and voluntary ones, ever regarded as excusing her from any of what are termed the calls of society?'[3] Behind Mill's rhetoric lies Florence Nightingale's *Suggestions for Thought*, which had been privately printed and circulated, and which Mill certainly saw.[4] Unlike the vast majority of Nightingale's contemporaries, Mill had the opportunity to register the ire with which she attacked the treatment of middle- and upper-class women's time:

> There are people being robbed and murdered continually before our eyes and no man sees it. 'Robbed' of all their time, if robbing means taking away that which you do not wish to part with, slowly 'murdered' by their families.[5]

One of the most radical parts of Nightingale's polemic was her suggestion that women were being robbed of 'their' time – that it was actually their own time to begin with. The strength of her metaphors – women 'robbed and murdered' by those closest to them – reflects the need to find new words, new phrases, and new conceptualizations that could expose these hidden conditions of domesticity. Nightingale reflects a larger cultural need to put interruptibility into words, even if *Suggestions for Thought* remained unpublished in her lifetime.

This chapter examines how contemporary writers narrated such a fragmented and fluid temporal medium. In the periodical press, we see writers responding to the problem through both fiction and non-fiction. The means by which interruptibility, porousness, and fragmentation are narrated, I argue, reveal the underlying urgency of representation that pushes at the boundaries of realism. While nineteenth-century advice literature was keen to emphasize order, logic, sequence, and manageability, the present discussion finds evidence in those very same sources of the opposite. Representation was stretched to accommodate a domestic time riddled with ambiguities, a time run through with calls for filling it up and giving it structure, at time impossible to control. Timetabling might be suitable for schools and prisons which were built and run to be impermeable except at certain set times. The domestic sphere resisted such control. As I explain below, earnest efforts in the periodical press and in advice manuals conceptualized domestic time in order to gain control over it. Writers were torn between representing the home as a mystic realm of invisible but all-pervasive 'influence', and acknowledging that, in the end, domestic time was pragmatic and discretionary.

After discussing interruption as a condition of domesticity, I address specific attempts to respond to the problem. The first response is the ideology of the 'spare moment' and how to turn it to good account; the second is the discourse that takes sewing as a strategy for tackling domestic time's porousness. Both approaches were meant to counter the dangers of unmarked, undisciplined time. But interruptibility continued to stretch and challenge representation, thus forcing writers to react by stretching genre and realism. My analysis concentrates on three main genres: literary fiction, didactic fiction, and advice literature. The three genres subscribe to similar truisms about domestic time: all suggest a catalogue of personal practices most likely to improve the chances of moral improvement (avowedly) and social mobility (less openly). While there is no single discourse of interruptible domestic time, the heteroglossia contains many pervasive assumptions about the porous nature of domestic time. However, the three genres differ significantly in their strategies of realistic representation, and this difference affects each work's ability to stretch genre and narrative in its grappling with domestic time's resistance to representation.

The discussion that follows looks at articles taken primarily (but not exclusively) from domestic periodicals published around mid-century. I have approached the material with a combination of keyword searches and the 'sideways' reading of longer runs of periodicals advocated by Linda K. Hughes.[6] Periodicals contributed to the persistence of ideals of domestic time management from the earliest decades of the century. These documents explicitly moulded domestic time and the cultural assumptions of its uses, for instance by promoting needlework and other crafts; and they allowed writers to link gender-specific domestic time to larger social and moral issues such as class belonging, economic conditions, and sexual purity. Moreover, by printing multiple genres, periodicals could voice many different conceptualizations of the every-day in response to the difficulty of representation. We see this particularly in periodicals that have a strong editorial line, such as the *British Mothers' Journal*, the *Englishwoman's Domestic Magazine* and *Mrs. Ellis's Morning Call*. Each of these journals has thematic cohesion, perhaps enforced by their respective editors, Mrs J. Bakewell, Samuel Beeton, and Sarah Stickney Ellis. Periodicals had a stake in regularly, serially, repeating the same points. The periodical was a moral and social enforcer of practice, and it is in this context that we should see the various genres that insist on the interruptibility of domestic time.

Time, interrupted

Interruptibility made domestic time hard to control and hard to conceptualize. Paradoxically, however, interruptibility also allowed for its representation. Since the realist novel calls for particularized time and place for most plot developments, domestic time is often narrated at the point of its interruption. At the beginning of chapter 51 of George Eliot's *Felix Holt, the Radical* (1866), Esther Lyon is immersed in domestic time when she is suddenly interrupted:

> One April day, when the sun shone on the lingering rain-drops, Lyddy was gone out, and Esther chose to sit in the kitchen, in the wicker chair against the white table, between the fire and the window. The kettle was singing, and the clock was ticking steadily towards four o'clock. She was not reading, but stitching; and as her fingers moved nimbly, something played about her parted lips like a ray. Suddenly she laid down her work, pressed her hands together on

> her knees, and bent forward a little. The next moment there came a loud rap at the door. She started up and opened it, but kept herself hidden behind it. 'Mr. Lyon at home?' said Felix, in his firm tones. 'No, sir,' said Esther from behind her screen; 'but Miss Lyon is, if you'll please to walk in.' 'Esther!' exclaimed Felix, amazed.[7]

Like the reader of *Felix Holt,* Esther is waiting for the resolution of her story. Felix has been pardoned and released from jail, and Esther has renounced her claim on the Transome estate and chosen poverty and love. She also seems to have renounced her French novels for more demure 'stitching'. She has also, notably, abandoned the showier parlour for the more homely kitchen – in the absence of Lyddy, the maid-of-all-works, of course. In order to reach Esther's resolution, the narrative sets the stage of domestic time – the where, what, and when of the everyday – before it is interrupted. The verbal forms create a relief of background and foreground actions: the past progressive denotes ongoingness, such as 'was singing', 'was ticking', 'was [...] stitching'. The foreground is marked by the preterite of 'laid down her work', which interrupts the background verbs, supported by temporal adjectives and phrases like 'suddenly' and 'the next moment'. Esther's actions also go through a transition: her 'stitching' is replaced by abrupt movements and even a 'start'. As we see in this example, novels often stage domestic time only to interrupt it. Structurally speaking, without interruptions there would be no plots.

Interruptions, then, are entangled in the conceptualization of domestic time: in order to describe domestic time realistically, writers have to handle the trope of interruptibility. This obligation is such an accepted part of domestic temporality that an enduring tradition of informal private letter-writing has been to register interruptions in the middle of the letter. Elizabeth Gaskell frequently makes the recipient of a letter aware of at least some of the interruptions that happen during composition: 'Lunch is just going in[.] There's the 2nd bell! After lunch! I ought to be out. Katie is in bed with a bad cold.'[8] Such recording of interruption gives the effect of immediacy, and acknowledges the informal intimacy between writer and recipient. Disruptions illuminate what they disturb, which makes interruption a powerful source of information about hidden temporalities. On the one hand, interruptions are subversive factors in the struggle to schematize domestic time; on the other hand, they can be motors of representation and signs of hidden structures. Frank Trentman argues of the everyday: 'Rhythms and habits are interspersed with disjunctions and connected via suspensions, interferences and repair work. Disruptions thus reveal the elasticity of everyday life. They also open up its politics.'[9] Repetition and return are, as Trentman points out, shot through with 'interferences'. In fact, even the incidents that ought to function as structural lynchpins of domestic time – daily foreseen occurrences – can seem like interruptions. In *War at a Distance*, Mary A. Favret provides a reading of William Hazlitt's 'The Letter-Bell', where she observes that even expected events have an ability to throw time into sudden contrast: 'In signalling the moment', Favret tells us, 'the letter bell also exposes the surrounding drift of unsounded eventlessness.'[10] While interruption is thus sewn into the very fabric of domestic time, it is also paradoxically the best means by which it can be 'expose[d]'. The sound of the dinner bell can cut into a lazy afternoon, an eager discussion, or the hemming of a shirt. Regular and rhythmical events continually slice through unmarked time, and can feel as much like interruptions as more unscheduled events such as a knock on the door, a spoiled supper dish or a torn sleeve in urgent need of repair.

Domestic time was encoded differently for men and women: men's domestic time was often equated with leisure, whereas for women, time in the home was a much more nebulous mix of work and leisure. Women's daily lives lacked clear boundaries between the two, resulting in fluidity. As a result, the received idea was often that any strict time schedules in the home were enforced for the benefit of, and sometimes at the direct instigation of, the men of the household. Dinah Mulock Craik gives an example of this view in her novel *Olive* (1850):

> The return of the husband and father produced a considerable change in the little family at Stirling. A household, long composed entirely of women, always feels to its very foundations the incursion of one of the 'nobler sex.' From the first morning when there resounded the multiplied ringing of bells, and the creaking of boots on the staircase, the glory of the feminine dynasty was departed. Its easy *laisser-aller*, its lax rule, and its indifference to regular forms were at an end. Mrs. Rothesay could no longer indulge her laziness – no breakfasting in bed, and coming down in curl-papers. [...] [Mrs Rothesay's] favourite system of killing time by half-hours in various idle ways, at home and abroad, was terminated at once. She had now to learn how to be a duteous wife, always ready at the beck and call of her husband, and attentive to his innumerable wants. She was quite horrified by these at first. The captain actually expected to dine well and punctually every day, without being troubled beforehand with 'What he would like for dinner?' He listened once or twice, patiently too, to her

> histories of various small domestic grievances, and then requested politely that she would confine such details to the kitchen in future; at which poor Mrs. Rothesay retired in tears.[11]

Female domestic time is described as floating, irregular, lazy, and comfortable. The description is morally loaded against them both: Mrs Rothesay is lax and flighty, but her husband is overbearing. Not only does he expect regularity and punctuality of his wife; her time also becomes his to command. Order is imposed from a male realm with its own set of rules, which are described as distant and alien ('creaking of boots on the staircase') and indifferent to excuses of indecision, improvisation or difficulties. The new regime of punctuality is only skin-deep – the Captain is wilfully blind to the work going on behind the scenes – but the housewife must surrender unconditionally. Punctual dinners, in this culture, were a man's prerogative; women's time yielded to a supposedly oppositional time discipline. While other representations of domestic time weighted the binaries differently, this debate about the inherent politics of timing in the home was widespread.

Such gender distinctions were, of course, far from stable or unquestioned, but Craik's novel suggests the different temporal experiences of men and women, as well as points to some of the strategies that demarcated boundaries or broke them down. While domestic arrangements were settled by individual negotiation, and while the gendered spheres were not as watertight as some nineteenth-century commentators (or indeed modern critics) would like to think, being male led to different experiences of domestic time, if by no other means than the different domestic practices that the genders performed. As both Mill and Nightingale argued, men's time within the home had a vastly different status to women's: men could shield themselves – as Captain Rothesay peremptorily does – from interruptions or petty domestic worries. Women rarely had this option. In fact, contemporary domestic ideology could be openly hostile towards activities that required concentrated attention if they distracted women from their familial duties. Sarah Stickney Ellis, unsurprisingly, identified the danger of too keen an enjoyment of undisturbed time in *The Women of England* (1839). The example she gives is of a brother and sister enjoying an evening of intellectual stimulation:

> If [...] they read some interesting volume together, if she lends her willing sympathy, and blends her feelings with his, entering into all the trains of thought and recollection which two congenial minds are

capable of awakening in each other; and if, after the book is closed, he goes up into his chamber late on the Saturday night, and finds his linen unaired, buttonless, and unattended to, with the gloves he had ten times asked to have mended, remaining untouched, where he had left them; he soon loses the impression of the social hour he had been spending, and wishes, that, instead of an idle sister, he had a faithful and industrious wife.[12]

As with the passage from *Home Truths* that opens this chapter, Ellis's passage emphasizes a woman's duty to attend to small details that resist methodical forward planning, and which lie outside the realm of intellectual study. The dichotomy between sustained attention and torn gloves is one between an ideological centre and its margins. The marginalization of detail, and the insistence that certain members of the household operate in the realm of the marginal, is in itself a conceptualization of domestic time. On both sides of this debate, the assumption is that time is shot through with conflicting, mutually exclusive claims and desires; that some activities require absolute attention and others require absolute readiness for interruption and self-denial. The gendered difference in the quality of domestic time marked itself in spatial differentiation: while a drawing-room and a dining-room were the first spatial signifiers of middle-class status, the next step was likely to be a (male) study or smoking-room. This organization of domestic space allowed the master of the house to close the door effectively on interruptions. The drawing-room, which was most likely the wife's only personal space, had no such cultural claim to impermeability. Women's time in nineteenth-century understanding was a medium into which interruptions entered.

'Odds and ends of leisure': mobilizing spare moments

The writing that urged the importance of spare moments had to continually stress the value of even interrupted time. Even more significantly, narrative realism had to be manipulated. In April 1852, the *Leisure Hour* (a monthly magazine published by the Religious Tract Society) ran an article entitled 'Hints about Timethrift'. In this journal, the anonymous writer muses that 'most persons do not rightly estimate the worth of the smaller fragments of their time. They have large ideas of what may be accomplished in years and months, but of the value of minutes, or even hours, they seem unconscious.'[13] The 'smaller fragments', discontinuous and snatched as they are, must be put to good use, the article argues. Thus, the tired breadwinner, instead of spending his evenings complaining that he never has time to improve his mind, could read to his wife, or perform, 'if he have a talent in that way, some little piece of handicraft skill'. Meanwhile, a slatternly wife, always run off her feet, would do well to take the advice of a hypothetical pattern household manager, given voice in the article:

> When I rise in the morning, knowing I have certain duties before me which *must* be done, I try to put these in the best order, and to keep for the intervals of leisure which are sure to occur, those other matters which I should *like* to accomplish; such as reading, writing, a call of charity, or a visit to a friend. By this means, and by taking that first which is most pressing, or best fits in with the space at command, I contrive to keep my children and household in order.[14]

The emphasis throughout the article is on these 'intervals of leisure' and the necessity of always keeping some activity in readiness for them. What is needed, it seems, are tasks which can be picked up and put down easily and with minimal fuss or preparation, and which do not require continuous concentrated effort. The article's model housewife emphasizes those Victorian virtues of 'order' and 'contriv[ing]', which are meant to make domestic time seem manageable and logical; the writer downplays the tendency of household tasks to overrun or get entangled. 'Hints about Timethrift' goes on to assure us that 'by adopting and adhering to [this plan] we *fill up* our working time, so as almost entirely to preclude those brief intervals of cessation which most people find so difficult to improve'.[15]

On the one hand, 'brief intervals of cessation' must be filled and eliminated; on the other hand, they *will* keep appearing. To deny their existence is to deny their ideological value: the impression left by 'Hints about Timethrift' is that the 'smaller fragments of time' are the only time left to busy Victorians. The writer scrupulously includes both male and female activities:

> There are [...] some occupations which leave a man no fixed portion of the day at his own disposal. Physicians, lawyers, ministers, men filling high public stations, and many others, are liable, at all hours, to the calls of professional or official duty. If such persons know not how to improve the 'intervals' before mentioned, or to profit by their odds and ends of leisure, they will have no time at all for themselves.[16]

The call to mobilize 'odds and ends of leisure' is thus directed both at female household managers and at the busy male breadwinner, flatteringly equating the interruptibility of women's domestic time with important male professions, even 'high public stations', which require the same kind of 24-hour readiness. One also notes the general fudging of boundaries between leisure, work and self-improvement. The specific aim of the article is, however, decidedly domestic: all of these 'intervals of cessation' occur in the home, and call for domestic activities like reading or handicraft. Even the periodical in which the article appears bears the title the *Leisure Hour; an Illustrated Magazine for Home Reading.* The periodical itself seems, if its title is any indication, to be published expressly to fill out some of those gaps with improving matter – the publishers were, after all, the Religious Tract Society. While 'Hints about Timethrift' does not explicitly mention periodical reading, the assumption is that the instructive nature of the periodical's articles will perform that ultimate moral good of 'filling up' time and 'improving' all those tricky leisure moments.

Domestic time is unpredictable. It has 'odds and ends', like fabric; interruptions seem to rip it to shreds. The writer of 'Hints about Timethrift' equates 'cessation' with 'leisure'. Leisure is, in other words, the absence of activity and of work, but the article is eager to emphasize the productive potential of such a temporal patchwork. The waste of even the smallest unit of time is to be avoided, and 'Hints about Timethrift' accomplishes this by turning value on its head: what has been marginalized is in fact the most valuable of all. Eight years later, a very similar idea is expressed in the words: 'Spare moments are the gold dust of time!' This sentimental maxim appeared in a number of periodicals in 1858–59, in publications as diverse as the *Theatrical Journal* (August 1858) and *The Sunday at Home* (September 1858), the latter a Religious Tract Society publication. In December 1859, the self-same maxim introduces an article by Anna Ritchie in *Reynolds's Miscellany*.[17] Ritchie's article proposes to teach its readers how to put this 'gold dust' to good use, by evoking a model woman named Mabel: 'Our Mabel is never fussy – never bustling – never hurried. She never flies, with a whirlwind rush, from occupation to occupation, and creates a tornado-like atmosphere around her. [...] In short, she never seems *oppressively busy*.'[18] It is essential, of course, that Mabel is completely unaware of her own perfection; she does not set herself up as a pattern, but nevertheless unobtrusively contrives to be a model to her sex. In this respect, she conforms to the stereotypical ideal of a Victorian housewife and her pervasive but unobtrusive influence. But how, the writer muses, does Mabel manage her home and her family without bustle, without seemingly doing anything at all? At first, it seems an impossibility:

> But, watching our sweet Mabel, as she glided noiselessly through her day, we plucked the secret out of this mystery. It lay in Mabel's use of her 'spare moments' – little 'odds and ends' of time – intervals between anticipated events – pauses which people generally allow to slip by unfilled, while they are waiting for what is about to happen – the summons to a meal not punctually served – the arrival of a belated friend – the coming of a dilatory carriage – the cessation of unwelcome rain – or a hundred similar daily occurrences.

While Ritchie is committed to her ethereal angel of a household manager ('glid[ing] noiselessly through her day'), she does give examples of the causes of fragmented domestic time (unlike the writer of 'Hints about Timethrift'). The examples of everyday delays – the meal, the friend, the carriage, and the rain – function as anecdotal evidence in Ritchie's attempt to convey time's mundane slipperiness. Oddly enough, the sentence structure in this passage mimics the subject matter by becoming, itself, delayed by a multitude of small irregularities, ones separated by an endless series of dashes. One explanatory interjection engenders another, and then another, and the sentence drifts off into disjunct musings about unpunctual meals, 'dilatory carriage[s]', and other everyday irregularities. Like the hapless housewife, the writer seemingly becomes distracted and loses sight of the task (or sentence) in hand. Ritchie is experimenting with the representation of interruptibility; in order to make her argument compelling, she must attempt to represent the slipperiness of domestic time.

While Ritchie describes the delays inherent in domestic time, she is less explicit about the actual means of putting '"odds and ends of time"' to good use. As is characteristic of much conduct literature of the period, the actual work is mystified and obscured into the 'gliding' and 'noiseless' trajectory of the ethereal Mabel. Rather unhelpfully, the article finishes with the following reflection:

> It is Mabel's thorough appreciation of the value of time, and the economical employment of these usually neglected, uncounted moments, which enable her thus to surpass others in undertaking largely and accomplishing proportionately, and have revealed to us the full interpretation of that poetically-expressed but practical truth – 'Spare moments are the gold dust of time.'

By concluding with a repetition of the opening maxim, emphasizing that it is 'practical', Ritchie deserts the specific for the general. This manoeuvre is of a piece with the article's disavowal of any actual signs of activity clinging to Mabel. While the repetition is a mark of the obscurantism of housework in contemporary domestic ideology, it is also a response to the difficulty of representing domestic practice. Readers, it is implied in Ritchie's article, are as well served by a recital of the golden rule, just as much as they would be by more solid instructions for practice. Similarly, the lack of clarity surrounding Mabel's practice is as much a recognition of the difficulty of representation as it is an ideological erasure of female work and productivity.

The representative detail: realism and genre

The articles 'Hints about Timethrift' and 'Spare Moments', both from the 1850s, valorize 'odd times' and emphasize their productivity. The ideology of spare moments underwrites the cultural assumption that the smallest details carry the largest significance. The periodical press – itself earning market dominance around this time, and changing the temporality of reading – was keen to suggest that its own perusal was valuable time use, and encouraged articles full of practical, yet normative advice. Writers experimented with the genres that could best convey the idea of domestic time's porousness, and tried to schematize it.

When Ritchie gives examples of daily interruptions and delays, her sentence structure disintegrates in mimicry of the subject matter: 'the summons to a meal not punctually served – the arrival of a belated friend – the coming of a dilatory carriage – the cessation of unwelcome rain – or a hundred similar daily occurrences'. Ritchie is making specific examples into representatives of the myriad mundane ways in which time slips away; she is making a pattern out of accumulated detail. In this sentence, Ritchie responds to a consensus about how unrepresentable things are represented. The accumulated details – the meal, the friend, the carriage, and the rain – come, by their very accumulation, precariously close to luxurious detail. There is a parallel between Ritchie's use of examples, and Roland Barthes's concept of the reality effect. Ritchie's carriage and rain are luxurious detail, prompted by the fluidity of domestic time – and it is precisely in such details that the struggle of representation is played out.

Barthes identifies 'superfluous' detail in the realist novel: detail not directly relevant to the plot. Although, cumulatively, these details can build up an indirect structural meaning, Barthes contends that some details belong to the reality effect. Superfluous details do not have a more direct link between signifier and signified than any other textual traces; they are not closer to the real. They are signs of the real because of a common consensus about the nature of representation. Since all theories realize that description can never be exhaustive – that any description of the real will always fall short of actually representing it fully – Barthes argues that exhaustive, extra-structural detail itself becomes a sign of 'concrete' reality:

> The pure and simple 'representation' of the 'real,' the naked relation of 'what is' (or has been) thus appears as a resistance to meaning; this resistance confirms the great mythic opposition of the true-to-life (the lifelike) and the *intelligible*; it suffices to recall that, in the ideology of our time, obsessive reference to the 'concrete' [...] is always brandished like a weapon against meaning, as if, by some statutory exclusion, what is alive cannot signify – and vice versa.[19]

Since reality can, in theory, only be approached through exhaustive, indeed never-ending, description, superfluity and meaninglessness itself becomes a sign of 'concrete' reality. The realist consensus is that the real does not 'mean' anything, and so meaningless details become signposts that by consensus denote the real. In using these details as signs, realist works seek to authenticate the real, according to Barthes.

The repetition I discussed in chapter 1 could be read as a reality effect – since reality is repetitive, repetitive narration is thus a sign for the real. In Ritchie's article, the accumulation of detail is part of a similar impulse to conceptualize the everyday through narrative luxury. In advice literature like 'Spare Moments', which uses traits from fiction, examples are signposts of the real, gestures towards the indescribability of the everyday. Such details help create a recognizable diegetic world which readers can agree is realistic – not closer to the real, but conceptualizing the real. Ritchie's derailed sentence performs exactly that work of signifying the unrepresentable.

The novels that form the subject matter for Barthes's concept of the reality effect aim to uncover truth by letting objects and characters unfold their nature over time by accumulating information. As Elizabeth Deeds Ermarth argues, since details in realist fiction are 'part of a hidden whole', 'the identity of anything – that is, its rational, structured, formal quality – can only be discovered in relationship, and so, in realism, discrete forms are replaced by continuities, stasis is replaced by implied motion, and hierarchy is replaced by horizon.'[20] In order to understand the object of inquiry, the realist novel places it before our eyes in many relations, in an accumulation of multiple viewpoints.[21] Ermarth goes on to argue that realism entails the shared assumptions of writer and reader that different viewpoints are indeed of the same object, and that conflicting opinions can be resolved:

> By the apparently innocent gesture of accepting the past-tense narration, then, we have accepted several rather more complex ideas: that time is a single continuum; that temporal continuities extend beyond the arbitrarily limited horizons of the text; that events point beyond themselves to a coordinating system; and that appearances are but aspects of hidden identities.[22]

Since description can never be exhaustive, realism merely presupposes that accumulated detail over time has revelatory potential. In *The Serious Pleasures of Suspense*, Caroline Levine argues that realist fiction, rather than attempting to paint a static image of the world, uses narrative as a process of discovery. Novels, Levine maintains, are structured to allow gradual unveiling over time. Nineteenth-century realists were fully aware of the epistemological gap between world and representation; George Eliot first and foremost strove for 'approximate truth'. When Eliot reviewed John Ruskin's *Modern Painters* (1843–60), she called, Levine observes, not for 'a style or effect of mimesis, but for the laborious act of attending to the world'.[23] Realist fiction accumulates details to build a representation of the whole, over time. As we have seen, Barthes's reality effect works exactly because a one-to-one relationship between world and representation is known, consensually, to be impossible. Superfluous details are gestures towards that impossible realm of complete, undiluted description. The material I use in this chapter – details, parts for the whole, reality effects – are significant because they attempt such representation of the unrepresentable.

All writing marks some details as insignificant, and how it does so sheds light on mid-nineteenth-century shared assumptions about domestic time. As I have noted, Ritchie's accumulated details are signposts meant to signify the slippery nature of unmanageable everydayness. Examples are markers set up to indicate that they, themselves, embody an entire body of practices. Meanwhile, incidental domestic time in fiction establishes a fabric of background time, a time that is always ready to slip away when the plot enters (in the shape of Felix Holt, for instance). There are differences, of course, to what is marginalized. Fiction and advice literature have different attitudes to tiny details. For example, in

Felix Holt, the Radical, a particular strand of domestic time occasionally emerges from the extreme background: the domestic time of Lyddy, the habitually distressed servant in the Lyon household. Glimpses of Lyddy's work and her time management are often given when Esther complains about her, as we see here in chapter 26:

> 'O, Lyddy, Lyddy, the eggs are hard again. I wish you would not read Alleyne's *Alarm* before breakfast; it makes you cry and forget the eggs.' 'They are hard, and that's the truth; but there's hearts as are harder, Miss Esther,' said Lyddy.[24]

Esther's tender quip about Lyddy letting the eggs boil too long is in all likelihood inaccurate for comic effect – Esther can be quite facetious about her loyal old Lyddy – but it is one of the few hints we are given about the servant's domestic time. The book she is reading is *An Alarm to the Unconverted* by Joseph Alleyne (or Alleine), a seventeenth-century Puritan whose work inspired John Wesley. Here, it signals Lyddy's somewhat outdated fatalism. But more than this, these luxurious details of Lyddy's domestic time are used because they are baffling and illogical. They refuse to resolve into a coherent picture.

In contrast, when advice literature luxuriates in detail, it does so for very different purposes. We see this in an article in a series called 'Economy of Dress' in the *Englishwoman's Domestic Magazine* from 1859. The article gives details of how to buy two lengths of cotton (the bulk-buying being more economical) and make a complete set of underclothes:

> When the set is completed, mark them neatly with red cotton. [...] Number each article, and wear them in rotation. It is advisable to get two other pieces of long cloth and commence a second half dozen, as soon as is convenient; by wearing them in turn, the dozen will last four or even five years.[25]

In this example, specifics – the minute instructions about the work – are very far from meaningless. Small details point towards a larger normative pattern. The article is probably a response to a letter from a reader, published in the same column two months earlier, asking specifically for instructions on how much '*must* be spent in under-clothing and shoes and what remains for the more showy parts, which are too often thought of first'.[26] The question and the resulting response operate in a moralistic dichotomy between inside and outside by juxtaposing clean, white linen (with its strong implications of purity) and 'showy' outerwear (with its connotations of worldliness). Unlike the details in Anna Ritchie's floating sentence, these details are very much imbued with a direct application to the world (wearing one's shifts in rotation). This may seem unnecessarily detailed, but it is not a reality effect. Advice literature has a tendency – due to its explicit normative purpose – to over-represent things that ought to be done, and to under-represent things that people do without being told. In other words, advice literature over-represents what is under-performed and under-represents what is over-performed. The great detail in which the *Englishwoman's Domestic Magazine* urges its readers to plain-sewing could very well reflect the writer's anxiety that plain-sewing is an under-performed practice.

Taking up sewing and putting it down

In the ideology of spare moments, one activity suffers intense over-representation: sewing. Advocated as an excellent filler for those pesky 'odds and ends of time', sewing was the primary mid-century response to domestic time's interruptibility. In other words, it solved a problem. While sewing could be taken up at spare moments, it could also easily be put down again. Although Talia Schaffer notes a brief mid-century enthusiasm for domestic sewing being efficiently machine-like, the overwhelming feeling was that sewing ought ideally not to be too absorbing.[27] Sometimes, rather than be put away, it simply retreated into the background. Most women kept some decorous needlework as a company employment – ideally not cumbersome sheets or mundane buttons. In Elizabeth Gaskell's *Wives and Daughters* (1864–66), Mrs Hamley confides to Molly Gibson: 'Now, I don't sew much. I live alone a great deal. You see, both my boys are at Cambridge, and the squire is out of doors all day long – so I have almost forgotten how to sew. I read a great deal.'[28] Sewing is a useful activity for company, whereas reading is solitary and selfish. Even ornamental sewing, which is surely all a squire's invalid wife could be expected to perform, is done for others. Frances Parkes's *Domestic Duties* advocated, as employment for the visiting hours, 'drawing, music, or light and ornamental needlework. [...] Indeed, any needlework with which you may be occupied at the entrance of morning visitors, may be continued without any breach of politeness towards them.'[29] While sewing can be used for filling interrupted time, it is also itself an interruptible activity. Women's domestic time thus becomes a tautology: they sew because they are interrupted; they can be interrupted because they sew. And in the periodical press especially, this response – take up sewing! – is urged, debated, and urged again throughout the middle decades. This urging repeatedly called for writers to conceptualize domestic time. Writers could agree that there were moments, minutes, even hours in domestic time that could not be timetabled, and that should most certainly be filled.

The knee-jerk activity promoted by magazines and conduct books alike was needlework. In fact, the word 'work', when referring to a middle-class woman's activities, never meant household work, but always sewing. The term made no distinction between fancy-work and plain-work. What constituted legitimate time use for women was always contested; but sewing enjoyed a special status. In 1842, Sarah Stickney Ellis could be surprisingly permissive:

> For my own part, I do not believe I have ever learned anything, even down to such a trifle as a new stitch, but I have found a use for it [...]; for either it has occupied what would otherwise have been idle time, it has used up what would otherwise have been wasted material, or I have taught it to others [...]. Besides which, there is the grand preventive this dexterity supplies, against ever being at a loss what to do – the happiness if affords, both to ourselves and others, to be perpetually employed – the calm it diffuses over a naturally restless temperament; but, above all, the ability this habit affords in cases of sickness, or other emergency, to turn all our means to account in the service of our friends.[30]

This advice from *The Daughters of England* reduces the worth of sewing to its time-filling capacities. Needlework fills up time, uses up materials, promises the practitioner that she can be 'perpetually employed' in the future, calms a 'restless temperament', and turns a woman into a good nurse in some unspecified way. I find this passage quite disturbing. First, it discounts any direct personal pleasure in the needlework itself. Secondly, it presupposes 'idle time' and 'wasted material' in an oddly tautological way: was the time 'idle' and the material 'wasted' before or after one sat down to learn a new, 'trifl[ing]' stitch? And thirdly, it shows that the 'new stitch' grows gradually larger and larger, until 'all our means' are turned over to others in denial of any personal fulfilment. The passage is dominated by a perverse pleasure in anti-usefulness, turning time to dust, in the face of woman's self-effacing duty. It would be wrong, however, to make Ellis the general representative of Victorian domestic temporal ideology. Ellis's talent is a particular kind of blunt misogyny, which feminists from Florence Nightingale onwards have denounced; most advice literature at the time was less blunt but more insidious.

Not only was it a convenient truism that women sewed in their spare time; several magazines that sprang up during this period were mainly vehicles for craft instructions. Needlework was supremely interruptible in a way that, for instance, glue-based crafts could not be. In their attempts to legitimize their own entry into domestic time, domestic periodicals suggested the many uses to which spare moments could be put. They used different genres to gesture towards a coherent, comforting view of domestic crafts and the time spent making them. There was a consensus in the mid-nineteenth century that the home was a site which 'held' time: the titles of periodicals for domestic use in the 1850s and 1860s often took care to imply not only the space into which they would intrude (*The Household Friend*, *Household Words*, *The Home Companion*), but also often the supposed temporality of this intersection into their readers' lives: *The Leisure Hour*, *The Sunday at Home*, *Once a Week*, *Mrs Ellis's Morning Call*, and *Timethrift*. These periodical titles suggest either their own temporal situation within domesticity or the leisure hour for which they are designed. While they seem to suggest – sometimes explicitly – when their readers will read, they also implicitly construct periodical reading as a timely, justifiable pursuit. Inadvertently, these titles reveal an anxious consciousness of the opposite possibility: that periodical reading could, itself, be construed as time-wasting, along with the crafts that were promoted. Periodical reading was a contested activity at the time, especially when it came to female readers.[31] Each periodical had to strike a balance between the desire to amuse and the urge to improve, and justifying its own interruptions of readers' domestic time could be a similar balancing act. What counts as good uses of time changes with each periodical, but it must always be supposed to include the periodical's own perusal. The question remains to what extent periodicals could negotiate the fine line between being good and bad employments of time. Not surprisingly, this question became more pressing as the number of titles grew over the course of the nineteenth century, and with the increasing dismissal of conventional female leisure activities, especially fancy-work, as pointless. Talia Schaffer identifies a shift around 1860, when handicraft came under attack for being an intellectually stultifying waste of time.[32] Periodicals had to negotiate these shifting balances.

One reason for the many conflicting discourses about women's sewing and handicraft was the ambiguous status of the final products of these efforts. Periodicals of the period were negotiating a tricky divide between production and overproduction, between meaningful work, on the one hand, and those endless antimacassars and doilies, on the other hand. The short-lived monthly periodical *Timethrift*, which folded after six numbers in 1851, was essentially a craft-oriented publication that sought to participate in the enthusiasm for consumer objects in the months leading up the Great Exhibition. A regular column entitled 'Exhibition Chat' lists items that will be on display – both professional work and amateur handicraft. Both homemade and professional object profusion became linked. The main business of the periodical was crochet and knitting, with as many as six pages devoted to work instructions and two pages of good-quality engravings of the finished products in every number. Possibly to counter any suggestions of frivolousness, the full name of the periodical was *Timethrift: Or, All Hours Turned to Good Account*. Evidently the editor, the successful craft author Mrs Warren, was trying to encode fancy-work as a good way of being 'time-thrifty', and the idea of turning 'all hours' to 'good account' echoes the ideology of the valuable spare moment. The discourse of time-filling became enmeshed in the domestic periodical's attempt to market itself.

But the artefact enthusiasm generated in the year of the Great Exhibition gave way to increasing misgivings about the pointlessness of all these objects. A few years later, *Timethrift*'s brand of dilettante products – doilies, imitations, crochet – was being ridiculed. It was no longer a good use of time. In 1858 the *British Mothers' Journal* ran an article entitled 'A Whisper to our Elder Daughters. By a Maiden Lady', lamenting the tendency of young women to consider themselves 'well and usefully employed' while they were, in fact, wasting their precious time with fancy-work, fashion frills and gossip over their work-table.[33] By this time, crochet and fancy-work had become shorthand for time-wasting. In the series of articles from *Chambers's Journal* that she collected in *A Woman's Thoughts about Women* (1858), Dinah Mulock Craik launched an attack against young women who 'prick [old Time] to death with crochet and embroidery needles'.[34] Craik's articles and resulting book appeared at the high point of a spirited debate about women's education and their access to work, which included the founding of the radical feminist periodical *The English Woman's Journal*, edited by Barbara Bodichon, in March 1858, but which raged in virtually all domestic periodicals of the decade. Craik's ire against those who prick time to death with crochet needles turns the idea of spare moments on its head, denying that domestic time is simply something that should be filled.

The semantic merger of work and leisure – the use of the word 'work' to cover all kinds of sewing – made it difficult to interpret the borders between worthwhile and worthless occupation. It is this nebulousness that prompts articles like 'Hints about Timethrift', keen to suggest both that spare moments do occur, and that they can be put to productive use; it is also this nebulousness that generates the confusion about what is productive. By the time George Eliot wrote *Felix Holt*, she could count on her readers sympathy with the narrator's condemnation of old Mrs Transome's embroidery: 'A little daily embroidery had been a constant element in Mrs Transome's life; that soothing occupation of taking stitches to produce what neither she nor any one else wanted, was then the resource of many a well-born and unhappy woman.'[35] *Felix Holt* was published in 1866, around the time of the Second Reform Act, but set in 1832 just after the passing of the First Reform Act. Eliot can thus displace Mrs Transome's unsatisfactory embroidery to a pre-Victorian past, while simultaneously denouncing the craft excesses of the 1850s. She is, of course, also denouncing the anaesthetic properties of sewing, the laudanum effect it has on the spirit of a healthy, intelligent woman with no scope for development. Sewing has effected that generalized boon that writers of advice literature brought out again and again: the 'soothing' of Mrs Transome, the 'calm' mentioned by Ellis. Sewing, too, was believed to encourage good habits: habits of patience, neatness, submission and industry. In other words, sewing was the means by which girls became accustomed to a sedentary and submissive life, as we saw in the passage from *The Daughters of England*. Kristie M. Allen defines the Victorian ethos of 'habit' thus:

> Though considered to be closely allied to instincts because of their durable and unconscious nature, habits, paradoxically, were also described as flexible dispositions, capable of being retrained through conscious effort. Thus for Victorian culture, one's habitual regimes were intensely moralized.[36]

When good and bad habits were discussed, there was always an earnest subtext of moral anxiety. For women, inevitably, the home became a site for disciplining actions into habits. Frances Parkes writes in *Domestic Duties* (1825) that 'an occasional effort will not form a habit; and it is habit alone that makes those things pleasant and agreeable, which, in the first instance, oppose our love of self-indulgence'.[37] Repetition engendered habit. Since domestic time is so permeable and nebulous, and since it resists exact timetables and schematization, correct instincts of time management, produced by habit, were crucial to self-control and efficiency. Fancy-work played an important part in contemporary understanding of the production of domestic habits. All these practices are responses to, and a construction of, the perceived porousness of domestic time.

Fancy-work, on the one hand, soon became a convenient shorthand for all the worst aspects of female domestic time: frivolity, uselessness and overproduction. Plain-work, on the other hand, occupied a more secure moral place in mid-century periodicals. However, plain-work engendered its own unique species of vexation (bordering on class paranoia). While writers were eager to portray plain-work as something unproblematically womanly – and hence middle-class – the articles themselves, when read against the grain, seem unsure about whom they are addressing. As I have pointed out, we cannot ignore the tendency for under-performed practices to be over-represented. The profound unease about the class status of plain-work reveals an even greater unease, within periodicals themselves, over whether they could actually address their readers' real experiences and inclinations. This anxiety makes domestic time a vexed ground for impossible fantasies of proper femininity and for the dramatization of a time-use deliberately placed outside capitalist economic structures.

Plain-work involved the making of personal linen (underwear, night-wear, shirts, handkerchiefs, baby linen) and household linen (sheets, cloths, towels, etc.). Because of width-restrictions in linen and cotton manufactory, bedsheets had to be sown together from two long strips of cloth, and then at some point unstitched and sewn back edge-to-edge when the middle became worn. This was work that was often done in the home. Personal linen had traditionally been made at home, too. As Amanda Vickery has observed, home-made linen was a primary caregiving gesture from a family's women towards its men. Georgian men who had no female relatives to make them shirts were pitied.[38] This symbolic significance of shirt-making endured into the Victorian era. Even with increased availability of ready-made shirts, or perhaps in response to it, advice literature around mid-century continued to urge women to sew their family's linen. And even if the linen was made up outside the home, there were still buttons to re-attach and torn cuffs to mend – all part of women's daily business. The menial sewing tasks of buttons, sheets, cloths and so on, were sometimes transferred to servants, preferably nursemaids, or to daughters, as part of their training in selflessness. The crucial thing, however, was that plain-work should be familial, private, and especially unpaid, in order to maintain this high moral status.

Plain-work, unsurprisingly, was suggested as a peerless activity for 'spare moments'. In the *Englishwoman's Domestic Magazine* article on making underwear, the writer sees no difficulty in finding time for making personal linen:

> To young ladies of limited means who say they have not time to do their own plain sewing without interfering with other duties, I would say, rise an hour earlier for the purpose, and always have some at hand to take up any spare minute that may occur during the day. [...] No one can be a true economist who wastes a moment of that time far more precious than the gold which perisheth. I hope those ladies who can well afford to purchase these articles ready-made will always do so, since the making them forms the sole subsistence of hundreds of their suffering sisters.[39]

The advice here is conflicting: those who have little time (probably domestic servants and other working women) are to use their spare moments; those who have money (and hence time) are to buy their shifts ready-made. Notoriously, domestic servants had little or no time of their own, and not always adequate lighting for sewing or reading. The idea that they can put their spare moments to such worthy use is a middle-class fantasy. As is implied in all the self-help literature, the ability to find time in scarcity (to mobilize spare moments) is, in and of itself, a mark of moral superiority and thus a social catalyst. The readiness to perform plain-work was imagined to spill over into all aspects of women's moral habits and psychology, which also always meant their class status. Meanwhile, 'ladies' – well-off middle-class matrons – were to buy ready-made underwear, thus supporting the impoverished needlewomen who were a particular worry in the 1840s and 1850s. In the *Englishwoman's Domestic Magazine* article, the social and personal benefits of plain-sewing are sung from a slightly awkward position: addressing working women who do not have the time, urging them to perform a task which is increasingly becoming a professional (or even worse, a sweat-shop) practice. Plain-sewing itself is encoded with such significance outside the cash nexus that the article cannot help but sustain its advocacy of private plain-sewing, even while it obliquely references an ongoing debate that middle-class women were undercutting the seamstresses' wages by sewing in their leisure time. There were two different kinds of time for sewing: the spare moments of the comfortable middle classes and the relentless slavery and fourteen-hour days of the poor wage-earner.[40] In this article, the benefit of plain-work on servants was seen from a middle-class perspective.

In her 1860 book *Homely Hints from the Fireside*, H. Wilson admits that 'good old-fashioned plain "white-seam" has gone so much out of fashion as ladies'-work, that it almost seems unnecessary to offer any hints on the subject'.[41] Wilson nevertheless urges plain-work as a vital part of working-class girls' education: 'It may seem absurd to talk of the moral effects of such a mechanical occupation, but there is something in the habit acquired of patiently and diligently finishing a dull piece of useful work, that is likely to make more steady servants abroad.'[42] Unpaid plain-work, and plain-work as familial care-giving, was, in other words, encoded as a middle-class activity, and only then projected onto domestic servants – but always in the face of deep-seated doubt. We see this again in an anonymous 1865 article in *Chambers's Journal*. Entitled 'Plain-work', it begins thus:

> 'Thank goodness, Lizzie! you were taught to work.' My husband is constantly repeating this sentiment to me, and I decidedly agree with him that it is a great cause for thankfulness. I may say in passing, that I don't believe I should ever have married my husband at all if I had not been able to work, for one of his very first questions to me upon our becoming acquainted, was as to what occupation I took most pleasure in, and upon my answering 'Plain-work,' a pleased smile came over his face.[43]

While this incident has an air of the apocryphal and frankly improbable about it, the sentiment it expresses is genuinely meant; the purpose of the article is to argue that education in plain sewing is essential to making a middle-class girl into a good wife. Not only does it induce good habits of tidiness, care of appearances, patience and, presumably, self-denial; it also has the more nebulous effect of making a girl 'womanly and sensible'.[44] All these attributes are encoded as distinctly middle-class virtues; the article's writer displays great unease about the state of working-class sewing skills. With no perceptible trace of irony, the writer confides that: 'I have often thought, if I had only time to spare, how much I should like to teach the rising [working-class] generation the little I myself know of the art of plain-work.' This wish rings particularly hollow, coming as it does in a shilling monthly clearly aimed at the middle classes. The sentiment, however, conforms to the general tendency to associate bad habits, wastefulness, sloppiness, and ignorance with the servant class, living in uncomfortable proximity within the very walls of the middle-class home. The writer urges that a middle-class girl must under no circumstances be taught sewing by servants, as lower-class instructors will probably give her 'vulgar', un-ladylike habits, such as 'clicking her needle with her thimble, pinning her work to her knee, biting the end of her thread, and sticking her needle into the front of her dress'.[45] Visible signs of servant influence – bad habits such as clicking thimbles against needles – are monikers for a more dangerous (because invisible) class-inflected moral corruption always just a few flights of stairs away. The many complaints that the working classes had insufficient sewing skills did not contradict the idea that sewing was a symbolic, if unstable middle-class activity. The very notion that middle-class women could instruct working-class girls in needlework reflects a desire to connote it as middle-class.

If plain-work stands for social and moral progression – for order and forethought – then its under-performance leaves domestic time unpinned again. The unease over middle-class rejection of plain-work, and the resulting confusion over who, exactly, should be taught plain-work, disturbs the comfortable fantasy that domestic time can be constructed in a way so that interruption is always answered by appropriate activity. In other words, the issue of class, and the question of whom the periodical is addressing (and how successfully), is bound up with the periodical's projection of itself into the reader's domestic temporality. The fantasy that domestic time's interruptibility can be countered with targeted fillers is destabilized.

Constant interruption: domestic time disturbed

The idea that the lessons learnt from industrious sewing were transferable to domestic time as a whole was a means by which the interruptibility of domestic time could be narrated in advice literature. In didactic fiction – which more than any nineteenth-century genre is invested in the significance of small details – this relationship between sewing and female duty becomes literalized. The *British Mothers' Journal* ran a didactic story in May 1858 entitled '"Duty First and Pleasure Afterwards": A Chapter for Our Daughters', which crystallizes the politics of interruptibility. It begins with a mother, Mrs Temple, reproving her young daughter for being too absorbed in her crochet (what else?), instead of finishing her father's new handkerchief: 'Had you not better hem the handkerchief at once, my dear, lest you forget it again in the interest of your fancy work?' When Emily demurs, Mrs Temple tells her: '"Duty first and pleasure afterwards" is the safest rule, Emily; so put that aside now, and fetch your work-box. You will enjoy your new patterns all the more by and by, when you have accomplished your morning's business.'[46]

Soon after, the story shifts its focus to the elder daughter, Janette, and Emily's lesson is a foreshadowing of the more formidable trials in store for her sister. Having left school, Janette 'had been gradually initiated by her mother into the mysteries of housekeeping, certain departments of which were her entire charge; whilst she also took care of her brother's linen – repairing, making, cutting out, and purchasing, as her skill and experience increased'.[47] This experience, it is clear, is to train her for her inevitable future as a housewife and mother. Working for her brother is encoded as one of the 'duties' that befall her as a woman-in-training. More momentous initiation is to come, however. Mrs Temple goes away on a two-week visit, leaving Janette in charge of the household. At first, all goes well. But then Janette becomes absorbed in a project of making wax flowers, 'and one little daily duty after another was put off till a formidable pile of needlework and unsettled accounts had accumulated'. Suddenly, Janette is behindhand with everything, and the disaster soon culminates in a day of complete unravelling, structured by a series of interruptions:

> 'If you please, Miss Janette,' said the housemaid, one Monday morning, 'the laundress has come for the linen.' 'Oh, dear! I have not written out her list,' exclaimed Janette, and she ran nimbly up stairs to prepare it. Here she met nurse, who remarked, 'Miss Janette, Dame Morland has sent up for the flannel gown your mamma promised her; the weather is so cold that the rheumatics have taken her, and the doctor has ordered her to wear flannel immediately.' Poor Janette was dismayed, for she had herself undertaken to complete this garment, and knew that it ought to have been in the old woman's chest a fortnight before. To add to her perplexities, her brother was now heard loudly complaining at the dearth of shirts and stockings in his drawers, and that the few he found there were minus one or two buttons. There was nothing to be done but to repair negligence as quickly and good-humouredly as possible. While doing this, time slipped away imperceptibly, till cook, thinking her young mistress must have forgotten the kitchen department, mounted in search of her to represent the empty state of the pantry, and the urgent need of some preparation for dinner. [...] The dinner-hour was near at hand, and Janette justly dreaded the remarks her meagre fare might excite.[48]

As if these accumulated catastrophes were not enough, Janette is shamed by a Bible District Committee lady, who has called for the quarterly subscription, which Janette has neglected to pay. Meanwhile, her wax flowers have been spoilt because she left them too close to the fire.

As in the Anna Ritchie article, this didactic story takes care to emphasize the serial nature of domestic upset – one thing after the other until the very worst happens: Janette's father must suffer an inferior dinner. Once Janette has gone through this purgatory of a day, however, she has learnt her lesson:

> [Janette] diligently persevered in the less agreeable, but more necessary, duties of darning stockings, sewing on buttons, and weighing out the contents of the store-room; making tarts and puddings, reading or playing with her younger brothers and sisters, and fulfilling all those nameless claims of 'kitchen, parlour, drawing-room,' which distinguish so obviously between the homes of the slatternly and the thrifty housewife. She no longer dreaded the consumption of the last cake of soap, or the ignition of the last candle! Janette then discovered that her leisure hours re-appeared, and by confining her recreative employments to the after part of the day, she pursued them with double zest.[49]

The temporal scheme is familiar: as long as there had been conduct books, women had been urged to get the 'business' part of the day done in the morning. The representation of Janette's new efficiency is structured by exemplary details: stockings, puddings, soaps, and candles. But the story also falls back on an easy excuse for mystification – 'all those nameless claims' on a household manager's time, the 'mysteries of housekeeping' in an earlier passage. The story that began with a neglected handkerchief ends with Janette's disastrous day, structured by necessary interruptions: laundrywomen, charitable cases, and the claims of religious observance all penetrate from outside the home and ignore internal schedules. The real lesson of the story is that while Janette can learn to anticipate interruptions, she cannot do away with this unavoidable quality of domestic time: its porousness. The spatial permeability of the middle-class home to other classes and to external economic mechanisms have to be countered by a corresponding temporal openness, on the part of the domestic manager, to meet these emissaries at the various thresholds and keep them at bay.

Didactic fiction represents the world not from an urge for realism, but from a desire to change it. The small details in didactic fiction are always overloaded with significance. A story in *Mrs Ellis's Morning Call*, for instance, begins with a rather lengthy complaint from a grandmother that her granddaughter is too absorbed by her crochet (of course crochet!) to attend to her.[50] This minuscule character fault becomes the occasion for the grandmother to tell the story of five sisters, who each of them choose to pursue only one talent: be it singing, languages or housekeeping. Each sister, once married, loses the ability to perform her particular talent, some through freak accidents that leave them each peculiarly and appropriately maimed. The upshot is that although they all catch a husband, each husband quickly tires of his wife once she can no longer sing/embroider/keep house, leaving her an idle, boring (and presumably bored) woman. In didactic fiction, the punishment, however harsh, always fits the crime. Minor details are significant in these stories; not only that, they are structurally significant, because they are the pegs upon which the plot hangs. Details that in realist fiction would be of secondary significance are here the very crux of the story. Didactic fiction refers to a different coordinating system, one in which details matter desperately. It is easy to berate the magazines for the peculiar quality of badness in their didactic fiction, but that would be to miss the point of these stories. Didactic fiction is not meant to be nuanced, realistic, or even controversial. Its purpose is to illustrate and enforce truisms of personal moral habit and social behaviour. Didactic fiction serves to fill up the pages of the magazine but also to shore up the expectations of gendered and classed behaviour. It is closer to a fantasy of practice than to the representation of it. This idealization results in over-functionality of detail when compared with realist fiction. When didactic fiction then tries to represent interruptibility, as we have seen, it does so by making the interruption over-signify. The story of Janette uses interruption as a primary structure of its narrative. Generic conventions – in this case, the didactic convention of the structurally significant detail – is not just a restraint, it is also enabling. Readers of didactic fiction understand that practice – whether thrift, industry or moral rectitude – will be crucial to the story. They find confirmation that there is virtue in small things (though the confirmation sometimes arrives too late for the main character).

Using genre to recognize and conceptualize the porousness of domestic time results in works that engage, in one way or another, with the modes of representation. One final example of this is from the diary of Emily Shore. In the 1891 edition, the appendix includes a short satirical play, apparently written when Emily Shore was 13, which would date it around 1832. The play is called 'The Interruptions'. In it, Emily and her mamma are trying to read *Sir Joshua's Discourses* (by the painter

Joshua Reynolds – a classic work of aesthetic self-improvement), but are constantly interrupted. First the housemaid comes in, saying that there is a man selling baskets, and then returns with a few of the baskets. This exchange follows:

> *Em.* Well, now, I hope I shall go on without interruption.
> *Mam.* I cannot answer for that.
> *Em.* 'As this principle is observed or neglected, our profession becomes either a liberal art or a mechanical trade. In the hands–'
>
> *Enter* WILLIAM.
> *Em.* (*aside*). How tiresome!
> *Will.* Did you ring, ma'am?
> *Mam.* No, it was not this bell, William. (*Exit* WILLIAM.) Now you may go on, Emily.
> *Em.* Well, we shall see in whose hands. 'In the hands of one man it makes the highest pretensions, as it is addressed to the noblest faculties–'
> (*The* COOK *pokes her head in*). The butcher has not sent the scrag of mutton, ma'am.
> *Mam.* Oh dear, cook! what shall we do?
> *Cook.* Why, I don't know, ma'am. There's the loin of mutton.[51]

The cook leaves, is called back, the nursemaid enquires about the children's clothes, a maid comes in because she cannot find the thimble, then a younger brother asks for paper, and finally a morning caller is admitted and Emily must leave off her reading. Domestic time was somewhat wryly accepted as supremely interruptible. The bathetic fall from 'the noblest faculties' to scrags of mutton underlines the sense of disruption. Shore chooses her genre – drama – to emphasize the sometimes farcical quality of domestic time's porousness. The affordances of genre play an important part in the representation of interruption. In this case, drama – with its written form that looks abrupt and fragmented on the page, and its long history of comedic comings and goings – lends itself to an accumulated series of interruptions.

And although this chapter ends with a play written at home by a precocious 13-year-old, it is again worth emphasizing how the representation of interruptibility, and the challenges it set to genre and realism, was a subject exactly suited for the nineteenth-century periodical press. Printing didactic stories with the same plot over and over again in never-ending numbers of periodicals had a purpose of its own: breeding familiarity and renewing pious ambitions in readers. Repetition also allowed each periodical to forge a coherence of voice and mission. The mid-century periodical was where all these genres met, and where many of them mutated and morphed. Advice literature becomes fiction (becomes didactic fiction...), employing the strategies of realism for which the devil was in the detail. Meanwhile, the periodical, in its very form, assumed its own interruption into the rhythms of the home, and played out its ability to direct and influence them. The greater and greater proliferation of domestic periodicals suggests that domestic time was increasingly encoded as addressable by print; the entry of printed matter into all aspects of domestic life, offering a variety of genres within each issue, similarly suggests the many ways in which domestic time could be read and narrated. Like the accumulation of superfluous details in realist fiction, and like the accumulation of identical plotlines in didactic fiction, the sheer accumulation of genres within the periodical shows the many avenues which representing the unrepresentable could take.

3
Division into Parts: Elizabeth Gaskell's *North and South* and the Serial Instalment

The evenings were rather difficult to fill up agreeably.
Elizabeth Gaskell, *North and South* (1854–5)[1]

At the opening of Elizabeth Gaskell's *North and South*, the protagonist Margaret Hale faces a problem with temporality. After living with her fashionable aunt in London and sharing the education of her cousin Edith, Margaret has returned, on Edith's marriage, to her parents' small parsonage in Helstone in the New Forest. Provincial domestic time, however, is difficult to adapt to. In the evenings, her mother tends to complain about the 'unhealthy' climate of the area, about Mr Hale's parochial duties that often take him out of the house, or about the family's lack of money. Margaret responds with demonstrative inattention: 'On such evenings Margaret was apt to stop talking rather abruptly, and listen to the drip-drip of the rain upon the leads of the little bow-window. Once or twice Margaret found herself mechanically counting the repetition of the monotonous sound' (21). Margaret breaks off disagreeable conversation to do nothing, but empty time in *North and South* tends to fall into a structure. The dripping raindrops on the window are at first a generic background noise, yet they gradually turn towards an unexpected sort of measurement – one that carves a rhythm ('drip-drip') out of that generalized passing of time. Margaret finds herself suddenly in this rhythm, hypnotized into 'mechanical' counting. Her instinct, then, is to fill time and to measure it, to trace a rhythmic structure onto unspecified duration.

Although *North and South* is a book about loss (of a home, of loved ones, of old social structures), Gaskell is not merely concerned with the contrast between a lost past time and an unmoored present time. Rather, Gaskell's interest is with time as it passes. Time is given texture

passing time

by narrative strategies of filling, counting, and measuring. Domestic time, in *North and South*, is noted and experienced as a meantime between upsetting events, a time when experiences may be discussed, contemplated, and assessed.[2] This domestic meantime may be eventless, but it has the potential to be recuperative for the novel's characters, who must sort their fraught memories into comprehensible narratives. When violent events happen, they are often shockingly sudden and disruptive, and so Margaret Hale and the other main characters need what I call domestic meantime to make sense of their pasts. The 'drip-drip' of the rain is just a precursor to the novel's intense interest with time as it passes. Whereas so far in the present study, I have been at pains to tease out domestic time from its contexts and show what it is made of, in this chapter I want to emphasize how enmeshed this temporality truly is. In *North and South*, domestic time can rarely be absolutely separated from psychological time, bodily time or the rhythms of language. In what follows, I argue that the serial divisions made in the weekly publication of *North and South* contribute significantly to the production of this recuperative meantime. Gaskell's way of dividing her story into parts draws into focus the rhythmic recurrences of time to think – not only for the characters and but also for Gaskell's readers.

Margaret, a parson's daughter with aristocratic connections, finds that her promised Eden in Helstone is of short duration. The first shock comes when Henry Lennox, a successful London solicitor, misunderstands her friendliness and proposes marriage to her. Soon afterwards, her father's religious doubts prompt him to leave the church and uproot the small family to a grim northern factory town, Milton. Here Margaret faces a series of confrontations with John Thornton, a self-made cotton manufacturer who takes Classics lessons with Mr Hale. Margaret instead bestows her sympathies on the working-class Higgins family. Her loyalties are challenged when the town erupts into strike action and rioting. In a moment of danger, Margaret defends Thornton and is herself struck by a stone meant for him. Thornton proposes to her, but she rejects him, ashamed that her actions should be interpreted as love. In a side plot, Margaret's younger brother Frederick, who is in exile after a naval mutiny, braves the risk of a court martial so that he can visit his dying mother in Milton but is recognized. Thornton, who remains in love with Margaret, sees her with Frederick and is mistakenly convinced that she has a lover.

While, as many have noted, the narrative structure of *North and South* bears some resemblance to Jane Austen's 1813 novel *Pride and Prejudice* (here contrasting the feudal and aristocratic social structure of the South with a more dynamic and disruptive industrial North), the result is a marriage plot that is far grimmer than this Regency predecessor. The novel contains no less than seven deaths. On the face of it, this is a novel characterized by dramatic, often violent events, and coloured by the political divisions of a newly industrialized society. The North, on the one hand, is defined as an active, vigorous, unsentimental environment, essentially endowed with conventionally masculine virtues and vices. The agrarian South, on the other hand, is soft, decadent, and fundamentally feminine in nature. Cousin Edith and her husband Captain Lennox represent the lazy, useless life of the moneyed aristocracy. They move to Corfu, but the Captain's military service there seems to consist mostly of troop revues and social engagements. In contrast, Milton experiences a cotton famine: a drop in sales that causes masters to underpay their workers, resulting in a strike. Like other social-problem novels (sometimes known as industrial novels), such as Charlotte Brontë's *Shirley* (1849), Gaskell's own first novel *Mary Barton* (1848), and Charles Dickens's *Hard Times* (1854), *North and South* describes political unrest in a factory town. Critical readings of *North and South* have often focused on its incorporation of large-scale historical events such as the Chartist movement, the European revolutions of 1848 or, more indirectly (because the novel does not refer to it), the Crimean War, a conflict that Britain entered in 1854 just before the serial publication of Gaskell's novel.[3] These major historical shifts are important, and I will return to the Crimean War below. If Gaskell's novel scrutinizes time, it does so, on the face of it, primarily in terms of massive temporal dis-synchronies caused by industrialization: conflicts between old and new, fears of future revolutions, and disputes about labour time and payment. However, in spite of these very public and politicized topics, I argue that this is also a novel that addresses the urgency of domestic time. *North and South* is knitted together by a near-eventless meantime, one that bridges the ostensible contrast between hasty North and slow South. Both North and South are equally prone to producing emotional shocks to which the characters must accustom themselves. The time when nothing happens is paradoxically productive, a pensive respite from the relentless forward motion of plot. The divisions between weekly serial instalments draw particular attention to this preoccupation with eventlessness, as I will show.

The concept of the eventless 'meantime' is one that I have taken from Mary A. Favret's book *War at a Distance*, in which she discusses Romantic poetry and the experience of living in Britain during the Napoleonic Wars. 'Wartime', Favret concludes, is a mode of daily living where the boundaries between war (geographically elsewhere) and peace (geographically here) are porous, and where one exists in constant oscillation between everyday routine and exceptional anxiety. War is diffused throughout everydayness, mingling news and non-news. Favret posits the existence of a meantime – a time between events. The value of Favret's concept for my purposes lies in her elucidation of the temporal medium through which home-front experience of wartime is filtered: 'the intimacies of the home and hearth, the wanderings of the mind, the interruptions and lapses – of time, knowledge, and feeling – that compose the everyday'.[4] In other words, though events of national significance are happening 'outside and beyond our reach', most people experience them through the everyday: an elusive and irrational duringness (irrational because it is liable to 'interruptions and lapses – of time'). Meanwhileness is slippery, not least because, according to Favret, it is affective: affect 'eludes the usual models for organizing time such as linearity, punctuality, and periodicity; it eludes as well the usual models for organizing history'. Favret's method for accessing the meantime, like mine for finding domestic time, is to look at the points of intersection between events and non-events. For instance, Favret asks, 'what about the time spent outside of news reading?' News from the front serves to highlight the way domestic time has of drifting, unsounded and unmeasured, into eventlessness.[5] The contrast between the two kinds of time – distant wartime and near meantime – highlights the dislocation, the oddness, and dis-synchrony of their interlacing. Something similar, I argue, happens in *North and South* with the intermingling of dramatic events in a quiet, interruptible, recuperative meantime.

In my analysis of *North and South,* I do not focus on its well-established contribution to the social-problem novel. Nor am I interested in assigning Gaskell's interest in eventlessness or meantime to the romance or to domestic fiction.[6] I understand genre as an emergent rather than a customary phenomenon. Genre is latent in the fabric of a novel, not something that binds or constricts it. John Frow stresses 'the open-endedness of genres and the irreducibility of texts to a single interpretative framework'.[7] If anything, Gaskell was a master at using and altering generic signifiers in her work. As Linda K. Hughes and Michael Lund have argued, 'throughout her career [Gaskell] was finding "vacant spaces" in the ideology of her day. [...] Taking on some of the fixed formulas of her culture in her narrative voice and novel structures, Gaskell "softened" their nature and reduced the rigidity of their applications'.[8] *North and South* is a richer work if we stop seeing it as belonging to only one type of fiction, such as the recognizable industrial novel.

Like Gaskell's approach to the class warfare of the northern industrial towns, her interest in generic markers emphasizes negotiation of, and not solutions to, existing modes of narrative representation. There are no quick fixes to the cotton famines which form the background to her novel; nor are there ready-made genres to describe them. In the context of *Time, Domesticity and Print Culture,* such pushing of boundaries is especially likely to produce complex conceptualizations of domestic temporality.

According to Jill L. Matus, 'Gaskell shows the turbulence, upheaval, and disruption in changing social conditions, all of which affect the mind in destabilizing ways'.[9] I contend that this destabilization is a result of desynchronized time as much as it is about social relations. In *North and South,* the national opposition between two geographical places and several different social ranks is played out on a background of everyday, domestic, personal time. On the personal level, characters struggle with the measurement of time – with its fraught and illogical nature, its fleeting fluidity in consciousness. As a consequence, their repeated counting, measuring, marking and recording of time becomes a central strategy both to calibrate events as they are happening, and to rewrite the past creatively in order to make sense of that past. When Margaret looks back on Helstone from her unhappy life in Milton, she reinterprets the unpleasant elements: 'The dull gray days of the preceding winter and spring, so [...] monotonous, seemed more associated with what she cared for now above all price' (169). She recasts her time spent petulantly counting raindrops as rest and tranquillity. Characters throughout *North and South* spend their domestic time revisiting, rewriting, and, more often than not, misremembering the past in light of their present situations.

Time is rarely an empty phenomenon in the novel. Margaret, as the adverb reveals, 'mechanically' counts raindrops. Similarly, poor sick Bessy Higgins experiences life on Earth as a dizzying, clicking machinery of 'hours and minutes, and endless bits o' time'. Her idea of Heaven is, essentially, a place where time has stopped (90). By reckoning time in this way, characters are itemizing it, dividing duration into comprehensible bits. Domestic time manifests itself on the body through sighs, heartbeats, and irrepressible movements. Accordingly, the body in *North and South* becomes a centre for the expression of affect when interior and exterior time reckonings collide. Bodies tremble, stutter, blush, fall; the interplay between feeling and body is often described in terms of delays, rushes, speedings-up or slowings-down. Emotional shocks in *North and South* are always registered in a temporally and spatially situated psyche and body. In a novel so intent on describing especially its heroine's physicality, these responses in both male and female bodies cannot help but be gendered.[10] But Gaskell's narrative challenges the traditional dichotomy of active men and passive women. *North and South* develops in a medium of heightened everydayness, intensely felt normality. Determinedly contemporary, Gaskell's novel expands the potential of the everyday for both its male and female characters.

One way of thinking about these different temporalities is as intersecting rhythms. The counting, pacing, and measuring act as rhythmic beats; there is also a consistent rhythm of characters revisiting and misremembering their pasts. The coincidence of timing, and the disjunction of irreconcilable timing, is a recurring narrative concern. In *Rhythmanalysis*, Henri Lefebvre describes the complimentary system of internal and external rhythms:

> Rhythm appears as regulated time, governed by rational laws, but in contact with what is least rational in human beings: the lived, the carnal, the body. **Rational**, numerical, quantitative and qualitative rhythms super-impose themselves on the multiple **natural** rhythms or the body (respiration, the heart, hunger and thirst, etc.), though not without changing them. The bundle of natural rhythms wraps itself in rhythms of social or mental function.[11]

In *North and South,* socially regulated rhythms such as factory time, railway time, and clock time run alongside rhythms of speech, bodies, and consciousness. The measured drip-drip rhythm of raindrops upon a windowpane is merely Margaret's interpretation: a cultural appropriation of a natural phenomenon. This sort of negotiation of external rhythms and personal interpretations occurs repeatedly in the novel. The distinction between bodily rhythms (which are 'natural') and social rhythms (which are 'rational') is the product of a naturalized language about the divide between body and society, in which the 'natural' emanates from the body and the 'rational' is imposed onto the body. Lefebvre qualifies the binary by adding: 'If there is difference and distinction, there is neither separation nor an abyss between so-called material bodies, living bodies, social bodies and representations, ideologies, traditions, projects and utopias. They are all composed of (reciprocally influential) rhythms in interaction.'[12] While acknowledging that the dichotomy of natural/cultural is useful, Lefebvre suggests that it would be possible to imagine time and rhythm spatially, as a three-dimensional field of superimposed rhythms. Rhythms wrap themselves together in complex strands and bundles that influence each other relationally. Such a field is a useful way of thinking about temporal experience in Gaskell's novel. *North and South* is intently concerned with the perception of different temporalities and rhythms, and their clashes. Rhythms are not always oppositional in *North and South,* but form a fabric that connects individual bodies with their surroundings. Sometimes, however, the connections are violent enough to form what I will call cataclysmic time: an oppositional clash of internal and external time reckonings.

In my previous chapter, I discussed Dickens's *Bleak House*, a novel that was written with serial instalments in mind. Here I turn to a work of fiction that Gaskell prepared for serial publication more or less under protest. What began as an amicable business arrangement between Gaskell as writer and Charles Dickens as editor turned into a vexed dispute, one that underlines some illuminating disparities between Gaskell's and Dickens's respective methods of composition. In the present chapter, I explore what happens to a material text external to its narrative logic, and how that impacts the work's conceptualization of time – specifically, domestic time.

Gaskell achieved an instant hit with her first novel *Mary Barton* in 1848, and Dickens was eager to secure her services for his new twopenny weekly, *Household Words,* which he launched in 1850. With *Household Words,* Dickens aimed to make the inexpensive weekly periodical respectable, in direct competition with especially G. W. M. Reynolds' sensationalist *Reynolds's Miscellany*. Gaskell wrote a series of successful 'Cranford' pieces for him between 1851 and 1853 (which she would reissue in volume form as the episodic novel *Cranford*), and so Dickens encouraged her to prepare her next novel for *Household Words*. On her part, Gaskell was hoping to produce a companion piece to *Mary Barton* which would feature a conciliatory portrait of a model mill-owner – *North and South*'s hero, John Thornton, is based on several of her reformist Manchester acquaintances.[13] Dickens was eager to secure quality serial fiction that suited *Household Words*'s ethos of social interrogation and reform. The periodical interpellated a readership that was happy to have its entertainment leavened with discussions of clean water and sanitation, living conditions, education, working-class recreation, and similar causes. On 7 October 1854, for example, *Household Words* led with an address 'To Working Men', urging them to make sanitary reform their primary, and joint, political goal, in light of the then ongoing cholera epidemic.[14] As Lorna Huett has demonstrated, the physical format of *Household Words* was designed to maximize its readership by combining low costs with high quality. Dickens's name, and the names of popular authors he could attract, was meant to compensate for the flimsy paper, tight columns, and lack of illustrations in his periodical.[15] Since her two previous full-length novels *Mary Barton* and *Ruth* (1853) were published in volume form, with *North and South* Gaskell was faced with an entirely new scheme of writing. She had to develop her story for the demands of serialization, with an editor who had himself made his name essentially dominating that very form of publication.

As is evident from her manuscript, which has survived, Gaskell composed a continuous text and only divided her story into chapters and serial instalments later.[16] It is this very problem – the contrast between how Dickens and how Gaskell wanted to divide the novel – that I analyse below. One bone of contention was the length restrictions. Gaskell overran her space allowance, forcing Dickens to allocate more columns to her story.[17] Still, she felt cruelly hampered by the restrictions, and she clearly thought that Dickens should have given her more than just twenty instalments. For her 1855 volume edition of the novel, she added extra material to the final chapters. She felt that the ending had been rushed because of the pressure Dickens exerted on her. *North and South*, being the main attraction in *Household Words* at the time, was in some ways responsible for its own circulation and that of the entire magazine; as Dickens's letters from the period show, the novel's value was calculated by the readers it attracted (or failed to attract) week by week. As I show in detail, Gaskell had to navigate Dickens's expectations and directions for what gave a serial novel 'interest', how one sustained it, and the topics it addressed.

Gaskell's struggles with word limits and her disagreement with Dickens over the best ways to sustain a plot became essential for the conceptualization of time within the novel. As Margaret Beetham has pointed out, the magazine form 'is deeply contradictory, simultaneously rooting its readers in the present while pointing them to the future'.[18] Because magazines both promise instant gratification and fantasize about a potentially endless series of future issues, they form a temporally charged relationship with their readership. Magazines and serials must always imply a continuing product; as James Mussell says: 'the success of a periodical or newspaper depends upon whether its producers can create an object that is recognizable and meaningful to its prospective audience'.[19] This promise is necessarily fraught with failure, as editors were well aware. However, while serialization can certainly be seen as another rhythmic quality added to an already rhythm-fascinated novel, the two aspects cannot be linked together by mere analogy. Serialization is not a universal metaphor, one to be imposed on any concept that shares its rhythmic qualities.[20] Rather, serialization is a material practice – unlikely to be metaphorically interpreted by mid nineteenth-century readers – that has clear consequences for the reading experience and the ongoing interpretation of the novel. Serial print culture helped construct, narratively, a sense of everydayness. An approximation of a common domestic temporality was interpellated by serial writing, but that representation was also influenced by the serial form itself. *North and South*'s concern with memory and the past complicates domestic time, and it does so serially. Things do not simply happen and go away; they are constantly referred to in the next number, and the next, to be questioned and reinterpreted. The 'now' in which characters suffer experience is often a domestic now: a private, insignificant and mundane temporal knife-edge. It is this intersection between the intra-textual and the extra-textual productions of time that the chapter will explore.

After discussing the publication scheme and the row between Gaskell and Dickens, I turn to an examination of the construction of domestic time in the novel, centred around rhythms, measurement, and around the idea of meantime. Then, I address Gaskell's composition of the novel during the first year of the Crimean War. I see elements of Margaret Hale's character, and her negotiation of women's work, in relation to Gaskell's friendship with Florence Nightingale. While the war is never mentioned even indirectly in *North and South*, any analysis with such a strong focus on the composition and publication of the novel as mine cannot omit what happened during this exact period: namely, that Britain entered into hostilities with Russia, and that Nightingale became a national celebrity when she travelled to the Crimean peninsula to organize the nursing effort in the fatally ad hoc military hospitals. Gaskell was a peripheral friend of the Nightingale family and wrote part of *North and South* at their family estate, meeting Florence herself shortly before she left for the Crimea. As I shall show, Gaskell's reaction to Nightingale's mission informed her vision, in *North and South*, of national redemption through female agency. Finally, the present chapter turns to Margaret and the conflict between trivial domestic tasks and strong emotion. I argue that domestic practice becomes a text through which the narrative 'reads' Margaret.

Falling to rest: the serial divisions in *Household Words*

It is evident from the letters exchanged between Gaskell and Dickens that Gaskell preferred to compose a continuous manuscript, and, unlike

Dickens, did not have explicit plans of individual numbers before she started writing. In February 1854, before Gaskell was writing in earnest, Dickens told her: 'Don't put yourself out at all, as to the division of the story into parts. I think you had far better write it in your own way', and suggested that he would be able to indicate points of division when he had some of the manuscript in type.[21] In mid-June, when he had received the first chunk of writing, he suggested divisions, summarized what would go into each number, and told Gaskell: 'According to the best of my judgment and experience, if it were divided in any other way – reference being always had to the weekly space available for the purpose in Household Words – it would be mortally injured'.[22] However, by contrasting his plan for the first 11 numbers, as set forth in this letter, with what was actually printed, we see that Dickens was overruled after the first three numbers. Dorothy Collins has examined the differences between the two plans of serialization for *North and South*, 'the divisions which Dickens recommended and those which were finally adopted'. The variations show, according to Collins, 'not so much differences in the technique of serialization between Dickens and Mrs. Gaskell, as emphasis upon one aspect of the novel rather than another'.[23]

In the first three numbers, Gaskell followed Dickens's plan; it was his decision to end the first number on a note of suspense as Henry Lennox comes to Helstone. In the fourth part, however, he suggested that the division should happen after Margaret had read her cousin Edith's letter and reflected on her changed life after the move to Milton. As Collins shows, 'the division was actually made a few paragraphs earlier with the Hales' arrival at their new house'.[24] The instalment thus ends with the reflection that, although Margaret and her mother may look on Mr Thornton as a vulgar tradesman, their landlord is in fact obliged to change their wallpaper 'at the one short sharp remonstrance of Mr Thornton, the wealthy manufacturer' (66). Collins concludes: 'It is an effective ending. Lingering with the reader, it suggests to him a set of northern values to which the Hales are strangers, directs his attention to the almost entirely unexplored territory of Milton, which is the novel's central setting, and opens the possibility of a developing connection between the Hales and Mr. Thornton.'[25] For the end of the sixth instalment, 'Dickens' division brought into prominence the working-class Higgins family, whereas Mrs. Gaskell continued [...] to direct the reader's attention as the part closed to the Thorntons'. Collins suggests that the growing discrepancy between Dickens's suggestions and the final choice of division was due to 'aspects of the novel which Dickens, for obvious reasons, could not foresee'.[26] Gaskell wished to emphasize the contrast between the Hales and the Thorntons.

It is worth bearing in mind that Dickens based his suggestions on a printers' estimation of Gaskell's handwriting that turned out to be wrong.[27] Dickens, however, evidently felt that the divisions actually adopted were damaging the novel. In mid-October, when sales of *Household Words* dropped, he attributed this to the failings of *North and South* and especially the serial divisions: 'Mrs. Gaskell's story, so divided, is wearisome in the last degree'.[28] He was possibly spurred on in this estimation by Gaskell's intractable behaviour in the previous months: she fell behind with the manuscript; the novel was too long and threatened, in Dickens's eyes, to overrun its number allowance; and she had refused to cut or compress the scene with Mr Hale's religious doubts, which worried Dickens.[29]

It is hard to guess why exactly Dickens felt that the divisions were so injurious to the novel's ability to sustain interest. J. Don Vann tentatively suggests that Dickens had not yet formulated a communicable principle that would explain his instinctive understanding of serial composition.[30] In a letter Dickens wrote to a female contributor more than ten years later, he explained that 'there must be a special design to overcome that specially trying mode of publication', and argued that 'the scheme of the chapters, the manner of introducing the people, the progress of the interest, the places in which the principal [events] fall' in her submitted work was 'hopelessly against' serialization.[31] Vann suggests that had Dickens presented such a set of principles to Gaskell in 1854, much aggravation could have been spared. However, it does not strike me that Gaskell significantly transgresses any of these principles in *North and South*. Characters and events are introduced regularly, and apart from a slow start there is always a development within each instalment. According to Dickens himself, it was the divisions ('so divided') rather than the structure that made the novel 'wearisome in the last degree'. Already two months earlier, he had made it clear to his sub-editor, W. H. Wills: 'when I read the beginning of this story of Mrs. Gaskell's, I felt that its means of being of service or dis-service to us, mainly lay in its capacity of being *divided at such points of interest as it possesses*.'[32] If by 'points of interest' Dickens means points of suspense, then it is true that the divisions fall short of this 'service'. Contrary to what Dorothy Collins believes, I would suggest that Dickens and Gaskell had different techniques of serialization.

The instalments of *North and South* are not structured by much conventional serial suspense. For instance, in the instalment that appeared around the time Dickens called Mrs Gaskell's novel 'wearisome', the final paragraphs address Mrs Hale's developing illness. Margaret tries to make her father aware of the pain her mother is in, and he refuses to believe her. The instalment ends: 'But she heard him pacing about [...] long after her slow and languid undressing was finished – long after she began to listen as she lay in bed' (105). Mr Hale's pacing marks time as something slow, unproductive and restless. This is hardly an exciting ending to an instalment, but not an uncommon one in *North and South.* The exception to this rule is the dramatic build-up to the riot, which starts with Margaret noticing 'an unusual heaving among the mass of people in the crowded road', a 'buzzing with excitement' and a 'thunderous atmosphere' (170). The instalment ends in ominous silence: 'There was no near sound, – no steam-engine at work with beat and pant, – no click of machinery, or mingling and clashing of many sharp voices; but far away, the ominous gathering roar, deep-clamouring' (171).

This is the closest the novel comes to a cliff-hanger. In the next (twelfth) instalment, the riot breaks almost immediately, and the instalment ends with Thornton's decision to ask Margaret to marry him, and, on Margaret's part, there is an interior monologue about her shame that anyone should suggest that she had an ulterior motive for shielding Thornton against the rioters. The contrast between Margaret's and Thornton's respective interpretations is thus abundantly clear to the reader and, in this way, suspense intensifies for the violent clash between the two characters' conflicting form of indignation in the next (thirteenth) instalment. The twelfth number, then, ends on a note of suspense. But before the thirteenth instalment is over, rather than linger on the proposal and refusal, a new subject is broached: Mrs Hale's anxiety for her health and her wish to see her son Frederick: 'Her voice was choked as she went on – was quavering as with the contemplation of some strange, yet closely present idea. 'And, Margaret, if I am to die – if I am one of those appointed to die before many weeks are over – I must see my child first. [...] Only for five minutes, Margaret. There could be no danger in five minutes' (201). This wholly new idea – that the as-yet-unseen Frederick must risk his life to say goodbye to his mother – points toward the next four instalments and the next dramatic peak in tension. Rather than simply contain the proposal, then, this instalment opens up a new avenue for serial suspense. It closes, though, on a decidedly low note, with Thornton's disclosure to his mother that Margaret has rejected him, and Mrs Thornton's ferocious words: 'I tried not to hate her, when she stood between you and me [...] But now, I hate her for your misery's sake' (208). The very last paragraph of the instalment is noticeably less loaded:

> And Margaret's name was no more mentioned between Mrs Thornton and her son. They fell back into their usual mode of talk, – about facts, not opinions, far less feelings. Their voices and tones were calm and cold; a stranger might have gone away and thought that he had never seen such frigid indifference of demeanour between such near relations. (208)

The instalment thus comes to rest before the end, finishing with this little vignette of the ways in which Thornton and his mother manage their emotions: they bury them under everyday, neutral concerns. As an ending to an instalment, it is decidedly anticlimactic.

All in all, *North and South* instalments have a tendency to finish just after a great release of tension. The next instalment, published on 2 December, contains Bessy's death and Margaret's insistence that Nicholas Higgins does not go out drinking in his grief. She brings him home to her father, and the instalment ends with a beautiful image of conciliation through grief, and a crisis averted: 'Margaret the Churchwoman, her father the Dissenter, Higgins the Infidel, knelt down together. It did them no harm' (230). This ending effectively closes down the events that occurred in the instalment, or at least defers their subtler consequences until much later in the novel.

Two weeks later, in instalment 16 (16 December), the subject is the great anxiety to get Frederick away. But all the dramatic events – his escape, the near-discovery by the drunken man Leonards, and Thornton seeing Margaret and Frederick together – occur before the instalment ends. In the following instalment (23 December), the threat of discovery by the police constable is both introduced and resolved before the number ends. In this number, which is the Christmas one, as in most of the preceding instalments, the chance for a dramatic cliff-hanger is passed up in favour of another dispiriting ending: 'And almost in proportion to [Margaret's] re-establishment in health, was her father's relapse into his abstracted musing upon the wife he had lost, and the past era in his life that was closed to him forever' (283). This release of tension (and the mixture of profound depression and quiet optimism) is symptomatic of Gaskell's use of serial divisions. Lingering on points of weariness, retrospection, and the winding down of dramatic tension, the instalment endings still introduce a note of quiet prolepsis. For example, the union in prayer between 'Margaret the Churchwoman, her father the

Dissenter [and] Higgins the Infidel' serves to hint at the transformative process in store for Higgins, who will exhibit true Christian spirit and honour Bessy's final wishes later in the novel. In other words, the serial suspense across instalments reaches into the greater arches of the story, rather than any immediate dramatic tension.

The longest such arch of suspense is Thornton's mistaken belief that Margaret has compromised her honour, a belief finally dispelled in the very last instalment. Jerome Meckier has claimed that Gaskell's prolongation of this misunderstanding is a parody of Dickens's sometimes absurd prolongations of suspense. However, Meckier's evidence is not entirely convincing. The strongest argument in favour of his view is that 'credible when met singly, obstacles in the way of union between Margaret and Thornton escalate into a parody of Dickens if totaled'.[33] My analysis of the instalment divisions and their emphasis on reflection points in another direction: the motivation for this narrative prolongation is that Margaret needs time to regret, and thus to re-evaluate, her antipathy towards Thornton.

What Gaskell ended up adding to the novel in its volume edition, free from Dickens's hated space restrictions, was more reflection, more delay. All of the instalment endings I have quoted suggest a significant need for time to process and categorize events. These endings also point to the fact that this necessary process is both a private and a social concern. In one ending, three people kneel down together, implying that there is both a personal and a communal benefit in prayer. Conversely, the past is often ignored or silenced, as in the ending where Mr Thornton and his mother return to their 'usual mode of talk, – about facts, not opinions, far less about feelings'. We see in the instalment endings two sets of double vision: a forwards-and-backwards perspective, and an internal–external perspective. Instalment endings that function as a release after tension underline the fact that things are irrevocably different after the latest development, and that characters need a period of adjustment to the new situation. It is important to repeat, however, that there is no evidence that Gaskell wrote with the instalment endings in mind, or that she intended chapters to end where they did. What Coral Lansbury has called the 'densely woven' quality of Gaskell's fiction meant that there were no 'natural' places to break, and so the divisions as they stand in *Household Words* are significant for what they more or less inadvertently highlight.[34]

The instalment endings underline one of the most fundamental aspects of *North and South*: most of the time, characters are simply trying to make sense of what has happened to them. In the process, they reinterpret the past. In the penultimate instalment (20 January 1855), when Thornton meditates on Margaret's imminent removal from Milton after both her parents have died, his version of events is hardly recognizable to the reader:

> Neither loss of father, nor loss of mother, dear as she was to Mr Thornton, could have poisoned the remembrance of the weeks, the days, the hours, when a walk of two miles, every step of which was pleasant, as it brought him nearer and nearer to her, took him to her sweet presence – every step of which was rich, as each recurring moment that bore him away from her made him recall some fresh grace in her demeanour, or pleasant pungency in her character. Yes! whatever had happened to him, external to his relation to her, he could never have spoken of that time, when he could have seen her every day – when he had her within his grasp, as it were – as a time of suffering. (349)

Seen in retrospect, and under the stress of watching Margaret disappear out of his life, Thornton's interpretation of the past is an idealized fiction loosely based on the alternating repulsion and attraction that has characterized their friendship. Looking back, Thornton sees potential where, at the time, he saw only Margaret's coldness. The time 'when he had her within his grasp, as it were', was never. But retelling the story allows Thornton to soften towards Margaret, in spite of his belief, at this point, that she has compromised herself. Looking back, re-evaluating, trying to puzzle out how the past fits in with the present – this is an imaginative, recuperative use of consciousness.[35] The painful separation of the past and the present is evident to Margaret very early on: 'Helstone, itself, was in the dim past. [...] She would fain have caught at the skirts of that departing time, and prayed it to return, and give her back what she had too little valued while it was yet in her possession' (169). Seen in contrast with the passage at the very beginning of this chapter, about the evenings in Helstone being 'rather difficult to fill up agreeably' (21), Margaret's nostalgia seems wilfully revisionist. From a traumatic present (Bessy's and Mrs Hale's illnesses, the impending strike), the past is transformed. But the opposite may also happen: looking back on her time at Milton, all the good seems to shrink and disappear under gloom and unhappiness:

> Looking back upon the year's accumulated heap of troubles, Margaret wondered how they had been borne. If she could have anticipated

> them, how she would have shrunk away and hid herself from the coming time! And yet day by day had, of itself, and by itself, been very endurable – small, keen, bright little spots of positive enjoyment having come sparkling into the very middle of sorrows. (104)

This is a reflection on the difference in perspective between immersed dailiness and retrospection: 'day by day' versus 'looking back'. It is a vision of time in portions, of periodicity in daily life. Gaskell invokes stark impossibilities in order to show Margaret's wounded relationship to time: praying for 'that departing time' to 'give her back' her past life (and she would value it more), imagining that her trials could have been 'anticipated'. Both are stock phrases and yet they are symptomatic of the slightly unreal and fantastical relationship that characters in *North and South* have to time. Embedded in this language is the irrational aspect of past and present, their relationship monstrously skewed by a perspective that cannot escape its own immersed vantage point.

Very early in the novel, dis-synchrony emerges as a major schism between measured clock time and an expanded experience of time, here in the scene where Margaret has received her first (unwelcome) proposal:

> It was well that, having made the round of the garden, [Margaret and Henry Lennox] came suddenly upon Mr Hale, whose whereabouts had been quite forgotten by them. He had not yet finished the pear, which he had delicately peeled in one long strip of silver-paper thinness, and which he was enjoying in a deliberate manner. It was like the story of the eastern king, who dipped his head into a basin of water, at the magician's command, and ere he instantly took it out went through all the experience of a lifetime. (32)

The peeling of the pear gestures towards clock time ('one long strip' indicating an unbroken duration), and yet 'all the experience of a lifetime' has rushed by Margaret at once. The reference to the Arabian Nights is significant: it underlines the unreal, fantastical aspect of time. There is a contrast between the everyday banality of peeling a pear, and the fairy-tale impossibility of a surge of emotion. Matus has commented on the novel's portrayal of the nightmarish unreality of real, everyday experience, and here we see the violent, unfathomable compression of lived time.[36] This dis-synchronization creates a fault-line in time, and it is along this fault-line that objective and subjective time are out of joint. This is what I call cataclysmic time. Over the course of the novel, Margaret will need to revisit and re-write many such inexplicable moments, many such small seismic shifts, and then try to heal the faultline between her memories and her forgetting. In the volume edition, one of the passages Gaskell added was this musing, by Margaret's godfather Mr Bell, on the by-gone days of his and Mr Hale's youth: 'Over babbling brooks they took impossible leaps, which seemed to keep them whole days suspended in the air. Time and space were not, though all other things seemed real. Every event was measured by the emotions of the mind, not by its actual existence, for existence had it none' (372–3). The unreality of time in memory is one of the themes that Gaskell chose to elaborate in the volume edition.

If *North and South* is a story about a process that can only develop over time (the slow transplantation of the outsider, genteel Miss Hale, into the new industrial middle class, which enables her to build a bridge between workers and masters), it is – as I mention above – also a story about remembering and misremembering, about reinterpretation and creative engagement with the past. As Alan Shelston points out of Gaskell's attitude to the past: 'If it is contiguous by virtue of its retention in the human consciousness it is nevertheless something distinctly distant and other in that we have to live in the here and now.'[37] The intermingling of past and present is illogical to the characters, and their necessary attempts to recuperate it are inevitably faulty. Margaret Hale is not the same woman in instalment twenty as she was in instalment one. Not only has she lost almost her entire family, but her personal history has also been rewritten. Frederick has settled in Spain, married his employer's daughter, and converted to Catholicism. Conventionally, when we see that Margaret, at the end of the novel, is the last of her family (on English soil, at least), we would expect her to have become the keeper of family memory. Yet Gaskell makes her the keeper of family *forgetting*. Stripped of her habitual prejudices, and of almost all of her emotional loyalties, Margaret must give up her attempts to clear her brother's name and resign him to Spain, Dolores, and Catholicism (a most effective severance). At the end of *North and South*, Margaret must emerge, traumatized but unfettered, into a new life.

And this unfolding rewriting, crucially, was first published serially. When we think of this narrative revision as a function of a serial novel, we see that issuing *North and South* in instalments aided the forgetfulness that allows the past to be rewritten. In a novel where interpretation of the past is the key to moving forward, the serial reader revisits events with Margaret and Thornton and watches them change with every act of memory. The shift in Margaret from shamed virginal queen to loving, longing heroine gradually unfolds. If the readers of a five-month serial need reminders of what happened before, they get them through Margaret's and Thornton's constant revisits of the strike, the proposal, the railway scene: all of which are angry and painful confrontations. For example, in instalment 13 Thornton remembers the moment when Margaret shielded him from the rioters in sensual terms: '[he was] almost sick with longing for that half-hour – that one brief space of time when she clung to him, and her heart beat against his – to come once again' (210). Such a perspective was surely not available to him in the anxiety of the actual moment, but could only come with hindsight. Slowly, rhythmically, over twenty instalments, the past is thus reinterpreted to allow for the future. At every revisiting of such moments, readers are confronted with a slightly different reading of events that they have already seen. As Elizabeth Starr has pointed out: 'in this novel, events don't exist apart from the narrative account of them'.[38] For this reason, the serial reader occupies a position similar to that of a character such as Margaret, who revisits and reinterprets events continually: 'For months past, all her own personal cares and troubles had had to be stuffed away into a dark cupboard; but now she had leisure to take them out, and mourn over them, and study their nature, and seek the true method of subduing them into the elements of peace' (336). This insistent revisiting (sometimes therapeutic, sometimes not) forms the fabric of the novel's everydayness, and it is the medium for Margaret's emotional growth. Retrospection, return and retelling make this a serial novel where the truth is constantly rewriting itself. The rhythm of memory and recuperation thus constantly intersects with the unfolding narrative in order to intermingle past and present time. In Lefebvre's terms, an internal psychological rhythm (of memory) intersects with the exterior rhythm of serial publication.

Gaskell uses the serial divisions to build a narrative that marries memory with futurity, a narrative that tells us how the future is reached through revisiting and revising the past. The drop between each division often coincides with a drop in events, with a relapse into eventlessness (rather than a cliff-hanger). The novel's double vision of everyday time – both forwards and backwards, both inwards and outwards – becomes the medium to which the narrative noticeably returns at each junction. The serial division, then, underlines the everydayness of the story, the periods of calm between events. The week that elapses between each number of *Household Words* can also be imagined as an (extra-textual) meantime, allowing the reader to forget or to re-evaluate the plot as the characters do. On each occasion when Margaret meets Thornton after the proposal, she takes a new step towards forgetting all that she felt before, and builds fresh feelings on top of her shame and regret. For the reader, these meetings are significant because they offer windows onto Margaret's changing feelings, revealing emerging emotions still hidden to Margaret herself. In the fifteenth instalment, she takes a significant step when the narrator divulges the questions passing though her mind: 'How was it that [Thornton] haunted her imagination so persistently? What could it be? Why did she care for what he thought, in spite of all her pride; in spite of herself?' (279–80). The reader can interpret this better than Margaret herself can. What this novel needs to create, more than anything, is time to think things through. This thinking through often happens in everyday, domestic time, and is thus, as we shall see in the next section, constrained by the politics of domestic time. If we now move from the longer dynamics of the narrative towards a discussion of intimate, personal time, we see that characters attempt to make sense of temporal experience by measuring time with direct speech. When characters revisit past events in their minds, time seems monstrously skewed. Direct speech can show exactly how this skewing happens.

Measuring time with bodies and words

Favret's concept of meantime will help us when we turn to the minutiae of lived experience: the moments when time in *North and South* becomes dis-synchronous to the minutest degree. Very small time intervals make evident how problematic the characters find it to measure time. What is actually happening when nothing is seemingly happening? The meantime of domestic time is anything but eventless in *North and South*, and is in fact the point of origin for cataclysmic, skewed, and troubling everyday-ness. Both the narrator and the characters are continually marking and measuring time, trying to come to some understanding of it. I would like to focus on direct speech as one kind of measuring device. In Günther Müller's terms, narrative time (the time it takes to tell a story) and narrated time (the time which passes within the story) stand in a dynamic relationship to each other. Sometimes events are compressed, and sometimes they are expanded.[39] It is my suggestion that direct speech, when narrated in the novel, brings narrated time and narrative time into near-synchronization. Direct speech approximately measures out the time that passes while it is being spoken.

In *North and South*, one crucial moment in Margaret's and Thornton's relationship uses direct speech to show heightened temporal awareness; here, we see internal and external time clashing in skewed simultaneity, showing the gap between thought and expression. In the proposal scene in instalment 13, Thornton's internal time overflows the bounds of direct speech:

> 'But you shall not drive me off upon that, and so escape the expression of my deep gratitude, my –' he was on the verge now; he would not speak in the haste of his hot passion; he would weigh each word. He would; and his will was triumphant. He stopped in mid career. (192)

Internal time expands the moment ('he would weigh each word. He would; and his will was triumphant') when Thornton struggles to gain control over himself. Each moment is 'weigh[ed]' in this battle between passion and will, playing out in hyper-aware time. Even the full stops and semicolons are employed to slow the pace. Narrated time is expanded, and breaks the temporal bounds of direct speech. But his stop 'in mid career' introduces a slight, almost imperceptible, delay in communication between Thornton and Margaret. This delay is symptomatic of the distance between feelings and their verbal expression, and thus also the distance between two minds, both of which are strongly controlled here.

The hyper-extended distance between thought and feeling furthermore leads into a temporal distance between language and its reception. In other words, the effects of this skewed simultaneity are echoed in Margaret's delayed comprehension of his halted speech. Margaret's grasp of what Thornton must be feeling – his love for her – comes parcelled out in delayed gasps of illumination:

> For, although at first it had struck her, that his offer was forced and goaded out of him by sharp compassion for the exposure she had made of herself, – which he, like others, might misunderstand – yet, even before he left the room, – and certainly, not five minutes after, the clear conviction dawned upon her, shined bright upon her, that he did love her; that he had loved her; that he would love her. And she shrank and shuddered as under the fascination of some great power, repugnant to her whole previous life. (195)

The smallest units of time – 'even before he left the room, – and certainly, not five minutes after' – which separate Thornton's declaration and Margaret's ability to grasp his meaning, are also the infinitesimal distances which separate their consciousnesses from each other. This intensification of the present moment, one highlighting tiny delays in understanding, occurs several times in the novel. When the narrative tells time in infinitesimal detail, it highlights the fact that time seems to be unable adequately to contain events – that the only reason characters can feel so much must be that time slows down.

The novel, then, measures shock by building a highly charged representation of irrationally expanded moments. As a counter-strategy, characters fall into practices of measuring time: Margaret counts raindrops and waves, and the novel is full of restless pacing. Gaskell uses the pacing to retreat from characters' interiority and instead show their exteriority: the narrative voice switches to a view from the outside, and the pacing becomes a sign through which the reader can infer the distress of the character in question: '[Thornton] kept on with his restless walk – not speaking [...], but drawing a deep breath from time to time, as if endeavouring to throw off some annoying thought' (142, 144). The reader does not know, but can guess, which past events Thornton is thinking over. Pacing is a marker of spiritual irritation, a compulsory bodily reaction to stress. The novel is full of characters who pace backwards and forwards in their homes: Thornton, Mr Hale, and Margaret find an outlet for their feelings in this way, and each time their pacing represents distress too great to put into words. Domestic time is thereby rendered strange – characters feel unmoored from it, and yet restricted by it. They have to pour tea and lock doors, answer to the demands of domestic time, while all the time feeling disassociated from it. As indicated above, this tracing out of interior stress often happens through speech: 'his will was triumphant. He stopped [speaking] in mid career.' The rhythms of speech become temporal markers. We see this early in the novel, when Margaret thinks back to Henry Lennox's unwelcome proposal and its (perhaps unwarranted) association with the new stress and uncertainty in her life:

> Margaret went along the walk under the pear-tree wall. She had never been along it since she paced it at Henry Lennox's side. Here, at this bed of thyme, he began to speak of what she must not think of now. Her eyes were on that late-blowing rose as she was trying to answer; and she had caught the idea of the vivid beauty of the feathery leaves of the carrots in the very middle of his last sentence. Only a fortnight ago! And all so changed! (54)

The sights before Margaret's eyes – a bed of thyme, a rose, carrot-tops – become aides of (reluctant) memory, bringing back her divided mind to the first real moment of cataclysm in her life. Tracing the length of a conversation across a kitchen garden (which she 'paced at Henry Lennox's side'), Margaret applies spatiotemporal markers to the remembered conversation: this passage is in fact an attempt at a kind of spatiotemporal linguistic measurement. If Margaret can only inscribe the conversation back onto the carrot-tops, she can attempt to understand the strangeness of the past, but without, at this point, engaging directly with 'what she must not think of now'. She essentially displaces the conversation from its meaning to its rhythm, one that is 'paced' out spatially.

In *North and South*, Gaskell creates a vision of domestic time as a highly charged creative medium for engaging with all aspects of past and present. If we follow Lefebvre's suggestion that we read rhythms spatially, as superimposed and mutually relational strands, we see that memory and interpretation are constantly brought back to past moments in order to wrest from them their meaning within the life stories that the characters weave for themselves. Dis-synchronicity is instigated both by the minutiae of temporal shifts, and by the chasm between past and present. Both of these levels become baffling and unreal to Margaret and Thornton. Since they make up such a dense fabric, the narrative rhythms and recurrences create a feeling of domestic time in which every moment can, imaginatively, be connected to every other moment by acts of remembering and misremembering. The rhythms of return therefore create an obstinate coherence between seemingly unconnected moments.

Into these layers of rhythm cuts the serial rhythm of weekly publication in *Household Words*, which is structured by the need to sustain and develop both plot and readership. The serial format not only expands narrative time artificially, but also lends each instalment a self-containment that it would not otherwise possess. Week by week, the serial must build an expectation of an ultimate ending, a place for all strands to meet, but there must be interest in individual instalments, too. For a serialized novel, those two logics (suspense and story-arch) have to be especially pronounced, each coming into focus every week in order to sustain circulation.

Against 'eventless ease': domestic time and women's labour

The focus on memory and rhythm is not gender-specific in *North and South*, but, as I have made clear, suffering is always situated in

Gaskell's work. Hence, domestic temporality is also situated in a gendered politics of time. Women's labour in the home is a focal point for the narrative. The final two sections of this chapter will discuss domestic time through the prism of women's work. This question has two aspects: first of all, there is the macrocosmic question within the novel of what women are working towards; secondly, there is the microcosm of domestic practice ('little nothings', as the narrative calls it) which occupies their time. In the macrocosm, which I treat in this section, Margaret Hale learns to combine familial duties with social reform; essentially, she learns how to bring humanism into labour relations. In this respect, Gaskell was influenced by events which happened while she was writing the novel: namely the outbreak of the Crimean War and Gaskell's meeting with Florence Nightingale before the latter took on the superintendence of the military hospitals in Scutari. The microcosm, which I will discuss in the final section of the chapter, is much more intricate, and centres on psychological experience. Women's work in the home, in *North and South,* tends to suppress internal feeling, but also to externalize feelings for outside viewers. Margaret becomes a canvas on which her emotions play. Her trivial household tasks are a text to be read by the narrator or by John Thornton. In other words, the microcosmic perspective is about the restrictions put on women's feelings by domestic time, restrictions in some sense imposed by the macrocosmic insistence that women maintain and uphold the emotional health of others.

The novel shows a preoccupation with what people, and especially women, do with their time. By contrasting domestic temporalities – different kinds of monotony and different kinds of activity – Gaskell works to formulate an ethics of behaviour for middle-class women, one that presupposes that women have time (both time given by God and by society) and thus need to find a way to spend it profitably. Towards the end of the novel, after she has lost her parents and has been taken in by her rich aunt and forced into luxurious inaction, Margaret concludes that she is now 'surfeited of the eventless ease in which no struggle or endeavour [is] required' (364). Before long, Mr Bell dies, leaving her an heiress. In the final instalment of *North and South* in *Household Words,* on 27 January 1855, Margaret realizes that 'she herself must one day answer for her own life, and what she had done with it; and she tried to settle that most difficult problem for women [...], how much might be set apart for freedom in working' (406). Edith interprets Margaret's determination to 'follow her own ideas of duty' as likely to make Margaret 'strong-minded' (a derogatory term in Edith's vocabulary), and cause her to dress 'in brown and dust-colour, not to show the dirt you'll pick up in those places'; as Edith phrases it, Margaret will 'go a figure' (407). Her simple-minded conception of Margaret's work is the only clue we are given of its nature. Edith exclaims: 'I'm sure I'm always expecting to hear of her having met with something horrible among all those wretched places she pokes herself into. I should never dare to go down some of those streets without a servant. They're not fit for ladies' (416). We have no better access to Margaret's London-based charity work than Edith's petty nothings; the novel remains curiously reserved about the exact nature and extent of it.[40] But Edith's comments add to a feeling towards the end of the novel that Gaskell's satire of aristocratic life is becoming more explicitly sharp and cruel. Edith's life in Corfu was filled with picnics and music, and now her motherhood consists of nannies and clean frilly caps, while Margaret takes all 'the semblance of duties off [her] hands' (363).

Edith clearly belongs to the old order. Modernity, in this novel, is represented not only by the railway and the factory but also by the middle-class woman who has learned to direct her own time. The novel also questions the value of men's industrial activity, work, leisure, scholarship and social consciousness. Mr Hale's scholarship is unproductive, while Thornton's emerging experiments with labour relations have promise. Implicitly, the novel asks a question: How do we put to use the time that has been given us? Much of Gaskell's ethos of usefulness and enquiry comes from her Unitarian upbringing. Unitarianism was influenced by the rationalism of the Enlightenment and such thinkers as Locke and Hobbes. It placed a strong emphasis on science, scepticism, and education.[41] Notably, Unitarians generally allowed their daughters access to education if they wished it. As a Unitarian, Gaskell presupposed that individual everyday time can be used for the common good – indeed, that individual progress is the key to communal progress.[42] As Jenny Uglow explains: '[Unitarianism] was essentially optimistic, assuming a dynamic of gradual progress to perfection, both in individuals and societies, and emphasizing personal action. Everyone should promote progress by questioning the status quo. Intellectual and scientific discovery was to be welcomed.'[43] For Gaskell, this meant that the smallest attempts at amelioration were part of a larger process of betterment. Such a credo sees no qualitative difference between familial caregiving, local charity, and the general advancement of society. As we saw in the previous chapter, domestic activity could always be the subject of moral judgement; Gaskell, almost uniquely among contemporary writers, both used the cultural system of signs and interrogated the way they were assigned.[44] The value of time, and of domestic work, is always understood in Gaskell's work to be underwritten by a painstaking, sometimes painful, negotiation. Margaret's self-interrogation about work and duty participates in a discourse about the purpose of women's labour at this time. Gaskell's heroine is by the end of the novel on course to become a mediator between classes through her personal emotional investment with workers and masters in Milton. This resonates with Gaskell's preoccupations at the time of composition. Her interest in Florence Nightingale's role in the Crimean War most likely informed her portrait of Margaret, as Jenny Uglow notes.[45] Not only was Nightingale a person of intense discussion in national newspapers from October 1854 onwards, but Gaskell and Nightingale were also personal (if recent) acquaintances.

Most scholarly readings of *North and South* acknowledge the fact that it was written during the build-up to and first months of what became known as the Crimean War, and that part of it was written at Lea Hurst, Florence Nightingale's family's home, just as Nightingale was becoming a celebrity. Gaskell wrote a series of letters while at Lea Hurst which show how fascinated she was by Nightingale and her mission to the Crimea. Nightingale had fought her family to be allowed to follow here vocational calling as a nurse, and the Crimean War gave her an avenue for her interest in administration. Her fame became a vehicle for her championship of nursing as a profession for middle-class women. Margaret Hale's transformation from a leisured upper-class 'lady' to an active middle-class social ameliorator in the latter half of *North and South* was undoubtedly influenced by Gaskell's reaction to Nightingale's mission.

Neither Nightingale nor the Crimean War is mentioned in *North and South*. This has not been a hindrance to scholars looking for parallels. Shelston concedes that 'Gaskell never refers to the war in her writing', although he quickly checks himself by asking: 'or does she?'[46] Stefanie Markovits, in *The Crimean War in the British Imagination*, observes: 'one might contend that the war had an unspoken effect on the plot of *North and South* by virtue of its effect on trade'.[47] At the same time, she acknowledges that 'Gaskell's novel obscures all [...] marks of the Crimean conflict'.[48] The unspoken assumption behind the verb 'obscures' is that this absence is somehow significant. Markovits goes on to see several parallels between the war and the novel, including a synonymy between Florence Nightingale, Margaret Hale, and Jane Eyre. By insisting that Margaret Hale is like Florence Nightingale, however, Markovits misses the opportunity to examine a much more subtle connection between *North and South* and the Crimean War. The link is the shared ground between Gaskell's interpretation of Nightingale and her simultaneously written fiction about a woman who claims a mission for herself and rejects society's attempts to keep her in 'eventless ease'.

Britain entered the war – initially a war between Russia and the Ottoman Empire over control of the Black Sea – in March 1854. In September, the British, Turkish and French expeditionary force landed on the Crimean peninsula and began the siege of Sebastopol. News reports travelled to England in approximately two weeks, telegraph reports in only a few days. The public in Britain was therefore informed of the shocking conditions in the camps and hospitals; all told, 90 per cent of British casualties during the Crimean War were due to disease and cold. The clamour for reform, sanitation, and proper medical care grew. In October, Florence Nightingale was named in *The Times* as the superintendent of the military hospitals in Scutari; this announcement caused something of a sensation in the press. However, in *Household Words* Nightingale was not mentioned while *North and South* was serialized, probably because the Stamp Duty prohibited a periodical from printing news.

At this point, Gaskell was already at Lea Hurst, avidly reporting her interactions with a sudden national celebrity in her private letters. Gaskell's first surviving letter from there is dated 11–14 October, and it includes a detailed description of Nightingale, which ends with the words: 'she is like a saint'.[49] However, Gaskell is not wholly uncritical. In a letter to Emily Shaen dated 27 October, Gaskell credits Parthenope Nightingale (Florence's sister) with the observation that 'F. does not care for *individuals* [...] but for the whole race as being God's creatures'.[50] Later in the same letter, Gaskell recounts an argument she had with Nightingale, who was of the opinion that all children ought to be brought up in crèches rather than with their mothers. Gaskell comments: 'that exactly tells of what seems to me *the* want – but then this want of love for individuals becomes a gift and a very rare one, if one takes it in conjunction with her intense love for the *race*; her utter selflessness in serving and ministering'.[51] As Shelston argues, Gaskell represents Nightingale as an 'institutionalising social-worker'.[52] Gaskell acknowledges the value of Nightingale's calling while still retaining a reservation about the extra-humane scope of Nightingale's ambition, which wilfully obscures the individual sufferer. It is in relation to this conflict between an institutional force for good and an individual one that I see Margaret Hale. Margaret represents the same deliberate rejection of aristocratic leisure; she also turns to the slightly patronizing role of class-traversing angel in a realization of her innate middle-class fitness for this work, and she interprets the choice as an expression of her freedom. In Gaskell's view, Nightingale achieved her status as 'saint' through her troubling rejection of direct one-to-one charity and, seemingly, the nuclear family. In contrast, Margaret Hale's interest in individuals is what makes her both goddess and woman at the same time. These likenesses and differences between Margaret Hale and Florence Nightingale cannot be relied upon as truths about the meaning of *North and South*. But they point in the direction of the questions that were emerging in Gaskell's writing at the same time as her narrative was developing in *Household Words*. How can middle-class and upper-class women contribute to social amelioration? How can their traditional role a caregivers be expanded? How can they find personal fulfilment in dedication to others?

Women like Margaret Hale and Florence Nightingale seemingly found their roles only in response to national distress. It may be no coincidence that where Favret identifies meanwhileness in wartime poetry, I see a similar hyperawareness of in-between-times in a wartime novel. It is conceivable that the everyday is mostly rigorously questioned exactly in that time of heightened eventfulness that characterizes a war. Although *North and South* is certainly a wartime novel, it concerns itself with the construction of a national identity that can somehow encompass the contradictions already inherent in modern everyday life. Domestic time is made complicit in the telling of those contradictions, just as it is the site of negotiations that aim to soften the conflict of interests between classes.

'Little nothings' and silent actions: Margaret Hale and domestic time

The parallels between Florence Nightingale's wartime work and Margaret Hale's positive influence on the class divisions in Milton are only present on an abstract scale. *North and South* makes few claims for genuine societal reforms or for alterations in the economic relationship between the classes. The role Margaret Hale devises for herself remains essentially unchallenging to the patriarchy, as several critics have noted.[53] Women's actual work in the novel is small, intimate, familial, and often completely ignored by male characters such as fathers and brothers. Gaskell's novel narrativizes silent labour, performed by women, which other characters are free to misread. The key point is that female labour, especially sewing and food preparation, presents a sort of text to surrounding people, and to the narrative, on which the interior feelings and qualities of a woman's mind can be traced.

Female practice is often associated with moral behaviour, as we saw in the chapter on sewing. The narrator's penalty on idleness, for example, is severe. Fanny Thornton, John's sister, can find nothing better to occupy herself with than a thoroughly irrelevant 'piece of worsted-work' from which she lapses into 'gaz[ing] at vacancy, and think[ing] of nothing at her ease' (143). Fanny's idleness comes to represent not just insufficient powers of self-management, but a complete absence of interiority ('thinking of nothing'). The narrator represents domestic practice, then, as a shorthand for mental processes (or the lack of them). Domestic practice and identity are powerfully aligned.

Suffering, in this novel, is always situated in the body or in a setting. Domestic routines must be kept up, domestic spaces put to right. After her mother's death, Margaret has two grieving men in the house and too much work to do to grieve herself:

> Her eyes were continually blinded by tears, but she had no time to give way to regular crying. Her father and brother depended upon her; while they were giving way to grief, she must be working, planning, considering. Even the necessary arrangements for the funeral seemed to devolve upon her. When the fire was bright and crackling – when everything was ready for breakfast, and the tea-kettle was singing away, Margaret gave a last look round the room before going to summon Mr Hale and Frederick. She wanted everything to look as cheerful as possible; and yet, when it did so, the contrast between it and her own thoughts forced her into sudden weeping. (247)

Immediately, Margaret is reprimanded by the family servant Dixon – 'You must not give way, or where shall we all be?' – and Margaret's duties even extend so far as to 'try and think of little nothings to say all breakfast-time'. Denying her own interiority, she must fill void-time with domestic time, with domestically related 'little nothings', with toast and tea-making. Domestic practice, then, crowds out Margaret's interiority by a supreme act of self-denial; it is impossible, the passage implies, to 'give way' to grief if you are 'working, planning, considering', let alone if you are thinking up little (domestic) nothings. Margaret is forced into this position of determined externality because of the selfishness of others, and it is the position in which she is most often misunderstood. The price to pay for her macrocosmic duty (to be a caregiver in her own home) is this minuscule but very real deferral of grief. Her menfolk – a father and brother who both have the leisure to 'give way to grief' – pay no notice to her labours. This is another kind of meantime: a time of actual work that is yet ignored because it crowds out or delays emotion. Frederick and Mr Hale are grieving; in the meantime, Margaret makes tea for everyone and tries not to weep.

Margaret's small working actions are repeatedly misinterpreted. When Mrs Thornton visits the Hales for the first time, Margaret is 'busy embroidering a small piece of cambric for some little article of dress for Edith's expected baby – "Flimsy, useless work," as Mrs Thornton observed to herself'. (96) Because Mrs Thornton keeps this thought to herself, Margaret has no opportunity to explain herself, and so the misunderstanding is allowed to stand. Significantly, the novel makes the practice of sewing a trope for this propensity for characters to overlook, misinterpret or misunderstand Margaret. On one occasion, she comes upon her father and Higgins in earnest conversation in the study: 'Higgins nodded to her as a sign of greeting; and she softly adjusted her working materials on the table, and prepared to listen' (222). During the conversation, she defends Thornton's decision not to prosecute the rioters. When Mr Hale comments, not knowing that Margaret has rejected Thornton's proposal of marriage, she retreats into womanly silence over her sewing: '"My daughter is no great friend of Mr Thornton's", said Mr Hale, smiling at Margaret; *while she, as red as any carnation, began to work with double diligence,* "but I believe what she says is the truth. I like him for it"' (228, my emphasis). Mr Hale, lacking the prior knowledge with which the reader is privileged, fails to read Margaret correctly, and she, to hide the tell-tale signs of her confusion, retreats into her safe position of silence and sewing. The move, by the narrative voice, to a position outside her consciousness allows the reader to read her blushes ('as red as any carnation'); paradoxically, the social loophole in which she is hiding serves to emphasize the readability of exterior signs, making her body the expression (through sighs, blushes, and trembles) of her distress. The narrative interprets her: the narrator repeatedly describes her exteriority as a series of signs. Actions in the physical world can delay or disguise feeling to other characters, but not to the narrator. Involuntary physical actions can reveal hidden feelings in the very moment they are being disguised. Sometimes, both the narrator and another character function together as interpreters of signs: most often, the other character is Thornton, whose love for Margaret privileges him as an observer. In a later instalment, after Thornton has insulted her, believing her to have compromised herself ('Is Miss Hale so remarkable for truth?'), the narrative again retreats to an outside view of her character; in this case, the narrative is told from Thornton's perspective:

> She sat quite still, after the first momentary glance of grieved surprise, that made her eyes look like some child's who had met with an unexpected rebuff; they slowly dilated into mournful, reproachful sadness; and then they fell, and she bent over her work, and did not speak again. But he could not help looking at her, and he saw a sigh tremble over her body, as if she quivered in some unwonted chill. (328)

Again retreating into safe silence, Margaret uses her sewing as a defence mechanism, a socially accepted escape that allows women to say nothing and reveal nothing. Thornton is finely attuned to her exteriority, but socially restrained to respect her retreat and unable to apologize or acknowledge his fault. The domestic meantime is composed of these checks and balances where the incommunicable is nevertheless communicated.

While sewing becomes a trope for the tendency of characters to misread Margaret, it is also a practice that allows her to hide in plain sight. For privileged readers of her body-as-text (primarily the reader and Thornton), this practice makes her interiority paradoxically more exposed. It is as if Margaret's true feelings are beyond her consciousness at certain junctures in the novel, and must be interpreted through the lines of her body. Domestic time and domestic tasks become markers for the collapse of consciousness and the reversion to seeming, surface, and silence. Instead of hearing Margaret's internal reaction to Thornton's insult, we are relegated to the outside, with Thornton, who merely 'saw a sigh tremble over her body'. Margaret's unrecorded thoughts stand for the novel's realization of the narrative failure of internal rationalization. The development of the plot defaults onto this unrecorded and intensely strung domestic time, the time when Margaret bends over her work in silence. Her emotional trajectory must be unconscious; unrationalized and unnarrated time is a necessary part of the time-scheme.

The serialization of *North and South* created a work that reflects on the experience of living through time, in time and with time. Serialization underlines the capacity for a novel to unite past and future, precariously. Moreover, seriality, while a pressure and strain on Gaskell's composition of the novel, served to emphasize the isolated-but-connected nature of each instalment, its link not just with the instalment immediately before and after, but also with the longer timescales needed for psychological development of the main characters. The weekly form lends an emphasis to this meanwhileness. In Gaskell's domestic time, strands of narrative are densely intertwined: so much so that every point in time can be connected to every other point in time through selective and creative acts of memory. In the very last instalment, Margaret sits for hours on the beach: 'All this time for thought enabled Margaret to put events in their right places, as to origin and significance, both as regarded her past life and her future' (404). By 'right place', Gaskell does not mean chronology, but a place of origin and significance – a place of causality and meaning. A moment can be expanded by its connection, through memory, to other moments. The domestic present, a time revisited and sorted into its right place, becomes a representative of an imperfect but nevertheless very real responsibility of the present to all other presents. In the domestic time of this novel, there is no correspondence between two moments, no possible return or repetition. Every moment is historically and spatially situated – domestic time asserts itself regularly and insistently. The serial divisions are used to emphasize the selective freedom of choosing to make moments count. By privileging the non-event and the mis-remembered event, Gaskell is revealing domestic time's dynamic and recuperative potential.

This focus on recuperative time reflects the novel's mixing of genres: *North and South* participates both in the 'social-problem' novel, the *Bildungsroman*, the psychological novel and the marriage plot novel. What Dickens was hoping for, and signally failed to receive from Gaskell's hand, was a suspense novel. Gaskell's instalment divisions reflect, as I have shown, the meantime in which psychological impact is allowed to resonate. There is no secret to be revealed. When Margaret in the final instalment puts 'events into their right places', the narrator asserts no opinion over how the pattern of events might fit together. Readers are encouraged to think that Margaret forgets as much as she remembers in order to make a liveable pattern of her past. Meaning is cumulative: sorting things by their significance is a puzzle that takes time.

While *North and South* is a novel defined by dramatic events, my focus on domestic time has revealed an emphasis on non-event: on a domestic meantime which saturates the emotional experience of living through social strife, personal losses, or spatial uprooting. The absence of the Crimean War in the narrative is understandable when you consider that the nation faced great challenges at home. This point is emphasized when we look at the surrounding material in *Household Words*. 'A Home

Question' on 11 November 1854, starts by mentioned the sanitary conditions in Sebastopol, but quickly turns to argue that more lives have been lost during a few weeks to cholera in London.[54] Just as *Household Words* cannot print news stories, *North and South* cannot incorporate the Crimean War. Margaret, in the end, rejects her charity work in London and, through her marriage and concurrent investment into the cotton trade, adopts a more directly personal responsibility for ameliorating the evils of global capitalism. Local structures are easier to change than global inequalities. Returning to *North and South*, for the serial reader, could be a kind of meantime that interspersed the dramatic events in the faraway Crimea. Turning the eye towards home, in Gaskell's case, means focusing on the impact of calamitous events to everyday temporal experience. To women especially, who had to manage seemingly small but vital functions of the household in order to provide food on the table, the minute-by-minute life in time was crucial, Gaskell seems to be saying. Women's work of nation-building, more than anything, is a question of absorbing and interpreting things which have happened. The act of memory, linking disparate moments together into a coherent causal whole, is in this novel a private experience not confined to women; but to women like Margaret Hale, the act of memory is interlaced with 'little nothings'. The domestic meantime may be illogical, but it is also highly charged because it is ultimately recuperative.

4
Decomposition: Mrs Beeton and the Non-Linear Text

Although, on the one hand, it sometimes seems that nineteenth-century novels were overflowing with details, there are limits to how much stuff a novel can describe without threatening the integrity of the narrative. A domestic manual like *Beeton's Book of Household Management*, on the other hand, is much less limited in its scope for detail. From a focus on narrative, plot and story in the first three chapters, *Time, Domesticity and Print Culture* now turns to a wholly different way of telling time. As I explain in this chapter, the *Book of Household Management* conceptualizes domestic time not primarily through narrative, but through the organization of information. Part of that organization relates to its serial publication. It was compiled by Isabella Beeton, and published in 24 monthly numbers (1859–61) by Isabella's publisher husband, Samuel Beeton. *Beeton's Book of Household Management* can marshal a multiplicity of genres, differentiate between them with different fonts, font sizes and chapter divisions, and administer specific information on foodstuffs, cleaning, behaviour, natural history and the material environments of the mid-nineteenth-century home. Given these features, the book has no need for an overall narrative progression. Instead, the high level of organization invites the reader to pick his or her own way through the printed text. Unlike the works I have discussed so far, this book is a-linear. It facilitates an endless choice of entry points and pathways, creating unique interactions between the writing on the page and the reader's domestic temporality.

However, while organization and navigation are such important principles for the use of the manual, the initial serial publication complicates the *Book of Household Management*'s usefulness, and for one reason: an a-linear writing genre was published in a linear format, and with disorienting consequences. Let me give some examples.

The second monthly instalment (December 1859) of the *Book of Household Management* ends in the following interesting place in the ingredients' list for 'Stew Soup II':

> Ingredients.– 1/2 lb. of beef, mutton, or pork; 1/2 pint of split
> [End of issue][1]

The next page does not appear until one month later, in the instalment for January 1860, and begins:

> [Start of issue]
> peas, 4 turnips, 8 potatoes, 2 onions, 2 oz. of oatmeal or 3 oz. of rice, 2 quarts of water.[2]

At the word 'split', the text literally splits up. It also has an unexpected grammatical effect. An accidental command is immediately obeyed, making 'split' a chance performative.

Why did this 'split' happen? The answer lies in the fact that the print block of the *Book of Household Management* was set, from the very beginning, ready for the culminating volume edition, as was common at the time. While this arrangement made financial sense for the publisher, it meant that the serial book was interrupted in peculiar places, often in the middle of a recipe or even mid-sentence, as in the example above. The serial 'split' in the *Book of Household Management* was therefore motivated not by an internal textual logic, but by an external material one. While in some serialized books of the nineteenth century (novels especially), the length of instalments determined the structure of each number, in the *Book of Household Management* no effort was made to make individual numbers into coherent wholes. The *Book of Household Management* failed to acknowledge the serial 'split' in either the letterpress itself or in the paratext.

Both extremes of serialization – careful planning versus arbitrary splitting – were common in mid-century publishing. Some authors and publishers happily used either of these approaches. Although Charles Dickens planned and wrote most of his novels with the intention of giving each separate instalment 'interest', the 1847 serial 'Cheap Edition' of his novels cuts off in the middle of sentences to keep down costs. Just because divisions were not compositionally motivated, however, it does not follow that they are insignificant. In the *Book of Household Management*, the organization of material – the physical layout of the page, the division into clearly defined chapters – is part and parcel of

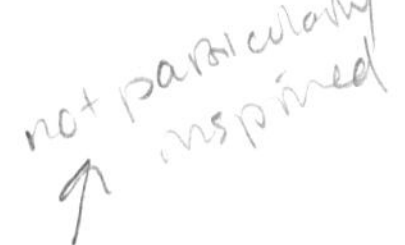

its message. The format is crucial to the success of the venture, both for sales and for impact; the arbitrary serial 'split' cannot, therefore, be ignored. The 'split' simply happens, and yet it is not at all simple. The one-month-long *enjambment* in 'split [...] peas' poses an important question: What does serial division mean when it is ignored by the writing itself? What does the 'split' mean to a work that prefers to position itself as a volume in the making? Here I argue that serial form shaped the reading public's first encounter with the *Book of Household Management*, and that the writing's ability to construct a representation of domestic time was affected by these unmotivated cuts. Since serialization situated the book's publication in a bustling print culture – and since the very fact of serialization was experienced as a sign of modernity – the first readers of *Beeton's Book of Household Management* experienced the book not as a codex, but as an unfolding process. This chapter will position the *Book of Household Management* in relation to the tradition of household manuals and their publication, and discuss its paratextual negotiation of becoming a volume. The work's representation of domestic time is interlinked with publication time in the printed text's formal organization.

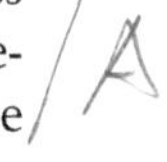

When we think of serialized nineteenth-century works and their relationship to time, we tend to think first of serial fiction. And yet serial non-fiction commanded a vast market in mid-century Britain, and weekly or monthly part-publication was often the first outing for a dizzying array of printed media in all genres. Part-issue was a popular form for selling general knowledge to a wide audience: some of the earliest serial ventures were encyclopaedias, spearheaded by the pioneering Charles Knight and his *Penny Cyclopaedia*, which commenced publication in January 1833.[3] Dictionaries, histories, bibles, songbooks, playtexts, classical literature and scientific works were all serialized and, judging by the proliferation on the market, sold well. Mark W. Turner has recently called for more attention to serialized non-narrative print matter, and he has posited that the way we understand serialization may be challenged by such a shift in focus.[4] Examining how a non-fictional work's representation of time is complicated because its arbitrary divisions into monthly parts have the potential to shed light on non-textual time – what we might call paper-and-ink time. I am interested in the way the material circumstances of print themselves make time, and in what happens to a text when it is split into parts. This approach offers a counter-intuitive perspective on the making of print time, the construction of genre, and the logic of using a serial instalment as opposed to a volume. Part-issue serialization was another

way of fitting into, and developing, a genre. In this case, it was a genre – the domestic manual – that spoke to practices which made the home a location of temporalized activities, and which itself was intended as a vehicle for the successful production of smooth domestic time.

In yet another way, *Beeton's Book of Household Management* is enmeshed in time: it stands as an embodiment of a particular historical tipping point. Seen from the twenty-first century, the significance of the 1859–61 publication of the *Book of Household Management* lies primarily in its immense subsequent success. The book's fate was to become a symbol of British national culture at the heart of the Empire, the best-selling cookery book in the latter half of the nineteenth century and a virtual bible for housewives well into the twentieth. By 1868, it had already sold nearly two million copies in various formats. Hence critics have tended to view the *Book of Household Management* in terms of its novelty, innovation and modernity, in order to account for its staying power for the next half-century. Dena Attar, for example, contends that 'historically [*Beeton's Book of Household Management*] marks the development from an earlier piecemeal approach to domestic work towards a systematic elaboration of the rules and routines which governed the daily lives of middle-class women'.[5] While not precisely wrong, this judgement is inaccurate. One can describe neither Anne Cobbett's *The English Housekeeper* (1835) nor Eliza Acton's *Modern Cookery* (1845) as piecemeal approaches to domestic work. Critics have tended to explain the *Book of Household Management*'s success in terms of its confident tone, the clever publishing schemes of Isabella's publisher husband Samuel (and, after he was forced to sell the rights in 1866, one year after Isabella's death of puerperal fever, the cleverness of Ward & Lock), or its all-encompassing, scientifically inflected and comprehensive scope.[6] All these are important factors, and yet none of them is unique to the *Book of Household Management*. Eliza Acton's cookery book was also highly structured, confident in tone, and a great bestseller in the 1840s and 1850s.[7]

The drive to publish totalising, encyclopaedic manuals of domestic work was widespread in the period; household manuals had been major sellers for decades. Throughout the genre, works attempted to lay claim to a wide and general inclusiveness. In 1844 Thomas Webster published *An Encyclopaedia of Domestic Economy* ('assisted by the late Mrs. Parkes, author of "Domestic Duties"'), a 1264-page tome on domestic building, servants, laundry, medicine and food preparation. In 1858 and 1859, the publishing house of W. Kent and Co. issued the two volumes of the *Household Encyclopaedia* 'by an association of heads of families and men of science'. These works (which Beeton freely plundered) had a very wide scope, and they combined scientific information with suggestions for domestic economy and management. Throughout these decades, writers attempted to encompass every imaginable aspect of a subject within the covers of one book. In this way, print culture was responding to the needs of a modern, recently urbanized, and socially uprooted readership. Andrea Broomfield has suggested the way in which readers approached these enormous books:

> Clearly, Victorian middle-class people accepted the fact that no household could operate smoothly all the time or along the ideal lines set forth in guidebooks. Thousands of men and women and children modified these social rituals and patterns to fit their own need and personalities, and certainly their own budgets. Nonetheless, Victorian guidebooks were numerous, and often [...] bestsellers. The speed of industrialization had left people with a somewhat shaky sense of their socioeconomic standing and how to keep it.[8]

In a modern world where individuals were uprooted from their backgrounds and had to find their feet in the growing middle classes, readers eagerly seized on printed media which offered them a wide selection of material, and adapted them to their circumstances. The totalising impulse of mid-century culture was clearly not restricted to Beeton's work. Much of Beeton's scientific information is actually taken from cookery books by Eliza Acton and Eustace Ude.

Similarly, the *Book of Household Management* was not the first household book to succeed at serialization: Robert Kemp Philp, who published a successful book called *The Practical Housewife* in 1855 full of material from his magazine *The Family Friend*, followed it with a serial household book, the landslide success *Enquire Within Upon Everything* (1855–56).[9] In her bibliography of household books, Attar notes that *Enquire Within* went into at least 124 editions, the last in 1970.[10] Philp was a mid-century pioneer of serial publication, at least five years before Samuel Beeton issued the first part of the *Book of Household Management*. The Beetons, therefore, were not the first to try serialization, nor the first to succeed with it. And if we look at the modernity of Beeton's writing itself – the contents, the recipes, the maxims, and the language in which it is all expressed – it takes only a few forays into the standard cookery books of the late eighteenth and early nineteenth century to realize that Isabella Beeton lifted recipes, instructions and sentiments from a score of older works and wove them together, in somewhat edited form, into a book of her own. As Kathryn Hughes notes, 'the various qualities ascribed to the *Book of Household Management* often turn out to be imprints left from the texts from which it was pieced together'.[11] On the cover, the reader is in fact told that the book is 'edited by Mrs Beeton'; a common moniker in contemporary print culture, indirectly acknowledging the composite nature of published works in this era of haphazardly controlled copyright. This detail explains the somewhat confusing shifts in tone and focus throughout the book. To speak about the modernity of mid-century printed media, then, we must also pay attention to the persistent echoes of earlier practices, and to the things that had changed little. Domestic time is rarely articulated, but maybe, for that very reason, it has a much longer memory than other practices in the nineteenth century. Whereas some routines changed utterly for the emergent middle classes, domestic time's practices were more likely to be inherited. This phenomenon did not prevent writers from presenting these practices proudly as new and original notions, but the genre of the cookery book grew out of, and grew alongside, older conventions of manuscript and print, in ways that constantly informed one another. The *Book of Household Management* stands as a temporal milestone, a marker between two epochs, if only because it unites inherited wisdom from the heart of the Georgian period with an immensely successful manoeuvring within mid-Victorian print culture. The manual was both a summing up of previous practices and a departure onto the terrain of print media from the 1850s and 1860s.

The date of publication for *Beeton's Book of Household Management* is often cited as 1861, which is indeed the year of the first volume edition. However, its publication actually began two years earlier, on 1 November 1859, when the publishing house run by Isabella's husband Samuel Beeton issued the first 48-page number, priced at 3*d*. Samuel Beeton was publisher-editor of two magazines, the *Boy's Own Magazine* and the *Englishwoman's Domestic Magazine*. Within a few years of their marriage in 1856, Isabella Beeton began to write and edit for the *Englishwoman's Domestic Magazine*, and out of this work grew the idea for a new publication in his *Beeton* series of books.[12] This series eventually included a dictionary, an illustrated Bible, and manuals for keeping pets and gardening. There was a clear contrapuntal rhythm to these volumes: the *Book of Household Management* started as a serial exactly one year after the first number of *Beeton's Dictionary of Universal Information*, and their publication schemes were standardized. Monthly parts were promoted with subscription lotteries; just as with the great magazines, there were quarterly and annual volumes; and at (or near the end of) the serial run, a bound volume edition was published. This was a standard method of publication, which, over the entire publication run, gave the buying public access to the book in various stages of completion. Thus publishers could, as Laurel Brake puts it, 'maximise a stratified readership'.[13]

Each monthly instalment of the *Book of Household Management* consists of 48 pages of letterpress, bound in paper covers with several pages of advertisements front and back. The front cover carries an elaborate engraving, and the instalment often includes a coloured plate, protected by tissue paper. All these serial-paratextual elements contrast with the book-paratextual elements, which were included in the final number in the autumn of 1861. These components consisted of the title page, the 'Analytical Index', a page of errata, the preface, and a list of where the illustrations should be moved if readers wished to have their edition bound. These two kinds of paratext pulled in different directions. This structure also means that the very first instalment start *in medias res* with the chapter entitled 'The Mistress'. At this stage, there is no indication of how the book will be structured or what it will contain. The idea was that the serial-paratextual elements could be stripped away, the opening matter in No. 24 moved to the front, and the serial origins of the book thus virtually erased. There is no editorial communication in the serial to explain this logic of publication; rather, it is assumed that readers are familiar with the principle. In spite of the many signs of ephemerality in the serial, this publication was intended as *Beeton's Book*, not *Beeton's Serial*.

Materiality, publication and time

The paratext gives clues to the *Book of Household Management*'s place within serial time. D. F. McKenzie's call for a 'sociology of text' makes the case that the readings which a text facilitates can be at least partly recovered from the physical format.[14] First, the physical format is dictated by certain expectations of what kinds of readings could be expected: the kind of reader, the spread of circulation, the wear and tear on the book and so forth. Secondly, the format gives modern scholars clues to the ways that readers could subvert such expectations. Michael Warner has suggested that texts dramatize the extent of their own circulation; paratext, presumably, does the same.[15] Beyond what the written text imagines, however, physical objects may enjoy afterlives long beyond their publication; the question of the uses of more or less ephemeral print media can reach beyond the immediate publication date if we take into account a printed work's shelvability. It is my argument that the temporality of ephemeral print objects can extend beyond the short life-span so often associated with the term ephemera. It is a question of what kinds of reading practices the specific printed format facilitates or complicates. Ending an instalment in the middle of a recipe, as Beeton does above, may just seem slightly comical to today's reader, who can easily access the volume edition and hardly ever reads cookery books in a linear fashion anyway; but such a serious *enjambment* must have affected the contemporary reader of a three-penny number, who may have set herself (it was most likely a woman) the task of reading attentively in order to glean as much useful knowledge as possible. Stacking up 24 separate instalments of the *Book of Household Management* on a shelf may seem unlikely for today's readers, but was probably not inconceivable in the mid-nineteenth century. Not just at the point of entry into the domestic everyday, but in its repeated use or defiant survival, the ephemeral print medium shaped time. The materiality of a cookery book influenced domestic time in particular.

While the structural paratextual elements of the *Book of Household Management* – the preface, index and title page in the last instalment – suggest that the work aspires to be a book, and not a serial, the serial-paratextual elements pull in the other direction, marking the *Book of Household Management* with contemporaneous dates. There is, for example, a year (1859) on the front cover, advertisements (including book lists), which mention the year or specific dates, and self-promoting paratext that encourages readers to subscribe to the serial itself. The front cover suggests that the serial will be 'completed in from 15–18 Monthly Parts' (a prediction which is abruptly changed to '24 Parts' in instalment nineteen). In instalments 8–14, the front cover also carries a 'Notice of Removal', dated May 1860, to inform readers that the publishing house of S. O. Beeton is moving to new offices in the Strand. Such markers tie the *Book of Household Management* to the timespan of its publication; these are the temporal urgencies of a serial venture, which subsequent volume editions are keen to erase.

In the second instalment, the advertising supplement includes the 'Prospectus' for the *Book of Household Management* and a subscriber prize draw. Both are modelled closely on the corresponding prospectus and subscriber lottery from the *Dictionary of Universal Information*, which began serial publication exactly one year earlier. The prospectus is so similar to the prospectus for the *Dictionary*, in fact, that it makes much more of the general knowledge dimension of the *Book of Household Management*, and hardly anything of the recipes. It includes what amounts to a catechism, promising answers to questions such as: 'Where are Raisins grown, and how are they dried? – In what Countries do Currants flourish most, and what Process do they undergo in order to be made suitable for the English market?'[16] This set of questions mirrors the similar advertisement for the *Dictionary* one year earlier, suggesting that the cookery book's (to modern eyes) somewhat incongruous informative bent was in fact meant to tie it stylistically with the *Dictionary*. These two advertisements are never repeated in the serial of the *Book of Household Management*.

When we compare the *Book of Household Management* with the *Dictionary of Universal Information*, we see that the *Book of Household Management* is extremely constrained in its self-promotion. Judging from the paratext, the *Dictionary* was much more invested in the novelty of serialization; it was clearly Samuel Beeton's flagship publication. It was edited by Samuel Beeton and a collaborator, John Sherer, and its glorious full title was *Beeton's Dictionary of Universal Information: Comprising A Complete Gazetteer of Geography; A Perfect Cyclopædia of History; A Comprehensive Compendium of Biography; An Interesting Epitome of Mythology; An Inestimable Treasury of Bible Knowledge; A Reliable Chronological Record; with the Correct Pronunciation of Every Proper Name.*[17] The elaborate title gives the clue that this is not a publication to hide its light under a bushel (the subsequent volume edition had a significantly more toned-down subtitle). While the *Book of Household Management* is muted in its self-promotion, the *Dictionary of Universal Information* is positively shouting at the reader from every corner of its brown paper covers. The lower panel on the cover puffs the main attraction of next month's part, often an impressive coloured map or chart. The *Dictionary of Universal Information* has a prize draw for which readers must collect vouchers from the inside back cover; readers are often directed towards the best ways to have their *Dictionary* bound; and overseas readers are, from the thirteenth instalment, advised of the *Dictionary of Universal Information*'s sellers in Calcutta, Madras, 'Barbadoes' (*sic*), Melbourne, Parramatta and Geelong. However, the paratext also reveals the publisher's scramble to keep up and manage the text. The projected size goes from 24 numbers to 36; from the thirtieth instalment, the parts are double in size (and price) in order to finish on time. It finally wraps up with a 37th instalment. The neat contrapuntal rhythm of the *Dictionary of Universal Information* and the *Book of Household Management* is disturbed by the former's runaway size. It is notable, however, that the letterpress of the *Dictionary* itself is laid out to be aloof from the scramble of the surrounding paratext. It seems that 'Universal Information' must be kept separate from the demeaning implications of buying and selling; and from the implications of ephemerality. The culminating two-volume edition is handsomely finished, with marbled pages and no advertisements.

In contrast to the *Dictionary of Universal Information*, the serial edition of the *Book of Household Management* makes few alterations to its covers, and hardly addresses its readers in the paratext. Beyond the prospectus and the subscriber lottery in the second number, the *Book of Household Management*'s self-promotion is virtually non-existent. The advertisements in the supplement are generally for cheap household goods, kitchen staples and home remedies, aimed at the lower middle classes: 'Slack's Electro-plate', 'Phillips and Company, Tea Merchants', a 'Hair Destroyer' and 'Borwick's Baking Powder' suitable for 'Families, Schools, and Large Establishments, where bread and other flour foods are extensively consumed'. As a consumer product in its own right, the *Book of Household Management* has at best a muted presence. However, within the wording of the *Book of Household Management* itself, this seeming restraint is somewhat compromised: the paratext has a tendency to creep into the letterpress. On page 4 of the very first instalment, Isabella Beeton refers her readers to the *Englishwoman's Domestic Magazine*, her husband's periodical: 'On the important subject of Dress and Fashion we cannot do better than quote an opinion from the eighth volume of the "Englishwoman's Domestic Magazine."'[18] Similarly, in the fifth instalment she refers to *Beeton's Dictionary of Universal Information* in her description of the spice mace (184); one of the few attributions of a source in the entirety of the *Book of Household Management*. Finally, and famously, Beeton includes blatant product placement of the 'Improved Leamington Kitchener' whenever kitchen ranges are discussed, giving the address of the sellers, Messrs. Slack of 336, Strand, London (27). The in-text advertising draws attention to some of the economic factors of publication, as well as the simultaneous composition and publishing cycles of Samuel's output. In the *Dictionary of Universal Information*, the letterpress itself is kept strongly separate from its hectic paratext. In the *Book of Household Management*, on the other hand, different print genres – such as magazine articles and advertisements – are lurking within the letterpress.

There are further complications to the serialized *Book of Household Management*'s relationship to time. While the *Dictionary of Universal Information* culminates with a two-volume tome (complete with marbled pages), the *Book of Household Management*, although it does appear in volume form in November 1861, is almost immediately re-serialized, this time in 12 instalments (1862–63); set from the same block as the first serial, and hence with the same erratic cut-off points, but with a new cover and 96-page instalments. Not only that, Samuel and Isabella Beeton also instantly plunder the *Book of Household Management* for recipes for two smaller volume editions for small households: *The Englishwoman's Cookery Book* and *Mrs Beeton's Dictionary of Every-day Cookery*.[19] The titles deliberately echoed other Beeton publications in order to reach as far as possible into the publishing house's existing readership; at every step, the Beetons were tying the *Book of Household Management* with the consumer appeal of their other books and magazines. Instead of culminating in a volume edition, the *Book of Household Management* effectively re-ephemeralizes as soon as it has de-ephemeralized. These unceremonious shifts between forms challenge the conventional temporal understanding of the relationship between serial and volume. The *Book of Household Management* was not going to be completed; it was not a self-contained and inviolate whole, but a latent collection from which endless spin-offs could be extracted.

The buyers of the first 24-month serial, however, were not to know this, and their attitude to the serial must mainly have been influenced by the front-of-cover promises of 15, 18 or 24 instalments, as well as the interest they felt in the work itself. We can conclude certain things from the format. The promise of a certain number of instalments (amended during the run) is certainly one motivation to keep collecting. The *Book of Household Management* was indeed, as the front cover promised, 'to be completed'. Another motivation may have been irritation at the arbitrary splits in the middle of recipes. A third reason for sticking with it, though, may simply have been the very fact that the work was so clearly a book, cut into pieces. The lack of explanation in the paratext may have made the reader more, not less, eager to find out what it contained. It was understood that the book would eventually become an authoritative whole. Laurel Brake argues, in *Print in Transition*, that the drive to 'complete' is 'part of the allusion of the attainability of closure': 'The notion of an ordered library, in which the collected series rests, masks an unequal scurry, fostered by the publishing industry, to keep up, in a market cleverly predicated on the assumption that it will *never* end.'[20] This fantasy of completion is the basis of the capitalist print marketplace. Brake's model does not touch on the post-purchase afterlife of the serial; yet for the individual buyer, purchasing the serial *Book of Household Management* was governed by more than open-ended deferral. The afterlife of ephemera suggests that the fantasy of completion could be pushed beyond the point of purchase; the material form of the serial, though constantly inscribed with prospectuses for the next venture and the next number, also held the promise that the book *could* be completed, and enjoy a long shelf life.

So far, this chapter has discussed the possible implications of material form on the temporality of the serial. Inherent in the form of the *Book of Household Management* are projections of the time made by serials: the complex intermingling of immediacy and longevity. But, of course, the *Book of Household Management* also intervenes into domestic time through the writing, by narrating domestic time and the time the reader must spend in domestic tasks, and, more subtly still, in the perusal of the book itself.

The cookery book: return, repetition and scale

Beeton's feat in the *Book of Household Management* is not one of originality, but one of organization. To compile such a confident and on the whole coherent work, Beeton had to rephrase passages from an impressive number of older conduct books, recipe collections and books of domestic economy. Such rephrasing had the effect both of creating a succinct and coherent tone, but also of disguising her borrowings. While Nicola Humble and Annette Cozzi concentrate on the multi-vocality of the book, it is surely noteworthy how uniform a tone Beeton actually achieves in spite of all her borrowings.[21] Beeton's compositional practice poses a dilemma for a modern reader: how does one perform a critical reading of a work in which virtually every passage one quotes may have been borrowed? The echoes from various sources are themselves significant. The sheer fact that the *Book of Household Management* united all these disparate sources, and that it was published and became successful, warrants close attention to the ways in which it constructs domestic time.

The *Book of Household Management* is roughly divided into three sections. First, there is a general introduction, addressed to the mistress, housekeeper and cook; then follows the longest section, the recipes; and finally we find an assorted series of chapters with 'Bills of Fare', instructions for various domestic servants, and medical and legal advice (previously printed in the *Englishwoman's Domestic Magazine*). Although there are chapters for different members of the household, they could all easily be read by the same person; someone who could not afford a housekeeper would not be offended by the polite fiction that she could. The first instalment, which appeared on 1 November 1859, begins abruptly with the chapter 'The Mistress', and contains no recipes; the reader must wait until the second (December) instalment before the soup recipes start.

The overall structure is not revolutionary for household manuals of the period. Where Beeton's innovative approach really shows is in the layout of the text. The *Book of Household Management* uses different fonts and font sizes to distinguish between textual elements. Not only recipe titles, but also the different elements within the recipes themselves – ingredients, preparation time and so on – are set in different type in order to ease navigation. The additional information which Beeton famously inserted within the body of the manual, and which is highlighted in the 'Prospectus' – natural history, classical history, anecdotes, origins of ingredients – is clearly set apart in a small font, meaning that it is easily skipped. Beeton was not the first to invent the list of ingredients (Eliza Acton is generally credited with this innovation), but she was the first to put the list at the start of the recipe.[22] Overall, the clear distinction in print between various textual elements made the *Book of Household Management* uniquely easy to navigate. As Margaret Beetham observes: 'the printed format here not only elevated a seemingly humble task but also presented it as part of a systematic body of knowledge. In organising her material as she did, Beeton demonstrated the task of management which she advocated.'[23] Beetham highlights the important link between the printed text itself and the practices it hopes to engender. Readers are not only being instructed how to cook, but also how to read the book itself. I will return to this below. Meanwhile, it is worth noting that the use of different typefaces to catch the reader's eye was, at this time, mainly seen in advertising – Samuel Beeton's advertisements for his various magazines certainly employ such tricks of the trade. As we saw above, *Beeton's Book of Household Management* did not keep itself aloof from magazine genres such as advertisements and product placement. It is entirely possible that the thing that set Isabella Beeton's book apart from its competitors was derived from its promiscuous mixing of high and low modes of print culture, including advertising.

Conversely, Beeton's conceptualization of domestic time takes the highest possible tone. For Beeton, time within the domestic sphere is symbolically connected to larger historical timescales: dinner is never just dinner, but always also an expression of cultural supremacy. Cookery itself was a mark of civilization:

> As in the Fine Arts, the progress of mankind from barbarism to civilization is marked by a gradual succession of triumphs over the

> rude materialities of nature, so in the art of cookery is the progress gradual from the earliest and simplest modes, to those of the most complicated and refined. (39)

It was through cookery that Britain had to assert itself. Dinner was the central event of the day, and the point in time to which all other temporalities were subservient. Everything in the *Book of Household Management* leads up to this point or takes its cue from it: 'it is in her preparation of the Dinner that the cook begins to feel the weight and responsibility of her situation' (42). Similarly, for the mistress of the house, 'the half-hour before dinner has always been considered as the great ordeal through which the mistress, in giving a dinner-party, will either pass with flying colours, or, lose many of her laurels' (12). The reason why the temporal framework of the day is so highly charged is that British middle-class dining, as Beeton makes clear, is positioned on the extreme cusp of human progress:

> The nation which knows how to dine has learnt the leading lesson of progress. It implies both the will and the skill to reduce to order, and surround with idealisms and graces, the more material conditions of human existence; and wherever that will and that skill exist, life cannot be wholly ignoble. (905)

It is not merely civilization that has 'reduced to order [...] the more material conditions of human existence'. It is also, by implication, a work undertaken each and every day in the kitchens of the nation. The brute vitality of nature must be made to yield its nutritional value, and erratically grown vegetables must be cut into pieces and arranged, aesthetically, on a dish, with croutons in diamond shapes.

The project of civilization rests on the daily practices of the household manager, and the very smallest details carry immense value for the continued progress of the empire. Domestic time is a mundane small-scale version of that progress. Beeton claims, however, that the skills necessary can be learnt when the cookery book is sufficiently detailed. When speaking of the artisan cook, whom she describes as male, Beeton says:

> all terms of indecision should be banished from his art. Accordingly, what is known only to him, will, in these pages, be made known to others. In them all those indecisive terms expressed by a bit of this, some of that, a small piece of that, and a handful of the other, shall

> never be made use of, but all quantities be precisely and explicitly stated. (39–40)

It is not genius that is needed, but a book which insists on precision and method. In order to work this system, Beeton advocates an organization of base, addition and scale, which is evident in her very first recipes. The basis of all cookery, and thus of the whole enterprise of domesticity, is a 'base' broth or stock. In the second instalment, the reader learns:

> *Note.*–It is on a good stock, or first good broth and sauce, that excellence in cookery depends. If the preparation of this basis of the culinary art is entrusted to negligent or ignorant persons, and the stock is not well skimmed, but indifferent results will be obtained. [...] In the proper management of the stock-pot an immense deal of trouble is saved, inasmuch as one stock, in a small dinner, serves for all purposes. Above all things, the greatest economy, consistent with excellence, should be practiced, and the price of everything which enters the kitchen correctly ascertained. The *theory* of this part of Household Management may appear trifling; but its practice is extensive, and therefore it requires the best attention. (54, author's emphasis)

The use of stock as a basis for cooking is derived from French cuisine – and, unsurprisingly, this passage is lifted from one of the best-known French chefs in England, Louis Eustache Ude. In his bestselling book *The French Cook*, first published in 1813 and continually in print up to the time of Beeton's work, Ude urges his readers:

> It is on a good first-broth, and good sauce, that you much depend for good cookery: if you have entrusted this part to persons who are negligent, and if your broth has not been well skimmed, you can make but indifferent work. [...] The theory of the kitchen appears trifling, but its practice is extensive: many persons talk of it, yet know nothing of it beyond a mutton-chop or beef-steak.[24]

Aside from these instructions, Beeton borrows Ude's system of base broths, but reduces their number to only four: 'Rich Strong Stock (1s. 2d. per quart)', 'Medium Stock (9d. per quart)', 'Economical Stock (3d. per quart)' and 'White Stock (9d. per quart)' (55–7).

These stocks are the foundation upon which not just a meal, but the entire practice of household management, is to be built. In order to achieve 'excellence', the inexperienced cook must return again and again to these origin recipes, and then, once the foundations have been laid, add ingredients according to instructions to obtain, for instance, 'Oyster Soup' or 'Pea Soup'. A significant number of soup and gravy recipes rely on this return to the base broths. Similarly, in the 'Pastry' chapter, no fewer than 14 different pastry recipes are given at the very beginning, and are then used in many of the subsequent recipes. The governing idea is one of base and addition. Within the moral system of the book, without this 'basis of the culinary art' (42), the whole sparkling edifice of the genteel dinner will topple, with disastrous consequences to home, family, and, by direct implication, civilization itself. Kathryn Hughes points out that 'soup was a moral food, the emblematic product of the well-run middle-class kitchen in which everyday ingredients were slowly transformed'.[25] Soup-making also implied that every little scrap of food could be used up, making good both vegetable peels and bits of meat that would otherwise have been thrown away; it was thus an embodiment of middle-class self-understanding, of economy and thrift. Beeton notes at the beginning of her soup chapter:

> We are glad to note [...] that soups of vegetables, fish, meat, and game, are now very frequently found in the homes of the English middle classes, as well as in the mansions of the wealthier and more aristocratic; and we take this to be one evidence, that we are on the right road to an improvement in our system of cookery. One great cause of many of the spoilt dishes and badly-cooked meats which are brought to our tables, arises, we think, and most will agree with us, from a non-acquaintance with 'common, every-day things.' Entertaining this view, we intend to preface the chapters of this work with a simple scientific *résumé* of all those causes and circumstances which relate to the food we have to prepare, and the theory and chemistry of the various culinary operations. (49)

Soup has become a sign of a scientific, knowledgeable approach to cookery, which extracts the most flavour and nutrition out of the basic ingredients. Knowing, in detail, what happens when you cook soup, means understanding the sophisticated modern world in all its complexity. Finally, the phrase we saw earlier, which recommends that 'the price of everything which enters the kitchen' should be 'correctly ascertained', also implies that the household manager has to curb another kind of waste, that of duplicitous servants and suppliers. 'Soup' becomes the topic upon which all the rigours of 'management' must be practiced;

if they are not, it will be detrimental to the running of the household and the nation. All these things, Beeton tells us confidently, can be mastered within the *Book of Household Management*.

The system of base and addition means that similar processes can produce results on a large scale simply by being added together. A larger dinner merely requires the addition of more dishes. Tellingly, in the 'Bills of Fare' section, the first example is for a formal dinner for 18 people. This general outline of an ideal dinner is preserved in most of the subsequent smaller bills of fare (909–60), except for the 'Plain Family Dinners', which look more like a modern three-course meal. Any entertaining, from cooking a meal for the extended family to giving a grand dinner, mainly differs in term of scale, enabled by adding or subtracting elements. The fact that this would invest food with a certain sameness is immaterial. Indeed, surprises are profoundly undesirable. The principle of repetition is very strongly urged in the *Book of Household Management*. In the first instalment, readers are told that:

> It will be found, by far, the better plan, to cook and serve the dinner, and to lay the tablecloth and the sideboard, with the same cleanliness, neatness, and scrupulous exactness, whether it be for the mistress herself alone, a small family, or for 'company.' If this rule be strictly adhered to, all will find themselves increase in managing skill; whilst a knowledge of their daily duties will become familiar, and enable them to meet difficult occasions with ease, and overcome any amount of obstacles. (16–17)

This repeated performance, playing at 'company' every day to instil the necessary habits in every member of the household, affirms the performativity of practice. Much later, in a recipe for sucking pig, Beeton assures her nervous readers:

> A sucking-pig seems, at first sight, rather an elaborate dish, or rather animal, to carve; but by carefully mastering the details of the business, every difficulty will vanish; and if a partial failure be at first made, yet all embarrassment will quickly disappear on a second trial. (399)

Everything, even the most complicated techniques, can be learnt with practice. In the passage about the tablecloth and sideboard we see, yet again, that the governing principle is that the highest level of organization (company dinner) is the standard against which lesser performances are measured. In order to avoid awkward formal dinners, all dinners are made formal. The passage, incidentally, is borrowed, with minor modifications, either from Robert Kemp Philp's 1855 *The Practical Housewife* ('servants should always be accustomed to lay the cloth and serve dinner as neatly when the family is alone as when company is expected'),[26] or from Anne Cobbett's 1835 book *The English Housekeeper*:

> Practice is as necessary to good waiting, as it is to create perfection in any of the higher accomplishments; therefore it would be well for the mistress to insist on the same particularity in preparing the table, in arranging the side-board, and in waiting at dinner, when her family dines alone, as she requires when there are visitors; because, in the latter case, an increase in number gives quite sufficient additional trouble to a servant, without her being thrown into confusion by having to do what she may have forgotten, from being out of the habit.[27]

On her side, Anne Cobbett may well be elaborating on Maria Rundell's suggestion from the beginning of the century that 'much trouble and irregularity are saved when there is company, if servants are required to prepare the table and sideboard in similar order daily'.[28] The echoes of advice reverberating through the different books bring into the mid-nineteenth-century era a blueprint by which an idealized system can be constructed. Significantly, Beeton's rewritten version of the passage varies from the earlier ones mostly in tone: the rules must be 'strictly adhered to', but the servant can then expect to 'overcome any amount of obstacles'. The ideas of domestic performance are sharpened, but also essentialized; they carry more symbolic meaning and are thus moved to a moral field of operation absent from earlier, more down-to-earth formulations.

The emphasis on repeatable systems and on the ability to scale up and down also has consequences for more humble situations. In Beeton's chapter on the maid-of-all-works, the template for the lone maid's duties is taken from a more affluent establishment. The authorial voice insists that this is not a problem: 'If the servant is at all methodical, and gets into a habit of "doing" a room in a certain way, she will scarcely ever leave her duties neglected' (1001). In order for this to work – for the maid-of-all-work to stretch far enough to replace three or four servants – her routine must be elaborately plotted, down to the last minute:

> After she has had her own breakfast, and whilst the family are finishing theirs, she should go upstairs into the bedrooms, open all

> the windows [etc.]. [...] The breakfast things washed up, the kitchen should be tidied, so that it may be neat when her mistress comes in to give the orders for the day: after receiving these orders, the servant should go upstairs again, with a jug of boiling water, the slop-pail, and two cloths. (1002)

Even in a tiny household, the 'orders for the day' must be given in the (swiftly tidied) kitchen, even though the maid is actually at this time supposed to be cleaning the bedrooms. Alison Light points out that often, two girls of 14 years of age would be made to serve dinner while pretending to be a staff of twenty.[29] A series of calculated movements through the house in a specified order is designed to minimize confusion and time-wasting, but follows the pattern of a substantial country house. As Beetham says, Isabella Beeton 'redefined the task of managing the domestic so that attention to the minutiae of daily life was not just given as a maxim to live by but was worked through in detail'.[30] We see that this detail comes from a unifying view of the unproblematically scalable household. The performance and re-performance of domestic practice within a system where Beeton has already organized the shortest possible route from task A to task B will thus produce a workable and maintainable machine with ambitions of social climbing. The high level of detail is not unique to Beeton. Servants' movements through the house had long been highly scripted in the manuals from which in all likelihood she borrowed these chapters.

The ease of scaling up and down, however, is repeatedly threatened with collapse. The chapter on the maid-of-all-work projects a cheery confidence that perfectly smooth operations are achievable, but troubling elements creep in nonetheless. We are told that the mistress may 'assist' with cooking dinner: 'Now she has gone the rounds of the house and seen that all is in order, the servant goes to her kitchen to see about the cooking of the dinner, in which very often her mistress will assist her' (1003). Similarly, on washing days:

> If the washing, or even a portion of it, is done at home, it will be impossible for the maid-of-all-work to do her household duties thoroughly, during the time it is about, unless she have some assistance. Usually, if all the washing is done at home, the mistress hires some one to assist at the wash-tub, and sees to little matters herself, in the way of dusting, clearing away breakfast things, folding, starching, and ironing the fine things. With a little management much can be

> accomplished, provided the mistress be industrious, energetic, and willing to lend a helping hand. (1004)

The fantasy that the mistress can maintain her amateur involvement with housework becomes increasingly implausible. Just keeping up this polite fiction of idleness is a full-time job in itself. Thus, at the low end of the middle class, the fantasy of effortlessly copying the time management of more affluent households becomes stretched to breaking point. We see a hint of tension between the minute detail of the domestic system and the class anxieties of the one-servant household.

Writers of household manuals find no difficulty in drawing up detailed plans for domestic staff. Robert Kemp Philp, in *The Practical Housewife* (1855), goes into minute detail when describing the outline of a servant's day and duties:

> A servant should be trained to rise about half-past five, throw open her bed, and her window, too, when the weather permits; unclose the shutters of the staircase and dining-room, open the windows of this latter to air it; pass into the kitchen, and open the shutters and windows there; light the kitchen fire; well rinse the kettle, and fill it with fresh water; see that the boiler is well supplied with water, and then proceed to prepare the room required for breakfast.[31]

Incidentally, Beeton copies part of this in her chapter addressed to the cook, telling us that 'she will thoroughly rinse the kettle, and, filling it with fresh water, will put it on the fire to boil' (42). This is a level of detail that is almost entirely missing from outlines of mistresses' days. The disparity probably springs chiefly from a regulatory impulse.[32] Pinning down every stray minute of a working day was imagined to produce better servants. Middle-class mistresses did not just rely on printed sources for the daily schedules they demanded of their servants. In the Sambourne Family Archive, for example, one finds a manuscript notebook from the latter half of the nineteenth century that specifies, in half-hour intervals, every single duty for the housemaids that the mistress can think of.[33] Such exhaustive detail is a question of class. For middle-class writers of household manuals, the fantasy of a machine-like, smoothly running household can only be played out by elaborately plotting the bodily movements of their servants. This is the closest we get to a 1:1 scale model of the nineteenth-century domestic day. By outlining the duties of their inferiors so rigorously, writers attempted to create a reproducible system of knowledge – a pattern for daily repetition. But this overemphasis on servants' time inadvertently reveals the inherent difficulty in plotting time: middle-class writers were trying to regulate the working classes in the face of the very real anxiety that such a schedule would always – could only ever – be unattainable. The fantasy of the smoothly run household is displaced onto mute paper servants.

Setting the text and reading the text: layout, textual organization and influence

While Beeton's authorial voice emphasizes the symbolic value of domestic time – the benefits of repetition, habit and scrupulous exactness – the print layout is also a significant part of the *Book of Household Management*'s ambition to influence its readers' domestic time. Beeton's book is not the first to offer a high level of organization; most of the older household manuals had been very far from haphazard. Anne Cobbett, in *The English Housekeeper*, organizes her early chapters around domestic spatiality, with a chapter each on the 'Store Room' and the 'Kitchen'. Philp, in *The Practical Housewife*, is a little more eccentric in his organization. He includes a very long section entitled 'Domestic Manipulation' which contains various proceedings such as cleaning, drying, corking, tying down, stoppering, and unstoppering, as well as recipes for cements, entries on the economy of heat, and suggestions for packing and cleaning various materials. His recipe section is divided by month – arbitrarily, to a large extent. 'Shortbread', for example, is given under 'February' with no particular reasoning. Some books had no organising principle at all. Susannah Reynolds, wife of the radical writer and publisher G. W. M. Reynolds, published a recipe collection in serial parts around 1847. Recipes follow no logical order in her work; three recipes for puff pastry are scattered throughout the book.[34] This was not merely a function of the time in which she published; much later books could be governed by the same surprising disorder. Philp's 1855–56 bestseller *Enquire Within* lacks any coherence of organization at all, and it remains unusable without the index. The year of publication of a book of household management seems to give no useful indication of how organized it was. *Enquire Within* appeared just a few years before the *Book of Household Management*, but is nowhere near as organized as Cobbett's book from 1835, or Acton's from 1845. Similarly, archaic forms show remarkable persistence: both early works (Parkes's *Domestic Duties*, 1825) and later ones (Soyer's *Modern Housewife*, 1849) can be written partly or entirely in dialogue or epistolary form.[35]

Beeton is not the only writer to aim for a complete and exhaustive book of household management. She is, as Hughes observes, merely one participant in the 'totalizing, categorizing culture that drove the early Victorians'.[36] In Beeton's book, however, the textual organization adds another level to the representation of domestic time: her attempt at a complete system of knowledge is embedded in print layout. Beeton even states explicitly how she expects print to influence practice: in a short 'Note' in the second instalment, immediately before the first recipes, Beeton introduces her 'system' of organization within the recipes (55). She recommends that the 'young housekeeper' should follow the instructions to the point of actually placing all the ingredients on the table before starting:

> It will be seen, by reference to the following Recipes, that an entirely original and most intelligible system has been pursued in explaining the preparation of each dish. We would recommend the young housekeeper, cook, or whoever may be engaged in the important task of 'getting ready' the dinner, or other meal, to follow precisely the order in which the recipes are given. Thus, let them first place on their table all the INGREDIENTS necessary; then the *modus operandi*, or MODE of preparation, will be easily managed. By a careful reading, too, of the recipes, there will not be the slightest difficulty in arranging a repast for any number of persons, and an accurate notion will be gained of the TIME the cooking of each dish will occupy, of the periods at which it is SEASONABLE, as also of its AVERAGE COST. (55)

Beeton is instructing the reader how to read the recipe. Since the layout of recipes is Beeton's own, we can in this case assume that the passage originates with her. The terms in small capitals designates the significant features of each recipe ('ingredients'; 'mode of preparation'). The recipe is imagined to transcend the page and reach into the physical realm of the reader; textual organization elicits a practical spatiotemporal response, mirroring the layout on the page. The micro-level of textual layout, and the everyday practice of domestic cookery, is in this instance imagined to be each other's doubles. We see Beeton pushing to the extreme edges of representation, to a level of synonymity between writing and reading that is almost utopian.

The reality of following a recipe is often that one scurries back and forth between stove-top and book, loses one's place in the instructions and hurriedly tries to find it before something burns, flattens or clots. To counteract such problems, the *Book of Household Management* fantasizes about direct usefulness and purpose that will reform its readers' households substantially, beginning with the most basic bodily movements of the reader. The *Book of Household Management* often suggests collusion between print and material world which would allow the latter to become more like the former. In the fifth instalment, a recipe for 'India Pickle' is followed, uniquely for the book, by a note that really belongs in an introductory chapter, entitled 'Keeping Pickles':

> Nothing shows more, perhaps, the difference between a tidy thrifty housewife and a lady to whom these desirable epithets may not honestly be applied, than the appearance of their respective store-closets. The former is able, the moment anything is wanted, to put her hand on it at once; no time is lost, no vexation incurred, no dish spoilt for the want of 'just a little something,' – the latter, on the contrary, hunts all over her cupboard for the ketchup the cook requires, or the pickle the husband thinks he should like a little of with his cold roast beef or mutton chop, and vainly seeks for the Embden groats, or arrowroot, to make one of her little boys some gruel. One plan, then, we strenuously advise all who do not follow, to begin at once, and that is, to label all their various pickles and store sauces, in the same way as the cut here shows. It will occupy a little time at first, but there will be economy of it in the long run. (217)

I have been unable to find a source for this passage, and so I am working on the assumption that Beeton wrote this herself. Quite possibly she simply elaborated on an earlier, less colourful prescription. In 1835, Anne Cobbett commented:

> The saving in time that is occasioned by observing order, and the waste of time that is occasioned by want of order, are incalculable. [...] The mistress of a house, when she sends her servant or a child to a store room, should be able to direct precisely where what she wants may be found.[37]

While Beeton has inherited Cobbett's sentiment, Beeton's passage is sparkling with wit. It evokes the distracted wife, hunting desperately, while her husband is plaintively requesting pickle; as the wording makes clear, this is surely not an unreasonable wish when faced with 'cold roast beef or mutton chop'. Beeton's little 'note', with its accompanying engraving, urges the reader to the same virtues as her own book displays: categorising, labelling, inscribing, ordering (see Figure 4.1).

to add to the pickle, do not omit first to boil it before adding it to the rest. When you have collected all the things you require, turn all out in a large pan, and thoroughly mix them. Now put the mixed vegetables into smaller jars, without any of the vinegar; then boil the vinegar again, adding as much more as will be required to fill the different jars, and also cayenne, mustard-seed, turmeric, and mustard, which must be well mixed with a little cold vinegar, allowing the quantities named above to each gallon of vinegar. Pour the vinegar, boiling hot, over the pickle, and when cold, tie down with a bladder. If the pickle is wanted for immediate use, the vinegar should be boiled twice more, but the better way is to make it during one season for use during the next. It will keep for years, if care is taken that the vegetables are quite covered by the vinegar.

This recipe was taken from the directions of a lady whose pickle was always pronounced excellent by all who tasted it, and who has, for many years, exactly followed the recipe given above.

Note.—For small families, perhaps the above quantity of pickle will be considered too large; but this may be decreased at pleasure, taking care to properly proportion the various ingredients.

KEEPING PICKLES.—Nothing shows more, perhaps, the difference between a tidy thrifty housewife and a lady to whom these desirable epithets may not honestly be applied, than the appearance of their respective store-closets. The former is able, the moment anything is wanted, to put her hand on it at once; no time is lost, no vexation incurred, no dish spoilt for the want of "just a little something,"—the latter, on the contrary, hunts all over her cupboard for the ketchup the cook requires, or the pickle the husband thinks he should like a little of with his cold roast beef or mutton-chop, and vainly seeks for the Embden groats, or arrowroot, to make one of her little boys some gruel. One plan, then, we strenuously advise all who do not follow, to begin at once, and that is, to label all their various pickles and store sauces, in the same way as the cut here shows. It will occupy a little time at first, but there will be economy of it in the long run.

INDIA PICKLE.

VINEGAR.—This term is derived from the two French words *vin aigre*, 'sour wine,' and should, therefore, be strictly applied to that which is made only from wine. As the acid is the same, however it is procured, that made from ale also takes the same name. Nearly all ancient nations were acquainted with the use of vinegar. We learn in *Ruth*, that the reapers in the East soaked their bread in it to freshen it. The Romans kept large quantities of it in their cellars, using it, to a great extent, in their seasonings and sauces. This people attributed very beneficial qualities to it, as it was supposed to be digestive, antibilious, and antiscorbutic, as well as refreshing. Spartianus, a Latin historian, tells us that, mixed with water, it was the drink of the soldiers, and that, thanks to this beverage, the veterans of the Roman army braved, by its use, the inclemency and variety of all the different seasons and climates of Europe, Asia, and Africa. It is said, the Spanish peasantry, and other inhabitants of the southern parts of Europe, still follow this practice, and add to a gallon of water about a gill of wine vinegar, with a little salt; and that this drink, with a little bread, enables them, under the heat of their burning sun, to sustain the labours of the field.

INDIAN CHETNEY SAUCE.

452. INGREDIENTS.—8 oz. of sharp, sour apples, pared and cored; 8 oz. of tomatoes, 8 oz. of salt, 8 oz. of brown sugar, 8 oz. of stoned

Figure 4.1 'Keeping Pickles': Detail from *Beeton's Book of Household Management*, p. 217

The illustration is in fact doubly inscribed: the pickle jar carries the legend 'Piccalilly', and underneath the engraving we see the words 'India Pickle'. Mistakes cannot possibly be made with this level of specificity. Print is infiltrating materiality, inscribing itself onto the reader's bottles and pickle-jars. The placing of the passage, however, seems decidedly unpremeditated; it is possible that Beeton is here suffering under her own organising principle, and can find no more appropriate space in which to advise on store cupboard management. Ironically, the passage imitates the pickle jar by hiding in the wrong place. The misplacement could be caused by the very oddness of this level of detail; in this passage, the *Book of Household Management* again moves into extremes of specificity, which the book cannot ultimately uphold. The store cupboard, which is the ultimate source for good housekeeping, is also the breaking point for realism.

But materiality not only threatens to overrun the powers of realism, it also destabilizes the domestic temporality in the *Book of Household Management*. Hidden within the work is another complication to the desire for a reproducible system of knowledge: the dangerous fluidity of a hastily decomposing material world. In this era before refrigeration, things are constantly running out or going off, requiring the diligent Household Manager to create a new supply, or hurriedly utilize something before it putrefies. Stock, on which Beeton's French-inspired system of cookery rests, takes six hours to boil under near-constant attendance and will keep, in hot weather, for only a few days (48). Milk and cream will turn sour in a matter of hours unless scalded once a day (812). The storeroom of meticulously labelled pickles, too, must be watched and planned for with remarkable prescience: a 'Mixed Pickle' is begun with a vinegar mixture in May, adding new vegetables over the summer as they come in season, but is not edible until twelve months later (226). All these different periodicities must be planned for, watched and inspected at regular intervals, and any imminent lack of one thing must be discovered and prevented in time. Domestic time is an intricate fabric of use-by dates and natural processes of consumption and decay, meaning that one is constantly working to new deadlines within a dense web of different periodicities. This is a temporality of multiple time schedules, all imminently coming to an end, necessitating constant return to the book and a constant repetition of finely honed actions, all to maintain the household in a (precarious) state of readiness. In this pressured temporality, the words cannot keep track of the material world. The need for an easily navigated system of organization is thus motivated by the need to keep on top of a worryingly unstable material world.

Beeton's representation of domestic time is tightly wound into her construction of a system of knowledge that the book elaborates both through words and through print layout. While the *Book of Household Management* fantasizes about infiltrating the material reality of its readers, and of influencing their bodily movements, it also acknowledges that in order for domestic time to work, in all its fluidity, the reader must be able to return to the book easily and navigate between recipes with judicious speed. The domestic time the volume constructs cannot, in the nature of things, follow the printed text linearly. The form instead facilitates these informed returns to the text.

Participating in genre: cut and paste

Just as Beeton's composition of the *Book of Household Management* was a cut-and-paste job, so reading and using a cookery book is an exercise in cutting and pasting. The use of a cookery book is rarely linear, but is structured by a self-informed pathway: a constant activity of choosing, adapting and discarding. Recent criticism is moving away from the idea that a work forces readers to read in a certain manner, and that any deviation from that norm is automatically anarchic or illicit. Leah Price has argued that eighteenth- and nineteenth-century readers were highly skilled at reading for what they found useful, and dispensing with what they deemed uninteresting. Readers were not passively led by printed media, but found their way competently through them.[38] This is especially true of readers of cookery books. Cookery books have an embedded suggestion of non-linear, pragmatic time. They hint at a larger temporal realm of individual practice. This also means that there is a parallel between using and compiling a cookery book. Just as readers pick and choose, extract and amend, so Beeton, as an 'Editress' of the *Book of Household Management*, had to decide which advice to trust and which to discard. It is more than a parallel, however: the printed recipe book undoubtedly grew out of private practices. Borrowing recipes is an immeasurably older practice than publishing them. Indeed, the boundaries between manuscript collection and printed books were often blurred. The most ambitious recipe collectors would sometimes make the transition into print: Maria Rundell's cookery book was a printed version of her private collection.[39] Rundell claimed authority exactly because hers was a private manuscript helpfully offered to the public. Conversely, as Andrea K. Newlyn has shown of America, private manuscript cookery books would often ape printed works by, for instance, including a mock title page.[40] This 'playing at publication' lent a sort of joke authenticity to private manuscripts and is evidence of the power of genre for personal expression. Mimicking publishing genres is not so much a blurring of boundaries as an imaginative engagement with genre. And while the *Book of Household Management* does not have a similar manuscript genesis, since it was a publishing venture from the start, its method of composition aligns itself with common manuscript practices of scrapbooking, transcribing and collecting, thus challenging our conventional ideas of authorship and of domestic time as constructed by print culture. Anne Cobbett in 1835 urged her readers to keep their own recipe book. She even announced with candour:

> I give some bills of fare, because such things are sought for in books of this kind, but not because I think they can ever be of much use; for, whether it be for a large or a small party, the person who cooks the dinner ought to be the best judge of the number of dishes required.[41]

Cobbett here characteristically undercuts the pretensions of her own work. Typically, she is the first to recognize the limits to what print culture can do to influence practice, and hence to gesture towards the large realm of individual experience that lies beyond her book.

There is increasing scholarly attention to print genres, such as scrapbooks, which subvert the classical author–text–reader relationship. As Ellen Gruber Garvey has argued, 'scrapbooks help us to understand reception as an active phenomenon'.[42] Readers were not necessarily passive; they actively participated in print culture, in a sense making re-publications. As Garvey says: 'scrapbook makers were engaged in homemade archive creation [...], literally producing a new text. Like editors, they re-circulated the materials they had collected, making the text available at least to their future selves and often to others.'[43] Compilers were re-authoring the print they read, actively re-forming an eclectic variety of material. Beeton wrote for an active print readership that could respond to advice literature and recipes by annotating, cutting out, transcribing and editing for themselves. Some readers practiced participatory reading that led them to ape publishing practices in their own private manuscript works. They based their editorship on what they found useful, and what they considered to be reliable information. Time is embedded within the *Book of Household Management* by these practices of flicking, choosing and adapting, which allowed readers to keep up with the rapidly dwindling store of pickles and the souring cream. In a sense, Beeton was writing for a readership that understood that practice had to be performed in order to be useful – even to the point of performing the genre of the cookery book itself.

My observations underline the suspicion that borrowings are endemic to the genre of cookery books. Beeton was not alone in this practice; cookery books were particularly susceptible to plagiarism and piracy. In a sense, the pilferings of *Beeton's Book of Household Management* serve to make more apparent how much genre is a question of inheritance, innovation and appropriation. Within the cookery book genre, unlike in narrative genres, inheritance is very literal, and actual innovation often more hit-and-miss. The interplay between persistent modes and modernity is extremely complicated. With the benefit of knowing about her book's subsequent success, and the further benefit of ignoring what went before, Beeton can seem like more of an innovator than she really was. This raises questions of time and print culture: a book that appears modern in 1859 is knitted together of echoes of previous books. It may have been its very recognizability that gave the *Book of Household Management* its appeal, since it was a neat summing up of received wisdom. If that is the case, the credit for the *Book of Household Management*'s astounding success lies with its formal qualities: the print layout and the imaginative use of serial publication. The echoes of older works are constantly reverberating through print culture, undergoing slight or substantial changes. Modernity, essentially, is inherited. Print culture is, and has always been, a meeting place where a multiplicity of temporalities linger – either acknowledged or unacknowledged – as they find new forms of expression.

Using the serial

As a genre, the cookery book challenges conventional ideas of authorship, textual progression and reading, by allowing and necessitating annotation, reader-editing, armchair reading and a non-linear pathway through the book. Beeton's *Book of Household Management*, however, poses additional problems because of the serial nature of its publication. While Beeton may start with boiling stock, for a mid-century housewife there would have been multiple possible starting points – an imaginative patchwork approach – which would enable her to produce a full menu or a single dish. As I have pointed out, cookery book is not a series of sequential moments; sequentiality in cooking must always be assembled from a variety of points in the book if one is to achieve a workable meal. The plainer menu plans towards the end of the *Book of Household Management* suggest the workings of this causality (incorporating leftovers into next day's dinner), but there is a tension between this logic, which is required by users of the manual, and the temporality allowed by serial publication. Embedded within the *Book of Household Management* are two kinds of time: domestic time and serial time. These two time schemes refuse to align with each other; the serialization of the *Book of Household Management* lends itself to a linearity that is alien to the cookery book genre.

The serial form made it more difficult to navigate through the *Book of Household Management* as a whole: if the most important temporal idea which governs the practice of owning a cookery book is return, then it is necessary to have the full set. The heedless serial splits and the sparse paratextual clues leave no indication of what the next instalment will contain, or how long a reader might have to wait in order to learn about puddings, or even if there will be any puddings. To enable the sort of individual pathway to a full meal that cooking demands, you would require a good few of the 24 numbers. Cross-referencing and linked paths through the recipes would otherwise soon become impossible; for instance, many fish dishes in the third instalment require 'Lobster Sauce', the recipe for which does not appear until the fifth instalment. This structure would not be a problem for an experienced cook who probably already had such sauces in her repertoire; but for an inexperienced cook or newlywed mistress, it must have been maddening. For the first twenty months of its publication, it was by no means even certain how long the *Book of Household Management* was going to be.

And yet having the book cut up into instalments may have made it more manageable for an ambitious reader, susceptible to the call of self-improvement, who would be spurred on each month to renewed efforts. Serialization drives and revives the consumer's impetus to read because of the very thinness of the 48-page paper-covered instalment. Probably an insecure cook would be compelled to read every word, whereas a more experienced cook would be more likely to browse, skim, and dip, making mental or actual notes of useful tips and recipes. So while serialization obstructs one kind of usefulness, it facilitates another kind of reading: the kind that is linear and progressive. Over the two-year run, the reader might familiarize herself with the work as a whole. Gaining familiarity with the book, the reader of the serial could decide to make a start at some point when she had assembled enough pages to feel confident. The layout of the printed text, and the encouraging language Beeton employs, ensures that any start is a step in the right direction.

Even a failed attempt is a valuable experience. Every single point in the cookery book can produce its own sequence, working with the available collection of instalments.

Since it was marked with ephemerality, the serial *Book of Household Management* became more liable to physical cut-and-paste techniques, scrapbooking, circulation and copying; readers were likely to collect only parts of the serial, and so to have a fragmented experience, or their collection could be made up of a combination of the 1859–61 serial and the 1862–3 serial.[44] Even if a reader collected all or most of the instalments of the serial of the *Book of Household Management*, he or she would still to a certain extent be working against the format (unless they went to the expense of having it bound). Finding a specific recipe or section would take some trial and error, as there is no way of knowing from the outside which of the 24 issues contains what. First the reader would reach for the last issue, which contains the 'Analytical Index', and then try to guess which issue contained the particular page they wanted. The number of starting points for using the *Book of Household Management* grew exponentially with the number of parts readers had collected, and Beeton's system of base, addition and scale meant that such starting points could, in principle, be adapted to most classes and conditions. For the reader immersed in the periodicity of the *Book of Household Management* throughout 1860 and 1861, each instalment would add elements to make the book more whole: serialization meant accumulation, and delay meant incompleteness. While serialized novels motivate the reader to keep buying instalments by building suspense and a promise of narrative fulfilment, a cookery book is not motivated by 'The End'. For the *Book of Household Management*, the motivating factor is to have the whole set. There is no suspense, no denouement, merely a gradual assemblage of equally valued fragments. Beeton's domestic time highlights accumulative knowledge, not least because her work is a cumulative collection of other people's recipes. However, inherent in the circumstance of serial publication is the projection of a future where the book can be finished, thus allowing the reader full access to all of the parts. Just as linearity is a serial logic, so the need to complete – to reach a unified, finished whole – is a serial need.

So little does the culmination of the *Book of Household Management* matter in economic terms, however, that immediately after the 24-month run, and after the volume edition, Isabella Beeton and Samuel Beeton re-issued the book in yet another serial (1862–63). This development suggests that readers did not resent the enforced stop-and-start logic of the monthly parts or the erratic cut-off points. This is a text which de-ephemeralizes itself into a volume, but then re-ephemeralizes itself just as easily, with no changes made in the body of the text during these shifts back and forth. This phenomenon shows us that domestic time is not unified or complete in the *Book of Household Management*, but is available in a piecemeal logic that borrows linearity from serial publication and then discards it just as easily. In the cookery book serial, one *can* return to the same place twice, and reproduce domestic time, and serial time, in politicized repetitive practice.

The *Book of Household Management* participates in a print culture where familiar practices (cookery books) were united with unfamiliar ones (serialization); where a book's genre was created by the intersection of asynchronous timeframes; and where both recipes and printed media were copied, recycled, de-composed and put together anew. The *Book of Household Management* was imprinted with these practices of splitting up and putting together, and, as a material object, the serial *Book of Household Management* itself was open to similar reader responses. The decisive serial 'split' – the failure to acknowledge the divisions when they happen, or to prepare for them – changed the way the *Book of Household Management* worked as a printed object. The practice of returning again and again to an object like a cookery book was complicated by this very real interruption introduced to the material text. Collecting the *Book of Household Management* was to participate in a print culture that promised accumulative knowledge and the possibility of constructive returns. While the 'split' cuts up the text, it also introduces a flexibility to the way information is disseminated. The first serial edition, and its subsequent reissues in various forms, marks a radical cut-and-paste approach to the relationship between print culture and domestic practice.

Coda: Scrapbooking and the Reconfiguration of Domestic Time

In 1850, a young woman with the initials M. A. C. began compiling an album. She used a pre-printed volume made especially for the purpose, and probably given to her as a gift. In making this album, M. A. C. produced a far from straightforward record of domestic time. Albums are unique among nineteenth-century print practices in that they represent a close proximity between consumption and production; the album's owner or contributors cut out, re-organized, pasted and embellished printed matter according to their own whims. Material was captured out of the flow of the print marketplace and fixed in the manuscript volume for a local, domestic readership. In this final section of *Time, Domesticity and Print Culture*, I will trace the conceptualization of domestic time that emerges from nineteenth-century albums. Of a necessity, the discussion will at times turn speculative – albums are apt to frustrate fixed interpretations – but in order to expand our understanding of the production of time by print culture, it is vital that we examine modes of representation even if the referents are hazy and the chances of misreading are high. Nick Hopwood, Simon Schaffer and Jim Secord have asserted that as serial culture became ubiquitous in the nineteenth century, 'newspapers and other periodicals defined knowledge as a material commodity distributed, consumed and disposed of on a regular basis'.[1] While this is an important insight, I want to offer a corrective to this model of regularity, simultaneity and timeliness. Print may enter the domestic sphere regularly, but what about the ways in which it is collected there? By extending the field of print culture to albums, we arrive at a more nuanced picture of two problems: how print was consumed, and how that consumption structured domestic time. Albums more than any genre dramatize the aesthetic and affective possibilities of reception, and shows print consumption to be dis-synchronous, imaginative, residual and irreverent. Albums follow print temporality on their own, highly localized, terms, making a fallible, composite, approximate record of domestic time lived through printed matter.

One of the assemblages in M. A. C.'s album is a page entitled 'Needles' (Figure 5.1).[2] It consists of a large cut-out of a printed frontispiece (from a book or periodical) with the three Graces on a plinth, surrounded

Figure 5.1 'Needles', page 169 of M. A. C.'s album

by Classical objects. The title and year of the publication have been excised, and instead M. A. C. has painstakingly printed a short discursion on the history of needle production, and a fragment of a poem by Edward (Ned) Ward:

> I tell thee, wife, I'll have our daughters bred,
> To book'ry, cook'ry, thimble, needle, thread;
> To knit, to spin, to sew, to make, to mend,
> To scrub, to rub, to earn, & not to spend.

Hovering in the top right-hand corner of the page is a glued-in wrapper from a needle packet ('Hall and English Superior Elastic Silver Eyed Needles'), surrounded by a dark blue border and grey shading to underline its three-dimensional state. The needle packet not only adds incongruity to the page – commercial packaging was one of the more rare forms of ephemera in mid-nineteenth-century albums – but also acts to literalize the theme. The page is not just concerned with words about needles, but also with the medium through which they enter the home. By including the packet, M. A. C. points towards the disconnection between representation and lived modernity: an entire realm of printed material often fails to make the pages of print culture.

The 'Needles' page is linked to temporality in at least three ways. First, it is a repository of printed material, ephemera and modes of knowledge that are all part of the temporal fabric of print culture. Secondly, it is a record of the labour it took to produce it. Thirdly, Ward's poem plays on the traditional registers of women's domestic time – not least in associating sewing with feminine docility and economy, as we saw in Chapter 2. But the poem also jars against its setting. The commercial needle packet points to the inescapable fact that even 'thimble, needle, thread' have become associated with the modern consumer market and will no longer preclude 'spend[ing]'. And M. A. C.'s album as a whole is very far removed from the 'book'ry' of Ward's speaker, who is undoubtedly referring to household accounts. The album in which this page is found delights in material culture: shining gold foil, colourful fabric scraps and all the colours of the rainbow abound in its pages. The album itself is compiled in a pre-printed volume made especially for the purpose. It is an incidental catalogue of domestic outlays on artist's supplies, decorative bits and bobs and printed matter. The album represents, furthermore, a labour far removed from 'scrub[bing]' and 'rub[bing]' – on the contrary, it is evidence of considerable expenditure of time on creative practices with very little household purpose.

It aligns itself with the idea of 'mak[ing]' and 'mend[ing]', but only in the sense that it puts spare bits of material culture to use. In fact, if M. A. C.'s album hovers somewhere between thrifty and sumptuous, it is very much situated on the latter end of that scale.

The element on this 'Needles' page that is most adrift is the engraved frontispiece with the classical theme, which has no resonance with anything else on the page. Since it has been worked into this manuscript volume, it has become unmoored from its symbolic meaning. The re-appropriation of print culture and its insertion into the domestic album alerts us to the composite nature of domestic time. Albums represent the ongoing labour within the domestic sphere which processes and edits the materials that enter it, and they juxtapose different temporalities on the page: in this case, a contemporary print of a Classical subject; an insistently modern needle packet; the year 1565 (when commercial needle production began, according to M. A. C.); and an eighteenth-century comic poem. By re-inscribing these materials into the album, compilers recorded aesthetic influences and the labour that made up domestic time. As Claire Farago suggests: 'nineteenth-century British scrapbooks provide rich material records of past daily lives [...] [The] practical memory that these scrapbooks record comprises an imaginary but physically embodied space filled with time past and time passed.'[3] M. A. C. captures past times out of the printed material that enters into her domestic life, and passes the time by labouring to insert scraps into her album in new and surprising juxtapositions. By re-appropriating a frontispiece M. A. C. re-evaluates print culture (valuing paratext rather than content). The nuggets of writing on the page suggests a valorization of facts, anecdotes and inclusion-by-association. In other words, M. A. C.'s labour on the album tends to categorize the material according to her own standards. These generic traits within her album, and those it shares with other albums, point towards a conceptualization of domestic time.

Scholars sometimes use the terms 'album' and 'scrapbook' interchangeably. Strictly speaking, whereas a scrapbook is almost entirely filled with material culled from print, an album is defined by the heterogeneous nature of the material it collects: between 1820 and 1860 this type of album could include sketches and watercolours, poems and prose (handwritten or printed), pressed flowers and seaweed, fabric samples, embroidery and decoupage, among other things. While the early albums were often in home-made or specially commissioned blank books, towards the mid-century they were often compiled in pre-printed, commercially produced volumes, such as the one used by

M. A. C. Commercial volumes generally had a printed title page with a special place for the owner's name, and a range of different paper qualities for different purposes. Some few, but by no means all, even contain pre-printed poetry. In albums, older practices such as the commonplace book continued into the nineteenth century. Similarly, the act of scrapbooking is a subcategory of album-making. The term scrapbooking pertains specifically to the collection of printed material, and it is the interplay between such an inclusion of print and the artistic decoration on the page of the domestic album that interests me here.

Time and the album

Even if, as Farago says, albums and scrapbooks are records of 'time past and time passed', they make no claims about the accuracy of that record. They may 'capture "lived time" in a material form', as Katherine Ott, Susan Tucker and Patricia P. Buckler suggest, and become a 'material manifestation of memory', but they also 'fracture chronology'.[4] The question is how we can read time – and domestic time especially – out of this fraught relationship with chronology. The album was a means of accumulating material as a response to modernity, as we can see from the inclusion of photographs from the 1860s onwards. But inherent in that modernity was also the need to preserve the past. In *Stranded in the Present,* Peter Fritzsche argues that nineteenth-century scrapbooks and albums became records of increasingly historicized domestic lives. They were tools to compile memories, identities and rituals that preserved the family or the community in time, while at the same time being inscribed with the inevitable loss of the past from which the scraps had precariously survived.[5] Like the friendship album, the album recorded not only presence – being written very often in what Samantha Matthews calls 'present tense presence' – but also, inevitably, absence. As Matthews points out: 'while albums typically start life at home, they are as mobile as their owners, and as records of brief encounters, album inscriptions express temporal as well as physical dislocations'.[6]

One way of understanding the urgencies which made albums into temporal records – and the inherent impossibility of fixing time to the page – is to compare them to another popular manuscript practice: the diary. Like albums, diaries are, superficially at least, shaped as records of private or familial activities over time. Unlike the album, the diary will suggest this by clearly marking dates at the top of every entry. Neither genre offers straightforward or reliable records, however. In her book *Time, Space, and Gender in the Nineteenth-Century British Diary,* Rebecca

Steinitz posits that in the period the diary was thought to demand 'the thorough representation of experience in time', but in practice diaries were often begun on a wry note of prospective failure.[7] It is simply impossible to record everything. Some diarists skipped whole days; some summarized missed days retrospectively; and some simply wrote a brief phrase such as 'Nothing particular' on certain days rather than leave them blank. As Steinitz notes, '"Nothing" stands in for something [...], a kind of synecdoche for "nothing out of the ordinary," that is, the fullness of daily routine.'[8] Such notation has a tendency to elide the ordinary, the everyday, and the mundane routines and habits of normal life, just as the daily schedules I discussed in the Introduction discursively empty out the day of any particularity. While it was almost impossible to achieve, 'writing in the present remained conceptually central to the diary's dailiness'.[9] Steinitz concludes:

> Even as diurnal form marks the fullness and persistence of time, it reveals the ever-present threat of the ever-imminent rupture of that fullness and persistence, thus highlighting a fundamental textual and ontological instability. Though the individual diarist's ever-imperfect attempts to achieve diurnal form may register that instability as personal failure, the failure at stake is in fact both generic and existential.[10]

Steinitz's book is a reminder that genres can never be taken at face value and that textual claims for chronology, even when they are emphatic, must be treated with caution. Diary practices are bound up in creative manipulation of temporality, thus making it likely that scrapbooking practices are, too.

The most basic thing in common between diaries and albums is the codex in which they are overwhelmingly composed. Both practices are defined by the volume form, but the way they differ in their approach to the codex is illuminating. Whereas diaries borrow chronology from the codex, most albums leave few traces of the order of their composition: in striving for aesthetic consistency they tend to weave things together, and often omit dates (sometimes even the year the album was begun). In one album in the Harry Page Collection, no. 166, illustrations of birds which look identical in colouring and stylistics are distributed a hundred pages apart.[11] Engravings of birds obviously taken from the same scrap sheet or book page are similarly spaced far apart in the album. This feature suggests that the owner either distributed entries evenly or laid material aside for later insertion. The same album also contains facing pages with illustrations dated years apart, as is quite common in albums. Patrizia di Bello discusses a striking example of similar practices: the album compiler Anna Birkbeck has pasted a poem written by her husband, George Birkbeck, into her album, next to a printed, dated card from his funeral in 1841.[12] The juxtaposition of his verses with the funeral proceedings is a poignant mixture of past and present, presence and absence, which underlines the irregular nature of album time. Di Bello's example shows the album's deliberate choice to make chronology subservient to memory. This phenomenon is by no means unusual in the albums I have seen: though the volume form suggests linearity, the practice of filling it was rarely linear. Time in the album is therefore composite.

Categories

We could fall into the trap of thinking, based on M. A. C.'s album, that album-making is inherently subversive and imaginative: that it always challenges and baffles the cultural centres and focal points. In fact M. A. C.'s album is unusual in its inventiveness. Another album, no. 56 in the Harry Page collection, is composed almost exclusively of pre-printed commercial sheets. Watercolours of butterflies and shells have been confined to separate pages; few attempts have been made to mingle the commercial scraps with artwork. The scrap sheets have merely been cut to pieces and re-assembled in unadventurous categories: crowned heads, eminent writers, Romantic poets, scenes from Shakespeare, etc.[13] What this scrapbook engenders more than anything is a feeling of sameness. The page devoted to the Royal Family tells us that we are in the reign of George IV, which puts the date between 1821 and 1830; significantly, this lone gesture towards dating the album is concerned with signalling allegiance to the ruling establishment. This is a scrapbook that does not so much record the passing of time as preserve the status quo.

In this preoccupation with categorizing and fixing, there is an important point to be made about domestic time in the album. Albums can be seen as a meeting place between what Raymond Williams has called 'residual', 'dominant' and 'emergent' cultural elements.[14] Williams says that 'it is in the incorporation of the actively residual – by reinterpretation, dilution, projection, discriminating inclusion and exclusion – that the work of the selective tradition is especially apparent'.[15] Such selection is happening in each individual album, when compilers take scraps out of the flux of print both for their novelty and for their safe familiarity. On the whole, albums are more often residual than anything else. As I said in the Introduction, print culture – and, by extension, its manuscript repositories such as albums – works with inherited forms and persistent ideas. But the condition for this work is always to operate with or against emerging modes. As di Bello argues throughout *Women's Albums and Photography*, albums were a multidimensional meeting of materials and quotations, both seeking to sustain and affirm residual culture but performed at all times as a negotiation of modernity.[16] The residual ideas in albums often take the forms of allegiance to cultural, political or national figures: many albums devote pages to the Duke of Wellington and Waterloo, sometimes up to fifty years after the fact. Byron is also a popular inclusion throughout the nineteenth century. And although these cultural residues show us the conservatism of much album work, they are at all times interspersed, sometimes intertwined with, the products of an expanding visual culture that, after all, made the very albums themselves possible.

In a sense, albums sort through residual elements in order to incorporate them into emerging schemata, and they do so by mediating the album genre. The act of arranging or classifying items is one of the basic modes of scrap collecting, before even reaching for the glue pot. M. A. C.'s album shows us the genre's allegiance to taxonomies. Not that she always pays particular attention to conventional modes of grouping knowledge: the taxonomies of the album are often surprising and idiosyncratic. M. A. C.'s page on 'Tea' is merely a way of assembling various scraps and quotations loosely associated with the two tea-producing countries, China and India. The common denominator, tea, unites wildly disparate elements on the page, producing M. A. C.'s very own system of knowledge. This collapse of geography in the face of album-makers' voracious appetite for a kind of imaginative taxonomy is evident in many albums. One example in the Harry Page collection, in a particularly stunning album from the early decades of the nineteenth century by Elizabeth Reynolds, is a piece of thin paper with Chinese script. The surscript tells us that this is a 'Card of Compliment left by a friend of Prince Le Boo at a gentleman's house in Clapham', and the signature itself has been rendered in both Chinese and Latin characters: 'Young Saam Tak'.[17] A little digging reveals that Prince Le Boo (more commonly 'Lee Boo') was a chief's son who came to England in 1796 from the Belau Islands (now the Republic of Palau) in Micronesia by getting passage with a Captain Henry Wilson. Unfortunately, Lee Boo died of smallpox six months after arriving in England; he is buried in Rotherhithe. Young Saam Tak, on the other hand, was Chinese, and came to England ten years later. The only connection between the two was that, according to the *Monthly Magazine* of 1 March 1805, the very same Captain Wilson brought Young Saam Tak to England.[18] It is perhaps not surprising that the album compiler links the two young men – Prince Lee Boo had made quite a sensation when he arrived in England – but the suggestion that they know each other is based on a misunderstanding. Even more tellingly, the visiting card is glued into the album next to an engraving of a Chinese abacus or 'Accompt Table'. Linked by exoticism, these two scraps show the suggestibility of the album compiler, on constant lookout for links between scraps. The calling card, on its exotically thin paper adorned with simple calligraphy, stands out from the rest of the album. The abacus seems insufficient to match it.

Whereas in these examples – of tea and Chinese – the chosen categories make a certain kind of sense, other instances can be rather baffling. An excellent example of this is page 102 of M. A. C.'s album (Figure 5.2). The page imitates an illuminated Bible page, beautifully coloured and decorated with at least three different kinds of gold cuttings. The title word is 'Charity'. The central illustration is a glued-in printed card – one of many religious illustrations in the album – depicting a priest in a Jesuit habit, bending over a prisoner. The words on the card are 'J'étais en prison et vous m'avez visité' ('I was in prison and you visited me'), a quotation from Matthew 25:31–46, the parable of the judgement. The underlying suggestion of the little card is that the priest, by showing charity to the prisoner, acts as a true Christian. However, when we look closer at the page, the ground begins to shift. The title word 'Charity' is the first word in a sentence that reads: 'Charity covereth a multitude of sin' – not the message one might expect to apply to the seemingly selfless priest. Further down we see: 'Charity loses its benign influence, when heralded by ostentation'. Is this meant as a reflection on the Jesuit? Most of the writing on the page actually defines charity by what it is not. If we read this page as a negative comment on ostentatious Christianity, maybe it is also a comment on the religious print culture embodied by the card, where Christian virtues are touted as colourful scraps?

Even more unsettling, on closer inspection, is the colourful border. Rather than painted, the illuminated Bible page is made up of cut-out figures between the snippets of gold paper. The figures turn out to be Aztec or Mayan icons: a parrot, a dog, and a demon-like double-headed figure (possibly a priest or a warrior – maybe a god). On something that is at first glance a Bible page, these New World figures are utterly incongruous. We cannot finally determine why M. A. C. chose to embellish her illuminated page on 'Charity' with Mesoamerican demons. Is it

Figure 5.2 'Charity', page 102 of M. A. C.'s album

a mischievous juxtaposition or merely an indiscriminate magpie-like interest in the exotic? But when M. A. C. later in the volume uses up the last of her demon icons, she again juxtaposes them with a Catholic Bible illustration.[19] What are we to make of this? Did M. A. C. simply have these two sources of scraps to hand at the same time, and so chose to mix Catholic imagery with Mesoamerican? This would certainly suggest the strangeness of domestic time and its surprising simultaneities of print. Incongruity could be wavered for the expediency of making up that illuminated border with whatever material was at hand. Or was there some point to be made, indirectly, about the Catholic Church? It is difficult to judge M. A. C.'s religion from her album, but there is a notable absence of Catholic iconography such as rosaries and the Virgin Mary, which can be found in other albums in the collection.[20] Based on the internal evidence, M. A. C. was almost certainly Protestant, although that in itself might not have made her critical of such Bible cards.

M. A. C. certainly may have received the Mesoamerican figures without any explanation of their provenance. And yet, as a well-educated middle-class woman, she was probably at least aware of their geographical origins. The ancient Mayan ruins had been under investigation for a good few decades at this point. In 1824, the *Literary Gazette* printed a review of a book about ancient cities of Mexico, illustrated with small engravings of the types of figures found in the Mayan scrolls – images not unlike those that made their way into M. A. C.'s Bible page.[21] The religious *Saturday Magazine* ran a series on Mexican ruins in their August and October 1842 supplements, illustrated by figures and plates.[22] An underlying fascination behind such articles was the near-total destruction of pre-Conquest culture as well as other Mexican cultures that had gone before. In this, the religion of the Spanish conquerors rarely went unobserved. An 1853 review in the *Gentleman's Magazine* discusses a book on Spanish Mexico. The author of the review is alike censorious against Mexican blood sacrifice and Catholic brutality:

> The Aztec priesthoods are accused of cruelty because of the human sacrifices made by them to the gods. But in the fires of the Inquisition perished more victims than on the sacrificial stone of the Mexican war-god. [...] If Christianity has held its ground in Mexico, it is because its salt of truth has kept it ever sweet in spite of the poisonous corruption of the superstitions under which it has been all but buried.[23]

The aforementioned *Literary Gazette* article from 1824 was similarly horrified both by the heathen sacrifices and the Catholic conquest. Admittedly, there is no reason to suppose that M. A. C. had access to, or interest in, this or any other account of Mexican history. But it is telling that the article in the *Gentleman's Magazine* so explicitly links Aztec and Catholic barbarity, undoubtedly because of an awareness of the devastation caused by the Spanish Conquest. For example, the reviewer shows outrage at the burning of the Mayan codices by Archbishop Zumaraga in the sixteenth century. Without drawing any firm conclusions on what could be a mere coincidence, it is nevertheless suggestive that both M. A. C. and the article in the *Gentleman's Magazine* see an alignment between Catholicism and Mesoamerican cultures, which had been intertwined for over three hundred years at this point. Maybe M. A. C.'s juxtaposition is not as incongruous as it first seemed?

The inclusion of one or several geographical 'others' in an album projects a local practice to global history, and links domestic time to a larger sphere of world history. Almost certainly M. A. C. gleaned the figures from a magazine article aimed to inform a domestic audience. The intermingling not only of disparate cultures but also of disparate geographical times produces startling spatial and temporal complexities. In this sense, albums produce a kind of album realism by the sheer incongruity of its scraps – not the 'reality effect', but the shock effect. Similarly, it is the incongruity of that commercial needle wrapper which gives it its power; this is what Caroline Levine has called the shock of the ordinary.[24] The 'real' suddenly pokes its head into the album. Juxtapositions of material taken from different branches of material culture make albums into records of the multiplicity of print. If print culture mediates time, albums remediate it, both pinning down material out of the flow of time and recirculating it in their own formalized setting: the commercially produced blank codex. This act of fixing is intimately linked with the sheer incongruity of Mesoamerican demons hovering above a Jesuit priest. Albums make things – and the domestic time that produced them – seem strange and surprising. They alert us to the fact that domestic time can be dis-synchronous, imaginative and irreverent, in a way that more than makes up for the limited circulation of these albums. Scrapbooking engages with the materiality of print on its own, highly localized, terms.

The volume and the assembly of time

The domestic album combines residual modes (highly visual and recognizable ones with a defined place in history) with emergent and often surprising modes. Emergence is always more diffuse than tradition, for obvious reasons; such emergence means that modernity in the album is not clearly marked, and often located in the combination of scraps, rather than the mere inclusion of them. Sometimes one finds a needle wrapper or a news story, but it is not so much the use of these temporalized items, but the way they sit within the album, that generates a conceptualization of time. Domestic time is narrativized in the album precisely as such diffuse emergence in forms. The way we read domestic time in the album relies less on dates, and much more on traces of the labour, and hence the kind of time, creating the genre in which each album participates, and which has plucked scraps out of their temporal contexts.

The needs of the genre speak of this labour of compilation. If albums do not strive for a transparent order of composition, they do, however, aspire to a kind of fullness. The full album is one where almost every page, sometimes every corner, has been filled. While M. A. C. succeeded with this goal, the failures in the Harry Page Collection tell us something about the process of filling up an album. We see that some paper qualities were more desirable than others, and that desirability structured the labour. Most commercial albums at mid-century contained a number of pages with embossed borders: these were raised designs of flowers or scrolls, into which the compiler's own art could be inserted, glued or drawn directly on the page. Even in half-filled albums with many blank pages, these embossed pages are almost always filled. The frames were clearly coveted, and were sought out, maybe from the outset, maybe even some time after the owner had otherwise lost interest in album-making. This is another clue to the non-linear approach to filling up the album. But even though these valuable pages had been sought out, the non-linearity did not necessarily bleed into the album labour as a whole. In one uncompleted album, the even distribution of embossed pages has not inspired the owner to disperse her other material evenly: beside the embossed pages (which have mostly been used up), the first half of the album is considerably more filled out than the second half.[25]

So while the volume form lent itself to linearity, the blank album's contingencies also influenced the labour of filling an album. The format extended restrictions and opportunities that shaped album-makers' approach to their labour. The ideal of a full album should remind us of the differently formed, and yet similar need within diaries to facilitate a full time. The full album does not aspire to the same kind of comprehensiveness as a daily diary, but it suggests a domestic time that can nevertheless be filled, purposeful, and integrated in its historical moment. A personal record which records very little that is tangible beyond its own making, it nevertheless narrativizes domestic time as a process with a purpose.

Uncompleted albums allow us to see the generic urgencies that structured this process: the finding and filling of desirable pages, for example. An album in the process of being filled would be the centre of ongoing labour: collecting scraps, soliciting contributions, thinking of amusing juxtapositions, and then setting aside the time for fiddly, glue-based assembly work (not something that could easily be squeezed into spare moments). But, conversely, the writing within albums tries to forestall accusations that the album-making has taking up too much of the compiler's time. The time-consuming nature of this labour is averred or excused by the album's insistence on its own insignificance. The term 'scrap', of course, highlights the small value of the items that fill the album, and nineteenth-century album compilers often emphasized the relative insignificance of their labours.[26] In M. A. C.'s album, a dedication by 'F. D. S. for M. A. C.' tells us something similar:

> I seek no praise, yet fear no blame,
> *Nil admirari* may be true;
> Still may a solitary Dame
> Unaided, working fairly claim
> The meed to independence due.

The archaic word 'meed' is defined in the *OED* as 'a person's deserved share *of* (praise, honour, etc.)'. *Nil admirari* means 'to be surprised by nothing' or to adopt an attitude of indifference to the world. With these words as her starting point, M. A. C. seems to be claiming said 'independence' by associating it with words like 'solitary' and 'unaided'. This is an album of individual labour, not a collective effort, and the verses both claim and reject outside praise for the work. There is, in this dedication, a pointed setting apart of the album-labour from the outside world. By using an authorial voice (through 'F. D. S') that both invites and rejects critical engagement, M. A. C. positions her album as a product of enmeshed 'independence'. By implication, this labour – the labour that produces scrapbooks and albums – is independent work at the edges of print culture. In this sense, the album claims a marginalized domestic time for itself. Maybe it is for this reason that the claim for independence is so insistent: to aver that no one else was inconvenienced in the making of this album. 'Solitary' time; using up leftovers of print; expecting no recognition beyond her own immediate circle: M. A. C.'s epigraph is an invitation to reassess print culture to a set of different standards. All of these elements align the album labour with the generic form – the album is, like the labour that goes into it, resolutely located in the margins. Not least, one might add, for drawing attention itself to its marginality – to claim it, in fact, as a virtue. The album is inherently and unapologetically self-referential.

Margins and domestic time

Album material was selected for any number of reasons; we cannot even say that albums recorded pre-existing artistic practices which, but for the fixity of the volume form, would have been lost to us. Rather, scrapbooking was a genre that produced its own needs for compiling. As Ellen Gruber Garvey notes; 'scrapbook makers generated a new form along the way, *creating* the usefulness of the scraps by saving and classifying, and thus making them available for reuse'.[27] This includes noticing the normally unnoticed parts of magazines, such as the decorative scrolls in corners of cover pages. On the page facing her epigraph, M. A. C. has included scraps from a greenish magazine cover as a frame around the edges. These borders are full of mottos from British institutions of state ('Dieu et mon droit', 'Honi soit qui mal y pense'), as well as several small lions and unicorns. They have clearly been chosen, however, for their decorative qualities, not their national significance. This, the least-noticed part of a magazine, is used to decorate the album page, and the title of the original publication has not even been recorded for posterity. In another part of M. A. C.'s album, on the other hand, the gold-and-blue masthead from the 1841 issue of a musical annual, *The Queen's Boudoir*, has been selected for its elaborate typeface and swirls. The *Queen's Boudoir*, which appeared every year between 1841 and 1854, had elaborate front and title pages embellished with gold designs; this is exactly the kind of thing that M. A. C. values as surroundings to her quotations and commonplaces. The front pages of the *Queen's Boudoir* could be recycled without injuring the songs within. It is very likely that M. A. C. has selectively gleaned from a number of annuals and gift books in this way (though mostly not including, as in this case, the title of the publication); such elaborate books appears to be a likely source for the snippets of gold swirls throughout her album. None of this is fuelled by the printed material itself, but by the needs of album-making. If the album records print culture, it does so by divesting that same print culture of markers and signs of origin, if it suits the purposes of the album assemblage.

Aesthetically, albums self-identify not only with leftovers and ephemera but also with, significantly, edges and borders. In other words, albums favour aesthetics that usually belong to the margins of things, including, as we just saw, marginal time. Throughout M. A. C.'s album, the scrolls and corners have received more loving attention than the centres and focal points. In a later album in the Harry Page

Collection, by Kate Aspinall (no. 74), the inserted photographs and engravings serve as the starting point for elaborate pencil or watercolour treatments, sometimes extending the illustration into the surrounding album page, sometimes framing it with flowers or rosaries. The two albums may treat margins differently, but the generic interplay between scrapbooking and album-making proper – in other words, a movement from cutting-and-pasting to surrounding and juxtaposing – suggests a self-alignment with marginalia. Appropriation is not merely a question of re-evaluating printed material, but it is also created by a kind of abhorrence of the blank page – *horror vacui* – that causes art to blend into the corners. There is a peculiar dynamic between seamlessness and surprise in the album genre. As a consequence, albums had very little interest in dating things, or in tracing them back to their origins.

The very aesthetic of album-making is concerned with marginal things that are not only divested of their original contexts but also necessarily taken pointedly out of time. Album-making brings to centre stage bits and pieces that were destined for the dustheaps. Although Brian Maidment points out the significant contribution scrap sheets played in the formation of mid-nineteenth-century print culture, scrapbooking and scrap-printing always associated themselves with marginal practices.[28] Album-making and scrapbooking showed an awareness of its own temporal marginality; the domestic time which produced albums stood outside regular narrativization. Cutting magazine covers into pieces, and pasting title pages into blank books, unmoors print culture from its temporal allegiance. This uncoupling of print from its historical moment shows us that the domestic distribution of print fed, more often than we realize, into a deliberately asynchronous engagement with print time. Albums create their own needs, and album-making conceptualizes a domestic time which can encompass those needs. Even more significantly, whenever the album has cause to write history, the compiler must rely on marginal scraps and personal anecdotes, often not dated. The visiting card from Young Saam Tak, which somehow travelled from the 'gentleman's house in Clapham' to the pages of a domestic album, has only the most marginal interest for the history of Anglo-Chinese relations in the early nineteenth century. Its inclusion is exotic, but far from historically significant; the assemblage shows the compiler's excitement with even this minor brush with history. On the recto of the same page, Elizabeth Reynolds has glued in a little scrap that looks as if it has been used by Young Saam Tak for testing his autograph stamps, as well as idle doodling. The thing to which she had access was literally waste paper. M. A. C. at one point draws a little ivory figurine, accompanied by an explanation: '"A pretty little ivory image, found in the ruinous part of the Castle of Dunstaffnage, or Stephen's Mount, in Scotland." Grose's Antiquities. M. A. C. Visited Dunstaffnage Castle, on Loch Etive, near Taynuilt, but did not see the image.'[29] M. A. C. identifies the source of her image – presumably, she copied her illustration from an engraving – and then tells her readers that she visited the place, but did not see the figure. The need to inform her readers that she has not in fact witnessed this historical artefact underlines the spectator–editor relationship of the album-compiler towards her world and its history-writing. She is both observing and recording, and balances between what she knows, and what she has only learnt second-hand. It is this very position outside official records that allows her to mischievously combine Bible cards with Mayan parrots. This combination dramatizes the way that history enters the home – the indirect and ephemeral brushes with history which most ordinary people experienced.

Such meetings with the historically significant are so rare that they stand out. Young Saam Tak's visiting card stands out even in the diverse album in which it now sits. Albums produce their own systems of knowledge, linking a Chinese signature with a Chinese abacus; but the example also shows the fortuitous way that they record history. The calling card represents a brush with a larger historical story, however tangential. An album-maker could not count on access to such material, which is why it sticks out rather glaringly from the fashion plates that form the backbone of this particular album. Many albums contain such marginal brushes with history; a late-nineteenth-century album in the Harry Page Collection, mostly devoted to the by-then ubiquitous greeting cards, suddenly includes an obituary of the Reverent W. M. King in Waterville, Quebec; two notices for the marriage of one of his sons in Montreal; and an 1895 photograph of the English church in Waterville, cut from a book or magazine.[30] The connection is not explained, but it is clear that when an album-maker sees an opportunity to commemorate family history when it has taken a sudden leap into public print, she takes it. The album accommodates these sudden incursions of history.

Just as albums focus on margins, so domestic time self-identifies with the marginal. Albums record a temporality which is filled and fractured at the same time; which occupies borders and edges (and spare moments) with varying degrees of enthusiasm, invention and taste; and which appropriates print culture alongside what we might call manuscript culture and domestic arts. It does all this through an active selection of the material culture that passes through the domestic centre: gold paper, fabric, foil, anecdotes, letters, jokes, profound philosophy, views of stately homes, etc. The material is remediated into residual or highly idiosyncratic categories. Albums are both registers of the individual, the domestic and the local, *and* of the regional, the national and the global. By editing the stream of stuff in the domestic setting, albums conceptualize the very idea of the fullness of domestic time. The thrift that lies behind a visually coherent album ties into the thrifty aesthetic of a smoothly running household, and its inherent inter-materiality.

Albums dramatize the multifarious ways in which readers can re-edit print culture. They also highlight the interrelation between print culture, private domestic time, and aesthetic recording and reordering. Just like the other works I have discussed in this book, they perform practices of modernity by recording and pinning down and, as an indirect consequence, conceptualizing domestic time. Imperfect and idiosyncratic they may be, but albums are testaments to the labour and aesthetic judgement that went into their making, and they demonstrate that domestic time is inhabited and remade. They suggest the myriad ways in which domestically situated practices engaged with, and reshaped, print culture; they suggest the importance of local practices and unpublished ideas. Albums are records of the marginalized time that made them, and which stands outside regular narrativization. Most important, albums challenge the misconception that real domestic time was merely a passive receptacle of print culture – that published print could simply be understood as powerful systems of knowledge, ones that built real time, willy-nilly, in their own image.

Conclusion

The co-dependence of form and representation is complex – shot through with genre demands, hidden assumptions and politics. As *Time, Domesticity and Print Culture* has argued, new forms and genres are evidence of a mid-century desire to expose all aspects of life to middle-class categorizing powers, and writers responded to the difficulty of representation with even more intense scrutiny. But it is entirely possible that the opposite was true, too: that proportional to the rate at which the mechanics of the everyday were described, writers realized that the everyday was difficult to pin down. As we have seen, once narratives zoom in and uncover the details of everyday time, it becomes strange – eerily mechanic or mysteriously shifty. This book captures print culture at the point where exhaustive detail and close observation were understood to be the most modern approach to understanding. While, in practice, societies do not necessarily move teleologically towards greater mechanization, greater regularity of time and greater genre mutability, those are often the terms through which modernity is understood. The aim of this study has been to trace the many points at which such textual teleology falls productively short. Taking the temporal turn while reading nineteenth-century print culture should be accompanied by a close attention to representation, as well as the representational power of forms and genres.

The forms which textual representation takes, as I have argued, facilitates what can be said. Novel formats and unsettled genres help construct new conceptualizations of temporal experience. For this reason, my study has traced a spectrum from fully coherent and linear literary fiction (*Bleak House*, *North and South*, didactic fiction) to increasingly fragmented and non-linear textual practices (a cookery book, a set of domestic albums and, more indirectly, the periodical form). The aim has been to show that writing about domestic time did not become more coherent and more assured in the nineteenth century, but the opposite: That print culture enabled a more fluid negotiation of experience. The practice of domestic time continually needed new models to describe itself with. Inherent in the textual teleology of greater and greater detail is a receding object of inquiry. Works which attempted to describe the practices which made the middle-class home temporal had to incorporate, at every point in their representation, an absence of representation. The household manual can enumerate an immense range of detail, but must always let the one stand for the many, the part for the whole, the jar of Piccalilly for an entire cupboard-full of jars, and that cupboard for a nation teeming with household spaces, all subtly different. Even books that can go into extreme detail must leave almost everything to be imagined. Only in that interplay can domestic time be portrayed; the sign for the real always signifies that the real cannot be contained in signs. As we saw in Chapter 1, the home is made temporal at the cost of narratively marginalizing the domestic servants of Bleak House; it is through their absence/presence that the time of domesticity can be suggested. Elizabeth Gaskell's strategy, on the other hand, is to saturate domestic time with experience, cramming time until it overflows the boundaries of measurement. This is a different kind of absence: an unmooring from external boundaries, making domestic time a painful site of dis-synchrony. Depictions of domestic time in the nineteenth century are constantly pushing at these outer edges of representability. It has been the aim of this book to show that these varying edges of representability are treated not as failures, but as creative spurs. It is on those very edges that the true possibilities of realism and representation are played out. It makes sense, then, to end with a genre – albums – which is far from traditionally representative.

Time, Domesticity and Print Culture has endeavoured to show how printed format situates a text in time, and complicates the ways in which it can narrate time. For the realist novel, expansiveness is not a problem; length is what defines the mid-century novel, more than anything. But for non-fiction, such as Isabella Beeton's 1,000-page cookery book, length – and especially a lengthy serial publication – complicates and alters the uses to which the text can be put. Twentieth-century archival practices have tended to obscure these important distinctions between formats, and there are still blind spots in our understanding of nineteenth-century serial publication of non-fiction. This should not keep us from acknowledging that there is nothing straightforward about the relation between form and longevity: the serial edition of *Beeton's Book of Household Management* may have lasted decades on a shelf before it was thrown out by the next generation. Ephemeral objects could have shelf lives long beyond their immediate publication. It may, on the other hand, have been immediately plundered for desirable recipes, while the bulk of each instalment went the way of all scrap paper. The ways in which printed media could be read, torn, dirtied, cut, pirated, preserved or re-circulated shows us how print culture feeds back into lived time.

Notes

Introduction: Timetabling and its Failures

1. Elizabeth Gaskell, *Wives and Daughters*, edited by Pam Morris (London: Penguin, 2003), p. 315.
2. Mrs William [Frances] Parkes, *Domestic Duties: Or, Instructions to Young Married Ladies, on the Management of their Households, and the Regulation of their Conduct in the Various Relations and Duties of Married Life*, 2nd edn (London: Longman, Hurst, Rees, Orme, Brown, and Green, 1825), p. 366.
3. Functional subdivision of homes – propounded by the architect Robert Kerr in his 1866 book *The Gentleman's House* – tried to separate activities, classes and genders as much as possible; there is an excellent discussion of Robert Kerr's work in Karen Chase and Michael Levenson, *The Spectacle of Intimacy: A Public Life for the Victorian Family* (Princeton and Oxford: Princeton University Press, 2000), pp. 156–78. For the history of the country house, see Mark Girouard, *The Victorian Country House* (New Haven and London: Yale University Press, 1979).
4. For timetabling, please see Elizabeth Langland, *Nobody's Angels: Middle-Class Women and Domestic Ideology in Victorian Culture* (Ithaca and London: Cornell University Press, 1995), p. 32; and Thad Logan, *The Victorian Parlour* (Cambridge: Cambridge University Press, 2001), p. 31. For cyclical time, please see Kathryn Allen Rabuzzi, *The Sacred and the Feminine: Towards a Theology of Housework* (New York: Seabury Press, 1982); Ann Romines, *The Home Plot: Women, Writing and Domestic Ritual* (Amherst: University of Massachusetts Press, 1992). For non-narratable time, please see Elizabeth Deeds Ermarth, *The English Novel in History, 1840–1894* (London and New York: Routledge, 1997); Elizabeth A. Campbell, *Fortune's Wheel: Dickens and the Iconography of Women's Time* (Athens: Ohio University Press, 2003).
5. Ermarth, *English Novel*.
6. Kathryn Hughes, *The Short Life and Long Times of Mrs Beeton* (London: Harper, 2006); Andrea Broomfield, *Food and Cooking in Victorian England: A History* (Westport and London: Praeger, 2007); Davidoff and Hall have traced the process of middle-class consolidation in *Family Fortunes*: Leonore Davidoff and Catherine Hall, *Family Fortunes: Men and Women of the English Middle Class, 1780–1850* (London: Hutchinson, 1987).
7. Rosa Mucignat, *Realism and Space in the Novel, 1795–1869* (Farnham: Ashgate, 2013), p. 40.
8. Nicholas Shrimpton, '*Bric-à-Brac* or *Architectonicè*? Fragment and Form in Victorian Literature', in Jonathon Shears and Jen Harrison (eds), *Literary Bric-à-Brac and the Victorians: From Commodities to Oddities* (Farnham: Ashgate, 2013), pp. 17–32.
9. Ermarth, *English Novel*, p. 10.
10. M. M. Bakhtin, 'Forms of Time and the Chronotope in the Novel', in M. M. Bakhtin, *The Dialogic Imagination: Four Essays*, ed. by Michael

Holquist, trans. by Caryl Emerson and Michael Holquist (Austin: University of Texas, 1981), pp. 84–258.

11. H. [Henrietta] Wilson, *Homely Hints from the Fireside*, 2nd edn (Edinburgh: Edmonston and Douglas, 1860), p. 112.
12. Sarah Stickney Ellis, *The Daughters of England: Their Position in Society, Characters and Responsibilities* (London: Fisher, Son, & Co., [n.d]), p. 35.
13. Elizabeth Shove, 'Everyday Practice and the Production and Consumption of Time', in *Time, Consumption and Everyday Life: Practice, Materiality and Culture*, ed. by Elizabeth Shove, Frank Trentmann and Richard Wilk (Oxford and New York: Berg, 2009), pp. 17–33, p. 17, author's emphasis.
14. Emily Brontë, *Wuthering Heights*, ed. by Ian Jack, Introduction and notes by Helen Small (Oxford: Oxford University Press, 2009).
15. Stuart Sherman, *Telling Time: Clocks, Diaries, and the English Diurnal Form, 1660–1785* (Chicago and London: University of Chicago Press, 1996), p. x.
16. Barbara Hutton, *Monday Morning: How to Get Through it. A Collection of Useful Practical Hints on Housekeeping and Household Matters, For Gentlewomen* (London: Groombridge and Sons, [1863], p. 10.
17. Maria Rundell, *A New System of Domestic Cookery*, facsimile of 1816 edn (London: Persephone Books, 2009), p. xii.
18. Parkes, *Domestic Duties*, pp. 354–5.
19. Anne Cobbett, *The English Housekeeper: Or, Manual of Domestic Management* (London: Anne Cobbett, [1835]), p. 85.
20. Hutton, *Monday Morning*, p. 13, author's emphasis.
21. Denis McKail, *Greenery Street* (London: Persephone, 2012).
22. Marshall Berman, *All that is Solid Melts Into Air* (New York: Penguin, 1988), p. 35.
23. John McGowan, 'Modernity and Culture: The Victorians and Cultural Studies', *Nineteenth-Century Contexts*, 22.1 (2000), 21–50, p. 27.
24. Trish Ferguson (ed.), *Victorian Time: Technologies, Standardizations, Catastrophes* (Basingstoke: Palgrave Macmillan, 2013); Stephen Kern, *The Culture of Time and Space, 1880–1930* (Cambridge, MA: Harvard University Press, 1983); Sue Zemka, *Time and the Moment in Victorian Literature and Society* (Cambridge: Cambridge University Press, 2012); Mary Hammond sees rail travel as a similar 'jolt' to the psyche with consequences for time experience: Mary Hammond, *Reading, Publishing and the Formation of Literary Taste in England, 1880–1914* (Aldershot: Ashgate, 2006).
25. Paul Glennie and Nigel Thrift, *Shaping the Day: A History of Timekeeping in England and Wales 1300–1800* (Oxford: Oxford University Press, 2009), pp. 408–9.
26. Margaret Beetham, *A Magazine of her Own? Domesticity and Desire in the Woman's Magazine, 1800–1914* (London and New York: Routledge, 1996), p. 9; Laurel Brake, *Print in Transition, 1850–1910: Studies in Media and Book History* (Basingstoke and London: Palgrave, 2001); Mark W. Turner, 'Periodical Time in the Nineteenth Century', *Media History*, 8.2 (2002), 183–96.
27. Nick Hopwood, Simon Schaffer and Jim Secord, 'Seriality and Scientific Objects in the Nineteenth Century', *History of Science*, 48.3 (September/December 2010), 251–85, p. 271.
28. E. P. Thompson, 'Time, Work-Discipline and Industrial Capitalism', *Past and Present*, 38 (December 1967), 56–97.

29. Logan, *The Victorian Parlour*, p. 115.
30. Michel Foucault, *Discipline and Punish: The Birth of the Prison*, translated by Alan Sheridan (New York: Vintage, 1995), pp. 215–16.
31. Charles Dickens, *Our Mutual Friend*, edited by Michael Cotsell, Oxford World's Classics (Oxford: Oxford University Press, 2008), pp. 128–9.
32. Hans-Joakim Voth, *Time and Work in England: 1750–1830* (Oxford: Clarendon Press, 2000), pp. 77–82.
33. Elaine Scarry, *Resisting Representation* (New York and Oxford: Oxford University Press, 1994), p. 65.
34. Bakhtin, 'Forms of Time', pp. 247–8.
35. Bakhtin, 'Forms of Time', p. 84.
36. Gaskell, *Wives and Daughters*, p. 224.
37. Nina Auerbach, *Communities of Women: An Idea in Fiction* (Cambridge, MA and London: Harvard University Press, 1978), especially p. 38.
38. Charlotte Brontë, *Shirley*, ed. by Margaret Smith, Herbert Rosengarten, and Janet Gezari (Oxford: Oxford University Press, 2008).
39. Ermarth, *English Novel*, p. 219.
40. Julia Kristeva, 'Women's Time', trans. by Alice Jardine and Harry Blake, *Signs: Journal of Women in Culture and Society*, 7.1 (Fall 1981), pp. 19–20.
41. Kristeva, 'Women's Time', pp. 21, 30–1.
42. Quoted in Henry Halliday Sparling, *The Kelmscott Press and William Morris, Master-Craftsman* (London: Macmillan and Co., 1924), p. 14.
43. Rachel Bowlby, 'Foreword', in *A Concise Companion to Realism*, ed. by Matthew Beaumont (Chichester: Wiley-Blackwell, 2010), pp. xiv–xxii, p. xviii.
44. Caroline Levine, *Forms: Whole, Rhythm, Hierarchy, Network* (Princeton and Oxford: Princeton University Press, 2015), p. 6.
45. Recent scholarship has worked to rectify this silence: see for example Moira Donald, 'Tranquil Havens? Critiquing the Idea of Home as the Middle-Class Sanctuary', in *Domestic Space: Reading the Nineteenth-Century Interior*, ed. by Inga Bryden and Janet Floyd (Manchester and New York: Manchester University Press, 1999), pp. 103–20; Elizabeth Langland, *Nobody's Angels*; Alison Light, *Mrs Woolf and the Servants* (London: Penguin Fig Tree, 2007); Leah Price, *How to Do Things with Books in Victorian Britain* (Princeton and Oxford: Princeton University Press, 2012), pp. 176, 199–202; and Carolyn Steedman, *Labours Lost: Domestic Service and the Making of Modern England* (Cambridge: Cambridge University Press, 2009).
46. Bruce Robbins, *The Servant's Hand: English Fiction from Below* (New York: Columbia University Press, 1986), p. 27.
47. Cobbett, *The English Housekeeper*, pp. 15–16, author's emphasis.
48. The only diary from a nineteenth-century maid-of-all-work, by Hannah Cullwick, was written for the eyes of her employer who was also secretly her husband. While that still makes Cullwick's diary a valuable text, it does change its status as a record of servant experience.

1 Repetition: Making Domestic Time in *Bleak House* and the 'Bleak House Advertiser'

1. Charles Dickens, *Bleak House*, ed. by Stephen Gill, Oxford World's Classics (London and Oxford: Oxford University Press, 2008), p. 408.

2. Dickens, *Bleak House*, p. 511. All further references will be given in brackets in the text.
3. Henry Lefebvre, *Rhythmanalysis: Space, Time and Everyday Life*, trans. by Stuart Elden and Gerald Moore (London and New York: Continuum, 2004), p. 6.
4. See Elizabeth A. Campbell, *Fortune's Wheel: Dickens and the Iconography of Women's Time* (Athens: Ohio University Press, 2003), p. xx.
5. Charles Dickens, 'A Preliminary Word', *Household Words*, Saturday 30 March 1850, p. 1.
6. Matthew Rubery, '*Bleak House* in Real Time', *English Language Notes*, 46.1 (Spring-Summer 2008), 113–18.
7. Laurel Brake, *Print in Transition, 1850–1910: Studies in Media and Book History* (Basingstoke and London: Palgrave, 2001), p. 30.
8. Gérard Genette, *Narrative Discourse* (Oxford: Basil Blackwell, 1986), p. 116.
9. Susan Stewart, *On Longing: Narratives of the Miniature, the Gigantic, the Souvenir, the Collection* (Durham and London: Duke University Press, 1993), p. 14.
10. Caroline Levine and Mario Ortiz-Robles, 'Introduction', in *Narrative Middles: Navigating the Nineteenth-Century British Novel*, ed. by Caroline Levine and Mario Ortiz-Robles (Columbus: Ohio State University, 2011), pp. 1–21, pp. 12–13.
11. I am grateful to Mary L. Shannon for pointing this out to me.
12. James Buzard, *Disorienting Fiction: The Autoethnographic Work of Nineteenth-Century British Novels* (Princeton and Woodstock: Princeton University Press, 2005), p. 109.
13. Alison Light, *Mrs Woolf and the Servants* (London: Penguin Fig Tree, 2007), p. 24.
14. D. A. Miller, *The Novel and the Police* (Berkeley, Los Angeles and London: University of California Press, 1988), p. 104.
15. Miller, *The Novel and the Police*, p. 102.
16. Emily Steinlight, '"Anti-Bleak House": Advertising and the Victorian Novel', *Narrative*, 14.2 (2006), 132–62, p. 138.
17. Dakin and Company, Advertisement, 'Bleak House Advertiser', 6 (August 1852), p. 1.
18. Dakin and Company, Advertisement, 'Bleak House Advertiser', 3 (May 1852), p. 1.
19. See Steinlight's discussion of this advertisement. Steinlight, '"Anti-Bleak House"', especially pp. 144–5.
20. Gerard Curtis, *Visual Words: Art and the Material Book in Victorian England* (Aldershot: Ashgate, 2002), p. 112.
21. Michael Slater points out that for the middle novels, *Bleak House, Little Dorrit* and *A Tale of Two Cities*, Chapman and Hall actually used blue-green rather than green covers. They returned to the green colour with *Our Mutual Friend*. Michael Slater, *Charles Dickens* (New Haven and London: Yale University Press, 2009), p. 526.
22. Andrew Williams, '*Bleak House* and the Culture of Advertising', in *Approaches to Teaching Dickens's* Bleak House, ed. by John O. Jordan and George Bigelow (New York: Modern Language Association of America, 2008), pp. 45–50, p. 48.
23. Salt & Co., Advertisement, 'Bleak House Advertiser', 7 (September 1852), p. 7.

24. See, for instance Steinlight, '"Anti-Bleak House"'; also Sara Thornton, *Advertising, Subjectivity and the Nineteenth-Century Novel: Dickens, Balzac and the Language of the Walls* (London and New York: Palgrave Macmillan, 2009).
25. E. Moses & Son, Advertisement, 'Bleak House Advertiser', 1 (March 1852), back inside cover.
26. Thos. Harris & Son, Advertisement, 'Bleak House Advertiser', 14 (April 1853), p. 15.
27. Curtis, *Visual Words*, note 35 to page 115.
28. Kevis Goodman, *Georgic Modernity and British Romanticism: Poetry and the Mediation of History* (Cambridge: Cambridge University Press, 2004), p. 72.
29. Karen Chase and Michael Levenson, *The Spectacle of Intimacy: A Public Life for the Victorian Family* (Princeton and Oxford: Princeton University Press, 2000), p. 217.
30. Charles Dickens, *Our Mutual Friend*, edited by Michael Cotsell, Oxford World's Classics (Oxford: Oxford University Press, 2008), p. 452.

2 Interruption: The Periodical Press and the Drive for Realism

1. M. B. H., *Home Truths for Home Peace: Or, Muddle Defeated: A Practical Inquiry into what Chiefly Mars or Makes the Comfort of Domestic Life. Especially Addressed to Young Housewives* (London: Effingham Wilson, 1851), pp. 83–4, author's emphases.
2. John Stuart Mill, *The Subjection of Women*, 2nd edn (London: Longmans, Green, Reader, and Dyer, 1869), p. 137.
3. Mill, *The Subjection of Women*, pp. 138–9.
4. Mary Poovey, 'Introduction', in Florence Nightingale, *Cassandra and Other Selections from Suggestions for Thought*, ed. by Mary Poovey (London: Pickering and Chatto, 1991), pp. vii–xxix, p. viii.
5. Florence Nightingale, *Cassandra and Other Selections from Suggestions for Thought*, ed. by Mary Poovey (London: Pickering and Chatto, 1991), p. 70.
6. Linda K. Hughes, '*SIDEWAYS!*: Navigating the Material(ity) of Print Culture', *Victorian Periodicals Review*, 47.1 (Spring 2014), 1–30.
7. George Eliot, *Felix Holt, the Radical*, ed. by Lynda Mugglestone (London: Penguin, 1995), p. 472.
8. Elizabeth Gaskell, *The Letters of Mrs. Gaskell*, ed. by J. A. V. Chapple and Arthur Pollard (Manchester: Manchester University Press, 1966), letter no. 175, p. 261.
9. Frank Trentman, 'Disruption is Normal: Blackouts, Breakdowns and the Elasticity of Everyday Life', in *Time, Consumption and Everyday Life*, ed. by Elizabeth Shove, Frank Trentman and Richard Wilk (Oxford and New York: Berg, 2009), pp. 67–84, p. 69.
10. Mary A. Favret, *War at a Distance: Romanticism and the Making of Modern Wartime* (Princeton and Oxford: Princeton University Press, 2010), pp. 19–20.
11. Dinah Mulock Craik, *Olive*, new edn (London: Chapman and Hall, [1877]), p. 37.
12. Sarah Stickney Ellis, *The Women of England: Their Social Duties, and Domestic Habits* (London and Paris: Fisher, Son, & Co., 1839), p. 212.

13. 'Hints About Timethrift', *Leisure Hour*, 8 April 1852, pp. 237–8, p. 237.
14. 'Hints About Timethrift', author's emphasis.
15. 'Hints About Timethrift', author's emphasis.
16. 'Hints About Timethrift', pp. 237–8.
17. Anna Ritchie is not to be confused with Anne Thackeray Ritchie, daughter of the novelist W. M. Thackeray. The article was almost certainly written by Anna Cora Mowatt Ritchie, an American writer, playwright, and former actress, who had a number of articles published in *Reynold's* and in the magazine *Bow Bells*.
18. Anna Ritchie, 'Spare Moments', *Reynold's Miscellany of Romance, General Literature, Science, and Art*, 17 December 1859, p. 398, author's emphasis.
19. Roland Barthes, 'The Reality Effect', in Roland Barthes, *The Rustle of Language*, trans. by Richard Howard (Berkeley and Los Angeles: University of California Press, 1989), pp. 141–8, p. 146, author's emphasis.
20. Elizabeth Deeds Ermarth, *Realism and Consensus in the English Novel* (Princeton: Princeton University Press, 1983), p. 16.
21. Ermarth, *Realism and Consensus*, p. 18.
22. Ermarth, *Realism and Consensus*, p. 42.
23. Caroline Levine, *The Serious Pleasures of Suspense: Victorian Realism and Narrative Doubt* (Charlottesville and London: University of Virginia Press, 2003), pp. 13, 24, 25.
24. Eliot, *Felix Holt*, p. 251.
25. 'Economy of Dress', *Englishwoman's Domestic Magazine*, July 1859, p. 94.
26. 'Economy of Dress', *Englishwoman's Domestic Magazine*, May 1859, p. 28, author's emphasis.
27. Talia Schaffer, *Novel Craft: Victorian Domestic Handicraft and Nineteenth-Century Fiction* (Oxford: Oxford University Press, 2011), pp. 36, 42–3.
28. Elizabeth Gaskell, *Wives and Daughters*, ed. by Pam Morris (London: Penguin, 2003), p. 64.
29. Mrs William [Frances] Parkes, *Domestic Duties* (London: Longman, Hurst, Rees, Orme, Brown, and Green, 1825), p. 366.
30. Sarah Stickney Ellis, *The Daughters of England: Their Position in Society, Characters and Responsibilities* (London: Fisher, Son, & Co., [1842]), p. 51.
31. For a discussion of gender and the periodical, see Laurel Brake, *Subjugated Knowledges: Journalism, Gender and Literature in the Nineteenth Century* (Basingstoke and London: Macmillan, 1994); Kate Flint, *The Woman Reader, 1837–1914* (Oxford: Clarendon Press, 1993) – especially p. 11, although Flint's book is about the reading of fiction, and not periodicals; Jennifer Phegley, *Educating the Proper Woman Reader: Victorian Family Literary Magazines and the Cultural Health of the Nation* (Columbus: Ohio State University Press, 2004), pp. 9–11.
32. Schaffer, *Novel Craft*, pp. 21–7.
33. 'A Whisper to our Elder Daughters: By a Maiden Lady', *British Mothers' Journal*, April 1858, pp. 87–9, p. 89.
34. Dinah Mulock Craik, *A Woman's Thoughts about Women* (London: Hurst and Blackett, 1858), p. 10.
35. Eliot, *Felix Holt*, p. 92.
36. Kristie M. Allen, 'Habit in George Eliot's *The Mill on the Floss*', *SEL: Studies in English Literature 1500–1900*, 50.4 (Autumn 2010), 831–52, p. 832.

37. Parkes, *Domestic Duties*, p. 357.
38. Amanda Vickery, *Behind Closed Doors: At Home in Georgian England* (New Haven and London: Yale University Press, 2009), pp. 120–2.
39. 'Economy of Dress', July 1859, p. 94.
40. For the debate about impoverished needlewomen, see Lynn M. Alexander, *Women, Work, and Representation: Needlewomen in Victorian Art and Literature* (Athens: Ohio University Press, 2003); Beth Harris (ed.), *Famine and Fashion: Needlewomen in the Nineteenth Century* (Aldershot: Ashgate, 2005).
41. H. Wilson, *Homely Hints from the Fireside*, 2nd edn (Edinburgh: Edmonston and Douglas, 1860), p. 122.
42. Wilson, *Homely Hints*, p. 123.
43. 'Plain-Work', *Chambers's Journal*, 16 December 1865, pp. 795–8, p. 795.
44. 'Plain-Work', p. 796.
45. 'Plain-Work', p. 797.
46. '"Duty First and Pleasure Afterwards": A Chapter for our Daughters', *British Mothers' Journal*, May 1858, pp. 102–6, p. 102.
47. '"Duty First and Pleasure Afterwards"', p. 103.
48. '"Duty First and Pleasure Afterwards"', p. 104.
49. '"Duty First and Pleasure Afterwards"', p. 105.
50. 'The Widow Wallace and her Five Daughters', *Mrs Ellis's Morning Call*, volume I (1850), pp. 286–8.
51. Emily Shore, *Journal of Emily Shore* (London: Kegan Paul, Trench, Trübner & Co., 1891), p. 353.

3 Division into Parts: Elizabeth Gaskell's North and South and the Serial Instalment

1. Elizabeth Gaskell, *North and South*, ed. by Patricia Ingham (London: Penguin, 2003), p. 21. I have chosen a modern edition for ease of reference, but the text I will be discussing is the first (serial) edition in *Household Words*, which lacks some chapters as well as any chapter titles and epigraphs. All further references appear in parentheses.
2. I use the word 'meantime' as suggested by Mary A. Favret in *War at a Distance: Romanticism and the Making of Modern Wartime* (Princeton and Oxford: Princeton University Press, 2010). I will discuss it in more detail below.
3. See, for example, Catherine Gallagher, *The Industrial Reformation of English Fiction: Social Discourse and Narrative Form, 1832–1867* (Chicago: Chicago University Press, 1987), which sees social problem novels, including *North and South*, as crystallizations of social debate. Recent studies which have focused on the influence of the Crimean War are Alan Shelston, 'Elizabeth Gaskell and the Crimean War', *Gaskell Journal*, 23 (2009), 54–63; and Stefanie Markovits, *The Crimean War in the British Imagination* (Cambridge: Cambridge University Press, 2009).
4. Favret, *War at a Distance*, pp. 4, 14, 18.
5. Favret, *War at a Distance*, pp. 11, 70, 20.
6. Nils Clausson correctly identifies *North and South* as an experimental novel, but in the course of his Proppian analysis, he characterizes its lack

of unequivocal genre beloning is a 'flaw'. I am more inclines to see genre mutability as a positive trait. Nils Clausson, 'Romancing Manchester: Class, Gender, and the Conflicting Genres of Elizabeth Gaskell's *North and South* in *The Gaskell Society Journal*, volume 21 (2007) pp. 1–20, p. 18.

7. John Frow, *Genre* (London and New York: Routledge, 2006), p. 28.
8. Linda K. Hughes and Michael Lund, 'Becoming Mrs Gaskell', *Gaskell Society Journal*, 14 (2000), 24–34, pp. 24–5. See also Deirdre d'Albertis, *Dissembling Fictions: Elizabeth Gaskell and the Victorian Social Text* (Basingstoke and London: Macmillan, 1997), p. 7.
9. Jill L. Matus, '*Mary Barton* and *North and South*', in *The Cambridge Companion to Elizabeth Gaskell*, ed. by Jill. L. Matus (Cambridge: Cambridge University Press, 2007), pp. 27–45, p. 35.
10. Hughes and Lund, 'Becoming Mrs Gaskell', p. 26; Terence Wright, *Elizabeth Gaskell: 'We are Not Angels': Realism, Gender, Values* (Basingstoke and London: Macmillan, 1995), 103.
11. Henri Lefebvre, *Rhythmanalysis: Space, Time and Everyday Life*, trans. by Stuart Elden and Gerald Moore (London and New York: Continuum, 2004), p. 9, emphasis in original.
12. Lefebvre, *Rhythmanalysis*, p. 43.
13. See Jenny Uglow, *Elizabeth Gaskell: A Habit of Stories* (London: Faber and Faber, 1993), pp. 343–5.
14. 'To Working Men', *Household Words*, 7 October 1854, pp. 169–70.
15. Cf. Lorna Huett, 'Among the Unknown Public: *Household Words*, *All the Year Round* and the Mass-Market Weekly Periodical in the Mid-Nineteenth Century', *Victorian Periodicals Review*, 38.1 (Spring 2005), 61–82.
16. I am indebted to Fran Baker of the John Rylands Library, Manchester University, for this point.
17. Uglow, *Elizabeth Gaskell*, p. 361.
18. Margaret Beetham, *A Magazine of her Own? Domesticity and Desire in the Woman's Magazine, 1800–1914* (London and New York: Routledge, 1996), p. 14.
19. James Mussell, *The Nineteenth-Century Press in the Digital Age* (Basingstoke: Palgrave Macmillan, 2012), p. 30.
20. An example of overenthusiastic analogy is to my mind Linda K. Hughes and Michael Lund, *Victorian Publishing and Mrs. Gaskell's Work* (Charlottesville and London: University Press of Virginia, 1999), in which (assumptions about) female sexual pleasure, the serial's more 'intimate' and 'interruptible' qualities, and finally the monthly format's analogy to menstruation, all coalesce to make the authors pronounce the serial form 'attuned to female experiences' (99, 105, 106–7). See also their article: Linda K. Hughes and Michael Lund, 'Textual/Sexual Pleasure and Serial Publication', in *Literature in the Marketplace: Nineteenth-Century British Publishing and Reading Practices*, ed. by John O. Jordan and Robert L. Patten (Cambridge: Cambridge University Press, 1995), pp. 143–64.
21. Charles Dickens, *The Letters of Charles Dickens: Volume 7: 1853–1855*, ed. by Graham Storey, Kathleen Tillotson and Angus Easson (Oxford: Oxford University Press, 1993), p. 278: To Mrs Gaskell, 18 February 1854.
22. Dickens, *Letters*, p. 355: To Mrs Gaskell, [15] and 17 June 1854.

23. Dorothy Collins, 'The Composition of Mrs. Gaskell's *North and South*', in Elizabeth Gaskell, *North and South*, ed. by Alan Shelston, Norton Critical Edition (New York and London: Norton, 2005), pp. 519–22, p. 519.
24. Collins, 'Composition', p. 520.
25. Collins, 'Composition'.
26. Collins, 'Composition', pp. 520, 521.
27. Dickens, *Letters*, p. 355: To W. H. Wills, 19 August 1854.
28. Dickens, *Letters*, p. 439: To W. H. Wills, 14 October 1854.
29. For Gaskell falling behind, see Dickens, *Letters*, p. 394: To W. H. Wills, 9 August 1854; For Dickens's concerns about Gaskell overrunning, see Dickens, *Letters*, p. 403: To W. H. Wills, 20 August 1854; For his concerns about Mr Hale's doubts, see Dickens, *Letters*, p. 402: To Mrs Gaskell, 20 August 1854.
30. J. Don Vann, 'Dickens, Charles Lever, and Mrs. Gaskell', *Victorian Periodicals Review*, 22.2 (Summer 1989), 64–71, p. 70.
31. Quoted in Vann, 'Dickens, Charles Lever', p. 70.
32. Dickens, *Letters*, p. 406: To W. H. Wills, 24 August 1854, my emphasis.
33. Jerome Meckier, 'Parodic Prolongation in *North and South*: Elizabeth Gaskell Revaluates Dickens's Suspenseful Delays', *Dickens Quarterly*, 23.4 (December 2006), 217–28, p. 221. Meckier even suggests that the reason Gaskell and Dickens fell out was the Dickens detected this parody: 'Dickens may have been offended by the anti-Dickensian way *North and South* goes on, not by elongation per se'. Ibid., p. 220.
34. Coral Lansbury, *Elizabeth Gaskell: The Novel of Social Crisis* (London: Elek, 1975), p. 97.
35. Lansbury makes a similar point: Lansbury, *Elizabeth Gaskell*, p. 99.
36. Matus, '*Mary Barton* and *North and South*', p. 38.
37. Alan Shelston, 'Elizabeth Gaskell and the Sense of the New', in *Elizabeth Gaskell: Text and Context*, ed. by Francesco Marroni and Alan Shelston (Pescara: Edizioni Tracce, 1999), pp. 11–38, p. 17.
38. Elizabeth Starr, '"A Great Engine for Good": The Industrial Fiction in Elizabeth Gaskell's *Mary Barton* and *North and South*', *Studies in the Novel*, 34.4 (Winter 2002), 385–402, p. 396.
39. Günther Müller, *Morphologische Poetic: Gesammelte Aufsätze*, ed. by Elena Müller (Tübingen: Max Niemeyer Verlag, 1974).
40. For the cultural background to Margaret's role as 'female visitor' to the poor, see Dorice Williams Elliott, 'The Female Visitor and the Marriage of Classes in Gaskell's *North and South*', *Nineteenth-Century Literature*, 49.1 (June 1994), 21–49. See also d'Albertis, *Dissembling Fictions*, especially pp. 62-71.
41. Uglow, *Elizabeth Gaskell*, pp. 5–7.
42. Lansbury, *Elizabeth Gaskell*, pp. 13–15.
43. Uglow, *Elizabeth Gaskell*, p. 6.
44. See Elizabeth Langland on *Cranford* and the semiotics of respectability in *Nobody's Angels: Middle-Class Women and Domestic Ideology in Victorian Culture* (Ithaca and London: Cornell University Press, 1995), pp. 121–30.
45. Uglow, *Elizabeth Gaskell*, pp. 362–5.
46. Shelston, 'Elizabeth Gaskell and the Crimean War', p. 56.
47. Markovits, *Crimean War*, p. 88.
48. Markovits, *Crimean War*, p. 95.

49. Elizabeth Gaskell, *The Letters of Mrs. Gaskell*, ed. by J. A. V. Chapple and Arthur Pollard (Manchester: Manchester University Press, 1966), no. 211 (11–14 October 1854), pp. 305–10, p. 306.
50. Gaskell, *Letters*, no. 217 (27 October 1854), pp. 316–21, p. 317, Gaskell's emphasis.
51. Gaskell, *Letters*, p. 320, Gaskell's emphasis.
52. Shelston, 'Elizabeth Gaskell and the Crimean War', p. 59.
53. See Elliott, 'Female Visitor', especially pp. 44–9; and d'Albertis, *Dissembling Fictions*, especially pp. 69–71.
54. 'A Home Question', *Household Words*, 11 November 1854, pp. 292–6.

4 Decomposition: Mrs Beeton and the Non-Linear Text

1. Isabella Beeton, *Beeton's Book of Household Management, Edited by Mrs Isabella Beeton* (London: S. O. Beeton, 1859–62), 2 (December 1859), p. 96.
2. Isabella Beeton, *Beeton's Book of Household Management*, 3 (January 1860), p. 97.
3. On the significance of Charles Knight's many publishing ventures, see Valerie Gray, *Charles Knight: Educator, Publisher, Writer* (Aldershot: Ashgate, 2006). For the serial publication of science, see Nick Hopwood, Simon Schaffer and Jim Secord, 'Seriality and Scientific Objects in the Nineteenth Century', *History of Science*, 48.3 (September/December 2010), 251–85.
4. Mark W. Turner, 'The Unruliness of Serials in the Nineteenth Century (and in the Digital Age)' in *Serialization in Popular Culture*, ed. by Rob Allen and Thijs van den Berg (New York: Routledge), 2014, pp. 11–32.
5. Dena Attar, *A Bibliography of Household Books Published in Britain 1800–1914* (London: Prospect, 1987), p. 12.
6. For a discussing of Beeton's confident tone, see Kathryn Hughes, *The Short Life and Long Times of Mrs Beeton* (London: Harper, 2006), p. 205. For the publishing schemes, see Margaret Beetham, 'Of Recipe Books and Reading in the Nineteenth Century: Mrs Beeton and her Cultural Consequences', in *The Recipe Reader: Narratives – Contexts – Traditions*, ed. by Janet Floyd and Laurel Forster (Aldershot: Ashgate, 2003), pp. 15–30, p. 16. For the scope and breath of the book, see James Buzard, 'Home Ec. with Mrs. Beeton', *Raritan*, 17.2 (September 1997), 121–35, pp. 123–6.
7. Eliza Acton, *Modern Cookery, in all its Branches: Reduced to a System of Easy Practice, for the Use of Private Families, in a Series of Practical Receipts, which have been Strictly Tested, and are Given with the most Exact Minuteness* (London: Longman, Brown, Green and Longmans, 1845).
8. Andrea Broomfield, *Food and Cooking in Victorian England: A History* (Westport and London: Praeger, 2007), p. 40.
9. Robert Kemp Philp, *Enquire Within: A Work of Practical Instruction Upon Literally Everything that a Housekeeper Ought to Know, for the Use or Ornament of a Home, and the Health and Comfort of its Occupants* (London: Houlston and Stoneman, [1855–56]).
10. Attar, *Bibliography*, p. 177.
11. Hughes, *Short Life and Long Times*, pp. 198, 217.
12. Hughes, *Short Life and Long Times*, p. 188.

13. Laurel Brake, *Print in Transition, 1850–1910: Studies in Media and Book History* (Basingstoke and London: Palgrave, 2001), p. 30.
14. D. F. McKenzie, *Bibliography and the Sociology of Texts* (London: British Library, 1986).
15. Michael Warner, 'Publics and Counterpublics', *Public Culture*, 14.1 (Winter 2002), 49–90.
16. Quoted in Nicola Humble, *Culinary Pleasures: Cook Books and the Transformation of British Food* (London: Faber and Faber, 2005), pp. 9–10.
17. Samuel O. Beeton and John Sherer (eds), *Beeton's Dictionary of Universal Information* (London: S. O. Beeton, 1858–62).
18. Because of access issues, I have used a facsimile of the 1861 volume edition for reference. The actual text is identical, as the serial and volume editions were set from the same block; only in its title does the Cassell edition deviate from the first edition, preferring the later '*Mrs Beeton's Book*' rather than the earlier version, '*Beeton's Book*'. Isabella Beeton, *Mrs Beeton's Book of Household Management*, facsimile of the 1st edn (London: Cassell, 2000), pp. 4–5. All further references in brackets in the text.
19. For a superlative account of the afterlife of the *Book of Household Management*, see Margaret Beetham, 'Of Recipe Books and Reading', particularly p. 16.
20. Brake, *Print in Transition*, p. 31, author's emphasis.
21. Annette Cozzi, *The Discourses of Food in Nineteenth-Century British Fiction* (New York and Basingstoke: Palgrave Macmillan, 2010), p. 83; Nicola Humble does in fact acknowledge this. Humble, 'Introduction', in *Mrs Beeton's Book of Household Management*, ed. by Nicola Humble, Oxford World's Classics (Oxford: Oxford University Press, 2000), pp. vii–xxx, p. xvii.
22. For more on this debate, see Kathryn Hughes, *Short Life and Long Times*, especially p. 218.
23. Beetham, 'Of Recipe Books and Reading', p. 21.
24. Louis Eustache Ude, *The French Cook: A System of Fashionable, Practical and Economical Cookery, Adapted to the Use of English Families*, 14th edn (London: Ebers and Co., 1841), pp. xli, xlii.
25. Kathryn Hughes, *Short Life and Long Times*, p. 222.
26. Robert Kemp Philp, *The Practical Housewife: By the Editors of the Family Friend* (London: Ward and Lock [1855]), p. 13.
27. Anne Cobbett, *The English Housekeeper: or, Manual of Domestic Management* (London: Anne Cobbett, [1835], p. 35.
28. Maria Rundell, *A New System of Domestic Cookery*, facsimile of 1816 edn (London: Persephone Books, 2009), p. xiv.
29. Alison Light, *Woolf and the Servants* (London: Penguin Fig Tree, 2007), p. 282.
30. Beetham, 'Of Recipe Books and Reading', p. 21.
31. Philp, *Practical Housewife*, p. 15.
32. Michel Foucault calls it 'the temporal elaboration of the act' which organizes the act into controlled successive stages, allowing complete control of the subordinate's body. Michel Foucault, *Discipline and Punish: The Birth of the Prison*, trans. by Alan Sheridan (New York: Vintage, 1995), pp. 151–2.
33. London, Sambourne Family Archive, Leighton House, MS ST/2/5/10.
34. Mrs G. W. M. [Susannah Frances] Reynolds and William E. Hall, *The Household Book of Practical Receipts, in the Arts, Manufactures, and Trades, Including Medicine, Pharmacy, and Domestic Economy. Illustrated with Diagrams*

(London and Paris: Printed for the proprietor, by John Dicks, at the office of Reynold's Miscellany, 1847).
35. Alexis Soyer, *The Modern Housewife or Ménagère*, 2nd edn (London: Simpkin, Marshall, & Co., 1849).
36. Kathryn Hughes, *Short Life and Long Times*, p. 189.
37. Cobbett, *English Housekeeper*, p. 33.
38. Leah Price, *The Anthology and the Rise of the Novel from Richardson to George Eliot* (Cambridge: Cambridge University Press, 2000).
39. Janet Morgan, 'Preface,' in Maria Rundell, *A New System of Domestic Cookery*, facsimile of 1816 edn (London: Persephone Books, 2009), pp. v–xix, p. vii.
40. Andrea K. Newlyn, 'Redefining "Rudimentary" Narrative: Women's Nineteenth-Century Manuscript Cookbooks', in *The Recipe Reader*, ed. by Floyd and Forster, pp. 31–51, p. 38.
41. Cobbett, *English Housekeeper*, p. 51.
42. Ellen Gruber Garvey, 'The Power of Recirculation: Scrapbooks and the Reception of the Nineteenth-Century Press', in *New Directions in American Reception Study*, ed. by Philip Goldstein and James L. Machor (Oxford: Oxford University Press, 2008), pp. 211–31, pp. 212, 213.
43. Garvey, 'Power of Recirculation', p. 219.
44. The incomplete copy of the *Book of Household Management* serial held by the Bodleian Library is put together of parts from both serials.

Coda: Scrapbooking and the Reconfiguration of Domestic Time

1. Nick Hopwood, Simon Schaffer and Jim Secord, 'Seriality and Scientific Objects in the Nineteenth Century', *History of Science*, 48.3 (September/December 2010), 251–85, p. 261.
2. Manchester Metropolitan University Special Collections, MS Page 144, p. 169.
3. Claire Farago, '"Scraps as it were": Binding Memories', *Journal of Victorian Culture*, 10.1 (Spring 2005), 114–22, pp. 114, 116.
4. Katherine Ott, Susan Tucker and Patricia P. Buckler, 'An Introduction to the History of Scrapbooks', in *The Scrapbook in American Life*, ed. by Susan Tucker, Katherine Ott and Patricia P. Buckler (Philadelphia: Temple University Press, 2006), pp. 1–25, pp. 2–3, 16.
5. Peter Fritzsche, *Stranded in the Present: Modern Time and the Melancholy of History* (Cambridge, MA and London: Harvard University Press, 2004), pp. 195, 198.
6. Samantha Matthews, '"O All Pervading Album!": Place and Displacement in Romantic Albums and Album Poetry', in *Romantic Localities: Europe Writes Place*, ed. by Christoph Bode and Jacqueline Labbe (London: Pickering & Chatto, 2010), pp. 99–116, p. 104.
7. Rebecca Steinitz, *Time, Space, and Gender in the Nineteenth-Century British Diary* (New York: Palgrave Macmillan, 2011), pp. 17–18.
8. Steinitz, *Time, Space, and Gender*, p. 23.
9. Steinitz, *Time, Space, and Gender*, p. 24.
10. Steinitz, *Time, Space, and Gender*, p. 28.

11. MS Page 166, for example, pp. 8 and 128.
12. Patrizia di Bello, 'Mrs Birkbeck's Album: the Hand-Written and the Printed in Early Nineteenth-Century Feminine Culture', *19: Interdisciplinary Studies in the Long Nineteenth Century*, 1 (2005), 13.
13. MS Page 56.
14. Raymond Williams, *Marxism and Literature* (Oxford: Oxford University Press, 1977), pp. 121–7.
15. Williams, *Marxism and Literature*, p. 123.
16. Patrizia di Bello, *Women's Albums and Photography in Victorian England: Ladies, Mothers and Flirts* (Aldershot: Ashgate, 2007), pp. 25, 151–3.
17. MS Page 178.
18. 'To the Editor of the *Monthly Magazine* [A Chinese in England]', *Monthly Magazine, or British Register*, vol. XIX, part 1, p. 139.
19. MS Page 144, p. 134.
20. For example, in an album by Kate Aspinall, MS Page 74.
21. 'Travels and Acquisitions in Mexico; By Mr. Bullock', *Literary Gazette*, 10 January 1824, pp. 25–6.
22. 'Ruined Cities in Central America and Mexico', *Saturday Magazine*, 28 August 1842, pp. 81–8; 'Ruined Cities in Central America and Mexico II', *Saturday Magazine*, 30 October 1842, pp. 169–76.
23. J. Doran, 'Memoranda on Mexico', *Gentleman's Magazine and Historical Review*, December 1853, pp. 547–55, p. 554.
24. Caroline Levine, 'The Shock of the Banal: *The Wire*, *Mad Men*, and Victorian Realism', unpublished conference paper, 2011.
25. MS Page 186.
26. Cf. Brian Maidment, *Comedy, Caricature and the Social Order, 1820–50* (Manchester: Manchester University Press, 2013), p. 78.
27. Ellen Gruber Garvey, 'Scissorizing and Scrapbooks: Nineteenth-Century Reading, Remaking, and Recirculating', in *New Media, 1740–1915*, ed. by Lisa Gitelman and Geoffrey B. Pingree (Cambridge, MA and London: MIT Press, 2003), pp. 207–27, p. 214, author's emphasis.
28. Maidment, *Comedy, Caricature*, pp. 78–86.
29. MS Page 144, p. 116.
30. MS Page 103.

Bibliography

Unpublished sources

London, Sambourne Family Archive, Leighton House, MS ST/2/5/10 22
Manchester, Manchester Metropolitan University Special Collections, MS Page 56
Manchester, Manchester Metropolitan University Special Collections, MS Page 74
Manchester, Manchester Metropolitan University Special Collections, MS Page 103
Manchester, Manchester Metropolitan University Special Collections, MS Page 144
Manchester, Manchester Metropolitan University Special Collections, MS Page 166
Manchester, Manchester Metropolitan University Special Collections, MS Page 178
Manchester, Manchester Metropolitan University Special Collections, MS Page 186

Primary sources

'A Home Question', *Household Words*, 11 November 1854, pp. 292–6
'"Duty First and Pleasure Afterwards": A Chapter for our Daughters', *British Mothers' Journal*, May 1858, pp. 102–6
'Economy of Dress', *Englishwoman's Domestic Magazine*, May 1859, p. 28
'Economy of Dress', *Englishwoman's Domestic Magazine*, July 1859, p. 94
'Hints About Timethrift', *Leisure Hour*, 8 April 1852, pp. 237–8
'Plain-Work', *Chambers's Journal*, 16 December 1865, pp. 795–8
'Ruined Cities in Central America and Mexico', *Saturday Magazine*, 28 August 1842, pp. 81–8
'Ruined Cities in Central America and Mexico II', *Saturday Magazine*, 30 October 1842, pp. 169–76
'To the Editor of the *Monthly Magazine* [A Chinese in England]', *Monthly Magazine, or British Register*, 1 March 1805, p. 139
'To Working Men', *Household Words*, 7 October 1854, pp. 169–70
'Travels and Acquisitions in Mexico; By Mr. Bullock', *Literary Gazette*, 10 January 1824, pp. 25–6
'A Whisper to our Elder Daughters: By a Maiden Lady', *British Mothers' Journal*, April 1858, pp. 87–9
'The Widow Wallace and her Five Daughters', *Mrs Ellis's Morning Call*, volume I (1850), pp. 286–8
Acton, Eliza, *Modern Cookery, in all its Branches: Reduced to a System of Easy Practice, for the Use of Private Families, in a Series of Practical Receipts, which have been Strictly Tested, and are Given with the most Exact Minuteness* (London: Longman, Brown, Green and Longmans, 1845)

Beeton, Isabella, *Mrs Beeton's Book of Household Management*, facsimile of the 1st edn (London: Cassell, 2000)

——, *Beeton's Book of Household Management, Edited by Mrs Isabella Beeton*, 24 monthly instalments (London: S. O. Beeton, 1859–61)

Beeton, Samuel Orchard and John Sherer (eds), *Beeton's Dictionary of Universal Information*, 37 monthly instalments (London: S. O. Beeton, 1858–62)

Brontë, Charlotte, *Shirley*, ed. by Margaret Smith, Herbert Rosengarten, and Janet Gezari (Oxford: Oxford University Press, 2008)

Brontë, Emily, *Wuthering Heights*, ed. by Ian Jack, Introduction and notes by Helen Small (Oxford: Oxford University Press, 2009)

Cobbett, Anne, *The English Housekeeper: or, Manual of Domestic Management* (London: Anne Cobbett, [1835])

Craik, Dinah Mulock, *Olive*, new edn (London: Chapman and Hall, [1877])

——, *A Woman's Thoughts about Women* (London: Hurst and Blackett, 1858)

Dakin & Co. Advertisement, 'Bleak House Advertiser', 3 (May 1852), p. 1

——, Advertisement, 'Bleak House Advertiser', 6 (August 1852), p. 1

Dickens, Charles, *Bleak House*, with illustrations by H. K. Browne, 19 monthly instalments (London: Bradbury & Evans, 1852–3)

——, *Bleak House*, edited by Stephen Gill, Oxford World's Classics (London and Oxford: Oxford University Press, 2008)

——, *The Letters of Charles Dickens: Volume 7: 1853–1855*, ed. by Graham Story, Kathleen Tillitson and Angus Easson (Oxford: Oxford University Press, 1993)

——, *Our Mutual Friend*, edited by Michael Cotsell, Oxford World's Classics (Oxford: Oxford University Press, 2008)

——, 'A Preliminary Word', *Household Words*, Saturday 30 March 1850, p. 1

Doran, J., 'Memoranda on Mexico', *Gentleman's Magazine and Historical Review*, Dec. 1853, pp. 547–55

E. Moses & Son, Advertisement, 'Bleak House Advertiser', 1 (March 1852), back inside cover

Eliot, George, *Felix Holt, the Radical*, ed. by Lynda Mugglestone (London: Penguin, 1995)

Ellis, Sarah Stickney, *The Daughters of England: Their Position in Society, Characters and Responsibilities* (London: Fisher, Son, & Co., [n.d.])

——, *The Women of England: Their Social Duties, and Domestic Habits* (London and Paris: Fisher, Son, & Co., 1839)

Garrett, Elizabeth, *Morning Hours in India: Practical Hints on Household Management, the Care and Training of Children, Etc.* (London: Trübner & Co., 1887)

Gaskell, Elizabeth, *The Letters of Mrs. Gaskell*, ed. by J. A. V. Chapple and Arthur Pollard (Manchester: Manchester University Press, 1966)

——, *North and South*, ed. by Patricia Ingham (London: Penguin, 2003)

——, *Wives and Daughters*, edited by Pam Morris (London: Penguin, 2003)

Hutton, Barbara, *Monday Morning: How to Get Through it. A Collection of Useful Practical Hints on Housekeeping and Household Matters, For Gentlewomen* (London: Groombridge and Sons, [1863])

'M. B. H.', *Home Truths for Home Peace, Or, Muddle Defeated: A Practical Inquiry into what Chiefly Mars or Makes the Comfort of Domestic Life. Especially Adressed to Young Housewives* (London: Effingham Wilson, 1851)

McKail, Denis, *Greenery Street* (London: Persephone, 2012)

Mill, John Stuart, *The Subjection of Women*, 2nd edn (London: Longmans, Green, Reader, and Dyer, 1869)

Nightingale, Florence, *Cassandra and Other Selections from Suggestions for Thought*, ed. by Mary Poovey (London: Pickering and Chatto, 1991)

Parkes, Mrs William [Frances], *Domestic Duties: Or, Instructions to Young Married Ladies, on the Management of their Households, and the Regulation of their Conduct in the Various Relations and Duties of Married Life*, 2nd edn (London: Longman, Hurst, Rees, Orme, Brown, and Green, 1825)

Philp, Robert Kemp, *Enquire Within: A Work of Practical Instruction Upon Literally Everything that a Housekeeper Ought to Know, for the Use or Ornament of a Home, and the Health and Comfort of its Occupants* (London: Houlston and Stoneman, [1855–6])

——, *The Practical Housewife: By the Editors of the Family Friend* (London: Ward and Lock, [1855])

Reynolds, Mrs G. W. M. [Susannah Frances] and William E. Hall, *The Household Book of Practical Receipts, in the Arts, Manufactures, and Trades, Including Medicine, Pharmacy, and Domestic Economy. Illustrated with Diagrams* (London and Paris: Printed for the proprietor, by John Dicks, at the office of Reynold's Miscellany, 1847)

Ritchie, Anna, 'Spare Moments', *Reynold's Miscellany of Romance, General Literature, Science, and Art*, 17 December 1859, p. 398

Rundell, Maria, *A New System of Domestic Cookery*, facsimile of 1816 edn (London: Persephone Books, 2009)

Salt & Co., Advertisement, 'Bleak House Advertiser', 7 (September 1852), p. 7

Shore, Emily, *Journal of Emily Shore* (London: Kegan Paul, Tench, Trübner & Co., 1891)

Soyer, Alexis, *The Modern Housewife or Ménagère*, 2nd edn (London: Simpkin, Marshall, & Co., 1849)

Thos. Harris & Son, Advertisement, 'Bleak House Advertiser', 14 (April 1853), p. 15

Ude, Louis Eustache, *The French Cook: A System of Fashionable, Practical and Economical Cookery, Adapted to the Use of English Families*, 14th edn (London: Ebers and Co., 1841)

Wilson, H. [Henrietta], *Homely Hints from the Fireside*, 2nd edn (Edinburgh: Edmonston and Douglas, 1860)

Secondary sources

Alexander, Lynn M., *Women, Work, and Representation: Needlewomen in Victorian Art and Literature* (Athens: Ohio University Press, 2003)

Allen, Kristie M., 'Habit in George Eliot's *The Mill on the Floss*', *SEL: Studies in English Literature 1500–1900*, 50.4 (Autumn 2010), 831–52

Auerbach, Nina, *Communities of Women: An Idea in Fiction* (Cambridge, MA and London: Harvard University Press, 1978)

Attar, Dena, *A Bibliography of Household Books Published in Britain 1800–1914* (London: Prospect, 1987)

Bakhtin, M. M., 'Forms of Time and the Chronotope in the Novel', in M. M. Bakhtin, *The Dialogic Imagination: Four Essays*, ed. by Michael Holquist, trans.

by Caryl Emerson and Michael Holquist (Austin: University of Texas, 1981), pp. 84–258

Barthes, Roland, 'The Reality Effect', in Roland Barthes, *The Rustle of Language*, trans. by Richard Howard (Berkeley and Los Angeles: University of California Press, 1989), pp. 141–8

Beetham, Margaret, *A Magazine of her Own? Domesticity and Desire in the Woman's Magazine, 1800-1914* (London and New York: Routledge, 1996)

——, 'Of Recipe Books and Reading in the Nineteenth Century: Mrs Beeton and her Cultural Consequences', in *The Recipe Reader: Narratives – Contexts – Traditions*, ed. by Janet Floyd and Laurel Forster (Aldershot: Ashgate, 2003), pp. 15–30

Berman, Marshall, *All that is Solid Melts Into Air* (New York: Penguin, 1988)

Bowlby, Rachel, 'Foreword', in *A Concise Companion to Realism*, ed. by Matthew Beaumont (Chichester: Wiley-Blackwell, 2010), pp. xiv–xxii

Brake, Laurel, *Print in Transition, 1850–1910: Studies in Media and Book History* (Basingstoke and London: Palgrave, 2001)

——, *Subjugated Knowledges: Journalism, Gender and Literature in the Nineteenth Century* (Basingstoke and London: Macmillan, 1994)

Broomfield, Andrea, *Food and Cooking in Victorian England: A History* (Westport, CT and London: Praeger, 2007)

Buzard, James, *Disorienting Fiction: The Autoethnographic Work of Nineteenth-Century British Novels* (Princeton, NJ and Woodstock: Princeton University Press, 2005)

——, 'Home Ec. with Mrs. Beeton', *Raritan*, 17.2 (September 1997), 121–35

Campbell, Elizabeth A., *Fortune's Wheel: Dickens and the Iconography of Women's Time* (Athens: Ohio University Press, 2003)

Chase, Karen and Michael Levenson, *The Spectacle of Intimacy: A Public Life for the Victorian Family* (Princeton, NJ and Oxford: Princeton University Press, 2000)

Clausson, Nils, 'Romancing Manchester: Class, Gender, and the Conflicting Genres of Elizabeth Gaskell's *North and South*', *The Gaskell Society Journal*, volume 21 (2007) pp. 1–20

Collins, Dorothy, 'The Composition of Mrs. Gaskell's *North and South*', in Elizabeth Gaskell, *North and South*, ed. by Alan Shelston, Norton Critical Edition (New York and London: Norton, 2005), pp. 519–22

Cozzi, Annette, *The Discourses of Food in Nineteenth-Century British Fiction* (New York and Basingstoke: Palgrave Macmillan, 2010)

Curtis, Gerard, *Visual Words: Art and the Material Book in Victorian England* (Aldershot: Ashgate, 2002)

d'Albertis, Deirdre, *Dissembling Fictions: Elizabeth Gaskell and the Victorian Social Text* (Basingstoke and London: Macmillan, 1997)

Davidoff, Leonore and Catherine Hall, *Family Fortunes: Men and Women of the English Middle Class, 1780–1850* (London: Hutchinson, 1987)

di Bello, Patrizia, 'Mrs Birkbeck's Album: the Hand-Written and the Printed in Early Nineteenth-Century Feminine Culture', *19: Interdisciplinary Studies in the Long Nineteenth Century*, 1 (2005)

——, *Women's Albums and Photography in Victorian England: Ladies, Mothers and Flirts* (Aldershot: Ashgate, 2007)

Dereli, Cynthia, 'Gender Issues and the Crimean War: Creating Roles for Women?', in *Gender Roles and Sexuality in Victorian Literature*, ed. by Christopher Parker (Aldershot: Scolar Press, 1995), pp. 57–82

Donald, Moira, 'Tranquil Havens? Critiquing the Idea of Home as the Middle-Class Sanctuary', in *Domestic Space: Reading the Nineteenth-Century Interior*, ed. by Inga Bryden and Janet Floyd (Manchester and New York: Manchester University Press, 1999), pp. 103–20

Elliott, Dorice Williams, 'The Female Visitor and the Marriage of Classes in Gaskell's *North and South*', *Nineteenth-Century Literature*, 49.1 (June 1994), 21–49

Ermarth, Elizabeth Deeds, *The English Novel in History, 1840–1895* (London and New York: Routledge, 1997)

——, *Realism and Consensus in the English Novel* (Princeton, NJ: Princeton University Press, 1983)

Farago, Claire, '"Scraps as it were": Binding Memories', *Journal of Victorian Culture*, 10.1 (Spring 2005), 114–22

Favret, Mary A., *War at a Distance: Romanticism and the Making of Modern Wartime* (Princeton, NJ and Oxford: Princeton University Press, 2010)

Ferguson, Trish (ed.), *Victorian Time: Technologies, Standardizations, Catastrophes* (Basingstoke: Palgrave, 2013)

Flint, Kate, *The Woman Reader, 1837–1914* (Oxford: Clarendon Press, 1993)

Foucault, Michel, *Discipline and Punish: The Birth of the Prison*, trans. by Alan Sheridan (New York: Vintage, 1995)

Fritzsche, Peter, *Stranded in the Present: Modern Time and the Melancholy of History* (Cambridge, MA and London: Harvard University Press, 2004)

Frow, John, *Genre* (London and New York: Routledge, 2006)

Gallagher, Catherine, *The Industrial Reformation of English Fiction: Social Discourse and Narrative Form, 1832–1867* (Chicago: Chicago University Press, 1987)

Garvey, Ellen Gruber, 'The Power of Recirculation: Scrapbooks and the Reception of the Nineteenth-Century Press', in *New Directions in American Reception Study*, ed. by Philip Goldstein and James L. Machor (Oxford: Oxford University Press, 2008), pp. 211–31

——, 'Scissorizing and Scrapbooks: Nineteenth-Century Reading, Remaking, and Recirculating', in *New Media, 1740–1915*, ed. by Lisa Gitelman and Geoffrey B. Pingree (Cambridge, MA and London: MIT Press, 2003), pp. 207–27

Genette, Gérard, *Narrative Discourse* (Oxford: Basil Blackwell, 1986)

Girouard, Mark, *The Victorian Country House* (New Haven, CT and London: Yale University Press, 1979)

Glennie, Paul and Nigel Thrift, *Shaping the Day: A History of Timekeeping in England and Wales 1300–1800* (Oxford: Oxford University Press, 2009)

Goodman, Kevis, *Georgic Modernity and British Romanticism: Poetry and the Mediation of History* (Cambridge: Cambridge University Press, 2004)

Gray, Valerie, *Charles Knight: Educator, Publisher, Writer* (Aldershot: Ashgate, 2006)

Hammond, Mary, *Reading, Publishing and the Formation of Literary Taste in England, 1880–1914* (Aldershot: Ashgate, 2006)

Harris, Beth, 'Introduction', in *Famine and Fashion: Needlewomen in the Nineteenth Century*, ed. by Beth Harris (Aldershot: Ashgate, 2005), pp. 1–9

Hopwood, Nick, Simon Schaffer and Jim Secord, 'Seriality and Scientific Objects in the Nineteenth Century', *History of Science*, 48.3 (September/December 2010), 251–85

Huett, Lorna, 'Among the Unknown Public: *Household Words, All the Year Round* and the Mass-Market Weekly Periodical in the Mid-Nineteenth Century', *Victorian Periodicals Review*, 38.1 (Spring 2005), 61–82

Hughes, Kathryn, *The Short Life and Long Times of Mrs Beeton* (London: Harper, 2006)

Hughes, Linda K. '*SIDEWAYS!*: Navigating the Material(ity) of Print Culture', *Victorian Periodicals Review*, 47.1 (Spring 2014), 1–30

Hughes, Linda K. and Michael Lund, 'Becoming Mrs Gaskell', *Gaskell Society Journal*, 14 (2000), 24–34

——, 'Textual/Sexual Pleasure and Serial Publication', in *Literature in the Marketplace: Nineteenth-Century British Publishing and Reading Practices*, ed. by John O. Jordan and Robert L. Patten (Cambridge: Cambridge University Press, 1995), pp. 143–64

——, *Victorian Publishing and Mrs. Gaskell's Work* (Charlottesville and London: University Press of Virginia, 1999)

Humble, Nicola, *Culinary Pleasures: Cook Books and the Transformation of British Food* (London: Faber and Faber, 2005)

——, 'Introduction', in *Mrs Beeton's Book of Household Management*, ed. by Nicola Humble, Oxford World's Classics (Oxford: Oxford University Press, 2000), pp. vii–xxx

Kern, Stephen, *The Culture of Time and Space, 1880–1930* (Cambridge, MA: Harvard University Press, 1983)

Kristeva, Julia, 'Women's Time', trans. by Alice Jardine and Harry Blake, *Signs: Journal of Women in Culture and Society*, 7.1 (Fall 1981), 13–35

Langland, Elizabeth, *Nobody's Angels: Middle-Class Women and Domestic Ideology in Victorian Culture* (Ithaca and London: Cornell University Press, 1995)

Lansbury, Coral, *Elizabeth Gaskell: The Novel of Social Crisis* (London: Elek, 1975)

Lefebvre, Henri, *Rhythmanalysis: Space, Time and Everyday Life*, trans. by Stuart Elden and Gerald Moore (London and New York: Continuum, 2004)

Levine, Caroline, *Forms: Whole, Rhythm, Hierarchy, Network* (Princeton, NJ and Oxford: Princeton University Press, 2015)

——, *The Serious Pleasures of Suspense: Victorian Realism and Narrative Doubt* (Charlottesville and London: University of Virginia Press, 2003)

——, 'The Shock of the Banal: *The Wire, Mad Men*, and Victorian Realism', unpublished conference paper, 2011

Levine, Caroline and Mario Ortiz-Robles, 'Introduction', in *Narrative Middles: Navigating the Nineteenth-Century British Novel*, ed. by Caroline Levine and Mario Ortiz-Robles (Columbus: Ohio State University, 2011), pp. 1–21

Light, Alison, *Mrs Woolf and the Servants* (London: Penguin Fig Tree, 2007)

Logan, Thad, *The Victorian Parlour* (Cambridge: Cambridge University Press, 2001)

Maidment, Brian, *Comedy, Caricature and the Social Order, 1820–50* (Manchester: Manchester University Press, 2013)

Markovits, Stefanie, *The Crimean War in the British Imagination* (Cambridge: Cambridge University Press, 2009)

Matthews, Samantha, '"O All Pervading Album!": Place and Displacement in Romantic Albums and Album Poetry', in *Romantic Localities: Europe Writes Place*, ed. by Christoph Bode and Jacqueline Labbe (London: Pickering & Chatto, 2010)

Matus, Jill L., '*Mary Barton* and *North and South*', in *The Cambridge Companion to Elizabeth Gaskell*, ed. by Jill L. Matus (Cambridge: Cambridge University Press, 2007), pp. 27–45

McGowan, John, 'Modernity and Culture: The Victorians and Cultural Studies', *Nineteenth-Century Contexts*, 22.1 (2000), 21–50

McKenzie, D. F., *Bibliography and the Sociology of Texts* (London: British Library, 1986)

Meckier, Jerome, 'Parodic Prolongation in *North and South*: Elizabeth Gaskell Revaluates Dickens's Suspenseful Delays', *Dickens Quarterly*, 23.4 (December 2006), 217–28

Miller, D. A., *The Novel and the Police* (Berkeley, Los Angeles, London: University of California Press, 1988)

Morgan, Janet, 'Preface', in Maria Rundell, *A New System of Domestic Cookery*, facsimile of 1816 edn (London: Persephone Books, 2009), pp. v–xix

Mucignat, Rosa, *Realism and Space in the Novel, 1795–1869* (Farnham: Ashgate, 2013)

Müller, Günther, *Morphologische Poetic: Gesammelte Aufsätze*, ed. by Elena Müller (Tübingen: Max Niemeyer Verlag, 1974)

Mussell, James, *The Nineteenth-Century Press in the Digital Age* (Basingstoke: Palgrave Macmillan, 2012)

Newlyn, Andrea K., 'Redefining "Rudimentary" Narrative: Women's Nineteenth-Century Manuscript Cookbooks', in *The Recipe Reader: Narratives – Contexts – Traditions*, ed. by Janet Floyd and Laurel Forster (Aldershot: Ashgate, 2003), pp. 31–51

Ott, Katherine, Susan Tucker and Patricia P. Buckler, 'An Introduction to the History of Scrapbooks', in *The Scrapbook in American Life*, ed. by Susan Tucker, Katherine Ott and Patricia P. Buckler (Philadelphia: Temple University Press, 2006), pp. 1–25

Phegley, Jennifer, *Educating the Proper Woman Reader: Victorian Family Literary Magazines and the Cultural Health of the Nation* (Columbus: Ohio State University Press, 2004)

Poovey, Mary, 'Introduction', in Florence Nightingale, *Cassandra and Other Selections from Suggestions for Thought*, ed. by Mary Poovey (London: Pickering and Chatto, 1991), pp. vii–xxix

Price, Leah, *The Anthology and the Rise of the Novel from Richardson to George Eliot* (Cambridge: Cambridge University Press, 2000)

——, *How to Do Things with Books in Victorian Britain* (Princeton and Oxford: Princeton University Press, 2012)

Rabuzzi, Kathryn Allen, *The Sacred and the Feminine: Toward a Theology of Housework* (New York: Seabury Press, 1982)

Ricœur, Paul, *Time and Narrative*, 3 vols, trans. by Kathleen McLaughlin and David Pellauer (Chicago and London: University of Chicago Press, 1984–8)

Robbins, Bruce, *The Servant's Hand: English Fiction from Below* (New York: Columbia University Press, 1986)

Romines, Ann, *The Home Plot: Women, Writing and Domestic Ritual* (Amherst: University of Massachusetts Press, 1992)

Royle, Trevor, *Crimea: The Great Crimean War, 1854–1856* (London: Little, Brown, 1999)

Rubery, Matthew, '*Bleak House* in Real Time', *English Language Notes*, 46.1 (Spring–Summer 2008), 113–18

Scarry, Elaine, *Resisting Representation* (New York and Oxford: Oxford University Press, 1994)

Schaffer, Talia, *Novel Craft: Victorian Domestic Handicraft and Nineteenth-Century Fiction* (Oxford: Oxford University Press, 2011)

Schivelbusch, Wolfgang, *The Railway Journey: The Industrialization and Perception of Time and Space in the 19th Century*, 2nd edn (Leamington Spa: Berg, 1986)

Shelston, Alan, 'Elizabeth Gaskell and the Crimean War', *Gaskell Journal*, 23 (2009), 54–63

——, 'Elizabeth Gaskell and the Sense of the New', in *Elizabeth Gaskell: Text and Context*, ed. by Francesco Marroni and Alan Shelston (Pescara: Edizioni Tracce, 1999), pp. 11–38

Sherman, Stuart, *Telling Time: Clocks, Diaries, and English Diurnal Form, 1660–1785* (Chicago and London: University of Chicago Press, 1996)

Shove, Elizabeth, 'Everyday Practice and the Production and Consumption of Time', in *Time, Consumption and Everyday Life: Practice, Materiality and Culture*, ed. by Elizabeth Shove, Frank Trentmann and Richard Wilk (Oxford and New York: Berg, 2009), pp. 17–33

Shrimpton, Nicholas, '*Bric-à-Brac* or *Architectonicè*? Fragment and Form in Victorian Literature', in Jonathon Shears and Jen Harrison (eds), *Literary Bric-à-Brac and the Victorians: From Commodities to Oddities* (Farnham: Ashgate, 2013), pp. 17–32

Slater, Michael, *Charles Dickens* (New Haven and London: Yale University Press, 2009)

Sparling, Henry Halliday, *The Kelmscott Press and William Morris, Master-Craftsman* (London: Macmillan and Co., 1924)

Starr, Elizabeth, '"A Great Engine for Good": The Industrial Fiction in Elizabeth Gaskell's *Mary Barton* and *North and South*', *Studies in the Novel*, 34.4 (Winter 2002), 385–402

Steedman, Carolyn, *Labours Lost: Domestic Service and the Making of Modern England* (Cambridge: Cambridge University Press, 2009)

Steinitz, Rebecca, *Time, Space, and Gender in the Nineteenth-Century British Diary* (New York: Palgrave Macmillan, 2011)

Steinlight, Emily, '"Anti-Bleak House": Advertising and the Victorian Novel', *Narrative*, 14.2 (2006), 132–62

Stewart, Susan, *On Longing: Narratives of the Miniature, the Gigantic, the Souvenir, the Collection* (Durham and London: Duke University Press, 1993)

Thompson, E. P., 'Time, Work-Discipline and Industrial Capitalism', *Past and Present*, 38 (December 1967), 56–97

Thornton, Sara, *Advertising, Subjectivity and the Nineteenth-Century Novel: Dickens, Balzac and the Language of the Walls* (London and New York: Palgrave Macmillan, 2009)

Trentman, Frank, 'Disruption is Normal: Blackouts, Breakdowns and the Elasticity of Everyday Life', in *Time, Consumption and Everyday Life: Practice, Materiality and Culture*, ed. by Elizabeth Shove, Frank Trentmann and Richard Wilk (Oxford and New York: Berg, 2009), pp. 67–84

Turner, Mark W., 'Periodical Time in the Nineteenth Century', *Media History*, 8.2 (2002), 183–96

——, '"Telling of my weekly doings": The Material Culture of the Victorian Novel', in *A Concise Companion to the Victorian Novel*, ed. by Francis O'Gorman (London: Blackwell, 2005), pp. 113–33

——, 'The Unruliness of Serials in the Nineteenth Century (and in the Digital Age)', in *Serialization in Popular Culture*, ed. by Rob Allen and Thijs van den Berg (New York: Routledge, 2014), pp. 11–32

Uglow, Jenny, *Elizabeth Gaskell: A Habit of Stories* (London: Faber and Faber, 1993)

Vann, J. Don, 'Dickens, Charles Lever, and Mrs. Gaskell', *Victorian Periodical Review*, 22.2 (Summer 1989), 64–71

Vickery, Amanda, *Behind Closed Doors: At Home in Georgian England* (New Haven and London: Yale University Press, 2009)

——, 'Golden Age to Separate Spheres? A Review of the Categories and Chronology of English Women's History', *Historical Review*, 36.2 (June 1993), 383–414

Voth, Hans-Joachim, *Time and Work in England: 1750–1830* (Oxford: Clarendon Press, 2000)

Warner, Michael, 'Publics and Counterpublics', *Public Culture*, 14.1 (Winter 2002), 49–90

Williams, Andrew, '*Bleak House* and the Culture of Advertising', in *Approaches to Teaching Dickens's* Bleak House, ed. by John O. Jordan and George Bigelow (New York: Modern Language Association of America, 2008), pp. 45–50

Williams, Raymond, *Marxism and Literature* (Oxford: Oxford University Press, 1977)

Wright, Terence, *Elizabeth Gaskell: 'We are Not Angels': Realism, Gender, Values* (Basingstoke and London: Macmillan, 1995)

Zemka, Sue, *Time and the Moment in Victorian Literature and Society* (Cambridge: Cambridge University Press, 2012)

Index

CPSIA information can be obtained at www.ICGtesting.com
Printed in the USA
BVOW06*0227180816

459406BV00011B/35/P